P9-DHM-878

Lost in the Spanish Quarter

Lost in the Spanish Quarter

a novel

Heddi Goodrich

HARPERVIA

An Imprint of HarperCollinsPublishers

This is a work of fiction. Names, characters, places, and incidents are products of the author's imagination or are used fictitiously and are not to be construed as real. Any resemblance to actual events, locales, organizations, or persons, living or dead, is entirely coincidental.

LOST IN THE SPANISH QUARTER

Original Italian language publication: Copyright © 2019 by Heddi Goodrich.
Original English language publication: Copyright © 2019 by Heddi Goodrich.

All rights reserved. Printed in the United States of America. No part of this book may be used or reproduced in any manner whatsoever without written permission except in the case of brief quotations embodied in critical articles and reviews. For information, address HarperCollins Publishers, 195 Broadway, New York, NY 10007.

HarperCollins books may be purchased for educational, business, or sales promotional use. For information, please email the Special Markets Department at SPsales@harpercollins.com.

Originally published as *Perduti nei Quartieri Spagnoli* in Italy in 2019 by Giunti Editore.

FIRST EDITION

Designed by SBI Book Arts, LLC

Library of Congress Cataloging-in-Publication Data

Names: Goodrich, Heddi, author.
Title: Lost in the Spanish Quarter : a novel / Heddi Goodrich.
Other titles: Perduti nei Quartieri Spagnoli. English
Description: New York, New York : HarperCollins, 2019
Identifiers: LCCN 2019003702 | ISBN 9780062910226 (hardcover) | ISBN 9780062910233 (trade paperback) | ISBN 9780062910240 (ebook)
Subjects: LCSH: Americans—Italy—Fiction. | Man-woman relationships—Fiction. | Naples (Italy)—Fiction.
Classification: LCC PS3607.O5922548 P4713 2019 | DDC 813/.6—dc23 LC record available at https://lccn.loc.gov/2019003702

19 20 21 22 23   LSC   10 9 8 7 6 5 4 3 2 1

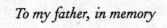

To my father, in memory

Lost in the Spanish Quarter

From: tectonic@tin.it
To: heddi@yahoo.com
Sent: November 22

I know you'd rather I was dead. I'm barely alive. I don't expect an answer to this email, and I won't write you again. I've been trying to write you for the past four years. I should write a hundred-page letter to try and explain. I would never be able to, so I won't try to explain myself now.

I'm a fool. I've always trusted my instinct but my instinct is a fake, a traitor, an idiot. A few years back I made the worst mistake of my life— unrecoverable, inexplicable, unimaginable. I lied to myself for a while (I can be quite good at that sometimes) that I did what my head, or my gut, was telling me to do. Maybe it was the right thing but it ruined my life. I just wanted to tell you that. Because you deserve to know that my life isn't worth a cent. You deserve to know that every time I sit down to eat with utensils in my hand for a moment I have the desire to gouge an eye out with my knife.

I hope with all my strength that these words will twist a little smile of satisfaction from your lips, just as I hope that for you I was just a bad dream, not your cross to bear. My other hope is that my life goes by quickly so that I can be reincarnated into someone or something better than my current self. Then perhaps I'll run into you in an airport in Stockholm or Buenos Aires.

Don't forgive me, don't answer, don't be sad. Be happy, have babies, write books, make mixed tapes, take pictures . . . it's how I always love to think of you. And now and then, if you can and if you want to, remember me.

p.

I

"HEDDI."

I heard my name pronounced as no one had said it in years, like a person might say the name of an exotic species. Rising into a question but mastered—subtle aspiration, short vowels, and all—as if it had been breathed in private again and again until it could roll off the tongue with startling casualness. No other sound in all the Spanish Quarter, not a woman screaming bloody cheater or a gun popping with the thrill of vendetta, could have made me turn away from the murmuring fireplace on such a cold night.

There stood a boy, a man, his mouth tightened like he'd said his bit and now it was my turn. His shirt was tucked in at the waist, rolled up at the arms, and strained at the heart, a handy breast pocket barely managing a pack of cigarettes. Nothing like the other guests, who with their face piercings and dreadlocks and pasty skin tried to cover up the wholesomeness of their childhoods spent frolicking at the beach and eating potato gnocchi. Despite the hour, their sweet scent, of patchouli and thrift shops and hashish, still hung in the kitchen, fusing with wafts of flat beer and saffron risotto. Clearly, he wasn't from our tribe of linguists, the centuries-old Istituto Universitario Orientale, so easy to get into and so much harder to graduate from. Yet there he was, as still as the water of a deep lake.

"Here, I made this for you," he said, fishing something out of his jeans pocket. Definitely a southern Italian accent, if not Neapolitan. His hand quivered, a slight ruffle, as he handed me a cassette tape in its homemade case. *Per Heddi*, it read, beginning with a capital *H* and ending with an inky splash, the dot on my long-forgotten *i*.

This threw me. It was actually the spelling of my name that derailed its pronunciation, for then it was easy to take it to its literal extreme, with a melodramatically elongated *e* and the *d* duly hardened by consonant doubling, which southern Italians took so very much to heart. That the *H* was ignored was entirely forgivable, for in Naples breathiness was reserved exclusively for laughter. "As in Eddie Murphy?" people would ask and I would simply nod. I didn't mind really. Heddi was before and Eddie was now.

"Music?" I asked, and he merely nodded awkwardly, his knuckles taut over an empty beer bottle.

My back was warmed by the erratic dance of the flames and by the oblivious laughter of the friends I affectionately called "the boys," *i ragazzi*. That I belonged there too and could turn back toward them at any time made me feel undeniably safe, a privilege that all of a sudden I perceived as unfair.

Downstairs the front door shook with a thud, probably the last of the guests staggering out, and my gift bearer looked jolted by the awareness that the party that had been whirling around him earlier was now gone. He tried to hide his embarrassment but I felt it all the same, a painful pinch followed by my own regret at being, once again, the only one sober.

"It's probably getting late," he said.

"I guess so, but there's only one clock in the whole house."

Abruptly, he shifted his weight from one leg to the other, and unintentionally I mirrored his asymmetry by tilting my head to one side. The better to see him with, at least, though his face was hidden every time he found solace in his shoes—comfortable, practical shoes—by a dark mane. I could honestly say I'd never seen him before, I could have sworn

4

by it, because if we'd ever locked eyes I surely would have remembered that determined look, a willingness to bide his time.

"I should probably get going." He set his bottle down as if afraid to break the glass, despite the fact that the kitchen counter was an invitation to make a mess, with its knocked-over bottles, greasy pans, and mugs stained with wine like old teeth.

"I'm sorry, what was your name?"

"Pietro." It was a rock of a name, straitlaced and somewhat hard, and he lifted his eyebrows apologetically.

"Thanks for the tape . . ." I said, but his name died in my throat. "So you're leaving?"

"Yeah, I have to get up early. I'm off to the farm for a few weeks. My family's farmland, in the province of Avellino. I go every Easter. Well, not just Easter, but you know . . ."

I didn't know but I nodded anyway, grateful for the string of phrases. I still held out hope that in those last seconds before his departure (and I would probably never see him again) I could solve the mystery of how he'd come to be on such intimate terms with my name and why he'd gone to such trouble to make me something.

"OK, bye."

"Bye, enjoy your farmstay. I mean, your stay at the farm."

I wished he would just go now, this outsider who was now a chance witness to my slip of the tongue. It was exasperating how my Italian, my favorite disguise, could still come apart at the seams whenever I was taken by surprise.

A round of goodbyes and he was gone. I reclaimed my seat by the fireplace, slipping the tape into the pocket of my vintage suede miniskirt. The flames felt their way boldly up the scavenged firewood, fondling what had once been the leg of a proper chair or the headboard of a single bed. Within seconds the blazing fire swept any trace of unease from my face.

"What was that guy's name again?" asked Luca beside me, tossing a cigarette butt into the fire and slipping a white ribbon of smoke from his mouth.

"Pietro, I think," I said, tasting just how solid the name was.

"Oh, yeah. He's a friend of Davide's."

"Davide who?"

"The short one with curly hair," said Sonia, the only other girl in our innermost circle.

Davide, now I remembered. Luca sometimes played in his band. Davide, Pietro, did it matter? The truth was we didn't need anyone else in our clan. We were fine just as we were.

I was fine.

Mesmerized by the flames, we let the night slide into a moonless, hourless limbo. We talked about Hinduism, the Phoenician alphabet, the Mani Pulite judicial investigation that was cleansing a corrupt government and making a killing at the newsstands. Now and then a chunk of wood caved into the embers, triggering a showy display of sparks and a few *ooh*s and *aah*s for that little moment of drama. When the fire started to nod off, Luca rummaged through the stack of makeshift firewood. Beside it was an acoustic guitar, which Tonino's hairy hand reached for.

"You're not throwing *that* in," said Angelo, another of the boys.

"No, Tonino, please!" said Sonia.

"Party's over, children," Tonino announced with a heavy Pugliese drawl as he propped the guitar on his knee. "About fucking time for your lullaby."

This was the part I loved the most. Tonino's foul language drawing us in closer, his glasses turning to golden rings in the firelight as he began playing a tune that sounded like Lucio Dalla's "Attenti al lupo," "Watch Out for the Wolf." He strummed with those small chunky hands covered in dark fleece, the hands of a garden gnome come to life. And he was hairy all over. Once Tonino had asked me to shave his back to deal

6

the final blow to some crab lice, incontrovertible evidence that he really had managed to get someone into his bed—a Spanish girl, or so he said. Underneath it all, shorn like a spring lamb, Tonino possessed almost fine features that made him look, in a certain light, like my own brother.

Tonino sang that ballad like a heavy metal front man, with death growls and all, managing all the while to tweak the lyrics to his needs. "There's this tiny little house . . . with a tiny little grapevine . . . and inside there's a tiny little professor . . . who won't fucking shift the deadline . . . And there's this tiny little student . . . with a brain the size of Einstein's . . ."

"Fuck me, that's a hit song," said Angelo. "You know what? Forget your studies. You should start a punk band."

"Yeah, maybe I'll ask my Sanskrit professor if she wants to be the drummer, what do you say? That way she can beat the shit out of something else besides me."

"Play us one of those traditional Neapolitan songs instead," said Luca.

Tonino handed over the guitar. "I'm not the fucking Neapolitan," he said. It was a compliment.

"I'm only half."

"The bottom half, naturally," said Angelo.

His shoulder-length hair falling over his face, Luca cradled the instrument and offered them an off-center laugh, but his eyes were on me. That half smile was in itself a compliment, for Luca was as selective with his smiles as he was with his words, as if he'd spent his last incarnation seeing all the irony in the world and in this lifetime had achieved Zen. Although technically he too was one of the boys, I had always thought of him as distinct from the other two. He was simply Luca Falcone.

"This one's for you."

It took only the first few notes for me to figure out that he'd chosen Carosone's old classic "Tu vuo' fa' l'americano." It was like I'd been caught out, the American incognito, and in fact Luca was looking my way, waiting.

I didn't feel like singing, and if I did from the second verse onward, it was only because I realized the others genuinely didn't know the words and that it was up to me to fill the silence. Perhaps I did it for Luca too. To show him that, if nothing else, I could put on an impeccable Neapolitan accent, a low-class growl rising from even lower in the gut than his. To see if I could make him smile. For his benefit, I crooned comically and gesticulated like a fishmonger, magically transformed into one of those poor women standing in the doorway of a typical inner-city *vascio*, a street-level, one-room hovel that some called a storeroom, others a store, and yet others unfortunately called home. I was every bit her, that mother or sister or girlfriend waiting for that good-for-nothing to return, her eyes narrowed and ready to snap . . . or burst out laughing. Oh, he thinks he's a hotshot, all loose in the tongue from whiskey and soda and loose in the hips from rock 'n' roll, but I'll show him as soon as he gets home, you bet I will, and I'll slap him good, or maybe I'll stroke his cheek, before cutting him down to size in front of the whole slum: "Look at you! You're nothing but a Neapolitan! *Tu si napulitan'!*" and if he so much as dared to come back at me with a lame "*Ailoviu*" I would really lose it.

Apart from the last expression that was supposedly in English, the lyrics were in dialect so I wouldn't have been able to spell them—nor was there any academic standardization for, or even interest in, faithfully capturing those sawn-off endings and tight-lipped sounds that disfigured Italians' famously operatic vowels. I wouldn't even have dared utter the lyrics without music. They were vulgar and truthful and sharp with that satire that Neapolitans were so skilled at turning inward upon themselves since the fall of their city. And it was the words themselves that were directing me, assigning me the part, to the point where, as I channeled the character through the dialect, I wasn't an American at all but a *vasciaiola* who could see through the Americanness and expose it for nothing more than an act.

The others tapped a foot and chimed in for the chorus. Finally Luca raked his fingers over the strings. "I can't remember how it ends."

I leaned back in my chair, sweating and giddy, almost tipsy. There was always a mimic in me, or maybe even a gambler, waiting to burst out. No sooner had the fire popped lethargically than I was already on my feet. "We need bigger pieces of wood. I'll go up on the roof."

"I'll come up with you, Eddie," said Sonia. "I could use the fresh air."

Luca and the boys shifted effortlessly into a Pearl Jam song. English rolled much more readily off their tongues than Neapolitan, but they butchered it, slurring the diphthongs and crumbling consonant clusters. Sonia and I climbed the spiral staircase beside the fireplace. The space was so tight and Sonia so tall that she had to duck, the black sheet of her hair dipping forward, her combat boots ringing the metal all the way up to the flat rooftop.

"My god, it's cold," I said, my words little clouds in the night.

"Freezing." Sonia hugged herself, adding in that Sardinian accent that was as crisp as the air, "So I guess you know Pietro."

"Pietro? From tonight?"

"Yeah, Pietro."

The name had rolled extraordinarily lightly off her tongue. It occurred to me, for an instant of folly, that we must be talking about two entirely different people.

"What do you think of him?"

"I don't really know him." I crouched to pick through the loose wood, a bookshelf dismembered and lumped against the protective wall of the roof. "Why do you ask?"

"Don't tell the boys." As Sonia sank to the spongy ground, her face as bare as a full moon, I grasped that it wasn't a breath of fresh air at all but a confession. Kneeling like that and looking considerably less tall, she reminded me of how young she really was, just in her second year at the Orientale. Although only the stars could have heard us, she fell into a whisper. "We've barely exchanged a handful of words. But there's just something about him, I don't know . . ."

"He seems nice enough." Instinctively I patted my pocket that held the cassette tape, as if to smooth out its conspicuous bulge.

"I really do like him. Next time I see him, I'm going to go up to him."

"You definitely should. You have nothing to lose."

Sonia had a way of biting her bottom lip when she was restless. She breathed out hard as if preparing for a sprint.

"Chin up, Sonia. You're beautiful, smart. This Pietro guy would be a fool not to give you a chance."

I loved Sonia's sweet doodle of a grin, but the word *fool* used in connection with this stranger named Pietro somehow felt like an insult to my own sensibility and filled me with remorse. Sonia offered to help, grabbing a broken plank and letting out a *brrr*.

"You're cold," I said. "Take those and I'll finish up here."

"OK."

But as soon as I was alone, I lowered the wood to the ground and leaned my elbows on the wall, the only barrier preventing a seven-story free fall to the street. "Tonight . . ." I whispered to myself in English, but I was unable to finish my own sentence.

A cold breeze pressed the smell of the gulf against my face, that unique infusion of fish and diesel and salt. Below me, the city shimmered its way down to the water, strings of yellow streetlights beaded here and there with the pearly glow of kitchens. Naples never really slept. Even in the dead of night, fluorescent lightbulbs shed their cheap, unforgiving light onto family members who were up and about and slapping the kitchen table in god knows what argument or joke or confession. But, like a moth, I was drawn to those white lights. If I could, I wished now as always, I would flutter toward them and slip in through a window. I would sit there soundlessly and seamlessly blending in with the wallpaper, trying to piece together the shards of their sentences into a narrative that made sense.

A foghorn blared. I couldn't tell which of the many ships it could have come from, vessels invisible but for their connect-the-dot lights suspended in the utter blackness of the bay. It was a rare clear night, and without a moon I couldn't even see the volcano. The only trace of it were the homes on its flanks sketching its silhouette as far up as they dared. Vesuvius hadn't made a peep in half a century, but I stared at it through the curtain of the night and tried to imagine what it might look like breathing fire as in so many of those eighteenth-century oil paintings. I stared so hard I almost believed I could will it back to life with my eyes.

My hands had turned to cool marble, yet I hadn't had my fill of Naples; I could have stayed there all night drinking in its scent and feasting my eyes. Still it would have been in vain. The city was water seeping through my hands, and my very love for it filled me with sadness, especially at night. It was a sadness I could never fend off or even put my finger on. I'd given myself over to the city, maybe even betraying myself to do so, but even after all these years it still held me at a distance.

Vir' Napule e po' muor', they say: "See Naples and die." A city so magnificent that once you've seen it there is nothing left in the world to see. The saying had become such a cliché that I would never have used it in conversation, but right then I whispered it to the night as the truest of truths. Then I collected the firewood before heading back downstairs.

From: heddi@yahoo.com
To: tectonic@tin.it
Sent: November 30

Pietro,

I don't know what to say. It's been four long years since I last heard from you. Time makes everything bearable, even waiting. Or maybe I simply forgot what I was waiting for.

I still don't know why you did what you did. Sometimes at night I look at the stars hoping for some kind of explanation from them. It's crazy, I know, to think that the constellations could read like a sort of story with a beginning, middle, and maybe even a happy ending. But to be honest, I can't make any sense of them. I can't even recognize the simplest of constellations: the sky seems jumbled, upside down, unfamiliar. And yet I like looking at the stars anyway. Every single one of them is, after all, a trace of a luminous object that is unique and perfect and no longer exists. A luminous memory?

I've worked hard at forgetting everything to do with you. A kind of self-induced amnesia, which has been quite successful. Of course it helps not having people, places, or things around me that could remind me of you. Except the Roman figurine. But that's not something I could regift or throw away. Maybe it would make more sense to one day give it back to the land . . .

My cat's on my knee, she's digging her claws in. She has beautiful gray fur. I rescued her from an animal shelter, so in a way I saved her life. But I think it's more accurate to say that she saved mine.

Things are good. I've found a place where I fit in, I have a great job and new friends that only know as much about me and my past as I'd like them to know. It's good to hear from you. It's good to hear you say you're sorry. Or have I put words in your mouth?

h.

2

THE DAY AFTER, the day of the hangover, I was sitting on my creaky bed turning the pages of my textbook when I heard Luca coming down the hallway toward me. I could tell it was him even before his voice broke through the mournful Bulgarian folk songs and the humming rain. It was the smell of his tobacco that gave him away. His smoke meandered in through my open door and danced before me as elusively as a wish.

For as long as I'd known him, Luca Falcone had always smoked those hand-rolled cigarettes: he was puffing on one when I was first introduced to him. Leaned against the dejected plaster outside the café across from my department, he was holding something very alcoholic and wearing out-of-fashion leather pants, seemingly oblivious to the historical era or the geographical location he'd wound up in. Luca was already in his third or fourth year and he was pockmarked, weathered like a traveler who had crossed the desert to get to that bar, that bourbon, that stopover.

That moment marked the beginning of my university life as I knew it now, for most unexpectedly Luca took a shine to me and slipped me into his inner circle—the alternative crowd majoring in Urdu or Swahili or Korean at the Department of Arabic-Islamic and Mediterranean Studies and the Department of Oriental Studies, whose remote Italian origins (Puglia, Basilicata, Sicily, Sardinia) branded them as outsiders too.

"The movie's starting," said Luca with the lilt of his native Varese, in the Lakes region.

"I'll be right there. I'm just finishing the page."

Up close, Luca smelled of lavender soap. He stamped a kiss on my forehead, a big one like he was farewelling me at the train station. Yet he didn't leave. He lingered in the doorway to bore his eyes into me, as he sometimes did, as if to hypnotize me. That prolonged gaze always threw me into confusion while at the same time giving me the strange certainty, at least for as long as it lasted, that our friendship was not limited to this moment or these circumstances, that we had a bond which would outlast the rest. I knew it was ridiculous, and that I was no exception: everyone wanted a piece of Luca Falcone.

On either side of the now empty doorframe were some of my black-and-white photographs, taken with a macro lens, hand-printed and taped to the wall. They were good shots, though somewhat abstract. Through the window, sandwiched up against another building and transformed by the rain into a game board of Chutes and Ladders, I couldn't even see my neighborhood being beaten down by the weather and by the passage of time. But it was Sunday and I knew that at that hour all the shops would be closed and the markets packed up, and every last soul would be back home for a marathon meal, followed by the compulsory nap. Sunday lunchtime was the only time when people felt *sorry* for me. Poor stray, so far from home.

Home. The word itself puzzled me. Didn't *home* mean my dad grilling steaks or my psychotherapist stepmom doing her on-the-spot dream analysis? Wasn't it my mom's shiatsu foot rubs, her chilly but soft hands, or my brother plucking the bass? The cats? Apparently not, because for all the other out-of-town students home was a place. Colle Alto in the province of Benevento, Adelfia in the province of Bari. Home was a red dot on the map, a reference point that was so very small and yet able to contain, it seemed, *everything*. People appeared to take it for granted, as if it were just another basic human emotion—happy, sad, angry, home—and yet their eyes lit up when they said the word. *Casa.* I struggled to grasp that extraplanetary sensation but in the end I couldn't really feel it. I had to resort to logical analysis to get my head around it.

I was from everywhere and from nowhere. Washington, DC, Maryland, Virginia Beach, the outskirts of Boston, Athens in Ohio, and a few other forgettable stop-offs. That was until, at sixteen, I was assigned a dot on the map by an international exchange program that landed me in the nation of Italy, the province of Naples, the town of Castellammare di Stabia, the apartment of a divorcée with two grown sons who told me to call her Mamma Rita. It was Rita, and not AFSAI, who begged me to stay on after the first year and who had the foresight to advise her "American daughter" to graduate from a *liceo linguistico*.

I became convinced that nothing in this world is random. It was that diploma, in fact, that got me into the Orientale. The admissions lady had narrowed her eyes. I wasn't Italian, but with that piece of paper I couldn't not be Italian. When she thumped my admission form with four glorious official stamps, she turned me into a university student like any other. And among Luca's friends, who were now mine too, the camouflage was almost perfect.

The boys and I had a fun little game, which would start with a request for a cold beer and usually end with a cup of hot tea.

"Ah, c'mon, gorgeous," pleaded Tonino that afternoon lying starfish on Luca's bed. In the spastic light of the TV, I could see that Tonino looked as miserable as the old wallpaper behind him, covered only partially by Luca's Arabic calligraphy. "If I don't inject more alcohol into my bloodstream, I'll never get rid of this bastard headache."

"You did ask for it," said Angelo.

"Like you asking for that bong . . ."

"Listen, boys," I said, putting on my sternest voice, in no way meant for Luca, who was rolling a cigarette. "You have class tomorrow, bright and early. C'mon, boys, it's the last week before the break. You can do it! Honey or sugar?"

Tonino cursed half-heartedly in three dialects (Neapolitan, Sicilian, and his own), but they both gave in straightaway. I smiled to myself on my way to the kitchen, knowing full well that what those two really craved was not a drink at all but a bit of mothering. I paused in front of Angelo's cracked door, catching a peek at his black-and-white cowhide rug we often lay across sipping green tea from Japanese cups while deciphering our respective codes, kanji and Cyrillic. I climbed the staircase, which had lost its railing, swerving at the top to avoid stepping on the crack in the floor, just in case there was some reality to that childhood truth. The fracture started at the fireplace in the kitchen, half a meter out from the wall, and shot through to the end of the living room, dissecting the tiles to where they met the terrace. I wondered, as brazen as that crack was, why I hadn't noticed it when I'd moved in with the boys. I'd probably been too distracted by the aging beauty of the once luxurious apartment, by all its fireplaces, frescoes, and bas-reliefs flaking and fading in the shadows.

I carried back beer mugs of tea and a pack of cookies; the bed sagged in the middle under our weight. I'd missed the opening scenes, but then again it was a movie we'd watched over and over, a New Zealand film I knew only by the name *Una volta erano guerrieri*, and I was very familiar with the plot. Tattooed Maori thugs bashing each other at night in parking lots and bars and on green lawns, spattered with blood and foul language dubbed in proper Italian with a northern accent.

"Man, what an awesome place New Zealand must be . . ." said Angelo dreamily.

"Awesome my ass," Tonino spat back.

"It can't be all that dangerous. Look at those wide-open spaces, they can do whatever the hell they want. I'd love to go there one day."

"Sure, blondie, better to get an ass whipping from a Maori gang than a kneecapping from the Mafia."

16

Angelo frowned, defiantly pulling up the plaid blanket. He had a nose ring and a proud Sicilian accent that should have lent him an air of toughness. But, whatever the situation, Angelo was like a kid in a candy shop and this was something Tonino just couldn't let him get away with. It certainly didn't help matters that Angelo had the complexion of a Swede, a washed-out color that didn't stop at his face and hair. I only knew this because I'd nursed him back to health once when he was suffering from excruciating neck pain. Angelo had turned facedown onto that cow rug and pulled down his pants; quickly, before I lost the nerve, I jabbed the syringe of anti-inflammatory into his right buttock.

"Well, one day I'm gonna go there," Angelo reiterated through a mouthful.

"You're as baked as that cookie," said Tonino.

"You should go. The world is a book . . ."

That last enigmatic sentence emerged from Luca's smoke. I hadn't even realized he'd been listening. Yet another night scene plunged the room into darkness, but Luca's Arabic pendant, carved out of what looked like bone, shone as if reflecting light from an unknown source.

"New Zealand's too far," I said, and in fact I preferred destinations like Sardinia, Umbria, the Netherlands, Kiev, Vienna—with or without my family. Or better yet, Capri, Procida, the Phlegraean Fields, the streets of Naples. "Who wants to come with me to the Maria Santissima del Carmine Church during the break?" I suggested. Another one of my "field trips," as the boys called them.

"A church over Easter?" said Angelo. "I'll pass. I'd rather be sitting around a table stuffing my face with cassata."

"It's also known as the Fontanelle Cemetery," said Luca. "Definitely worth a visit."

Hope swelled up inside me. Maybe, just maybe, this time Luca would set aside his band practice or research for his thesis to wander with me through the city that was his by right of blood. But he said nothing more and slipped definitively back into the darkness.

"Well, I wouldn't be able to go for all the pussy in the world," Tonino said. "March is when we prune our olive trees . . . Oh, that's right, you intellectuals wouldn't want your hands getting dirty, now would you? But it would actually do you some good. Check out these muscles. You think they're just for show?"

The boys burst out laughing and I sat up with a jolt. *Pietro.* I hadn't even looked at the tape since he'd given it to me the night before. I had a habit of doing that, setting aside letters and packages from home, sometimes for days on end, savoring the anticipation of opening them. Or maybe I'd just wanted to forget all about it after Sonia's confession. But now I was beset by a sense of urgency. Where had I put it?

"Hey, where are you going?" Angelo called out behind me. "This is the part where Nig gets initiated into the gang!"

My suede skirt hadn't forgotten last night: it smelled like a bonfire and was still holding on to the fragile little package I'd entrusted it with. In good lighting I could now see that the neatly written song list was framed by cartoonish drawings of ladybugs and fish in rust-colored ink, a detail of such playfulness, kindness, and undeniable intimacy as to make my head spin.

I sat on the bed and put the cassette into the tape deck. The first song was Aretha Franklin's version of "Son of a Preacher Man." I let out a sigh. My love life up until then had been a series of melodramas and misunderstandings.

In Castellammare di Stabia I met Franco, a rookie in the Camorra, the local Mafia. At the time it felt a lot like love. Or a movie about love, with scenes of gripping his thick waist on the back of a Vespa that snaked through the ruins of his ghostly neighborhood, which over the centuries had taken one too many punches from earthquakes and landslides. Watching his mother in their poorly lit *vascio* wail with chronic pain in legs as swollen as tree trunks. Listening to the story of how his friend had been shot dead by a rival gang. Holding Franco in my arms as he broke every code of honor to cry and cry against the backdrop of a friend's uninhabited apartment that didn't even have electricity. I was sixteen and I wanted to save him. One day without an explanation he broke it off. The ending was unsurprising, even desirable. After that, those adolescent sunsets over the polluted sea became even more beautiful and raw, like blood oranges.

Cesare was an error in judgment I paid dearly for. In hindsight, I could have guessed that his brilliance and eccentricity were the early symptoms of schizophrenia. But at the time I was enamored with how enamored he was with me, his searing gaze, his crooked teeth. He was disheveled, possibly even ugly, but he possessed a blinding confidence and wrote terse, dense poetry that read like haiku. Cesare quickly betrayed signs of obsession: only later did I learn he'd given me the cheap, useless gift of his virginity. Long after he left the university to be hospitalized back in his hometown of Catanzaro, he continued to send me packages, even to my dad and Barbara's house in DC, containing self-published volumes of love poems or top-secret instructions for building a bomb. Those declarations of undying passion, which became more and more grandiose, intensified my bouts of cold sores and also my shame, verging on disgust, for how I'd played the part of the carefree girl and used sex as an intellectual experiment in carnality, for how careless I'd been and how easily my instinct for self-preservation had won out over my compassion.

And then there was Luca. Or rather, there wasn't. Late one night while watching a movie on his bed we'd drifted into sleep and he tangled himself around me. I woke up. The movie was over and Luca's torso was rising and falling in a faraway, untroubled rhythm that seemed extraordinary in itself. His hair had come loose from his ponytail and his lips were slightly parted, but even in his sleep Luca was still ruggedly handsome. I was only pretending to sleep. Paralyzed with pleasure and awe, I let the night tick away with the flashing green of Luca's digital clock as his pendant pressed its cryptic script onto my skin. I was afraid to wake him. I wanted to lie next to him for as long as the universe had miraculously granted me, to absorb everything about him. His esoteric knowledge, his composure, his patience and faith in himself. During that long magical night, I gained an important insight: what I felt for Luca was not a crush, it was far more than that. I didn't want Luca Falcone, I wanted to *be* him.

I dropped back on my pillow and listened. There was a certain euphoria, and an unmistakable sensuality, to the song that I'd never noticed although I'd heard it a thousand times. I wondered if Pietro could fully understand the lyrics, if he was aware he'd given me a love song.

3

I COULDN'T QUITE picture Pietro's face. Our encounter had been so very brief and I'd even rushed it to a premature conclusion. The harder I tried to conjure up his image, the more it slipped away, until it was no more than a collection of indistinct features blending with the many eyes, noses, and mouths all around me, like those in the audience at my glottology lecture in the Astra Cinema. Fearing I would lose it forever in the crowd, I told myself not to dwell on it and to focus on my lesson instead.

The theater was warm and dark, womblike, the comfy seats upholstered in red velvet, my professor's voice a low frequency. I couldn't be dragged away from here even by wild horses, I thought to myself before realizing it was not a thought at all but a line from the second song, by the Rolling Stones, on Pietro's mixed tape.

I refocused on my notebook, where I was attempting to transcribe every word coming from the stage. "All the world's languages vary according to what we call taxa, or language families," I jotted down in tidy, compact letters. "Colors are a type of significant taxonomy: in fact, we might even say there is such a thing as ethnic chromatism . . ."

"Please shoot me now." The dark-haired girl next to me widened her made-up eyes, adding in a low whisper, "Signorelli's head looks like an Easter egg, don't you think?"

"He's really good, though." Actually, to me he seemed like a rock star.

"Sure, but he can't teach. He just reads straight from the textbook."

It wasn't entirely true, but I found myself once more trying to shake the familiar fear that I'd enrolled in a university in shambles.

"I've seen you a bunch of times in Russian class. What's your name?"

"Eddie, and yours?"

"Are you the foreigner?" My classmate leaned in close, too close, like I had something magical that could rub off on her. I didn't know her but I recognized that hunger, so widespread in the Department of European Languages, that yearning to be beamed up to a galaxy far, far away. She fired breathless questions at me: "Where are you from? Are you German? Why did you come to *Naples*, of all places?"

"I'm from . . . the Spanish Quarter."

I Quartieri Spagnoli. I knew how to lop off the final vowels and palatalize the *sp* in the Neapolitan manner and I'd learned to tame the awe in my eyes when I roamed the city, but there was no hiding my un-Italian features. In fact, the girl didn't fall for it, but at least she steered her attention off me and back to my professor, who deserved it far more.

". . . a distinction between bright white and dull, plain white. In Greek, *melas* is a radiant black, a concept that was completely lost in the shift from ancient to modern languages. And it's not clear why. In antiquity there was a particular focus on luminosity . . ."

"That's all I can take; I'll just read the book at home." The girl closed her notebook, murmuring with palpable joy, "In Sala Consilina, that is. I'm catching the train tomorrow morning."

"Sala Consilina . . ."

"It's in the province of Salerno. You wouldn't know it, it's just a nothing town . . ."

I could see she was embarrassed. I wanted to tell her not to worry because if anyone was provincial it was me, having grown up in one characterless suburb after another. But she wouldn't have understood.

It would have been an unthinkable concept for an Italian: hailing from the provinces was such a historical and deeply ingrained humiliation, but mine was a modern shame—tangled up with that typical American uneasiness of knowing that I was, on some fundamental level, one of the privileged.

"Have a safe trip then."

"Happy Easter."

I turned again to look at my professor. Excluding the bald head, I thought, one day that will be me. Signorelli truly was a brilliant man, endowed with the ability not only to convey fascinating tidbits on the evolution of language but also to trigger surprising insights into humanity itself. These nonverbal, or perhaps preverbal, inspirations would come to me during class or even in the most unlikely of settings, sparks of knowledge I could never catch hold of and write down before they were gone like fireflies.

But once in a while something amazing would happen. Several of those wordless sparks, which I'd been unable to capture but apparently hadn't left me for good, would start to gather on their own and whisper to one another. Secrets in a foreign language, maybe an animal language, that all together made a low, humming sound. Within seconds that buzzing would grow in intensity, a strange and exciting cacophony like instruments warming up before a concert. Gradually those unintelligible sounds would begin to slide into place and consolidate into one overriding idea that would explain everything. And it wouldn't be just a simple statement but a roar, something so unheard of, so astonishing, it might even be deafening. *The truth*.

If only I could hold my breath that long, I thought, for that crescendo of notes to meld into one whole and boom their mysterious message, then I would *know*. I would understand the primeval urges of man, the true reasons why people do what they do and are who they are, since the dawn of time. Art, war, religion . . . love.

I started humming "Wild Horses" to myself. All at once I felt trapped by my seat, by that windowless cinema. I wanted to break free, run home, and listen once more to the tape. To listen between the lines.

I got up and left. University students streamed out of cafés and used bookstores, forcing the cars to slow and bend to their will. Here the city was ours. From our tribe I spotted Costantino, a Japanese major, and Rina, who studied French, but unable to stop in the crowds we simply waved excitedly to each other. I was going against the current. It seemed almost as though all the other students were heading away from the center, toward the train station. By the end of tomorrow they would all be back in their hometowns. People brushed past me, even pushed me, but it was never done with malice, only familiarity. Yet I kept to my path, the street known as Spaccanapoli, a long and deliberate cut through the heart of Naples that would lead me back to the Spanish Quarter.

The Easter break freed me to visit the Carmine Church. I didn't know the way there, so for once I'd taken the bus. The Sanità neighborhood felt run down, almost unwell. A knife struck a cutting board a few stories up, a motorbike stirred lethargically in the distance. Certainly not the kind of place to use my camera, the Minolta my dad had passed down to me. Instead I pulled out my well-worn map, waking it from its comfortable folds. Then I veered left.

The streets tightened around me like vises and had a mind of their own. With every step my shoes gave me away, clapping on those typical Neapolitan cobblestones—volcanic *basoli*, large flat slabs with chisel marks that turned the streets into giant, moth-eaten quilts. My footsteps were regular, almost a musical rhythm. I realized that I had, in fact, yet another of Pietro's songs in my head, a U2 song that was dictating my pace: "Where the Streets Have No Name."

I came to a stop before sheer yellow cliffs of volcanic tuff. It was like being inside a desert canyon. Everything there was the color of sand, but the sun had no business here. Oozing from natural caves were houses, very poor dwellings without windows that appeared pinned down by the weight of the rock. A pregnant woman in her pajamas stood in a doorway. Sometimes, thinking myself invisible, I gave in to the luxury of staring. When she saw me coming, she shut the door.

I walked along that far edge of the neighborhood until I came to a church. Although it too was half inside a cave and as yellow as the cliff above it, the church seemed not so much a product of the rock as an ornate statement of uprising against circumstance.

I went in seeking refuge more than anything; I doubted this was the right church. There was nothing out of the ordinary about the place: just the usual tinted marble and frankincense, a few old women sitting in the pews fingering rosaries. One of the women got up and made a beeline for me.

"You're here for the dead, aren't you, my dear?"

"Actually, I am." How could she tell? From my breathless entrance, or the fact that I'd neglected to puncture the surface of the holy water with my fingers?

"I'll take you down." She talked in a manner typical of Neapolitan widows, drawing out the syllables as if to mourn each and every one of them, yet she was smiling generously. As I followed the woman toward the altar, she turned to say, "You're not from here."

"No."

At the far end she took me down a stairwell. It was musty and so dark that my feet had to make tentative guesses until, at the bottom of the steps, they hit packed earth. As I got used to the dim light, the space grew before me. A dirt path carved through piles of what my eyes could only see as kindling, unstable mounds pushed hard against the sandy walls of the cave. Above was a single hole of sunlight, a square choked with weeds. In that swampy light the mounds gradually, horrifically, began to take their true shape.

"Whose are they?"

"Only the good Lord knows," said the churchwoman, her voice echoing. "They're the unnamed dead. Folks who died in earthquakes. Or the plague. People used to drop like flies back then."

Among all those random pieces of people, I could make out thighbones, vertebra, and smaller bones that might have been fingers. Only once had I looked death in the eyes, at my step-grandmother's funeral, and it had stared back at me blankly, like a mannequin. I wasn't afraid of death but only of saying the wrong thing, of taking the wrong step.

"Our women here dedicate their prayers to these people," the woman added, "in the hopes they'll see them in a dream."

I went up to a particularly slender, curved bone. What had she meant by *see them in a dream*? But when I turned around to ask her, she was gone.

Finally alone, I stepped deferentially through the cave. So the real church was down here. The path narrowed, the bones thickened. It was not scary but simply quiet, a stroll through a forest of felled pines, my trail scattered with branches, twigs, needles. But my imagination ran wild. Maybe one of Naples's many cholera epidemics had killed a woman, perhaps married with two or three children, who then in the dead of night was thrown like a rag doll into that cave. Or maybe the volcano had sputtered during a Sunday market and a boy selling persimmons, hard new-season ones that make paper of your tongue, had suffocated in the poisonous gases. No, that was impossible: Mount Vesuvius had long been dormant; it was just a backdrop on the other side of the bay. Maybe an earthquake had toppled a wall on top of him, flicking the fruit like orange marbles across the street stones.

The dampness of the cave began to pinch my bones, an arthritic sort of feeling I knew well from years of living in unheated rooms where the paint peeled from the walls like bandages and the plaster still bore earthquake wounds that refused to heal over. I lingered in front of a coffin, built from wood that looked just as salvaged as the firewood the boys collected. I peered inside. Finding it empty filled me with gratitude mixed with an unspeakable disappointment. But just behind it was a much smaller coffin in a more advanced state of rot, only big enough for a baby.

I didn't belong there, that was clear to me now. But I didn't stop, for my eyes were too hungry, and eventually I came to a stack of skulls. They shone like varnished wood, as if caressed daily over the years; some were housed individually in crude wooden boxes with crosses gouged into them. I kneeled before one.

The face, the only earthly access to the soul. Big black eyes looked at me, astonished by their fate, the mouth releasing one long scream that I couldn't hear. This was no longer an excursion and I no longer felt excited or even curious. I wanted to stay there with that person and find the courage to run my hand over their skull, like putting a baby to sleep, to watch over them as they slept. I wanted to prove that I wasn't afraid of death because fate knew what it was doing. Didn't it?

"Everything all right?" The churchwoman's voice punched through the stillness. She'd obviously come to check on me, and perhaps I wasn't even really allowed there on my own. "Each of these skulls is the responsibility of a parishioner," she explained with a slowness that I now understood was not mourning at all but simply the effort to speak in Italian. "They take one or two in their care. It's like they become part of the family. They clean the skull, build an altar. Every day they pray for that person to get out of purgatory."

I listened without saying a word. I'd always pictured purgatory as something of a waiting room, and in my life I'd never known hell . . . or heaven, for that matter.

"Everybody needs somebody to look after them," the woman went on, letting out a bit of Neapolitan this time. "Someone to hassle the heavens for them." Some truths could only be spoken in dialect. If I'd been a Catholic I might have said *amen*. From my anthropological studies, I knew she was right—we are social creatures after all—yet I only grasped that her words were meant not for all of humanity but for me personally when she added in the raspy whisper of a smoker, "You got a boyfriend?"

"Me? No."

It was the only possible answer, and yet at the same moment my heart leaped inside my chest. Because along with that no, which came out more like a protest than a fact, an image of Pietro had appeared before me with a clarity I didn't think my memory was capable of. His lean body and solid gaze, his distinguished and slightly crooked nose, his mouth sealing a mysterious pleasure.

"Pretty little thing like you. There's gotta be someone," answered the woman, slipping into the dialect now like into a pair of old clogs and cradling my hand in hers, which were coarse and warm. "Someone's waitin' for you, I'd bet my bottom lira."

A man waiting for me? I met the old woman's eyes. There was something in them, a warmth easily tapped into with true-born Neapolitans that made me almost want to trust this stranger, in the middle of a mass grave, with the story of how someone had given me a gift that I couldn't get out of my head. A young man whom I didn't know and would probably never see again but who must have seen something—in me, in *us*—that I simply couldn't see.

Instead I said, "I like being on my own."

"On your own, huh?" She patted my hand—too hard, almost a slap—before letting it go. The moment was gone. And yet hadn't she just read my mind—and maybe even my future?

Outside the cemetery, the sun was unbearably bright and the neighborhood unbearably alive despite the premature siesta, the closed shutters, the lazy graffiti. Did the streets even have names here? A shield of tears—of discomfort or emotion, it was hard to tell—welled up in my eyes, turning the neighborhood into a molten, unreal landscape. Was the world bending to my vision or was it my own very atoms whirling like a dervish and fusing with the world around me? For an excruciating and beautiful instant there were no boundaries. Anything was possible.

From: tectonic@tin.it
To: heddi@yahoo.com
Sent: January 3

Dear Heddi,

I should have written back earlier. I'm trying again now, for the hundredth time, unsure of whether I have mustered enough courage over the years to tell you the truth about my life.

I dislike the life I lead. For the past two years I've been working on an oil platform in the middle of the Adriatic Sea. I'm a laborer. I work fifteen days a month and then the other fifteen I'm free (so to speak). The work doesn't give me any form of gratification. I'm afraid of being the same person day in and day out.

I'm still looking for a job abroad, but every time I send off my résumé I spend entire days fantasizing about finding work somewhere not far from you and maybe popping over to your house for a cup of coffee and a chat.

I constantly think of the mistakes I've made, which all converge into a sort of large basin of failure. You're probably wondering what it is I want from you. I don't know. But you're the only woman I've ever really loved. I hurt you, and even after all these years I'm unable to find an explanation as to why I ran away from you. I can only find excuses with myself. I'm well aware that I threw away my only chance of a peaceful and happy life, with you. It's an awareness that grows deeper over the years, that I ferociously walked all over the feelings, respect, and love of the most beautiful person I've ever met and will ever meet. It's the certainty that I folded my cards at a time when I could have walked away with the whole pot.

This makes me come back to the question: What do I want from you? I want you to know that my self-esteem is reduced to a few scraps; I want you to know that there will never be another woman like you in my life. I've had a few flings, which I've come out of feeling more aware, more certain than

29

ever, of the amount of shit I've buried myself under. I want you to see what a useless existence I have; I want to be sure I've shown you that you were right.

It's good to know you haven't completely buried my name, it's good to hear a bit about you and your cat. It's a gift I don't deserve. I hope you'll want to tell me more. I'd love to be able to imagine you, what you do every day, where you buy your groceries, what you cook, how you spend your weekends. Please write soon. And in the meantime, say hello to those Mexican cowboys for me and, if you think it's not too inappropriate, to Barbara and your father.

p.

4

G UESS WHO'S COMING TONIGHT," said Sonia as we set the table, which had been carried out to the terrace for the occasion. "Angelo invited him," she whispered. A crescent of a smile lit up her beautiful Mediterranean face as warm blasts of wind made strands of her hair go suddenly weightless like black seaweed in the water.

The scirocco had started to blow a few days earlier, creeping up on us without a sound. The Saharan wind always turned up around that time of year, and yet somehow it continually took us by surprise. Like a tropical mudslide it rolled down the streets of the Spanish Quarter, pressing itself indecently against everything in its path: the thighs of married women, the fur of stray dogs, cabbages sliced in half. Once inside the quarter, it strayed down the side streets, now left and now right, north and south, for it had no real aim there other than to blow the finest desert sand through the lace of panties hung out to dry and the engines of scooters parked for too long, and to blanket every last soul in a twisting, grating warmth.

Still, there was a raw pleasure in the scirocco: in its temporary lawlessness, in the sense of powerlessness and the heat it brought with it. It was finally warm enough to eat outside. The desert wind was a sign that summer was on its way, shepherded slowly up from Africa, and now more than any other year it made me yearn for that long, laid-back season. A desire that, upon hearing Sonia's words, became a dull ache in my gut. I heard a murmuring in my ear. It was the wind: *Hurry up*, it was saying.

"I've made up my mind. I'm going to talk to him tonight."

"Great, Sonia. You really should."

"Oh, the pasta!"

"I'll go."

At least in the kitchen there was no one around, not even the wind. I stirred the bucatini, the clumsiest of all pastas, long pasty limbs that went all awry and refused to be tamed, especially tonight, by my big wooden spoon. Before long I heard voices rising up from the front door. Then footsteps on the stairs.

Angelo was squealing, "Wicked, this stuff is the bomb!"

Then a vaguely familiar male voice. "Yeah, my grandparents make it too."

Finally, a deep, soulful voice. "It's not as good as last year's. I hope you like it anyway."

How had I not been moved, the night of the party, by the power of his voice? Pietro came up the stairs first, holding an unlabeled bottle of wine. I didn't look at him but at the curly-haired boy behind him, whom I recognized as Davide, followed by Angelo carrying something wrapped in butcher paper.

"Look what Pietro's brought from the farm," chirped Angelo, opening the brown paper for me to see. "Homemade soppressata, how about that?"

"Great," I said, stealing a glance at Pietro as he waited in the living room under the ceiling medallion. He just stood there awkwardly, leaning heavily on one leg as if the other was lame.

I put down the steaming spoon. "It's this way," I said under my breath and, whether he'd heard me or not, he followed me outside.

"Jesus Christ," were his first words. "What is this place, the royal palace?" He was looking at the chipped stucco waterspout attached to the terrace wall. In better times, water would have poured from the mouth of the devilish face into the basin.

Tonino greeted Pietro with a manly pat on the shoulder, taking the wine from him. "Whoever built it was probably just some prick trying to look like King Ferdinand the Fourth. Have you seen the frescoes? Fucking cheesy."

"In other words, the apartment's an illegal addition," said Luca, "built on top of the original building from the 1600s. It probably dates back to no earlier than the 1930s."

"Well, whenever it was built," Pietro replied, "the owners must have been rolling in cash."

"Yeah, maybe years ago when this neighborhood might have been halfway decent," said Angelo. "But the current owners are just a bunch of *vasciaioli*. They're trashy as hell, and they're crooks too. You should hear what fine Italian they speak when they call to put up the rent."

"They spend the day in the *vascio*," Luca clarified. "But their private rooms are on the next floor up."

"Big fat difference . . ."

"How the fuck do you always know all this shit?" Tonino said.

"I couldn't help noticing your delightful neighbor," said Davide, and in fact no one ever missed the transvestite standing outside the ground-floor home across from our building, with legs like a horse's. It wasn't easy to walk past without slowing down and at the same time tear your eyes away from the innards of the room, which, with its blood-red couch, faux marble, and fake gold fittings, tried to suck you in like a Chinese brothel.

"Enough to make a straight guy turn gay," said Tonino, his machismo perfectly intact.

Angelo was shaking his head. "Why anyone would choose to live down there instead of in an awesome place like this is beyond me."

"To avoid the fucking stairs," replied Tonino. "I swear, one day these six flights are going to be the death of me."

"Or to be right in the action, in the heart of it all," said Luca, extending a pack of tobacco to Pietro.

Pietro politely waved it away, pulling out a pack of Marlboros instead. He looked more relaxed as he took his first lungful. "They're Lights," he said, turning toward me. It was an apology.

Sonia came out carrying the pot of bucatini *alla puttanesca*, its bare-cupboard ingredients and uncertain origins—Sicily? Rome? Ischia?—the perfect dish for our motley crew. We all took a seat around the table, Pietro across from me. His red wine was served around. I hardly ever drank—alcohol only made me nauseated—but tonight I let my glass be filled, halfway . . . all right, three-quarters. I took a sip out of politeness and no sooner had I than liquid heat charged through my veins in the same pleasurable but invasive way that the scirocco was now furrowing its warm, fat fingers through my hair. I wrestled it back into an unsuccessful bun.

"Buon appetito."

We ate in customary silence, as good food required; the chaotic wind, too, imposed a certain solitary focus. It was the best chance I had to study Pietro unnoticed, to see if my memory matched reality. I had remembered his features after all, but now I was struck by their singularity. Pietro had the huge, expressive eyes of a deer in the woods, yet his long, bony nose lent a Babylonian majesty to his profile. As for his mouth, my eyes wouldn't go there.

I watched him as he topped up Davide's wine ("It won't win any awards," he was saying, "but it's better than water"), deciding that his attractiveness was well out of the ordinary, a kind of exaggerated beauty that bordered on ugliness. But although Pietro constantly toyed with the boundary between inaccessible beauty and easy vulgarity, he never crossed it. He was strange and magnificent. I studied his features so closely that, though separated by the table, I swore I could feel the warmth released through his nostrils, the tingling feather of his eyelashes. Again the wind went, *Hurry up.*

I took a big sip of wine and noticed that Sonia was clearly studying him too. She was watching his lips. Slightly reddened with tomato, they were moving, and it was only then I realized Pietro was speaking. Tonino had asked him a question.

"Hydrogeology," Pietro was saying, "is useful if you want to find water; for example, if you need to figure out where to dig a well."

"Do people still dig wells?" asked Sonia.

Tonino said, "Aren't you supposed to be from Sardinia?"

"Ah, the urban youth of today . . ." said Angelo, feigning a resigned sigh. He enjoyed teasing Sonia good-naturedly for the fact that she too was born at the far reaches of Italy.

"Can't you just use one of those sticks to find water?" asked Davide.

"The old folks in the village do," Pietro answered.

"You mean those wife-beating sticks?" chimed in Tonino. "My dad has one of those."

Everyone laughed so I did the convivial thing and joined in. Pietro was laughing, too, that is, until he wrapped his long fingers over his mouth in a rather contemplative gesture and rested his eyes on me. I could feel the weight of his gaze: it was as though he'd been waiting all evening for this racket, this rowdy opportunity when everyone was distracted, to unload it onto me. Any lightheartedness I might have had instantly abandoned me. I couldn't even hear all the happy chatter because in reality I was no longer with my friends around the table but with Pietro in a deep and clear world, a seabed where silence throbbed in our ears to the slow, inevitable rhythm of the waves.

There the two of us were alone. Pietro was anything but a stranger. He was looking at me, *inside* me, with the spear of his gaze puncturing everything I held dear, and without having to utter a single word he was telling me, *I came here tonight for you.* Understanding this, the fork still poised between my fingers turned to lead—I could hardly hold on to it—and the blood drained violently from my face until all that was left of me was a wandering spirit. The scirocco was now having its way with

35

me but I had no strength to fight it, or to hold Pietro's gaze even a second longer.

I turned away. The laughter flooded back into my ears. Pietro looked away, too, and gone was the certainty, unassailable only a moment ago, that we'd had a dialogue without speaking. Clearly I was delirious, perhaps even drunk.

"Have you taken volcanology?" Luca was asking.

Pietro answered, without emotion and without addressing anyone in particular, that he'd taken it for a year only. "It's not my field. But I do have great respect for volcanoes, let's put it that way."

So he was a geology major. That breast pocket, those shoes: it all made sense now. What could be intimidating about a geology student?

"What about Vesuvius," I said, surprised to hear my own voice. "Have you studied it?"

"A little. It's a perfect example of a stratovolcano."

"What does that mean?" asked Sonia, and he explained that they were the cone-shaped volcanoes, built up over hundreds of thousands of years from all the lava flows, with basalt and rhyolite and other enigmas coming to the surface.

"Basically, a giant zit," said Davide, chewing on a piece of soppressata.

Pietro smiled and again covered his mouth, rubbing his clean-shaven jaw. "You could say that. But it's the most dangerous type of volcano on Earth."

"Oh god, should we be worried?" asked Sonia.

"Maybe. Almost half of the world's volcanoes that have erupted recently have been stratovolcanoes."

"Define *recently*," said Tonino.

"In the last ten thousand years."

Davide and Angelo were now guffawing at something at the other end of the table. The noise drew my gaze to the edge of the terrace and out over the city all the way to the volcano, looking radiant in the orange light of the scirocco.

"But that doesn't mean," I found myself saying, "that Vesuvius is going to erupt *now*. It could be thousands of years away, right?"

"Who knows, but there's no point worrying. It's the law of chaos. There's not much we can do about it."

Pietro had spoken with a fatalism that poorly matched his baritone, which was firm yet reassuring like the voice of a news weatherman announcing the perfect storm. In fact, Sonia said, "Well, I'm not going to freak out about it then."

Seeing her light up like that had a sobering effect on me. It was Sonia's night. Maybe she'd even told her secret to Angelo, who was now conspiring to help her by inviting Pietro over. It also occurred to me that Pietro might not have understood a single word on that entire mixed tape of American songs, that for him it was merely a sharing of tunes with a native from the land of rock 'n' roll. Now I was doubly convinced that what I'd earlier perceived as a silent exchange across the table was nothing more than a glance in my direction, and like most glances it had in fact lasted only a few seconds. It was even possible that Pietro, on his own accord, had come here tonight for Sonia, or for no one at all. I vowed to avoid any future dramatization—and to not take even one more sip of his wine.

Pietro sliced more soppressata for the table. "But anyway, we'd get some warning, in the form of earthquakes."

"That's what Pliny the Younger described too," offered Luca, and, as was the case whenever he decided to speak, everyone went quiet. "The residents of Pompeii felt the earthquakes in the days leading up to the eruption. But they made no connection at all to Vesuvius."

"And the water tasted like sulfur before the wells suddenly dried up," added Pietro, "but they made nothing of it. They didn't have the science. The people didn't even know it was a volcano. For them it was just a mountain that gave them good grapes to make wine with . . ." As if to restrain inappropriate laughter, or for having said too much, his hand was back over his mouth.

His knowledge must have impressed Luca, for after that he collegially, almost gentlemanly, deferred to Pietro for every geological detail of his historical tale. Perhaps Luca's greatest wisdom was knowing what it was that he did not know, and Pietro added or corrected with the very same humility. One day around one in the afternoon, as the story went, came the blast, along with an eruption column about thirty kilometers high. When it hit the top of the sky, the column spread out like an umbrella pine, according to the eighteen-year-old Pliny watching the disaster from Misenum. Eventually though, the earth took back what rightfully belonged to it and all the erupted matter came back down—ash, pumice, rocks. Darkness fell like a sudden midnight. All afternoon and all night, rocks hammered the city, a malicious rain that made roofs cave in and filled up bedrooms and the streets of Pompeii and Stabiae, all the while sparing Herculaneum so as to leave it to the mercy of mudslides. Clouds of suffocating ash caught any who had survived. Just as the sea had pulled away from the coastline, leaving fish and shellfish on dry sand, so too were the gods deserting man.

As Luca spoke, the scirocco brushed his cigarette smoke east and then west before blurring it into the yellow night. "On top of that, there were toxic gases."

"And intense heat," added Pietro. "Pyroclastic surges."

Luca nodded gratefully before concluding, "That day over ten thousand people lost their lives."

I listened as if strapped to my seat. For years when I'd lived right there, in what was ancient Stabiae, where Pliny the Elder himself had died suffocated by the ash, like everybody else I gave little thought to the stories beneath my feet. Now, for some reason, that familiar truth filled me with an electrifying fear that bordered on euphoria: maybe it was the shimmering threads Luca had woven into the story, or maybe something else entirely.

I glanced over at Pietro, whose eyes, too, were on Luca as he drank from his cup, unperturbed by the Saharan wind teasing strands of hair from his ponytail. It was the way I often looked at Luca myself, with an admiration I was desperate to hide, all the more in moments like this when his tongue was loosened—by the wine or by the wind, I couldn't tell. Everyone else, though, was craning their necks to catch a glimpse at the volcano beyond the city lights, as though they'd only just now noticed it was there.

"Not to mention the devastating eruption of 1631," Luca said finally.

No one dared to ask about 1631. Someone shouted in the streets below, a motorbike skidded: it all seemed so far away. Pietro reached for his shirt pocket swollen with the perfect rectangle of his Marlboro Lights. As he did so, his shirt stretched opened a little, giving me a peek at a silver pendant. A sun?

Quickly I turned away. It wasn't my gift to unwrap. And yet the wind was fiddling with the collar of my moth-eaten jacket, breathing onto my neck, breathing my name. *Hurry up, Heddi, hurry up.*

The wine was gone, the soppressata, too, but the evening wasn't over. The mismatched chairs had moved like checker pieces away from the table; Davide sat on the edge of the fountain talking thick as thieves with Luca. The conversation shifted to lighter topics. At one point, Angelo took a breadcrust and balanced it on his upper lip. "How do I look with a mustache?"

"You look like Signor Rossi," Tonino said drolly.

"Oh yeah, Signor Rossi, that cute little cartoon guy," said Sonia. "I loved him when I was little."

"So people in Sardinia already had television then?" Angelo teased her.

Again laughter. I didn't look Pietro's way to see if he was laughing or not. Surely he, like everyone else, knew who this childhood hero Signor Rossi was. I stood to clear the table.

"I'll give you a hand." Pietro was already at my side piling the dirty dishes. I thanked him, gesturing him to follow me toward the kitchen. Behind me he said, "I hear you're a talented linguist."

"Where did you hear that?"

"Is it true you speak five languages?"

"Four, actually. My Russian's terrible," I said, putting the dishes beside his on the kitchen counter. I never counted Neapolitan—no one did—though it, too, was technically a language, Vulgar Latin steeped in Oscan, Greek, and even Arabic.

"Russian, I'm impressed. And a whole other alphabet too."

"It's actually not that hard to learn. I could teach you to read Cyrillic in five minutes."

"I'd like that."

Had I been so bold as to offer him a private lesson? I hadn't meant it that way. But I *had* asked him to follow me inside, away from all the others, when surely I could have cleared the table myself. All I knew was that out of the restless wind talking seemed easier. I beckoned him over to the sooty, cold fireplace. Up close I could smell his cologne. A breath of fresh air, a pine forest.

I pointed to the brown flowers on the tiled floor. "What do you make of this crack?"

"I see," he said. "How far does it go?"

"All the way to the terrace." I watched him as he stepped along the crack, cautiously as if on the edge of a crevasse. "I think it's getting wider," I added. "But the boys don't seem to pay any attention to it, not even Angelo, who has a crack in the ceiling in his bedroom."

"I'm not sure. But it doesn't look good, the way it follows the outer wall like this." He paused above it, squatting now.

I followed suit. I didn't know what I wanted from Pietro, who was neither an engineer nor an architect but a scientist of the Earth, but all I knew was that it was good to be able to crouch beside him, not looking at each other, in such a domestic stance.

I caught a glance of Sonia outside on the terrace. She was so good-hearted, and from a good family. Despite her cranelike frame, she retained that wholesome baby fat in her cheeks that I'd lost abruptly, overnight it seemed, some years back, unveiling a raw pair of cheekbones like rocks after the tide has pulled away, a vestige perhaps of the Cherokee blood that coursed through my veins and that, even in a small dose, could one day reawaken the nomad in me.

I thought about Sonia's solemn confession on the roof that night, but I didn't know how much weight to give it. Was it like in that card game where the first person to play their cards has the implied right to win the hand? Somehow it seemed so and that, according to these rules, it didn't matter that Pietro had given me a gift, and that the old churchwoman in the cemetery mysteriously seemed to have known about him, and that the memory of his gentle nature was a music that wouldn't give me rest, and that now his far-fetched face, with that nose appearing oddly delicate up close, was looking back at me with a rather serious expression. Was he worried about the crack in the floor or was he having the same thoughts as I was?

5

I RAN INTO PIETRO two days later near my university. Without much small talk, he invited me for a coffee that afternoon at the house he shared with his brother. Around four o'clock, he suggested, scribbling on a scrap of paper "Via De Deo, 33. Iannace." Their place was in the Spanish Quarter, apparently only four or five blocks from mine.

Yet on the way there I got lost, just as the neighborhood had hoped I would. Its grid pattern of streets had been designed for just that since their conception as Spanish military barracks. Nearly identical cafés, fruit vendors, and makeshift stalls with eggs or contraband cigarettes on every corner heightened the mirror effect of that grid, which was ideal for keeping the outsider out and the insider in.

To overcome this problem, I'd memorized paths through the quarter. For example, from my building to the Orientale it was left, left again, then right at the street shrine, then straight, sidestepping the puddles under the trays of octopus and mussels, until the street exhaled me out of the quarter and onto the main boulevard, Via Roma. Guided by a sort of muscle memory, I could walk through it all unscathed, even untouched, as if balancing on a tightrope drawn past the antennae and the hanging laundry, through the smog and the hollering. The Spanish Quarter couldn't be conquered, yet by following such routes I maintained the necessary control to navigate it practically with my eyes closed. But Via De Deo wasn't on any path I knew. I held on tight to my book bag, occasionally letting my eyes dart up to the street plaques.

"Hey, toothpick!"

It was a young girl who'd checked me out and summed me up and was now staring me down, raring for a catfight; she may have only been nine years old, but in Neapolitan years that was something like nineteen. It was always hard to tell what the locals thought of us university lodgers. It was said that they tried to shield us from their criminal dealings, but who knows. Sometimes they appeared curious, at other times violated. But mostly they looked at us the same way they looked at the neighborhood's stray dogs, with annoyance but not without tenderness, and kept us at arm's length.

The girl gave up and moved on. Out of the corner of my eye I saw something black and white run up a side street and into a *vascio*. A goat, I was almost sure. And I thought I'd seen everything there was to see in the Quartieri, including a white rabbit living in the woodpile under a pizza maker's oven. The goat seemed like a good sign and I dived into the alleyway after it. There was a farm smell but no trace of the animal. Locals were glaring at me from their doorways. I kept my eyes glued to the volcanic street stones, but I could already feel panic digging into my bewildered feet with its small, desperate claws.

I recoiled into the first right-hand alley. A deli, thank goodness. I took cover under the dangling meat and stole a glimpse at the street sign. *Via De Deo*. So much like *Dio*, it occurred to me. Real or not, the goat had shown me the way. Naples always came through for me in the end.

My thighs tensed up as I made my way up the steep incline. It gave the motorbikes a good workout too: men drove up it with their heads down in concentration, fat widows rode on the back, sidesaddle as their skirts and their years required. Women heaved uphill the burden of their shopping and of their children. Twenty-three. Twenty-five. Twenty-seven. My heart was racing. I blamed it on that ridiculous street, which, if it didn't ease soon, would take me all the way to San Martino, the monastery just beyond the Spanish Quarter that appeared to hover above it like the very gates of heaven.

Thirty-three. Through the gate I could see a courtyard sunken in darkness but positively thriving with potted plants. My gaze slid up the dizzying face of the building. Above was a blue rectangle, a hint of vastness that made me feel I was about to burst.

I tried to remind myself that it was just a coffee. And yet, as I pressed the button and heard the instructions to go to the top floor, the ensuing click at the gate sounded like the nonnegotiable voice of fate.

Pietro looked up from a table. The buttery smell of coffee was already permeating the house and a cigarette smoldered next to several others that were doubled over in the ashtray. He stood to greet me with a tight-lipped grin, his shirt tucked in hard. He seemed poised to shake my hand: he didn't, but neither did he kiss me on the cheeks.

"It's very . . . sunny up here," I said, out of breath.

"It's our Monte Carlo." He let out a short laugh. "Have a seat. Wherever you like. The coffee's ready. How do you like it?" He was firing words at me as he made his way to the adjoining kitchen.

"With a splash of milk, if there is any. Otherwise don't worry."

I took a seat at the table and looked around the spacious living room. Other than the size and the similarity of being on the last (and likely illegal) floor, the apartment was nothing like ours. As if it had just been moved into, there were no pictures or posters, just a sigh of white space interrupted only by the metal of a desk and a line of books. Above a vinyl sofa was a modern staircase that led to a second floor. Windows and still more windows allowed the sun into the deepest recesses of the room, even under the stairs, cottoning everything in a soft glow.

"Sugar?"

"Yes, please."

"Gabriele, coffee!" Pietro's call reverberated in the uncluttered house. "My older brother," he added as he put a cup before me. His hand was shaking slightly: Was it too many cigarettes or the fact that we were now truly alone together for the first time?

"I never asked you," I said, stirring my sugar with undue care. "How was your stay on the farm?"

"Same old same old."

"What do you mean?"

"Hellish as always!"

This clarification came not from Pietro but from an equally deep voice. A man with thinning black hair and a familiarly sharp, if slightly subtler, nose came toward me. Still standing, he said, "Gabriele, pleased to meet you. Let me tell you now, if you ever get invited to the farm, just say no. It'll save you a lot of grief."

"Don't listen to him. It's not that terrible."

"No, it's not that terrible," said Gabriele theatrically. "How should we call it then, bucolic? Elegiac? Evocative and thought-provoking?"

"I have to apologize for Gabriele. He doesn't appreciate fresh air. He prefers smog."

Gabriele lit a cigarette and appeared to draw life-giving oxygen from it. "My baby brother is a bit blind. It's not his fault: he's the favorite. And he deserves it." Then he looked at Pietro with a kind of love I'd never seen before, a furious adoration that made me lower my eyes. "Now, I'd love to ask you a zillion questions, but I'm sure my brother here would rather ask you himself, and anyway I have a design to finish by the end of the week. So I'll be out of your hair now." He downed his coffee.

"Are you an artist?" I asked, because suddenly I couldn't bear for Gabriele to go off and leave us alone.

"I study architecture."

"My brother's an architect too."

"Lucky him. I'm afraid for me it's only a dream. Farewell for now, Eddie, but I'm sure I'll see you again soon."

With a heavy gait, Gabriele disappeared up that staircase. What had he meant by *see you again soon*? I had the distinct feeling that Pietro had told his brother about me. And yet, what was there to tell?

Espressos take such a painfully short time to drink. After a difficult pause Pietro asked me if I liked rocks. The question was hopelessly generic but I clung to it nonetheless. I told him about how when I was little my father would sometimes take me to the beach to search for fossils, and about his many film canisters of sands, treasures collected around the world. He too had studied geology before having to change majors, something that secretly made me feel I had a privileged, almost genetic, relationship to rocks. "On the beach my dad used one of those, what's it called, a kind of hammer . . ."

"A prospecting pick," Pietro said excitedly. "Yes, I have one."

"Really?"

"All geology students have to own one. It's a tool of the trade, like a sword to a knight." He was laughing but looking intently now into his empty cup, like he was reading his fortune in the swirl of sugar crystals. All of a sudden he leveled his eyes with mine. "Would you like to see it? It's upstairs."

It wasn't just a coffee. Despite my wild heartbeat, there was a certain relief in giving in to that knowledge. As I followed him up the staircase, I had to restrain a smile. Wasn't it just like fourth grade, inviting a girl into your room to see a rock pick or a butterfly collection? Couldn't he have come up with something better? But it was in fact the childishness of that fib that made the invitation acceptable. And the comfort brought on by that lovely little lie, of which we were both willing participants, wiped away all doubt, there wasn't even a shadow of it now, that, on the third occasion that we'd ever spoken, once upstairs we would kiss.

———

Pietro's room was the size of a closet, or at best a cabin on a ship, with the port mounted like a jewel in the window. There was hardly enough space for a single bed, a makeshift bookshelf, and a Jimi Hendrix poster. Pietro lifted his prospecting pick off the shelf and offered it to me as if it were made of the most translucent porcelain. He showed me how his name was carved into the handle, by his own hand. As I listened to him, I stole glances at his fleshy lower lip, wondering how on earth we were going to shift from a pick to a kiss.

"Sorry it's such a small room," he said. "If you want to sit down, you can use the bed."

So this was how it was going to happen. I sat down, surrendering to that little twist and turn of fate. But I was out of my depth. I couldn't comprehend how I'd ended up there, in a stranger's room, on his bed. A slippery dip in blood pressure made my head go light and my body heavy like a bag of stones I suddenly had to bear. But at this point I was committed to seeing it through. I was already imagining being back in the safety of my own room, retasting the kiss that hadn't happened yet—or, it now occurred to me, trying to erase the memory of it.

Pietro sat next to me, saying simply, "I might lie down." He lowered the prospecting pick to the floor and stretched out comfortably, his legs pointing toward the sea.

I lay down, too, and this somewhat eased my light-headedness. We stayed there on our backs on that tiny bed, the kind children sleep in, while each and every pretense rose like steam up to the ceiling. For a long while we looked at the slanting ceiling, a mirror in which I could see reflected back to me a dizzying array of possibilities.

I asked, "Are you a Jimi Hendrix fan?"

"Not really. I just thought the poster looked cool." His voice was as close to me as it had ever been, and at such low volume it sounded deeper still. I wanted him to say more, and more. Instead he asked me what kind of music I liked.

"I don't know, quite a range." I shrugged at the ceiling. "I liked the songs you taped for me."

He laughed uneasily. "I thought a lot about what I was going to put on that tape. It took me hours."

"But you didn't even know me."

"It was like a sixth sense, Heddi."

There was a grave silence. I couldn't possibly turn my face toward him now, with his breath so close I could taste it. All at once, the ceiling went dark and there was a collision of sandpaper with my mouth. Startled, I pulled away. Oh god, it had gone horribly wrong, it had all turned out very high school . . . very *liceo*.

"What's wrong? Are you all right?"

"You just surprised me, that's all."

"You mean you didn't think I was going to kiss you?" And he fell dejectedly back on the bed.

Part of me wanted to walk out then and there and forget all about it. But a voice deep inside—and perhaps it was nothing but my familiar thirst for knowledge—told me I had to stay, to push through the awkwardness and the shame. I had to *know*. So I leaned over him, a rush of blood to my head instantly curing my low blood pressure, and I brushed his lips with mine as if to shush him. Pietro craned his neck to reach me with his mouth, like he was passing me a Halloween apple with his hands tied. I pulled back, burned by his stubble. Was this how they kissed in the province of Avellino?

I was still looking at his plump lower lip and without thinking I gently bit it. He let me. He just lay there, eyelids shut and breathing heavily, perhaps afraid of what I might do next. I didn't know myself.

In a show of goodwill, again I pressed my lips against his. And this time his mouth opened soft and sweet like a fresh fig. It was warmed by the sun and ripe, just right, and I wanted more. Another kiss, and yet another, and soon our mouths were feeding off each other, one taste leading inevitably to the next but never satisfying. Before long we were scrambling for them, greedily, individually, as they disappeared one by one like cherries from a bowl. In the end there might even be a winner and a loser.

I was not in any way transported: I was almost too present, a purely physical being hyperaware of every movement, every sensation. There was my upper lip becoming raw from Pietro's stubble, the balm of his tongue, the porcelain of his teeth. His belt buckle pressing into my hip-bone, the stubborn buttons of his shirt, his long fingers getting caught in my hair. His scent of cologne and coffee, tomatoes and sweat. I had to keep my eyes shut: that was the only way I could limit the number of senses flooding me with information I couldn't reconcile.

I lost my grasp of time, or perhaps time had lost its linearity. When had we started kissing: two minutes ago, two hours ago? I didn't have the faintest idea. The beginning had slipped into oblivion and the end was no longer inevitable. One kiss led to another and the only certainty was that we couldn't stop.

Then out of nowhere, something came over me—an inspiration, though not a flash of light but rather a flash of darkness, like a power cut. I was blinded, plunged into the deepest night. I was suspended there, sto-len out of my own body, stripped of my sense of self, and yet it was such an incredible feeling that I could have stayed there forever, floating in the universe. Was this why people took heroin? But if it was so, then it was also true that he and I had shot up with the same drug, the same needle, for in that very moment we both opened our eyes.

We looked at each other for an eternity, or maybe just a breath. A transparent and peaceful gaze that went beyond judgment or embarrass-ment, even beyond curiosity. Our mouths still attached, we watched each other as if someone else were doing the kissing, our bodies carrying on without us. We had nothing to do with it, we were merely witnessing the beauty of the world.

We closed our eyes, letting the kisses rock us like so many exploding stars. Decorum was gone. Lips wandered to the cheekbones, chin, neck. I rubbed my cheeks across his stubble, wishing now for rawness. He rolled on top of me, murmuring things that made no sense, a warm mist breathing into my hair and my ear, not words at all but a spirit moving me. My god, was *this* how they kissed in the province of Avellino? It was a divine, primordial chaos that seemed to be building up to a great upheaval of the elements. I became afraid, and as if to brace myself, to ground myself, I searched for his mouth so that I could take in his breath once more. I'd forgotten where I was and how I'd come to be there, I'd even forgotten his name or that he was like any of the other people on the planet who had names, pasts, and daily concerns. He was simply him, this *man*, whose mouth was mine to kiss, every warm and rich corner of it, and whose chest was pressed, sternum and ribs and heart and all, up against mine.

When the sun began staining the port soda-pop orange, we looked into each other's eyes again and there was a renewed awareness that we were two separate individuals. We started laughing, at nothing, perhaps with relief. I leaned against Pietro's chest. There it was, the pendant I shouldn't have seen when his shirt had opened up on the terrace, a smiling silver sun. I asked him if it had any special meaning to him.

"I bought it in a market, just a couple of months ago. And I thought while I was buying it that I wished I had someone to give it to. It's pathetic, I know."

"Not at all." I held the sun in my hands. Around a grin of fulfillment were rays with tips almost too sharp to touch. "I find it moving."

"You're such a good person, Heddi," he said rather solemnly.

"How did you learn my name?"

"I asked around. It wasn't that hard." Brushing the hair off my face, he added, "You're beautiful too. But I bet you've heard that many times before."

50

The truth was that, like all girls, I'd heard it plenty. When it came to the female form, at least in the slums a Neapolitan man wasn't a man unless he vomited his private thoughts in the streets. But hearing it from Pietro was another thing altogether.

"I don't know what you see in me," he said. "I'm just from a small village. You're a big-city girl."

"A big city?" As if American cities were ranked by their verticality, I cut Washington down to size by telling him there were no skyscrapers, and that my dad and stepmom's neighborhood was full of undocumented Mexican immigrants in cowboy hats, out of work and far from home, some who were so drunk by midday they couldn't even stand up. I didn't mention the Polish and Ugandan embassies just down the road: I didn't want the capital of the United States to steal my thunder. But neither did I mention the other half of my life spent in the suburbs with my mom and stepdad.

Pietro's particular dot on the map went by the name of Monte San Rocco. His parents were farmers, he told me, and poor—or at least they acted like they were. His mother hadn't finished elementary school, and it was Pietro who'd taught his father to sign his own name. "Before that he used to sign with an *x*."

"You mean he's illiterate?"

Pietro turned toward the wall. "I don't think you'd have given me another glance if you saw me on a tractor." He turned back to me. "And yet, Heddi, I can't help but want to be with you, from the first time I saw you."

I hoped he couldn't feel the drum of my heart against his chest. "Who knows? Maybe someday I'll get to see you ride a tractor . . . or is it drive a tractor?"

"Fly a tractor." He wiped his laughter away with a hand. As for me, the joke had not just saved me from a linguistic slipup but also broken the tension, and I burst out in heartfelt laughter. He said, "I'd sure like to fly to Washington someday."

"I'd rather be here."

"Really?"

"I love living by the sea."

I laid my head on his chest. I hardly knew him but his smell was familiar even in its exoticness—a new spice, but one as earthy as salt, one I might no longer be able to do without. It came from his now crinkled shirt, his dusty hair, and his fading cologne that was now on my face too.

The slippery, molten sunlight cast sharp, geometrical shadows against the surrounding rooftops. The insidious sand of the scirocco really seemed to have gone. Maybe it wouldn't be back again until next year.

I bolted upright. "I have to get back home."

"Now?"

"It's late. The boys will be worried." But I wasn't really thinking about the boys. I was thinking about Sonia.

From: heddi@yahoo.com
To: tectonic@tin.it
Sent: January 14

Dear Pietro,

How strange to be writing to you after all this time. How strange to be writing, period. I exchange letters with only a handful of people, I don't have a diary. Sometimes I think I haven't really made my peace with words and I'm more comfortable in the woods listening to the chirping of birds. Can you believe it, me in the woods? I like to immerse myself in their world and listen to all those unintelligible and at times haunting languages that overlap like verses sung in a round. It's like being inside a beating heart . . .

Funnily enough, my job consists of words. I teach English to foreigners, mostly Chinese, Korean, and Russian immigrants. Learning is a game; we even go on field trips together and become quite close. Then they get into the university or find the job they were aiming for, etc., and I don't see them again. I'm happy at least to have helped them make their dreams come true. I remember the dreams you had. Where have they gone?

It's true, at times I do think about my own aborted dreams and it makes me suffer. But you shouldn't beat yourself up, Pietro. It's not your fault: blame destiny. Or rather, blame the lack of destiny and order in the world, blame chaos. I too have to accept responsibility for what happened. Besides, over the past few years I've come to realize something important: it's possible to live without having any answers. You survive, life goes on. The world, with its tides and natural rhythms, is beautiful anyway, stunningly beautiful, even though (or maybe precisely because) it's indifferent to our ups and downs and broken hearts.

I really would like it if one day you dropped by for a chat, but I think it's unlikely. I'm not living in Washington, as you may believe, but in New Zealand. Maybe the constellations really are upside down here, on the other side of the world . . .

h.

6

THAT KISS, THAT KISS . . . Was this what tasting the forbidden fruit was like? Only one last moment of hesitation and then the immediate reward for throwing your better judgment to the wind: an explosion of god almighty on your tongue and a surge of the most perfect, unstoppable pleasure, so much so that you can't distinguish the juice of the fruit trickling down your chin from the saliva from your own mouth, nor do you care.

I didn't know much about Bible stories, but it did seem to me that there was something in that kiss that was so good it had to be against the law, maybe even against nature. And now that I'd tasted it, now that I *knew*, there was no going back. I couldn't undo what I'd done, I couldn't unknow what I now knew. And yet I didn't even remotely want to go back. I was only shocked, incensed even. How had this been hidden from me my entire life?

I replayed that kiss over and over in my mind. Unlike with a cassette tape, there was no wearing or warping: the more I played it, the more it deepened in detail and emotion. By reliving it, I could slow it down and thus savor its many little components, some of which I'd very nearly missed the first time around: the salinity in the folds of his neck, his eyes, a tender yet vibrant shade of brown like a branch that has just shed its bark, his graceful yet broad hand spanning the back of my head as he pulled me in. That kiss was something that deserved to be relived, for I'd gone twenty-three years without it only to be granted half an hour.

If that. Besides, I didn't know if I would taste it ever again. A kiss like that, I reasoned, couldn't repeat itself, just as the forbidden fruit couldn't be tasted but once. In fact, in my head it did not automatically equate that in order to experience it once more all I had to do was be alone with Pietro again. That kiss was not specifically connected to the person. It was much greater than him, than us. And we couldn't re-create it because the kiss had created us.

"Leaving for Guangzhou soon?" I heard beside me.

"Sorry?"

Luca nodded up at the colossal ancient map of China flattened behind glass, the pride of the Department of Oriental Studies. Who knows how long I'd been sitting in that study hall, staring with unfocused eyes at that map and not my semiotics book.

"I was just studying."

"I know my Cancerians." Luca tossed his tattered bookbag on the table and scraped the floor noisily as he pulled out a chair. A few students looked up from their books. "Roberta is like that too."

"Like what?"

"A shell that's never empty."

Being compared in any way to Roberta was a huge compliment. Luca and Roberta had been together so long, long before my arrival in the Spanish Quarter, that it seemed out of the question that they would ever part. But then, some time ago now, Roberta had left for a Greek mountain village to translate ancient Greek poetry into Italian for her thesis. I wondered if Luca missed her, if he still *loved* her. Yet such topics were not part of our shared vocabulary.

"Do you have a minute?"

"Of course."

Luca pulled a cassette tape from his bag. He wanted help deciphering the English lyrics to a song that his heavy metal band was hoping to perform. As he scooted his chair closer and uncoiled some earphones, I was deeply flattered that Luca Falcone needed me, even if just for a moment. He always had some creative project on the go—Arabic calligraphy, astrological charts, ancient runes, restoration of samurai swords—but in the cultivation of his crafts he devoted an almost meditative focus that carried him far, far away from me, the boys, the university, Naples.

Through the earphones, the tape barked unintelligibly. It was a terrible song, but because Luca liked it there had to be something sublime in it that I just couldn't grasp. Once Luca had shown me how to cook saffron risotto. The saffron, like fragile branches of red coral protected from the world by a tiny glass capsule, didn't seem even vaguely edible, especially with that odd, musty smell. Carefully he broke off a miniature twig and blew it like a kiss into the pot. As if by magic, the simmering rice—and, I could almost swear, even the steam above it—exploded with yellow. Luca was an alchemist, so there had to be gold in this song too.

I jotted down the words as best I could. All the while Luca followed my handwriting, sitting so close that I could smell the lavender of his soap and hear the scrunching of his leather jacket. At the end he said, "What would I do without you, Heddi."

My name was Nordic and outmoded, but I loved it on Luca's lips. He was an exacting linguistic who was fluent in Arabic, French, and English, and he didn't merely pronounce my name: he pulled it out from somewhere deep within, like a sigh. I had the sudden urge to tell him about Pietro, but I held back. I was afraid of killing the magic of that afternoon, which still tingled in my head like a secret whispered against my ear. Besides, what if Sonia had confessed her feelings for Pietro to Luca as well? I didn't want to have any flaw, moral or otherwise, in Luca's eyes.

The window of opportunity closed when he started buckling up his bag. "You keep on studying. At this pace you'll get your degree before any of us."

"Who cares about a degree?" I said. "In the end it's just a piece of paper."

"True, but to almost everyone else that piece of paper is worth far more than a precious Islamic scroll. Especially to my father." Luca had thrown his bag across his shoulder but remained seated at my side. Dropping into a confidential and somewhat aggrieved tone, he added, "And anyway, whether I like it or not, at some point this chapter has to come to an end."

"What chapter?"

Luca gave me a crooked smile. "Have you ever been to Tunisia? It's a fascinating place, I'd love to go back there. My friends in Japan are always inviting me over too. But first, graduation . . . and the military."

The military was a profanity that was never uttered among our group of friends, and hearing it now felt like an insult. But he explained in a peaceful (or perhaps resigned) voice, that he'd chosen not to fulfill the yearlong compulsory military service straight after high school, unlike most of his classmates. Perhaps this had been a mistake, though, because at this age life in the barracks would be unbearable. Therefore, he'd made the decision instead to complete the civilian service as a conscientious objector.

"Either way, a year is too long, Luca!" Unthinkably long, just as it was unthinkable that after that year Luca wouldn't simply return to Naples.

"A year and a half," he clarified. "Otherwise it would be the easy way out."

"There's nothing easy about it . . ."

I wanted him to pull out one of his magic tricks to make it go away, or at least to find a loophole. But Luca simply laid his eyes on me in that way he had of trying to communicate on another plane of existence. I was stumped as to what it meant, deciding instead that it was best to not make a big deal out of something that was still far off in the hazy future.

He stood to go, asking me to walk him back to the Quartieri. Without a moment's hesitation I shut my book and grabbed my bag. That we'd just had one of the most personal conversations Luca and I had ever had somewhat alleviated its heaviness. And as we walked down Spaccanapoli in a sweet cloud of tobacco, our arms tightly locked and walking very nearly in step with each other, I felt sure everyone would think we, little old me and Luca Falcone, were best friends.

"Luca, what did you mean by *The world is a book*?"

"The world is a book and those who do not travel read only one page."

"Your words?"

"You overestimate me. Saint Augustine. But to me it also means that the things that are truly worth learning can't be found in books."

I was determined to be more prepared when I faced Sonia, but perhaps I overdid it by asking her to meet me at Caffè Gambrinus. Its gilded mirrors and their multiplying effect on the well-to-do only made me slouch further into the antique chair, velvety and reassuring like the gray-green underside of olive leaves. Yet that day I needed the pitiful comfort of my favorite refuge, where I could order a cappuccino after midday without so much as a flicker of disapproval on the face of the bow-tied waiter, and indulge my adolescent fantasies about what Italy was supposed to be. A literary hub in the 1800s, Gambrinus was one of the few last reminders that at one time Naples had been a major European capital. Gabriele D'Annunzio had lived in Naples (and was a frequent patron of Gambrinus), Degas and Goethe too. And hadn't the Marquis de Sade himself called Naples an infernal heaven?

Sonia took a seat. I felt a few stares in our direction, at my shabby jacket, at Sonia's black uniform. "Wow," she said, "it's so fancy in here."

I remembered Pietro at our rooftop dinner saying something like that about our place. It wasn't hard to imagine Sonia and Pietro as a couple. They spoke with the same candor; they came from the same world and had watched the same cartoons. As if I'd deprived her of her one true match, I was struck by the idea that I'd left Sonia to the wolves. And I didn't like being that person.

We sipped our coffees and talked about our strictest lecturers. Hers was a Portuguese grammar zealot and mine an elegant Bulgarian native who from day one had banned our class of two from uttering a single word of Italian, but who soon had us calling her by her first name, Iskra, and visiting her grown daughter while on a scholarship to Bulgaria. As Sonia and I chatted away, through the window I stole glimpses of Piazza Plebiscito, which up until my first year there had been a massive inner-city parking lot. The recent urban renewal had rid it of cars, revealing, in addition to lewd graffiti and peeling posters, an unexpected spaciousness, a place open to a thousand possibilities.

Sonia's empty cup came down on her saucer with a final, devasting clank. It was now or never. But I didn't know where to begin. I hadn't spoken to a soul about Pietro. Now I could either trivialize what had happened between us or tell the shocking truth that since that kiss I could hardly read a line in a book—or sleep.

"You look so serious. You're not in some sort of trouble, are you?"

"No, I'm fine, I'm fine . . . Remember when you told me about Pietro, up there on the roof?"

"Oh, yeah, he's so gorgeous." Sonia rolled her eyes upward as though recalling something heavenly, before adding, "I mean, gorgeous in a kind of unusual way, don't you think? And he has such beautiful hands, the hands of a gentleman . . ."

The observation shook my resolve, and I started a string of sentences without finishing a single one. I felt like a rambling fool, a circus clown rummaging through a rickety suitcase and tossing out item after useless item—a shoe, an umbrella, a banana—until he finds what he needs. And what I needed was vagueness. "I have feelings for him," I said finally.

Sonia's smile dropped ever so slightly. "And I would imagine he has feelings for you too."

"I'm sorry, I—"

Sonia stopped me midsentence, conveying in her fast, almost urgent, Sardinian way how happy she was for me and wrapping me in a hug that smelled of watermelon shampoo.

It was like a puzzle piece gloriously clicking into place. Outside the café, the midday sunshine ricocheted off the shop windows as I walked the short distance back to the Spanish Quarter. I turned into its alleyways, where I was welcomed back by the call of fish sellers, the purr of motorbikes, and the canopies of laundry. My legs effortlessly drove me up the incline of Via De Deo. Aromas of roasted peppers and seared steak came steaming out over the balconies, enveloping me in a mouthwatering mist. I remembered I hadn't eaten anything all day and my stomach reawakened. This only accentuated the lightness in my head, and in every fiber of my being, as I slid through the gate left ajar and sprinted up the stairs two at a time. I hadn't called, I hadn't even buzzed. I was going to show up at lunchtime, uninvited, without even the courtesy of a loaf of bread. But still I rushed there as if I were running late.

7

PIETRO SET ABOUT cooking for me, chopping the onions like he was afraid to cause them pain and gently adjusting the flame under the frying pan. He sure knew how to maneuver in that tiny kitchen and how to make do with the few ingredients he had, as though he were used to having guests turn up unannounced for lunch. He didn't want any help; he was simply glad that I'd come back, he insisted, sitting me down on the terrace step with a cape of sunlight on my back. He also put a glass of wine in my hand, and what harm could it do? The wine was in fact a medicine that cleared my head instead of clouding it. I understood that my concern over talking to Sonia had been blown out of proportion, and now all the drama fizzled into a sweet pulp like those onions sautéing with pancetta.

"You're a man of many talents. Geologist, cook . . ."

"I'm not a geologist yet. And anyway, wait until you try this amatriciana before you say I can cook." He let out a hoarse laugh.

The wine on an empty stomach made me uncharacteristically bold, and I said, "You didn't cover your mouth this time when you laughed."

"You have an eye like a hawk's."

"You have a nice smile. Why hide it?"

Pietro took a while to answer. He emptied a jar of home-bottled tomatoes into the pan and stirred them thoughtfully. "Can't you tell? It's my teeth."

I beckoned him over, and reluctantly he kneeled before me, that silver sun jingling. When he parted his lips slightly, all the wine I'd drunk slipped its long red tentacles around me, wrapping me in a hot, stinging pleasure.

"Let's have a look." I tried to focus on his teeth. They were straight and somewhat boxy, pearly white corn that I felt an overwhelming desire to run my tongue over right then and there. He smiled. I hadn't noticed it before, but in fact on one of his front teeth there was a faint gray shadow. "It's hardly noticeable," I said, and we kissed, an intimate mixture of wine and smoke and hunger that made a commotion of my heart.

He stood up. As we waited for the water to come to a boil, out of the blue he said, "Did you know I used to live in Rome?"

My eyes went involuntarily big. "Then why did you come to *Naples*?"

I knew it was hypocritical of me to ask him the very question that had been put to me countless times, as if my answer might justify why *any* of us were there. But it was true: Naples was never a choice. It was a gift that had to be forced on you, by birth or by fate.

Pietro told me that his brother was the one who'd chosen to go to Naples, to study architecture. Their parents had readily given Gabriele their blessing. School was all he was good at. But Gabriele didn't stop there: he told them he wouldn't leave without Pietro. His younger brother, too, he argued, had the right to fulfill his own dream of studying geology. This time they refused, unwilling to let go of their only son who knew how to turn olives into emerald liquid and wheat into golden powder. But Gabriele was headstrong, and eventually the old folks gave in.

Pietro didn't stop there either. He told them he wanted to study not in Naples but in Rome. It was as far away as he could imagine going. And perhaps it made no difference to his mother and father, as they were losing him anyway, to one city or another. The farthest they had ever been was Schaffhausen, where both he and Gabriele were born, but all any of them ever saw of Switzerland was a dairy factory and a toy-strewn hallway of a rental apartment. More than a hallway, it was a babysitter: with the doors securely shut, it was a safe place to keep the little boys when shifts overlapped. Sometimes when their mom got home, she'd bring them ice cream from the factory. Once they were tall enough to reach the doorknobs, she took them back to Italy to start their first day of school in the same class, as though they were twins.

Pietro had great expectations of Rome. But the reality of it was that the only accommodation he could afford was a one-room unit bordering a highway. It took over an hour by bus to reach La Sapienza University. To solve this problem he bought a secondhand moped, thus spending much of his monthly allowance on gas. Not wanting to prove his parents right, he didn't ask them for more funds. There was no one to go out with anyway for a coffee or a pizza: his classmates were too cliquey; some openly snubbed him. The only friend he had there was Giuliano, a fellow geology student who shared his origins, the mountainous Irpinia district around Avellino, but unfortunately Giuliano lived on the other side of the city.

Pietro studied and studied. He excelled in geophysics, did well in mineralogy but failed mathematics twice. He became plagued with doubt. What the hell was he doing there, in the capital? Did he really think that someone like him, who'd come from nothing, was going to become a geologist? Looking back on it now, he was probably depressed. If it hadn't been for Giuliano, who knows how far he might have spiraled . . .

That's when he called his brother, who didn't hesitate to say, "Come to Naples then." University life was a blast, Gabriele said. They all lived in the center of the city and walked everywhere discussing politics, literature, art. They drank wine at lunch, studied at night, slept all day. In Naples it was possible to live like kings on very little money. Students were given discounts to see plays and movies, and vouchers for three-course restaurant meals at only two thousand lire. Not to mention the dirt-cheap rent in the Spanish Quarter.

Pietro's story took only as long as the penne took to become al dente. We sat at the table. "Another day, another meal," he said. "And who knows what tomorrow will bring." Then he laughed without emitting a sound.

I loved the way he played with the language, like no one else I knew, but it was never affected. And I had been right: he could really cook. Yet after only a few bites I was no longer hungry. Maybe I'd had too much to drink, though my full glass was proof to the contrary. And I was sober enough to tell that the surface of the wine was skewed, due certainly to the table itself, which dipped significantly at the center. Not only, but the liquid itself was quivering: Was it the ripple caused by his neighbor's television turned up too loud or was it the stirring I felt inside?

I put my fork down. "You fought for what you believed in, Pietro." For the first time I'd addressed him by name, a slip of the tongue that startled me and moved me as much as if I'd made a love confession. "And now here you are."

"Here I am, with you. Amazing." Pietro too lowered his fork. "Thank goodness I left Rome. Best move I ever made."

We looked at each other and I could see he'd lost his appetite too. Who needed food now, or ever again?

Pietro led me up the staircase but this time there was no fourth-grade awkwardness. We were giants in his little room. He cupped my face and kissed me like a long-lost lover, with both pleasure and heartbreak. Then his hands curled around my ribs, drawing me hard against him.

I surprised myself by pushing him backward onto his tiny bed. He surrendered easily, taking me down with him. The full pressure of my body against his—the crushing weight, the complete closeness—gave me a brief moment of relief, until I felt him go hard underneath me, a pressing heat, and I grasped that nothing in me, absolutely nothing, was at peace or under control.

Again we kissed, not like we had the other day but like we were simply picking up from where we'd left off—straight into the most perfect darkness where we could exist once more, where maybe we had always existed—and yet we kissed as if we couldn't wait a second longer, like travelers so thirsty from wandering through a vast wasteland that, now with water finally before them, drink without stopping for breath. When I moved my lips down to his now perspiring neck, he tried to undo my hair tie but could only get halfway before the kissing overpowered us again, and we couldn't stop, we just couldn't, even if a landslide had begun rolling down the Spanish Quarter to swallow us whole. It was only *this* that mattered, only him and me, and we were trying to devour each other with our mouths, our hands making fists of the other's hair, and soon we were begging each other, begging God, whom I didn't even believe in, and I grasped that it might actually be possible to die of pleasure.

We were breaking more than a few rules: shoes on the bed, girl on top, window wide open in broad daylight. But it was the siesta, and the only one watching was the volcano.

The afternoon sun lit our clothes thrown like laundry on the floor. We looked at each other and laughed, a hearty laugh, teeth and all, like we'd both suddenly gotten a brilliant joke. Through the window, the ships waited under the sun on the silver platter of the gulf. It really did seem that the heat the scirocco had promised was finally inching along in its wake.

"Summer's coming," I said. "I can smell it in the air."

"I want to spend every day of it with you, if you'll let me." I nestled into the crook of his arm and felt his lips moisten my forehead. "Come closer," he said in a raspy whisper. "Sleep with me."

The last thing I wanted was to sleep, but there was something about the late sun spreading across us like a second bedspread, the wine having gone lukewarm like a forgotten bath, and the tempo of Pietro's breathing that eventually lulled my racing mind.

I was standing outside a lone house: perhaps I lived there. It was a beach house, maybe somewhere near Castellammare; behind it was a slope of olive trees as pilly and gray as a much-loved wool blanket. Yet on closer inspection, I realized that towering behind the olive grove and the house was a breathtaking wall of rock, something not from our world but from the world of giants. Vesuvius. Why hadn't I noticed it before? It seemed to grow before my eyes, so I dared not lose sight of it as I backed away toward the sea, but the more I watched the volcano, the more I became mesmerized by it.

Out of nowhere came clouds, gray and laden like fieldstones being nested one on top of the other. The sun vanished. I was getting trapped in by the very sky, and when the ground rumbled beneath my feet, I no longer had any doubt as to what was happening.

I turned my back to the volcano and staggered toward the sea. There was a rowboat resting on the beach. I pushed it out into the water with a single shove, grinding the beach pebbles underneath. I rowed out far, disconcerted as to how the sea could be so very glassy and calm when disaster was imminent. The sea and the sky now mirrored each other, of the same ashen color that was neither day nor night, the color of the end of time. All at once, in a fit of fury or passion or folly, Vesuvius un-leashed molten rock down its sides like hot wax from a candle, maybe even destroying itself in that unstoppable act. I watched as the lava, dazzling even in its apathy, rolled toward the olive trees and the house. Why hadn't there been any warning, not even the slightest sign? But none of that mattered now; I had to keep going. Keep rowing, rowing, away from there.

All of a sudden, I heard screams as people began pouring out from the olive grove, most of them women and children. Where had they come from? I had the only rowboat, the only salvation. I had to go back and save them, as many as I could. And yet now the volcano was spitting rocks, too, and the rocks were pelting the water all around me. *Go back for them and you'll die*, I heard a voice in my head. I sat in the rowboat rigid with terror as I understood what I was about to do.

All I saw next were the sparse hairs on Pietro's chest rising and falling with his breath. The room was still ignited with sunlight; it seemed I'd only been asleep for a moment. I reached over to touch his jagged silver sun.

"Hi there," he said, his voice heavy with sleep.

"I had a bad dream."

"Are you scared?"

"Not anymore."

He turned to kiss me, a whirlpool pulling us in deeper and deeper until it ejected us, breathless. "One day . . ." he said in a hard whisper as though he didn't have enough air in his lungs. "One day I'm going to marry you."

8

THE NEXT FEW NIGHTS we were inseparable. During the day—in class, the library, or the study room—I did my best to study but I felt as though I were suffering from a mild fever. I was underfocused and overheated, and I counted the hours until I could finally quench my thirst in Pietro's arms, and yet it still wasn't enough. I didn't quite know what was happening to me. Still, I managed to pass my cultural anthropology exam, though with a score I wasn't eager to advertise.

"It might not be a thirty, gorgeous," said Tonino as I came upstairs into the kitchen. "But it's twenty-eight more points than I got in Sanskrit."

"You do know that you actually have to take the exam, Tonino, in order to pass it," said Angelo, congratulating me with a full, fleshy kiss on the cheek.

"But even if I pass it, wiseass, what the hell is it for anyway?"

"It's knowledge, Tonino," I said. "It doesn't have to be *for* anything."

With all the commotion, I couldn't tell if the boys were even aware that I had Pietro in tow, or whether they made anything of the two of us showing up there on our own or paid any notice to his silver pendant now hanging so conspicuously around my neck. I could only tell that Pietro, now standing in the exact same spot where he'd handed me that trembling cassette not so long ago, was greeted by the boys with a mere nod and without a glint of surprise. I took their lack of astonishment as acceptance and their silence on the matter as the ultimate sign of brotherly love.

I'd actually come by only to get some clean clothes and was, for some reason I couldn't grasp, relieved that Luca was out. But the boys, still in their pajamas with cigarette ashes as thick as snowflakes on their splayed books, weren't in any hurry to let us go. They pulled out a few chairs and a bottle of whiskey, like they'd been waiting all day for no better distraction from linguistic philosophy or the history of calligraphy than a discussion about rocks. Rocks, sand, dust: now these were real things. At one point, Angelo asked Pietro how oil was found.

"Well, you have to study the sedimentology and the stratigraphy of the area first," he answered. "Then if it looks like there could be hydrocarbons under the surface, you have to drill these exploration wells."

Tonino asked, "Any chance that while I'm out in my wheat field I could stick my pitchfork into some black gold?"

"What, in Puglia?"

"You're a communist," shot Angelo. "What the hell do you need the money for?"

We all cracked up, some whiskey spilled. Pietro had effortlessly slipped right in with the boys, who began calling him all sorts of names, which for them (and particularly for Tonino) was the greatest sign of affection. It was more than I could have hoped for. As usual when he laughed, Pietro cupped his mouth in a movement I now saw as well-mannered, even graceful. I had the sudden awareness that in Pietro I'd found something of dazzling beauty—a precious, and maybe priceless, stone among all the other gray, drab ones on my path—and I could hardly believe that in that treasure chest of a bedroom he was mine.

Pietro, more talkative than ever, went on to say that there were plenty of opportunities in oil, if you were willing to travel, and that he had a good rapport with his petroleum geology professor. He wanted to do his thesis with her, and she, being well connected in Italy and abroad, had already mentioned the possibility of landing him a job with an oil company. Pietro added that there were lots of countries to work in, some places you wouldn't even know had oil. "Like the Gulf of Mexico, off the coast of Louisiana," he said, looking over at me just then in what seemed like more than a pronunciation check. "It doesn't matter to me. I'd go anywhere."

"Anywhere but this shithole," said Tonino.

Everyone nodded in agreement. And I knew that feeling, the need to pack my bags and discover the world, but at some point out of love for Naples I'd set aside my gypsy spirit. Yet now, while everyone was going on about all the things the city was notorious for, its unlivability and backwardness, my love for Naples, my *need* for it, struck me as childish and indulgent.

"My parents have no idea," Pietro said. "They think getting a degree in geology is like taking a course in the mineral components of fertilizer or something, that afterward I'll just go back to the village and run the whole farm."

"Oh yeah? How many hectares do you have?" asked Tonino, an unlit cigarette between his lips.

Pietro lit Tonino's cigarette before his own. Puffing symbiotically, they talked in complex measurements of land. Angelo and I shrugged at each other across the table.

"It's tough living on the land, though," Pietro said. "Eight months of the year you're cold to the bone."

"And you're always worrying about the damn weather. Is it fucking going to rain or not?"

"Let's be honest, the work is backbreaking. The landscapes are pretty, it's a nice place to go for a visit once in a while. But go back and live there? No way in hell. I've already done my time."

The window beside us cooed with nosy pigeons. Under the table Pietro's hand landed warm on my thigh, a private signal. I finally got up to get my clothes, and when the two of us left together, there was again no amazement on the boys' faces, only disappointment that now they would have to get back to staring at the pages in their books.

Once, instead of spooning in that tiny bed, we slept in Gabriele's queen-size bed while he was away in Monte San Rocco for a few days. Despite how comfortable that futon was, set directly onto the floor under the sloping roof, I awoke with a start. I could hear hollering in the thickest form of dialect—insults, I was sure, but they didn't belong to a human language. It may well have been rabid dogs tearing each other to pieces or violent coughing fits spewing possibly infectious matter from the lungs. Whatever those sounds were, they came from the lower, darker floors of the building, becoming amplified as they made their way up the chimney-shoot courtyard. One final blast and the storm blew over.

"God, you look beautiful, baby," mumbled Pietro, awake now too. "My grandmother always said you should judge a woman's beauty by looking at her first thing in the morning."

I had to laugh because it was only technically morning, because I'd skipped a conference on the history of theater, and because I lay naked between the sheets belonging to my lover's brother. Behind the bed, right at our eye level, was a little window overlooking the neighborhood. On the windowsill Gabriele had placed an aquatic plant inside a wine bottle. On that threshold the plant seemed in great peril. It was so very moist and delicate, enclosed in its green refuge, yet it teetered on the edge of a sheer drop over a jumble of treeless, sunbaked houses, like a Tunisian medina. All it would have taken was to open the window.

I zoomed out to take in Gabriele's large, book-lined room with its drafting table in the corner. In addition to his countless volumes, the shelves housed so many small inviting objects—etched pencil cases, inlaid boxes, swirly marbles, amphorae, feathers, pine cones—that, had Pietro not been there, I would have likely given in to the temptation to snoop.

72

I sat up, pulling the sheet over my breasts. "Are you sure it's OK to be in here?"

"I told you, Gabriele won't be back till six tonight. Besides, he'll be so psyched about the job my folks have given him that he won't even notice we've slept in his bed."

"What, is he tilling or plowing or something?"

"Are you serious? Gabriele wouldn't be able to steal an egg from a chicken. No, he's just designing something for my mother." At my puzzled look, Pietro added, "Ask him about it sometime. I'm sure he'd be deeply honored to tell you all about his avant-garde design. But right now what I really want is a shower. Let me see if Madeleine's here."

Madeleine was their roommate, who'd come to Naples on an Erasmus scholarship, but so far we hadn't crossed paths. Halfway down the stairs, Pietro whispered, "I should warn you: she's a bit nuts. Though Gabriele prefers the term 'architectural genius.'"

"What does she have to do with the shower?"

"Just wait, you'll see." He called out her name once, twice, and was about to give up when a door at the foot of the stairs opened and out came a girl.

She was like a small, perfectly formed tornado, with an unsettling allure that came from her stormy too-short hair, her crumpled too-short T-shirt, and flirtatious navel. From the way she was rubbing her eyes with her fists and cursing the neighbors for disturbing her sleep again, from her husky voice with an unmistakable French accent. From her Japanese flip-flops and white socks, her tiny frame and big exasperated eyes.

Madeleine's gaze crawled up the staircase and came to rest on me. Looking suddenly awake, she gleamed with a strange voraciousness, as if she could smell our lovemaking. After we introduced ourselves, I stared at her almost to the point of rudeness. Madeleine was devastatingly beautiful. And she was the only other foreign student I'd ever met in Naples.

73

Madeleine frowned comically at Pietro. "You want my help with the shower, no? OK, but what about me?"

"I'll owe you one."

"And a handmade coffee?"

"Sure. As soon as I'm done."

"You do have a way with the ladies," she said with an even huskier voice, making Pietro go red in the face as he made his way back up the stairs.

Madeleine didn't seem crazy at all, I thought as the shower quickly steamed up. Rivulets of hot water took jagged paths down Pietro's chest, some puddling in the little dip where his chest caved in slightly. I observed him openly, as if looking at a photograph of him: the slender body, the long runner's legs, the pitch-black hairs between them. He was almost too gorgeous to touch.

Then there came a thundering from downstairs.

"What's that?"

Pietro laughed. "It's a water pressure thing, which pretty much sucks up here on the seventh floor. So when the flame in the hot water cylinder goes out, it has to be kicked back to life. But that French girl, man, she whacks it like she's practicing for a kickboxing match. Anger management issues, I'd say."

"Sounds like you need a plumber."

"I just need you."

We kissed, and as the warm water trickled into the cave of our mouths, Madeleine started pounding again. Laughing, we resisted the desire to linger in the heat, and the growing desire to make love standing up, and hurriedly shampooed each other's hair.

Gabriele returned from the village weighed down with almond biscotti, stuffed peppers, and red wine. Before closing the door behind us, he grabbed one of the bottles for the party he'd invited us along to.

Night was a watercolor bleeding down onto the Quartieri, but none-theless the timid warmth of that spring afternoon remained trapped in the streets, caught in the webs of forgotten laundry and in the clouds of frying squid and sickeningly sweet trash. We heard a thud behind us and spun around. Enormous rats (referred to by the locals as *zoccole*, a name they shared with hookers and other man-eaters) scattered out, their nails scratching across the cobblestones, just as a bag of garbage, still trembling from its fall, was starting to leak its sharp, greasy secrets onto the street. Whichever wise guy threw it from above, just to avoid the stairs, was already closing the balcony doors behind him. Did it re-ally matter? By morning the trash truck would have swept it all away.

"Would you two mind terribly if I stopped for some cigarettes on our way?" asked Gabriele.

"I'm out, too," said Pietro.

A fluorescent light drew us in, a beacon in the dark. With all the shops closed for the night, ground-floor homes could now open for business. This *vascio* was particularly lavish. Just outside the door was a small table displaying candies; dangling above them were bunches of potato chips. They were inviting signs that helped dissolve the boundary between street and home, between public and private, in the same way that the swampy night air melted the distinction between the warmth I felt out-side my skin and the heat I was nurturing inside.

In the *vascio* an elderly man eating his cutlet at the table looked straight through us, like we were invisible. There was no need to go to any trouble for any old customers, and the night was young. His wife rose from the bed behind a partition, shuffling out in her slippers. I didn't want to look at that bed with its cougar blanket, its disheveled and still warm sheets, its sloppy intimacy, but the pull was irresistible. In the end I gave in and looked at the couple's bed with the fascinated horror with which one might watch a TV screen flashing scenes of passion or blood-shed. The woman, however, was relaxed, perhaps indifferent. Wearing a pink dressing gown, she nimbly walked the razor's edge between business and pleasure, selling and sleeping, day and night. She squeezed in behind her husband, who was still busy chewing, to rummage through a utensil drawer and hand over her black-market cigarettes. The cash did a magic trick, vanishing into the pocket of her gown.

"They taste nasty but they're cheap," said Pietro, slipping the Marlboro Lights into his breast pocket.

We kept walking, the tapping of our shoes muffled by television sets turned on in people's homes. Suddenly Gabriele stopped in his tracks. "Oh god, now what?"

Pietro and I also stopped. Before us was a massive dog, so black he might have been just a figment of the dark. Under the feeble glow of the streetlight, the dog lay across a bed of cardboard, looking straight at us with mirrory eyes that reflected splinters of artificial light. Pigeons fat as chickens circumambulated his body, a map scribbled in scars from who knows what battles. He was breathing through his nose like a wild horse and rolling his eyes with us, now left, now right, following our every tentative movement. I gripped Pietro's arm.

"Now that's a beast if I ever saw one," he said.

The dog lay there with, it seemed, a sense of purpose, and it took me a few moments to understand that he was standing guard. Behind him was a series of low cement walls that trailed behind him like large graffitied dominoes, barricading the road before us for the length of the entire block. In that space, the flow of the city was cut off and, as if to build a haphazard dam, lawn chairs had been laid out, Vespas parked, undershirts hung out to dry. Above it all, scaffolding crossed out the sky, making a metal cage of this corner of the neighborhood. The dog let out a low rumble, or maybe it was a motorbike in the distance.

"Are you sure this is the right direction?" Pietro said to his brother in a low voice.

"I do believe so." Gabriele pulled out a limp piece of paper, the invitation.

"We'll just have to scoot past him then."

"But even if he lets us through," I said, "how are we supposed to get past the walls?" It would have been an obstacle course: the only visible opening, in the first wall, was obstructed by a parked scooter.

"Indeed. Unstable buildings in need of reinforcement," said Gabriele contemplatively. "Hence the barricade."

Pietro mouthed the words *Hence the barricade*, lifting his eyebrows mockingly. I frowned at him, hoping Gabriele hadn't noticed. Couldn't Pietro tell how much, how *hard*, his brother loved him?

We looked down the left-hand street, but another series of low walls blocked that too.

"Unfortunately, according to this map," said Gabriele, "to get to Anna's house we must get to the other side." Glancing at the dog, he ran a hand through his thinning hair. "But I fear the direct route is not an option tonight."

We had no choice but to backtrack and try another path, and that's when we became lost. Pietro wove his fingers through mine as we tried to chisel some sense into those indistinguishable streets. At one point, recognizing a distinctive pair of purple pants hanging from a balcony, we realized we'd gone full circle. Pietro suggested we ditch the whole thing, saying he wouldn't know anyone at the party anyway, but then, entirely by accident, we found the right building.

We followed the laughter and music to one of the upper floors. In the entranceway Gabriele kissed the hostess, a classmate of his who was delighted with the home brew; then he disappeared. Loose tiles creaked under our feet as Pietro and I inched our way through the guests. The apartment was a series of candlelit rooms without a corridor that simply flowed from one into the next. It was loud with voices and bittersweet with pot. Cats moved soundlessly between rooms, letting themselves be caught momentarily, only to slither out of my hands. I followed one of them into a less crowded room, losing Pietro in the process. Before me were chairs lined up awkwardly against the wall. Moved by their solitude, I sat down.

Soon enough Gabriele had settled into a chair beside me and was handing me a plastic cup of red wine. "Here, this will help you relax."

"But I'm OK without it," I said, taking a sip anyway. "Life is enough of a high for me."

"I know. And it's infectious," Gabriele said, downing all his wine at once. "Aaah. All that walking in circles made me thirsty."

"In squares, actually."

I would have gladly given Gabriele my wine even without that pretext. His eyes lit up as he emptied the contents of my cup into his, a gesture that was an admission both of fastidiousness in matters of hygiene and of an emerging intimacy between us. This made me want to open up to him in some way, and for some reason I decided to tell him about my visit to the Fontanelle Cemetery.

As I spoke, Gabriele leaned in toward me, ever closer, so as to hear me better in the midst of all the noise. I found the closeness pleasant. I could see every detail of his face: his unshaven jaw, his lips already a shade darker from the wine. Despite his excessive attention to cleanliness, Gabriele paid little mind to his appearance. His hair was always a mess, his eyebrows, too, and he dressed shabbily, with missing buttons and baggy pants that dragged on the ground. And now, having him right up next to me, so close I could smell the spicy complexity of his wine as though I'd drunk it myself, I felt a tipsy sort of desire to straighten the strands of his hair and the cords of his corduroy jacket.

"Unfortunately, Eddie, I have little time for outings myself. However, I do know it's not the only area in the city with caves like that," he said. "There are many, many more. Underneath our feet, Naples is almost completely empty."

"What do you mean by *empty*?"

A flicker of fire passed over Gabriele's eyes, as though he'd concentrated in them the light of all the candles in the room. I could see he was relishing my confusion at his words, and I let him have that desired effect in the same way I'd let him have my wine.

"Look around you. This building, all the other old buildings around it: they're all made of stone. They go on as far as the eye can see, with hardly a patch of green. But where do you think they get this construction material from?"

"I've never thought about it before."

Holding that flimsy plastic cup as if it were a fluted wineglass, Gabriele explained that while other cities had risen with the help of material shipped in from the countryside, Naples had not. From Greek times it had been known that the land was almost entirely made of yellow tuff, a stone of volcanic origin that is excellent for construction purposes due to its high workability. So they simply began dragging it up from underground, as well as from the surrounding hills. And as they dug and emptied the land invisibly beneath their feet, the city aboveground grew noticeably. Yellow tuff was so easily accessible that the practice continued beyond the late 1800s. Hence, added Gabriele, the Spanish Quarter was built in the same manner, even though the masonry walls weren't up to the standard of thickness used in the stately palaces, located elsewhere in the city. Perhaps in order to cut building costs even further, the thickness of the walls diminished on the upper floors.

"Upper floors like your place," I said, not to mention my place.

"Well, keep in mind that the structures in the Spanish Quarter rose to no more than four or five floors. The others are all raised floors."

"Raised?"

"Illegal floors, dear Eddie, without any building supervision. Just think about it for a minute. You've already got the thinnest load-bearing walls they could get away with: add to that the compression caused by the weight of the extra floors, and what you've got is major structural fragility. Neapolitan tuff is particularly soft and brittle. Have you ever noticed that, when you touch it in spots where the plaster has come off, it crumbles between your fingers?"

Gabriele extracted a cigarette and, as he fumbled for his lighter, I suddenly grasped the true meaning of the adjective *illegal*, so commonly and nonjudgmentally used in Naples. *Illegal* didn't mean *unwelcome* so much as *precarious*.

He lit up and took a puff. "For this and other reasons, Naples is incomparable. There's nothing like it anywhere else in the world."

An explosion of laughter and clapping came from another room, and all at once I felt overwhelmed by the facts I'd just learned, alluring and at once disconcerting details like a bunch of Lego pieces that I just couldn't put together and were thus running through my hands with a clatter as deafening as that laughter. I didn't *get* Naples, not really. I was missing the bigger picture, a true map. The Spanish Quarter, then, wasn't on the outskirts of society but the very quintessence of Naples. A place that on the surface appeared simple to unravel but that in reality followed its own mysterious logic that twisted it into a knot you couldn't untie. My knowledge of my adoptive city was so full of holes that I knew for sure I would never be like Luca, wise and at ease in the city. Because despite all the years I'd been there, despite the *liceo* and the excursions, despite all the passion I'd poured into it and my desire to surrender to it and lose myself in it, there was something about it that managed to elude me. Love wasn't enough.

I looked over at Gabriele. Smoking in profile like that, he looked so much like Pietro—the long, hard lines of his nose, the gray curve of his stubble—and the flickering, uncertain light of that room further blurred the boundaries between the two brothers. I became pleasantly aware that Gabriele and I were developing a degree of closeness, maybe even affection for each other, and that seemed very important to me though I couldn't yet figure out why. At the same time I didn't trust myself to dose that affection because, even without alcohol in my system, even without the physical presence of Pietro, that night as always I could feel his words set my mind on fire, his caresses ignite my skin, his kisses intoxicate my mouth. What we were doing wasn't having sex; it was like surrendering to an illness. And the most glaring side effect was that I released a sensuality I wasn't sure if I wanted or didn't want others to notice. A larger-than-life sensuality that was simply gushing from my pores and spilling sloppily around me, especially on Gabriele, who was genetically a part of Pietro and who was now sending a silky river of smoke to the ceiling, lost in who knows what thoughts.

"But isn't it dangerous?" I asked.

"What?"

"I mean, all these buildings and streets built on top of what is effectively hollow land?"

"Quite the opposite." Gabriele leaned in toward me excitedly, conspiratorially, as if about to reveal a secret. "Some people actually believe it has given Naples an advantage by making it more 'elastic' and saving it from more severe earthquake damage. Our village, the glamorous Monte San Rocco, was nearly razed to the ground in the 1980 earthquake and, as you know, all the other towns along the coast south of Naples were hit very hard. So why did Naples only suffer the collapse of a few structures here and there? Certainly, my brother would be able to give a more technical explanation. But basically, they say, the underground cavities absorbed the seismic waves. Actually, let's go ahead and ask him now. Look, there he is."

It was always the same when I caught sight of Pietro. First I would experience the thrill of vertigo—the world bending, even creating itself from nothing, and I was just an awed spectator. Then would come the fall as if from a great, great height, but giving in to that fall gave me the most intense, alarming happiness.

From: tectonic@tin.it
To: heddi@yahoo.com
Sent: February 23

Dearest Heddi,

*I've just returned from the platform to find your email waiting for me, all
the way from New Zealand! It's truly amazing! Why New Zealand? How
long have you been there? What season is it over there right now? Do you
have a tattoo? How long has it been since you've seen your parents? So many
questions. I'd love to see some of your pictures of the landscapes; you must be
an even better photographer than before.*

*Here everything is the same: nothing is good but everything keeps moving
along thanks to an unpleasant sense of inertia. Since receiving your email,
all I do is reread it, in the hopes of finding something between the lines. But
what? I don't know. You're a wonderful person. I don't know if, actually I
know perfectly well, that I would never be able to forgive or even have kind
words for a coward like me.*

*I'm not even a shadow of the person I was a few years back. I'm more cynical,
disillusioned, tired and—you're right—maybe a little depressed. You were
my adrenaline, my hot chocolate, my woolen scarf, my wine bank, my
English teacher, my best friend.*

*Sometimes I reflect upon humanity, people's behavior, their madness. When
I'm feeling particularly kind, I can even find some plausible explanations
for what I did to you, but when I'm feeling spiteful (that is, most of the time)
I can only kick myself. I gave you up because I felt strong. Because I thought
I could live without you. Nothing of the kind. You are and always will be,
even if you don't want to be, the only woman who has made me happy. I
understood this too late, extremely late in the best Hollywood tradition.*

*I get by. I trick myself into believing (only when I'm feeling kind) that there
will be some peace for me. But I'd really like to see you again. Recently I've*

82

had this recurring thought: I keep seeing myself as the owner of a farmhouse in Tuscany or Piedmont and imagining a couple of blond children and you writing at the computer. Very picturesque, don't you think? Hallucinations like I had long ago? Will I see you one of these days?

p.

9

THERE WAS A CERTAIN courtyard hierarchy in the Spanish Quarter. On the sixth or seventh floors, there was a surplus of light, sweeping views, sometimes even sea breezes. From those upper floors, the anarchy of the streets often seemed far away. Those one hundred and sixty-eight stairs were at once a test of the survival of the fittest and our Great Wall.

But already on the third floor, not to mention the second—or, heaven forbid, the first—it was like being inside a house of cards. Balconies were stacked upon balconies, sheets were hung upon sheets, and the buildings themselves, as if they weren't already close enough together, were shackled to each other by electrical wires, from which streetlights dangled, as though to keep them from drifting apart. Until death do you part. On those lower floors, sunshine could be measured in centimeters. A bar of gold would appear once a day on the kitchen table, like something left behind by a guest, but before you could slip it into your pocket it would warp into a rhombus, its edges nibbled away by the dark, until there was nothing left but a nugget—and then it was gone. As for living on the ground floor, that was a concept we couldn't even contemplate.

The locals made ample use of that wicker or plastic breadbasket called *il paniere* (*'o panaro* in dialect). I liked watching the *paniere* forced to bungee-jump from the higher floors down to the street, where it would pick up bread or drop off forgotten keys or money. It reminded me of a spider dropping fearlessly down its silky strand, accompanied by hollered, and often misunderstood, instructions. But the *paniere* was too ghetto for us university students. The rope we used to make contact with the noisy and often unruly world below us was much subtler and far more modern: the intercom.

"Hey, Pie', is Eddie there?" crackled a voice one day.

"Tonino. For you."

I ran to press the speaker button with a pang of guilt. I'd hardly been at home with the boys of late, thus jeopardizing that undisciplined daily routine on which our entire relationship was founded, not to mention leaving them at the mercy of their upcoming exams. As if to confirm my fears, Tonino's tone was harsh.

"You need to come home now, Eddie. There's no time to explain."

I rushed down the stairs. Even with those short legs, Tonino was practically speed-walking through the neighborhood, which had gone into hibernation after the midday meal; I struggled to keep up with him. All the while the sun pendant under my shirt jingled more and more persistently as I pressed Tonino for an explanation, but all he said was, "We couldn't find your camera."

"What do you need my camera for?"

"You'll see with your own eyes. But you're going to think you're tripping."

We summited the stairs and stepped inside the house. Immediately I noticed, through Angelo's wide-open door, that inside his room was a thick haze like when a movie cuts to a dream sequence. And yet it was all very real: the air tasted like lime, and I could make out Angelo himself standing by the window in a rather pensive pose but dusted ridiculously in flour like a pizza maker. Sonia, too, was covered in powder; seated on the bed leaning against the wall, she was as white as a geisha. Both were frozen in position like actors waiting for the curtain to lift.

"What's going on here?"

From the hallway came Luca's voice. "Look up."

Above Angelo's bed, the ceiling was gouged with a large, deep wound fringed with inlets like Sardinia. Below it, right on top on Angelo's now virtually unrecognizable cow rug, was a massive slab—of plaster or stone, I couldn't have said—and everywhere chunks, shards, dust. I should have understood, but the scene as a whole was one of such devastation that I couldn't wrap my head around it.

"Sonia and Angelo were just sitting there on the bed watching the usual crap on TV," said Tonino, "when out of nowhere a piece of ceiling came down on them."

"It could have broken our necks," added Angelo, trying hard to contain his enthusiasm. "It was a close call. It grazed my leg."

"Are you OK?" I made to step over the rubble toward them, but Tonino stopped me.

"Don't move anything, gorgeous. We need to take pictures first, to show the landlords, or the insurance company, or whoever the hell needs to see them. Otherwise no one will believe us."

"I'm all right, Eddie," said Sonia. "It just scratched my arm. We could have cleaned ourselves up a bit but we were waiting for you to take pictures."

"The camera's in the drawer . . . the one below the dictionaries," I said distractedly to Tonino. "But it has a roll of black and white in it."

"Doesn't matter. It's all white in there anyway."

I focused my Minolta and only then did I begin to make sense of the scene before me. *Click*, and I captured the rebel stone that on its trajectory from the ceiling had broken its edges against the bed. Angelo with bits of plaster in his hair. The bedspread covered in debris. Sonia's combat boots that were no longer black but white. If she had been a few centimeters farther from Angelo, it probably would have broken her leg. And if Angelo in that moment had leaned over to change channels . . . Angelo was right: they had both narrowly escaped serious injury—or worse. So then why did it hurt so bad to be safely behind the lens instead of right there with my friends, in that room I knew so well, covered from head to toe in dust? It was an absurd envy.

No sooner had I finished than Angelo was already making his way around the slab in the direction of the kitchen for a well-deserved coffee, while Sonia was heading to the bathroom for a shower.

"No," said Luca, "we need to get out of here. This house is no longer safe."

"The damage is already done, Falcone," protested Tonino. "It's not like the ceiling's gonna fall again."

"The crack upstairs is only getting bigger. It's obviously connected. This place is falling apart."

And with that, he sent us out to the corner café so that he could go talk to the landlady. Only Luca knew which *vascio* in the Spanish Quarter was hers, since he was the one who had rented the apartment in the first place, before any of us had come along.

He joined us half an hour later. He told us that the landlady had followed him all the way back to our place in her bathrobe and slippers, looking around and listening poker-faced to Luca's account. Goodness knows what cards she had up her sleeve, but what she ended up pulling out was a pricey cell phone, with which she called her nephew, shouting through it in a rapid-fire, rabid form of dialect that not even Luca, whose father was Neapolitan, could penetrate. She hung up with a saccharine smile, passing on to Luca the results of what was not a heated dispute after all but an off-site building assessment. She trusted her nephew like her own son, and anyway he was the best engineer in the Quartieri, or at least he would be once he finished his degree. Her nephew had recommended that a series of steel beams be installed to brace the floor to the outer wall, which was in effect detaching itself from the house. The reconstruction would take about six months, in Neapolitan time: until then, the place was uninhabitable.

For a while the deafening coffee grinder pleasantly filled our silence. Slumped in his chair, Angelo was the first to speak. "Damn, I love that house."

I freed a clump of plaster from his hair. "So do I," I said, but at the same time I felt something quite different pulling at me, something willful and irresistible like a rip current, and part of me knew the worst thing to do was to fight it.

"There's got to be a bright side here," said Sonia.

"Yes, you're right!" Angelo nearly jumped out of his chair. "Summer's coming and most of us are going home anyway. So I say we pack up the necessary items and just be homeless for a few months."

"Yeah right, blondie, I'd love to see you, all prim and proper, squatting with those real street punks," said Tonino.

"What the hell would you know? No, I was thinking I could stay with Davide, and you could stay with whoever will put up with you. C'mon, guys, we'd save a ton of rent, and then the place should be ready to go by the time classes start again in October." And with that, he sat back with a triumphant smile.

For once Tonino agreed with Angelo. From across the table Luca gave me one of those stares, powerful enough to put me under a spell, and this time I was sure that he was trying to tell me, in his infinite wisdom, to just let them talk—and to just *let go*.

I moved into Pietro's place. There was a naturalness, a predictability, in that decision that I didn't want to read into. In the heat of the moment I didn't stop to consider that we might be rushing into things, or to analyze the possible consequences. The future wasn't an issue, it never really had been, but the past was even less of one. Once I'd let go of that decrepit old palace that I'd so loved, I could suddenly see it for what it was and what it had been from the very beginning: a stop along the way.

Pietro pulled his mattress to the floor, dragged away the frame, and brought in a second single mattress. The already cramped room seemed to shrink even further. I stood in the doorway, unsure of how to help him in that block puzzle of sliding furniture and preoccupied with thoughts of the boys, of where and how often we'd see each other now.

"I think they'll fit best over here," Pietro said, before heaving the mattresses one by one into the corner under the window. Now there was only enough space left to open and close the door.

"Are you sure . . . ?" I began again.

"Without a doubt."

"I can pay—"

"Out of the question."

"It's just for the summer . . ."

"We'll see."

I stood there in awe of his one-man strength and his absolute certainty on the matter, as though all he'd ever dreamed of was to share a room the size of a wardrobe with another human being. He was wearing an expression of humble satisfaction, perhaps for having solved a geometrical puzzle, and standing heavily on that leg he preferred, hands at his hips. All at once I remembered him as he was that first night he came to dinner at our place: awkward and breathless from the stairs, he stood there under the ceiling medallion as if waiting for something to drop from the sky.

That image of Pietro as a stranger sent a chill through me. Wasn't that less than two months ago? But it seemed more that I was a stranger to myself, for how rashly I'd gone to stay with him when I still knew so little about him; for how easily his touch transported me, maybe even transformed me; for how gladly I'd skipped lessons and conferences to be with him; and for all the ways in which I'd proven myself to be impulsive, irresponsible, and maybe even foolhardy.

Together the mattresses formed a queen-size bed slit down the middle. "It's too bad about that crack, though," he said.

"It'll be fine."

The crack did grow larger throughout the course of the night. When I woke up the next morning, the first thing I saw was the long blue pencil of the sea. From that new angle, the Spanish Quarter seemed to have vanished into thin air. Pietro was still asleep when I got up.

I used the downstairs bathroom, which housed the boiler Madeleine had beaten to a pulp as well as a bathtub that had no difficulty filling up with hot water for when no such assistance was available. I put the coffee maker on the stove and stepped out onto the terrace. Two more steps and I was on the tar-sealed roof.

What a beautiful morning. All around me, TV antennae were trying to pierce a sky white with sun. I wondered how many of those decaying towers were balanced on hollow ground, as Gabriele had said. I wondered if this one was. Who cares, I thought. Up there I felt tall as never before, in a world without a ceiling. It was early and the neighborhood was making only muffled little noises as soft as slippers. The air too was half-asleep, smelling of newly lit cigarettes and freshly melted tar, hot bread and cool sea. I could have gorged myself on those scents, drunk it all in with my eyes, covered myself in the glitter of the gulf. On its calm surface, the container ships looked unreal: they quivered like mirages and were of a dusty, rusty brown, the same fragile color as the volcano behind them.

When the coffee gurgled, I stepped back into the kitchen. I was surprised to find Madeleine standing there with turbulent hair and minimalist clothing, but what surprised me even more was that she smiled generously and kissed me. She seemed so unlike the grumpy girl who had helped us with the shower. Clearly, with a solid eight hours she was positively charming. Pietro came downstairs, too, and all three of us sat down at the slanted table to have our coffee.

Any doubts about Pietro had melted away. I felt at home, and I loved him.

I could only imagine how shaken Sonia and the boys must have been after having experienced the collapse of the ceiling firsthand, but my reaction was to go in search of proof that Naples itself wasn't falling to pieces. One Sunday morning I took Pietro with me on an outing to Capodimonte Park, on one of the city's tallest hills. We might as well have been in Bali. Tunnels of trees trembled with exotic chirping, the grass was moist and freshly cut, and there were palm trees. To me, every palm tree in Naples was a vital sign, a symbol of its innate and indestructible beauty, and there were plenty up there.

"Now this is a sight for sore eyes," said Pietro. "Why have I never been here before?"

"There's no shame in it," I teased him. "Being shown around your own country by a foreigner."

He pulled out a pack of Marlboros, squinting as he lit up. "I love that you're from somewhere else. That you're not stuck in the same old mind-set as everybody else."

"Everybody who?"

"Most people, especially the people where I come from."

We wandered around the grounds, hand in hand or shoulder to shoulder, past reassuring traces of civilization like lampposts and iron benches. Now and then we crossed paths with normal-looking people: elderly couples stopping for a rest, parents pushing strollers, people enjoying healthy pastimes like biking or jogging. I looked at all of them barely suppressing a smile, hoping they couldn't read on my face the unchecked pride I felt walking beside Pietro. It seemed rude to flaunt it, to flash them with my wild joy over something I had and they didn't.

We walked for a long time, until one of the pebble pathways opened up onto a panorama of the urban sprawl that stopped only at the volcano, and the ever-present, ever-changing gulf.

Pietro nodded with approval. "I only wish I could have driven you up here in my own car. Treated you like a real lady."

We'd made our way back to the Capodimonte Museum, the city's second royal palace. It was painted in a fickle red, which, between sunrise and sunset when the park gates were open, would sometimes look the color of a sun-faded beach umbrella, or fresh blood, or old spilled wine. The huge lawn before it was spectacularly green.

I unbuckled my sandals and stepped onto that color-saturated carpet. It was something I hadn't done in years. I lay on my back, feeling Pietro sink into the grass beside me. The grass was so cool that I was reminded of the snow angels I used to make when I was little, and I wondered if there was such a thing as grass angels. The clear sky was an infinity rolling over us.

There came a low rumbling. "Thunder?" I joked.

"I swear it's not my stomach."

Within seconds, the rumbling grew into a sound so unnatural that it was like the very air was being sucked back up into the sky. Then from behind the palm trees came an enormous black plane. Flying at shockingly low altitude, it passed over us as if in slow motion; I could see its wheels locked into place, the silvery scratches on its black underbelly. Instinctively I pressed myself deeper into the lawn so as not to be grazed.

"Holy crap!" cried Pietro. "What the hell was that?"

Excitedly we went through a few hypotheses, finally agreeing it had to be a military plane.

"I've never been on a plane before," Pietro said.

"Not even once?"

"No."

I ran my palm over the little swords of grass. "Do you think there'll be another one?"

"I hope so. Let's wait a little."

We were gripped with suspense. It was like waiting for the next set of fireworks on the Fourth of July; it was the desire to play with fire. Our patience was rewarded when shortly afterward another airplane appeared. The air was ripped apart, the earth shook. I thought our luck had run out and this time there might very well be a collision, maybe with the roof of the museum itself, and I let out a silent scream. And then it was over.

We let the park settle back into place. The birds eventually got back to their chirping.

"You could take me away with you," Pietro said. "Hide me in your suitcase."

"Where would you want to go?"

"How about America?"

America was many things, but what came to mind to me right then was suburban America. I'd fled from it not because something bad had happened to me there: in the suburbs nothing ever happened at all. It was a slow painless death. I turned on my side, leaning on my elbow. "You know where I'd rather go, Pietro?"

"Where?"

"Norway."

I told him about how, when I was filling out the application form to be an exchange student so many years earlier, I'd written down Norway as my first of three choices. Italy was my last. I'd seen a photograph in the brochure of a Norwegian house nestled in a blue snowy landscape, its windows invitingly orange: that was my fifteen-year-old rationale. But just before putting the application in the envelope, I showed it to my best friend, Snežana, the daughter of a dissident writer from Bulgaria. She scoffed at Norway and told me to swap it with Italy. I wasn't convinced, but Snežana had dark circles under her eyes and had been to the Black Sea, so I followed her advice. It had seemed like such a haphazard and insignificant choice at the time, crossing out *Norway* and writing *Italy*. But it wasn't.

Pietro too had turned toward me, his hair tousled and looking so handsome that I wished with all my strength that he would just forget his usual public composure and kiss me. "Let's go to Norway then. Did you know they have oil there, in the North Sea?"

I let out a *brrr*. "Or maybe Iceland. At least they have volcanoes there to warm us up."

"Mexico. They have volcanoes *and* beaches. You and me, we could sit by the sea sipping giant margaritas."

"And Fiji! I've always wanted to go there, even though I don't know where it is."

We were joking, of course. Or maybe not. Pietro said, "Wherever it is, I'll take you there." And despite all the passersby, he leaned over to kiss me, though with guarded passion, right then and there on the damp lawn.

We made ourselves into grass angels again, clutching hands, surrendering to happiness. There wasn't a cloud in the sky. There was just a layer of blue, a layer of green, and the two of us in between like fallen angels. It seemed I could suddenly, finally, see the world—and love too—in its underlying simplicity. And I had the sensation that, instead of being flattened against the earth, we had uprooted ourselves and even shaken off gravity. Like feathers.

Pietro sighed. "And to think I got rid of my Swiss passport, like an idiot." He explained that he'd had to give up his Swiss citizenship when he was eighteen, in order to avoid the military service. "If it weren't for my brother, I wouldn't have any ties to the place at all."

"But I've never once heard him mention Switzerland."

"In fact, Gabriele's always talking about Posillipo," he said with a laugh, referring to the lofty part of the city with its double-barreled inhabitants. "Giampiero from Posillipo says this, Pierluigi from Posillipo says that . . ." He sat up to put his shoes back on. "No, not Gabriele. I was talking about my older brother Vittorio."

"You have another brother?"

"He's the eldest. No one really talks about him." Vittorio, he said, was married to a Swiss girl and had a couple of kids. He used to work in the same dairy plant as their parents: he had the night shift, and when he'd come home at five in the morning, he'd wake up their father so he could take his turn using the bed. Vittorio was seventeen when their mother started packing up to return to Monte San Rocco. "My folks argued with him but it was no use. He didn't want to go back to Italy. Anyway, my father was staying on in Schaffhausen, too, so that he could keep sending money home. So what could my mother say?"

I pondered the existence of yet another man who looked like Pietro, and it occurred to me that he could be repeated infinitely like in a house of mirrors. A delirious thought that was probably just an effect of having gone so long without food.

In fact, Pietro said, "I'm starving, baby. Let's go home."

Let's go home. Andiamo a casa. I loved the sound of that. I would have asked him to say it to me again and again in my ear. *Andiamo a casa. A casa.* But Pietro was already on his feet, holding out my sandals enticingly as if to remind me that if I didn't put them on soon I'd lose the last weight anchoring me to the ground and float away.

Yet Luca was always one step ahead of us, for once we were back in the Spanish Quarter we found out that he'd hopped on a ferry. He'd gone to Greece.

10

I COULDN'T MAKE SENSE of Luca's abrupt departure. Surely he had gone to Greece to see Roberta, but if he'd done so to coax her back to Naples, why now and not six months or a year ago? All Angelo said was, "A lot of stuff can change when a ceiling falls on you." The boys possessed pitiful information about his departure and they had no clue as to how long he'd be gone. I wanted to be *that* person, the one Luca most trusted, but I knew it was far from the truth.

Far more foreseeable was that Pietro would be taken from me. On his parents' land there was work to be done: trees to prune, farm equipment to fix. He was only going for a few days, but the prospect was alarming nonetheless. At the door Pietro kissed me goodbye and said, "When I'm missing you, you know what I'll do? I'll send you a little sign. So if you hear a fly buzzing around you, or a window whacking shut, or a car slamming on its brakes . . . that's me reminding you that I'm here, and I always will be."

Because Pietro was gone and I was still puttering around the apartment, my presence there became more solidified. Every day I came down the staircase still in my pajamas; I mopped the tiles, exchanged a few words with Madeleine, and studied at Pietro's metal desk right in the living room. But the pages of whatever book I was reading never seemed to turn.

The neighbors fought like cats. Once or twice a day a woman would start pleading with the Madonna, sweet mother of Jesus, only to turn up her voice like a drill and curse to eternal damnation another neighbor's dead relatives going back several generations. Any retorts shot back at her in the courtyard just fueled her fire; sometimes her screams intensified to the point where I'd have to get up from the desk and peer over the balcony. Was the end of the world nigh? In the depths of the courtyard, residents in dressing gowns and clogs threw themselves against the balcony railings, shaking revolutionary fists at each other in an explosive and vulgar uproar that was meaningless to me. All I could ever catch of their dispute, delivered in the densest dialect, were a few words: *scurnacchiato*, son of a bitch; *tutta chella fatica*, all that work; *tutte strunʒat'*, load of crap; *ommo e' merd*, piece of shit; *janara*, witch. Patched together like that, it didn't amount to much of a story.

I realized that my whole life I'd never truly known what it was like to miss someone. When the sun burned through my dreams in the morning, I'd open my eyes to find his crinkled half of our bed brutally empty. At first I spent as many hours as I could away from that room: I'd have my coffee on the roof or head out to the university, or to the deli to ask for a hundred and fifty grams (sorry, just a hundred this time) of prosciutto. Still, the emptiness followed me around like the moon chases you through the streets at night, staring at you around every corner with an unreadable expression—perhaps concerned, or perhaps quietly pleased, about your anguish. I soon realized that I couldn't outrun it because the emptiness was inside me, a perfect hole as round as the moon, a wound in my gut that had a weight all its own. It was not unlike the visceral pain I'd have just before getting my period or whenever I lay in a too-hot bath. A sickening wave of heat would rise up, making me feel at once overly full and ravenously hungry, brimming over with passion and starving for more. Eventually I chose not to push the sensation away. With Pietro gone, all I had left was that emptiness, and I would happily accept it if I could not have him. Missing him, I grasped, was as much of a privilege as loving him.

Giving in to it ended up providing me some relief. In the morning I lay in bed no longer averting my gaze from the tortuous folds of the sheets. I sought out Gabriele, to study his profile, to lose myself in his voice. This made me suffer but at least it hinted at Pietro's presence in the world. On the other hand, being in the city on my own only made my symptoms worse, maybe because out there were throngs of individuals busy shouting, kissing, laughing, and none of them was even remotely like Pietro. In the city center, that hot wave of nausea I harbored inside would completely take over and radiate out from my belly to every corner of my body, without ever finding a release. I felt feverish; my face was surely flushed. It was in plain sight of any passerby, like I was walking around engulfed in flames. I was obviously, painfully in love.

At the same time, it seemed, the Spanish Quarter felt for me, felt *with* me, shedding the tears that my pride made me swallow. Peddlers mournfully called out their wares—wicker baskets, roasted nuts—through streets as tight and clammy as hugs of condolence. Melancholy church bells rang off-key. One day a child inside a *vascio* cried and cried (over a broken toy, I think) and the adults, instead of telling her off as per tradition, were for once quietly respectful of her pain. Another time the steam from a pine-scented shower drifted down from a balcony, a cheap bodywash that managed nonetheless to move me like a real kiss smelling of Pietro's fresh, bitter aftershave. Never in my life had I been so delusional. In my state of feverish delirium, I began to suspect in fact that what we had was so good, but so far away, that I might have dreamed it all up.

One morning on my way to my Bulgarian class with Iskra, just as I'd slipped out of our neighborhood onto Via Roma, I noticed a homeless man. Washington was ashamedly bursting at the seams with homeless people (many of whom were suffering from mental illness), but not

Naples. True, the streets in the central city were littered with gypsies, who begged for money with tragedy in their eyes, and with heroin junkies lost in their selfish pleasure, but the gypsies had trailer camps to go back to and the junkies didn't appear to be living on the streets. But this man was neither a gypsy nor a drug addict nor a lunatic.

He was seated in a wheelchair outside a café; with sun-bleached hair and a leathered face, he had no legs from the knees down. On an untouchable piece of fabric beside him was a mutt with canines protruding from its mouth in all the cardinal directions. It was actually that unattractive dog that made me approach its man.

"Is he yours?"

"Good dog," he answered.

The man had an unwavering gaze, with eyes the slippery blue of a glacier. And hadn't I heard, in that unrolled *r* in *bravo*, a slight accent? Like his dog, the man had a disastrous mouth. It was hard to tell how old he might be. There was no alms cup or sign asking for anything.

I bent down to stroke the poor dog's matted, oily fur. "Would you like some money, to care for your dog?"

"Yes, please. Thank you."

Definitely a foreign accent, I thought, probably German. I gave the man some change before plowing onward toward the university. The next day I made a point of passing by the same spot during the morning rush. The hollowness in my stomach had nothing to do with hunger, so when I entered the café to order a cappuccino and an apricot croissant to go, it wasn't for me.

"Careful. It's hot," I said to the man.

His blackened hands grazed mine in the exchange, but I felt neither fear nor disgust. Then, instead of digging eagerly into the food, he looked up at me from his wheelchair with a rather mournful expression. I was flooded with shame for offending him by assuming he was poor and hungry when maybe he wasn't. Yet in those eyes all I really saw was compassion *for me*, as if his solitude and disability didn't bother him a great deal and the only pain he felt was mine, the pain that had been sapping my strength since the day Pietro left.

That look disarmed me and all I could do was mumble an excuse before handing him some coins and heading off. Maybe he really was an eccentric with a home to go back to, a mad artist or someone's visiting German uncle. Whoever he was, I knew that by giving him breakfast I'd started something I couldn't, or didn't want to, put a stop to.

It was hard to believe that Luca could return from Greece, crossing the Adriatic Sea and the entire girth of Italy, before Pietro could bus back from the hinterland of Naples. But it was most definitely Luca Falcone that I saw before me, pieces of him filtered through the usual stampede outside Palazzo Corigliano and through a light veil of rain. There was no need to call out to him: he'd already seen me and was making his way toward me, parting the mass of students and motorbikes and pigeons with the unhurried gait of a drifter, his backpack over one shoulder and beads of rain in his hair.

Luca told me he'd come back the night before and had stayed over at his aunt's house in Barra, in the industrial area outside the city. He asked me to walk him back to the old house, and less than ever was I able to say no to him. As I followed him along his own unique route through the Quartieri, we frequently bumped shoulders, every collision unleashing the smell of wet linen. With a rattle of keys we stepped into the house. There was the stench of damp basement, of abandonment. I remarked without astonishment that the renovations hadn't started yet.

"It doesn't matter, Heddi. Neither you nor I are coming back to live in this place. But I think you already knew that."

I solemnly followed Luca into his bedroom. The disheveled bed was crystallized in the state it was in when the ceiling had fallen. An espresso cup still sat on the bedside table, but the books were gone and so was the Arabic calligraphy, unpleasantly highlighting the old-fashioned wallpaper, a floral pattern stained with moisture. I tried not to linger on the memories of all of us lying on that bed watching the same old videotapes.

"You look tan."

Luca didn't reply, pulling out instead a bottle of Greek ouzo and releasing its complex scent of anise and cardamom into the stale air. Sitting down on the bed, he poured some ouzo into the espresso cup and offered it to me, surely a rhetorical gesture, and in fact when I waved it away he downed it himself. I was just standing there feeling, perhaps unreasonably, left out—from him, his motives, his intimate relationship with those forces greater than us.

But the ouzo was a fast-acting potion that soon coaxed the words from his lips. "I went to Greece for Roberta. Not to be with her, not exactly. I just wanted to see her again, find out what was left of us. And now we can put it behind us."

He stood, planting a kiss on my forehead with a smack, followed by a barely audible hum. I took it as my cue not to comment, out of respect. He opened the wardrobe, whose mirror as it swung captured a piece of daylight from somewhere and smuggled it into that dark room. "But now I have to leave again," he said. "For Varese this time." His mother wasn't well and he was an only child, he explained, laying a couple of shirts out on the bed. I realized he was packing.

"Of course you should go," I said, stumbling over my tongue, which had gone numb despite not having touched the ouzo. "And when you come back, we can find a new place."

"I'm not coming back to Naples, Heddi."

I might have guessed that myself if only my head had had time to catch up with my heart. The last thread attaching Luca to Naples was the presentation of his thesis; after that he would be sent away to complete his civilian service. Without warning, Luca pulled me toward him and wrapped his arms hard around me.

My knees felt weak. Was this it then? The end of a period of friendship I'd thought was immune to the laws of time or to erosion? I'd been lying to myself. And yet all my actions of late had hastened its end. I squeezed my eyes shut, letting myself dissolve into Luca's coarse shirt, his wild hair, his calm heartbeat.

We stayed like that for a long time, until the sprinkle deepened into rain. When I opened my eyes, I caught our reflection in the wardrobe mirror holding each other so unguarded. We did look like best friends. But there was still so much I hadn't told him.

Pietro called me every night. In the dark, even darker behind my closed lids, his voice enfolded me in a universe of its own. Was this what my professor had meant by the ancient Greek *melas*, radiant black? Pietro told me about the jobs he was getting done, the pig who ate like an emperor until the fateful day, the Roman coins he'd dug up in the fields, the childhood room he now sat in whispering into the receiver so as not to wake anyone.

"I'd love to take you here," he said to me one night, "to show you around these parts."

Wonderful scenes flashed before my eyes. His family calling us to lunch, a joyous note carried off by the wind. I could just see the house between the wheat stalks—the wide terrace, the plentiful table—coming more and more into focus as Pietro and I waded toward it through a golden field as soft and tickly as cats' tails. Then all of us sitting around the big wooden table, scarred with age and woodworms, under a filigree of olive branches, everyone looking tanned and pleasantly drained from the sun and from a good day's work. The images were so rich, in colors and sounds, that I could almost taste the bite of freshly cut lemons and smell the heat of freshly baked bread. I had a shiver of belonging like I'd never experienced before.

"Heddi, I've never had anyone to show around my hometown."

"Don't tell me you've never brought a girl home."

"There's no one I've wanted to bring home. Besides, you know what southern Italian parents are like: you bring a girl home and they already start embroidering pillowcases."

I paused. "Are you sure you want me to come?"

"Of course I am. There's no need to be scared, baby. Just be yourself and they'll love you."

"You're not nervous?"

"Not at all." He breathed out hard and long, perhaps the end of his cigarette. "With you I feel invincible. Like Superman."

After we hung up, I sat for a while on the vinyl couch in the stinging silence. Then, although I knew it was selfish, I walked upstairs and knocked on Gabriele's door. He cleared his throat and called me in. He was sitting at his drawing table, unseasonably wrapped up in a cardigan and woolen scarf, his face illuminated unkindly by a single lamp.

"Are you all right?"

"It's just a cold. Or maybe a flu. Or mad cow, I'm not too sure."

"If you like, I have a homeopathic remedy that might help."

"You're too kind, Eddie, but for what I'm suffering from there's only one cure," he said pointing to his usual companions on the floor beside him: a bottle of wine and a glass.

I took the last few steps toward his drafting table, making an effort to hide the intimacy I already had with his bedroom and the curiosity I felt for all his little treasures scattered throughout. "What are you drawing?"

"Nothing, a design for a building that will never be built." Gabriele beckoned me closer, close enough to feel the intense heat from the light-bulb that lit up his sketch. He ran his fingers over the crisp paper, pointing to the roof that was "aerodynamic, ideally like a bird in flight," the grand entrance and a cross section of the hallways that tapered toward the top "like inside the towers of the Sagrada Familia."

"It's beautiful," I said, at which he burst into a fit of laughter that turned into such a violent cough that even his ears went red. I waited for him to recover before asking him what kind of building he was designing for their mother.

"For our mother? Did Pietro say that?"

"I'm sorry, was he not supposed to tell me?"

"On the contrary. You're his beloved; he should tell you everything." He leaned over to rummage through a series of rolled-up sketches, pulled out one, and unfurled it. "But I'm not exactly designing a *building* for my mother."

I knit my brow, tilting my head to one side. "Is it a piece of furniture or something?"

"Well, it's still in the early stages. I've told her over and over again that it's a ludicrous thing to design. I've tried everything to dissuade her but she won't take no for an answer."

I still couldn't tell what it was. Gabriele took a sip from that medicine of his and then searched my face attentively, combing it for the same mixture of painful irony and delicious amusement that was on his.

"It's her gravestone."

From: heddi@yahoo.com
To: tectonic@tin.it
Sent: February 29

Dear Pietro,

Thanks for your last email. You write so well, from the heart. I only hope I'm able to do the same in my reply.

I've been in New Zealand for four years; it's here that I welcomed the new millennium. Nothing like the New Year's we experienced in the Spanish Quarter (do you remember?). In the period leading up to it everyone here was very excited, mostly because this tiny little nation was going to be the first to see the sun rise over the second millennium. And the closest you can possibly get to the dateline is a peninsula called East Cape. Hardly anyone lives there, and those that do are mostly Maori, and it's covered in rain forest and endless beaches. It was on one of those beaches that I went with a friend to wait for that momentous sunrise so full of expectation. It was hard to get to sleep: once the sun went down, the fine white sand went cold and all I had was a sleeping bag and no tent. You can imagine how many stars there were . . . it was like a roof. The sound of the waves was deafening (and they call it the Pacific?!), but I was still afraid I wouldn't wake up in time. I needn't have worried: I ended up being one of the first witnesses to the first sunrise of the new millennium. In reality it was nothing monumental, just a little newborn light, a bit pink and a bit orange, popping out from behind the clouds on the horizon. But it did give me some comfort to see that light, so unaware of its value, come out and do what it needed to do, what it has to do every day. That's what the future is to me now: just a new day, and I take it one day at a time.

On first impression, New Zealand is the epitome of the New World: it's a peaceful, convenient, and modern country with just a brief colonial history. And maybe this is the case in Auckland, where I live in a wooden house with a German doctor, a postal worker, and a Maori girl who teaches English like me. But as soon as you get out of the city, as I do at every chance I get, to visit the volcanoes and beaches and walk beneath those primordial fern trees, you realize that New Zealand does in fact have a history, one that's much more ancient than us little human beings.

It's impossible to capture with a camera all the stunning views that are around every corner. I almost always shoot with my macro lens: the veins in leaves, a white feather on a black beach, you know me. Recently I had a photographic exhibit (nothing special, it was just in a café in the city), but they're not digital so I can't attach any of them. But I'll attach this snapshot of me on the shores of Lake Taupo.

I'll write more later, I promise. In the meantime, please take care of yourself.

h.

I I

To get to Monte San Rocco, we took a bus from Naples to the town of Borgo Alto, where we picked up his uncle's car parked in front of a bakery, the keys hidden under a seat. We drove past the shops and houses until there was nothing left, just a naked undulation of land in a muted shade of green. Pietro said his hometown was only ten minutes away, but the road dragged us uphill and downhill, clockwise and counterclockwise, like in a spin cycle, and we never seemed to be gaining ground.

"Nervous?" asked Pietro, changing back into third gear before sliding his long, tapered fingers around my thigh. "There's nothing to worry about. My folks are old and completely harmless. Just offer to wash the dishes and my mother will love you."

Wasn't I just supposed to *be myself*? I turned to look out the window. With all those dark clouds, rain seemed certain. There was just one small piece of clear sky in the middle.

"What is that, the eye of the storm?"

"Don't worry, baby. It's just a bit of rain." Pietro looked in his element, with one hand loosely cupping the gear stick and an elbow sticking out the window. Soon the bare land became speckled with houses, and without warning the houses thickened into a village. "Welcome to Monte San Rocco, in all its rustic splendor."

The car ached up the steep road, passing in front of a butcher's, a café, a piazza. I suddenly longed for that endless, aimless road. We turned into a backstreet. An old woman peered at us through her window. A dog barked. The car grunted up a rocky driveway until the hand brake jerked it to a stop in front of a two-story stone house.

"Here we are."

Stepping out of the car, I was hit by the cool, damp air. It smelled of burning firewood and wet rocks, a promise of rain. Pietro grabbed our bags from the back as a chicken ran in a panic behind the house.

We walked in through the door to find Pietro's parents in the kitchen, his father bent over the fireplace unloading an armful of wood. Twigs and dried leaves clung to his sweater, but he didn't appear to take notice of them or of our arrival. His mother, however, who wore a kerchief knotted behind her neck, was on her feet ready to receive us but without saying a word.

"Ah, you're back, boy," Pietro's father said. "And you've brought a friend." At least, I was fairly certain that's what he said. Though related to Neapolitan, their dialect had thrown me.

"Papà, this is Eddie," Pietro nearly shouted, putting our bags down like there were champagne glasses inside. That balancing act he'd just performed, maintaining such delicateness in his gestures while simultaneously injecting such power into his voice, was deceptively tricky. Or maybe the power was an intrinsic part of the dialect. I also noticed he'd purposely simplified my name for his elderly father's benefit, undoubtedly a show of good manners and respect.

"It's a pleasure," said his father in Italian and at full volume. Was he partially deaf, or did it have something to do with the extraordinary amount of hair growing out of his ears? His father grabbed my hand to squeeze it between his own, which were large and rough like bark. He said something, a mesh of dialect in which I clearly heard "pretty girl" as I looked into his smiling eyes, made larger than life by thick lenses and framed by wrinkles that branched out like an old oak tree.

Pietro's mother was a matryoshka standing there, her hands one on top of the other and her face reddened by too much wind and sun. She unfolded a limp hand toward me. As I took it and leaned in to kiss her cheeks, I caught a glimpse of her dangling gold earrings, a vestige of girlhood decorating a face deeply marked by time.

"So happy to meet you," I said, still holding on to that hand as rough and flaccid as a gardening glove. "You live in a beautiful spot, *signora*."

"It's a pleasure to make your acquaintance," she answered in a slow, deliberate Italian. She rested her eyes on me with a somewhat concerned expression before rolling up her sleeves and turning back to her chores.

"Come with me. I'll show you around the house," said Pietro.

Was that it? After all the anticipation, the worst was over. I followed Pietro's willowy figure through the house. The rooms were prematurely dark. Lowered blinds let in only droplets of light that bounced off the facets of the whiskey glasses on display in the dining room, a formal lounge with 1970s-style furniture facing a darkened television set. An even darker hallway led upstairs. The landing was bare except for a window overlooking the now gray countryside and a telephone, whose cord Pietro had stretched every last curl out of to reach his bedroom and call me all those nights in Naples.

His bedroom was painted a frosty blue, with old posters, a wardrobe, a small bed, and a desk with a shelf above it groaning with rocks. I wanted to linger in that room of the boy I loved but at an age that I couldn't picture, yet he was already leading me down to the basement.

"It's not really an apartment yet, but it will be someday." More precisely, it was a cellar with concrete floors, some sacks, and a wooden chair. "You see this? This is where my mother prefers to cook." Pietro was pointing to a sort of coal range. I thought I ought to know what his mother needed two stoves for, so I didn't ask as we walked back upstairs, past the kitchen and out the front door to the terrace.

I took in that sweet fusion of black earth and cow dung. "The air here is heavenly!"

"Every time I go back to Naples my eyes sting the first day because of the smog," said Pietro, leaning his elbows on the railing. "You know, Heddi, my father likes you."

"Does he?" I reached for him and he grabbed my hand, burrowing it in the secret warmth of his jacket.

"Definitely. I can tell." He looked out in the distance. "You see that house over there?" My gaze followed Pietro's finger over the chickens in the driveway to a dirt road. Behind a splash of freshly budded trees were a few houses.

"You mean the brick one?"

"The brick one is my Aunt Libertà's house. They haven't finished rebuilding it yet, after the earthquake. No, the one behind it, the gray one with the terra-cotta roof."

They all looked like that. Those orange roofs stood out in brilliant contrast against the dark clouds, and I suddenly regretted leaving my camera behind. Pietro released my hand to pull his cigarettes from his breast pocket, explaining that that house was owned by his uncle Stefano, with whom his father had had a falling-out fifteen years ago over an unpaid debt. Since then the entire family was forbidden to even speak to him. I struggled to imagine Pietro's father, with those substantial lenses magnifying the kindness in his eyes, getting that pissed off and ranting and raving, maybe like they did in the Quartieri.

"It's insane. My parents are so hung up on money. Everything else is worthless to them." He talked while squeezing the cigarette between his lips, which now curled up at the corners. "And you see that house right next door to it, the one with the pine tree in the yard? That belongs to the girl my mother thinks I ought to marry." And he let out a soundless laugh, of unease perhaps, and yet his face went red.

I acted blasé. "What, like some kind of arranged marriage?"

"A bit like my parents'? Not on your life! No, this girl and I have known each other since we were eight years old. My brother and I used to go over and climb up their pine tree. A totally stupid idea, let me tell you, because we'd get scratched all over from the needles." He was still looking straight ahead, watching the footage of his memories.

"Your mother doesn't honestly think you're going to marry her, does she?"

"Who knows what goes through that woman's head. The only reason she wants us to get married anyway is because the girl's family owns land that borders ours."

Where was all this land that Pietro's family owned, anyway? I had to quickly come to terms with the fact that living in a town and having land beside your house were two irreconcilable concepts.

"Besides, just between you and me, she's as ugly as a mussel," he added, burying his half-smoked cigarette in a potted plant.

Brutta come una cozza. Not at all unpleased about the neighbor girl's genetic misfortune, I pointed out lightheartedly that it wasn't like him to give up a good Marlboro Light. But he'd had to put it out, he said, because his parents didn't know that he smoked. I couldn't help laughing at this explanation, given the rectangle so blatantly embossed into the plaid of his shirt pocket.

"Let's put it this way, baby. They pretend not to know that I smoke. So out of respect for them turning a blind eye, I smoke outside."

"That's complicated."

"Don't you have something like that that you want to hide from your family? Or are you always this honest?" he said without a hint of malice: if anything, with awe.

"Well, when I was little and my dad fed us meat, I'd brush my teeth before going back home so that my mom couldn't smell it on me."

"A Texan and a vegetarian," he said. "Now that's a match made in heaven."

"In fact, it ended in divorce."

"You and me, we're never going to get divorced." Pietro winked at me, saying he was popping into the kitchen to grab me a wool hat. He wanted to take me to a place he loved.

The village dissolved back into countryside. Pietro drove leisurely. The hills settled down and for some stretches the road straightened out into tunnels of mathematically spaced trees, behind which I saw flashes of unimpressed cows and unidentifiable crops. The clouds still hadn't burst: maybe the storm was just in my head after all. The sun even made an appearance, so bright as to turn those tree tunnels into fire hoops that we sped through unharmed. But the sun didn't last, and neither did the plain, and again the hills made it harder to drive and stole Pietro's warm hand from my thigh so that he could change gears. Soon we were up so high that the hood of the car was cutting through fog.

Pietro pulled over onto the grass. We sat there in the trembling car; we could feel the wind, as strong as anything, but we couldn't see it. "From up here there's a terrific view of the valley. But, damn it, the visibility sucks today. I'm sorry."

"It doesn't matter. It's like being inside the clouds, at the top of the world."

"I love how you see the good in everything. You make me feel good about my life, about my future." And we kissed with passion, and a touch of despair, as though over the last few hours it had been forbidden.

When we got out of the car, the rough weather overwhelmed us, tossing about our hair. "I knew you were going to need that hat," he said and we quickly retreated into the car. The engine started up with a gurgle.

It was true that we were both still young students financially dependent on our parents. But for a moment in time in the falling darkness, as we rode over the folds of the land in his uncle's car that we might never have to give back, just the two of us, with my hand stroking the nape of his neck and his squeezing my inner thigh, we could have been married and this might have been our car as we drove back home together after a day trip to the countryside. Pietro was smiling with his eyes glued to the road before him, trying hard not to show me, it seemed, how brightly they shone with pride. Perhaps he was having the same fantasy too.

That evening we ate dinner around the kitchen table mostly in silence, save the Italian voiceover coming from the television in the adjoining room. It was a bad Hollywood movie and I tried not to feel personally responsible for it. Nonetheless, Pietro's parents seemed so involved in the plot that my compliments to the chef went unacknowledged. I decided to wait for the ads to start a conversation. But Pietro's mother took advantage of every commercial break to get up—to slice more bread or turn the sausages in the pan—and so did his father, to tend the fire. With dinner nearly over, my last chance to speak was lost when, during a particularly zealous laundry detergent ad, Pietro's father burst into dialect, a series of sentences fired at Pietro from which I could only catch "land" and "tomorrow morning."

With that accent, it was clear that the affinity between their dialect and Neapolitan was of little use to me. As I listened to his father, I allowed my mind to wander to phonological considerations. Their Irpinia dialect melted the distinction between the liquid consonants, *l* and *r*, almost like Mandarin. Compared to Neapolitan, it was less drawn out, less visceral, resulting in speech patterns that were truncated, hurried, practically breathless. But what struck me the most was the way in which, when Pietro answered back, the dialect dropped his voice lower than I'd thought it could go; it sounded like someone else's voice. I had a flash of him as that little boy who, on his first day of school, didn't speak a word of Italian.

Everyone stood up, leaving the tablecloth scattered with breadcrumbs and balled-up paper napkins. Pietro looked as anxious as I was to turn in for the night, to carve out a space of our own. But first, I remembered, I would help his mother with the dishes. I stacked the plates and copied

Pietro in throwing the napkins into the insatiable fire. All the while his mother stood over the steaming sink. I went up to her. It turned out that she was the petite one, not me.

"Let me do these, *signora*."

"Don't go to such trouble," she replied with palpable tiredness but in clear and formal Italian.

"You've cooked a wonderful meal and I'm sure you've been on your feet all day. The least I can do is wash the dishes."

But his mother was a tiny statue in front of the sink as she said with a surprising amount of energy, "No. You two go to sleep now."

Pietro shrugged. I hoped that, despite her refusal, my offer had still fulfilled the magic formula he'd recommended. He guided me to the dining room sofa. We sat there for some time bathed in the colorful lights of the TV: the movie was over and an inane variety show had taken over. I squeezed my chilled hands between my knees as the dishes clanked and rattled in the kitchen. It seemed like an eternity before Pietro said it was time for bed.

No sooner were we alone in his room than Pietro told me that during dinner his father had asked him to help out the next day. "I need to go with him to drive the tractor to one of our plots of land. We'll need to head off early in the morning."

"Can I come?" He was already shaking his head so I quickly added, "You won't even notice me. I'll just sit there quietly and watch the scenery, I promise."

"Sorry, baby, it's too far away. About an hour's drive. And, anyway, where would you sit? Here's my idea: you can hang out with my mother in the morning, or just relax and read your book. Make yourself at home. And when I come back, we'll have the whole rest of the day together." As if we were being watched, Pietro kissed my forehead.

I didn't like the idea of spending an entire morning alone with his mother; on the other hand, I figured it might be the perfect opportunity to get to know her. I said I'd do my best. Pietro looked satisfied and pulled a pair of flannel pajamas from his wardrobe, for me.

"What do I need these for? I have you to keep me warm."

"But I'm sleeping in Gabriele's room," he said, but the disappointment must have been written all over my face, for he added, "It's a bit like the smoking thing. They pretend not to know we're together. For them, only old married couples can sleep in the same room without arousing suspicion. Don't forget, my parents were born in the last ice age."

I changed into the pajamas, saying, "Of course I get it, but it's just ignoring the obvious, isn't it? I mean, we sleep in the same bed in Naples."

"Heddi, my parents don't know we live together."

A smile escaped my lips. *Living together?* Is that what we were doing, not me just staying with him for a while? I'd never loved him more than in that moment. My immense joy was spoiled only by the growing awareness that we were up to our necks in trouble.

"Pietro, please . . ."

"Look, I will tell them. Just not right now, the first time they meet you. They'd judge you for it." A dog barked somewhere outside, and Pietro gave me a lopsided smile, leaning hard on his favored leg. "All right, love of my life?"

Yes, it was all right, more than all right, wonderful actually, with that term of endearment that, at just hearing it, had tipped over my heart like a cup that runneth over. I was already missing him, I could feel the first symptoms coming on, and in that moment he could have asked me for anything and I would have said all right; I would have lied for him, cheated for him. But fortunately he didn't ask me to: all I had to do was avoid bringing up our living situation in his parents' presence.

I loosened the tightly tucked covers to slip into bed, and Pietro tucked me in, running his hand over the dated but freshly laundered comforter, which seemed to blossom under his touch with yellow and green flowers. Then there came a soothing hum from outside. The rain was finally here.

12

IN THE MORNING the rain was still drumming on the roof. What woke me, though, was not the rain but the muffled voices from downstairs. I threw on my clothes and went straight to the kitchen. Pietro, fully dressed and wearing a black wool hat, was clinking a teaspoon around in his coffee. I caught him midsentence as he spoke with his parents.

"Good morning," he said. "Did you sleep well?"

With the same formality I greeted the whole kitchen. I noticed that his mother was still wearing her kerchief, like she'd slept with it on. In a voice meant only for Pietro, I said, "I think I've slept in."

"It's only eight o'clock."

"Let's go, boy," said his father sternly, but it was probably just an illusion created by the dialect because his eyes were again making lovely little branches.

"We've been waiting for the rain to stop, but it looks like we'll just have to leave anyway," said Pietro, downing his coffee. "There's some of my mother's biscotti on the table. Help yourself."

"Thanks, I'm not hungry." I wished I could at least kiss him goodbye but I never would have dared to in front of his parents, just as he hadn't called me baby.

"Try to eat a little something," he said.

Then his mother muttered a sentence that I clearly understood in spite of the dialect. *"Edda è troppu sicca."*

Interesting, I thought to myself. So *edda* meant what *essa* did in Neapolitan ("she"), and both dialects shared the same word for "skinny," *sicca*. Only afterward did I grasp the true meaning of the phrase. *She's too skinny,* she'd said, and in the third person: it was that detail that hurt me more than the aesthetic judgment. She had talked about me as though I weren't even in the room, as though I weren't merely thin but insubstantial, like a breath melting into the cold air of that kitchen. Like a ghost.

We women duly stood side by side as the men put on their raincoats at the door. I watched as Pietro mounted the growling tractor with his father. Even through the tulle of rain, he was painfully handsome and, judging from his embarrassed smile, wholly unaware of it as usual. As soon as he returned, I would ask him to take me for a ride.

His mother closed the door with a thud. "Bad weather," she mumbled as she sat by the lethargic fire. "Eat some breakfast."

I found it even more demoralizing that she'd gone back to addressing me with *voi*, the formal "you." My mouth was dry; I hadn't even been to the bathroom. But I pulled out a chair to face the fire and sank my teeth into a hard almond cookie. "They're delicious, *signora*."

She answered with a painful moan. I wondered if they were time-consuming to prepare and asked her how she made them.

"It's nothing," she said to the fire. "Just some old recipe."

"Let me see if I can guess the ingredients," I said with fake bubbliness, in reality needing to pee. "So, let's see, almonds of course. Then eggs, or not?"

She seemed not to have heard my question and, in all honesty, I didn't care to know the answer. She broke a branch on her thigh and threw it to the fire. Tiny, voracious flames ignited on the split edges like flies rushing to a wound. I spent some time watching them grow until they'd coiled their way up the entire branch.

Fearing that the silence between us would settle in definitively, I started telling her about the cookies my mother used to bake when I was little. They were made not with sugar but molasses (not knowing the correct term, I unsuccessfully Italianized it as *"molassa"*) and they had a line of jam down the middle that resembled a little road. That's why my mom had named them Jelly Roads, which I also poorly translated, even selling them at the local health food store.

I came to a sudden stop, sensing I was rambling on nervously. Why had I chosen such an inappropriate and semantically challenging story? What was I thinking? I was already exhausted from the effort and decided it was best to quickly wrap it up. "They were quite a hit, actually. But then macrobiotic people will eat anything . . ."

"It's just as well," his mother said without a clear logic and without looking at me.

What else could I bring up that would spark, if not enthusiasm, at least a bit of interest? I racked my brains as I gnawed on the nearly unbreakable cookie. Then it came to me. "Well, Pietro . . ." I said. "He sure looks like a natural on that tractor. Has he been driving one for a long time?"

"Yes."

"You mean, since he was a boy?"

She nodded.

"Do you need a license?"

"Of course not."

I jabbered on more rapidly than ever, due partly to my ballooning bladder, which was creating a sort of psychological pressure. At one point, I mentioned that I didn't know how to drive a car—and, thank god, she didn't either. A shared failure was just what I needed, and my bladder could wait. "You know," I said animatedly, perhaps to a fault, "sometimes I think it just looks impossible to change all those gears and keep your eyes on the road at the same time. How could I ever learn?" I scanned his mother's lined profile for the smallest sign of complicity, of sensitivity to my admission of weakness.

"It's probably not that hard."

After a little while, she announced she was going out to get some more firewood. As she stood up, I could see that her apron was, despite the early hour, already stained with tomatoes and soil. I asked if I could help; she shook her head. Hopefully soon she would tell me to stop calling her *signora*. I didn't even know her name.

This was my chance to go to the bathroom. The tiles were icy even through my socks. No wonder everyone was always in the kitchen: it was the only warmish room in the house. As the late spring rain tapped on the roof, I looked at my blotchy reflection in that silvered mirror, to make sure of my existence, however faint it might be, in that house.

Pietro's mother uncradled logs and branches from her apron, before sitting down to position them in the fireplace. I dared to place a couple of branches according to the pyramid structure that the boys had taught me. She let me. The fire grew, emanating a pleasant heat.

"What do you do with the wheat you grow on your land?" I hazarded after a while.

"We grind it into flour. I used to make my own bread with it."

"Why don't you make bread anymore?"

"Too much hard work. I'm old now."

I remembered the gravestone design that Gabriele had shown me. No, she wasn't ill, he'd said. Maybe she was just a tired old woman. Encouraged by that good long sequence of words, I asked her about their olive harvest. But this time she answered in monosyllables, looking straight at the fire. I asked about their grapes, also to little effect. Still, I nodded and smiled, going along with it all, feeling like a fool. I wasn't trying to work my way into her heart, to ferret her out or unnest her like a Russian doll. I wasn't that ambitious. All I wanted was the most basic of conversations, a chat, and that was something that, despite the humiliation, I was unwilling to forgo.

"So, I hear you have two beautiful grandchildren."

"They don't speak the language."

"Young people can learn so fast."

"What would I know."

"It must be nice to see your eldest son, when he comes over from Switzerland."

"Vittorio?" said his mother, turning up the volume. "Eeeiihhh . . ." It was a drawn-out, mysterious interjection, followed by a gesture of annoyance, like she was shooing a mosquito. And then nothing.

The light outside was unchanged, filtered as it was through clouds that unleashed torrents of rain like thick sheets of metal, dousing everything in sight. It was hard to tell what time it was. The hours were as sticky and sluggish as the mud in the devastated yard. All at once I became concerned about, of all things, the chickens outside. Had one of them been caught in the downpour, or had the coop flooded? Yet I didn't go to the window to check on them. I sat stubbornly next to Pietro's mother, diving aimlessly from subject to subject, swallowing each of her blunt replies. Sometimes she didn't even bother answering but just stared at the fire. Between the various attempts, I too gave in and observed the flames. After a bit, I began to see the fire as a friend, or a home base like in hide-and-seek, a safe place to go to where I was allowed to be, at least for a while, out of the game.

A long time went by before I had the brilliant idea that I could walk away from the fireplace. I could hide away under the daisies of Pietro's comforter with a book until he came back. But it was an extraordinarily difficult decision to make. First, I had to mentally consult with the fire on the matter, and even once I'd made up my mind it cost me a superhuman effort to stand up, push the chair back, and straighten my knees.

"*Signora*, I'm going to go read for a bit."

"Where are you going?"

"Upstairs."

"Sit down. It's too cold up there."

I was trapped. I couldn't fathom why his mother might want me there by her side if she didn't want to talk to me. Did she in some way enjoy the company? The many conversation starters I'd come up with had entirely drained me of words, and finally I just stared into the fire too.

That was when I realized that there was a sort of plot unfolding in the fireplace, and that the flames were as spellbinding as television. They told gripping, but strange and unspeakable, tales. Flashy orange flames, stained blood-red in the middle, billowed and deflated like laundered sheets hung out to dry; they snapped and whipped in the hot wind. Smaller flames as yellow and eager as tendrils danced, sashayed, licked, whispered, spat. The embers smoldered with latent fire, with menacing jealousy. Now and then a collapse of wood would trigger a tiny explosion, a brief climax followed by a lavish release of heat. And all the while I didn't move an inch. I sat as if in prayer with Pietro's mother, incapable of shifting my gaze from the fire even for a second, for fear of missing a line, a twist, the ending.

The rain thickened, washing the tractor shed and the neighboring houses into oblivion, and still there was no sign of Pietro and his father. I was certain he'd said the land was only an hour away. That would make the trip two hours, three at worst with the weather. I didn't know the time, but it might have been four hours since they'd waved from the tractor. A repulsive thought wormed its way into my head—and once I'd thought it there was no ignoring it—the possibility that Pietro and his father had had an accident, that the man of my dreams was lying bloodied in a ditch under the indifferent rain. And to think the last thing I'd said to him was *I'm not hungry.*

I hadn't used my voice in a while and it came out hoarse. "It sure is raining hard."

Pietro's mother mumbled an agreement, and I turned to look at her. Actually, she too looked worried. I may have been judging her unfairly. Maybe she was incapable of making small talk when all that was on her mind was the fate of her husband and son. For the first time I felt a connection between us, not a bond of affection but one of ancestral memory, a torturous affinity that only two waiting women could share.

"*Signora*, do you think they'll be all right?"

"Of course they will."

"But the storm—"

"What storm?" she snapped. "It's just a bit of rain." Then, tossing a branch into the fire, she announced it was lunchtime.

We ate leftovers, even yesterday's bread. The fire crackled by the table like a third guest. Afterward when I went to the sink to begin washing up, without a word Pietro's mother edged me away with her hips. To be honest, though, I'd acted with little conviction and didn't stand my ground.

By the time Pietro and his father came back that afternoon, my cheeks were hot from the fire. When the two men walked in through the door, a gust of wind blowing in with them, I would have leaped into Pietro's arms if I could have, even soaking my clothes in all the rain dripping off his jacket and his hands. We didn't say a word to each other, but his face shone so brightly I could tell that he too was greatly relieved to see me again.

He clouded over as he turned to address his mother in their harsh dialect. His father, wiping his glasses with a dry cloth, joined in on the storytelling. I picked up the most basic words: "rain," "couldn't see a thing," "tractor," "car." I glanced out the window and saw a little white car parked behind his uncle's car. They must have picked it up after dropping off the tractor. It was a detail I hadn't bothered to ask the night before, nor did I know what crop, if any, was on the land or why they needed to leave the tractor there.

Pietro's mother began preparing cups of tea for the drenched men, without offering me one. There was a sort of intimacy in that exclusion, as if through our troubled day together we had developed an unspoken understanding. The initial awkwardness between us was gone, and now at least she no longer felt it necessary to feign any interest in her son's girlfriend or conceal her true priorities.

With a wink in my direction, Pietro said he first needed to get changed. Mumbling something about grabbing my book, I followed him up the stairs. We hadn't even reached his room and already he was kissing me. In the semidarkness I could feel his face as cold as ice and his mouth as surprising and scorching as a secret love letter.

"I'm sorry we were so late," he whispered. "The rain really held us back. It was driving into our faces; I could hardly steer."

"I was so worried about you. I thought it was only an hour's drive."

"An hour by car. That's three by tractor. The land is all the way in Puglia. And the whole time all I could think about was you." He kissed me again and led me by the hand into his room. He pulled clothes from the wardrobe and quickly changed into them. "How did it go with my mother?"

"Not too bad."

He didn't press further. He said he was tired and in desperate need of a nap. It was the last thing I wanted to hear. I wanted him to take me out, even in the rain. We could go to a café in the village or just sit in the car watching the raindrops cut tentative, idiosyncratic trails down the windshield. Anything to get out of that house. But Pietro's hair was wet, his hands numb and clumsy as he tried to button up his jeans, and I felt for him. I went to tidy his bed that I'd left unmade that morning in my haste to get downstairs.

"Don't bother, baby. I'll just lie down on the couch downstairs. Besides, it's too cold up here."

"They'd think we're up to no good anyway."

"Exactly. You're catching on fast," he said with a playful smile.

By the time Pietro woke up, dinner was on the table. The rain was still droning on. As we ate homemade pasta with the television rigorously on, I allowed myself the luxury of disregarding his mother. It was simply too much work to try to make conversation. Instead, I focused on becoming like Pietro, on making myself as quiet and unremarkable as possible so that his parents' lack of interest in me would appear natural.

Just one more sleep and then in the morning we'd be on the bus back to Naples. I was so thrilled by the thought of leaving that I didn't regret not having hunted for Roman coins or gone for a spin around the town. Gabriele had been right from the beginning: the fresh air didn't compensate for the silence and the cold. I could almost picture the gloomy irony on his face as we walked back into the apartment, laden no doubt with hard almond cookies, aged cheese, and wine, as he had been after his last visit. I could see now that those culinary spoils were in reality reparation for the suffering endured.

And still I couldn't help but feel optimistic that, if I could only get back to the city—to my books, our bed, our budding collection of *National Geographic*—I would be able to refuel. Then I'd have the energy required to face his mother again and perhaps woo her in a more deliberate way. With this in mind, I couldn't resist the irrational instinct to offer, for the third time, to do the dishes.

From: tectonic@tin.it
To: heddi@yahoo.com
Sent: April 2

Dear Heddi,

You've moved to a beautiful place with beaches and palm trees, like a page out of National Geographic. I think of you over there like a bee on a flower. I'm happy that, in a way, due to the laws of chaos I too have contributed to your new life, simply by running away from you. But once again I find myself at a loss in my reply . . . where should I start?

Last summer I had the illusion of a normal life, as normal a life as one can have in a small, isolated, and dreadful town like Monte San Rocco. It all began one night mid-June. I was in a pub when I ran into a girl I knew. I was alone and so was she. We spent an evening together, exchanging a few kisses, nothing more. But to me it felt like the start of something new . . . it was probably the alcohol mixed with the euphoria of trying to have fun in such a way that it would make a good story to tell. Anyway, nothing ended up happening with this girl. A few weeks later at the nightclub I always go to (I'm practically a wallflower), I met a girl from here who's been living for years in Rimini. A bit of an oddball, slightly hippieish, really nice, friendly, but that's all. So I started thinking, well, well, this summer might just turn out to be all right after all. That was my first mistake.

But then, ever a sucker for punishment, I launched into renovating my house . . . I thought: OK, now I'll fix up the ground floor for my old folks, they'll be more comfortable there, they'll move downstairs . . . second mistake.

I went through two months of hell with builders and plaster everywhere, but my parents won't give up the house . . . a nice empty apartment . . . Then came the fall . . . and then winter: a total void, no vacation, no flirting, nothing at all.

A shitty life, that's what it is. The worst part, though, is that I'm such a creature of habit. By now I think all my disappointments, mistakes, and troubles have healed over like old wounds. I think of myself as a man in voluntary exile, but my spirit is at times retching . . . I can't see a way out.

At the same time, in a sort of cynical and mean way, I've come to believe that much of my grief and anguish stems from my parents, who have plotted with the idiotic part of me to make me monstrously similar to them.

On the one hand, I could never wish them ill: they're old and can't live forever. On the other hand, I can't help but experience the unmentionable feeling that I'm waiting. With some shame, actually quite a lot, I feel that the only purpose of my life here is to prepare for a funeral. When I project my desires onto the future, I start to see some possibilities . . . and it doesn't look too bad . . .

Though it may be hard for you to believe, I often think of you . . . with shame, believe me. Maybe I'm ashamed of my fate. I often think of how my life could have been different. I had my big chance. But it came too soon (even though deep down I wanted it). It was that ill combination of youth and lack of experience, too much too soon . . . and too soon even to feel an immediate regret . . .

As usual, I feel like I'm raving, but I'm sure you'll read these lines carefully, because that's what you're like. And that's enough for me, I couldn't ask for anything more. I feel superior to those around me because I met you. Because I hold inside me the memory of your immense love. Because I was privileged. Because you're my touchstone and I'm doomed to never be satisfied . . .

I hope these words go some way toward describing the affection I have for you. For me it's enough to know that you won't throw them in the trash.

With affection,

p.

13

WHENEVER I RETURNED to the Spanish Quarter, my senses would become so overloaded with data that my nervous system had to urgently reacclimatize. Despite the oppressive, stormy sky, Monte San Rocco had landscapes like wide-angle photographs and an air so sweet you could eat it. But our neighborhood, thrown into perennial shadow by its very being, required a certain myopia, a nearsightedness that allowed you to focus only on the street slabs laid out one by one under your feet, thus blurring any peripheral distractions. Your ears had to relearn to discern different sounds, isolating the useful ones and blocking out others that were nothing but background noise. You had to remember how to breathe, shallowly so as not to be overwhelmed by the clashing odors that brought the air to life while spoiling it at the same time. However, the warmth of those streets, especially this time, I did find welcoming: it was like sinking back into an old armchair.

We threw together a dinner. With our decrepit palace now gone, Pietro's was the only rooftop. Our steps and the feet of the table left short-lived impressions in the tar like footprints in black sand. It was a lovely evening and the salty air made the ship lights flicker in the bay. Vesuvius was still there, a black abstraction against the unnaturally bright sky, but I tried not to look at it because, depending on the night, the volcano could make me feel uneasy, or euphoric, or simply insignificant and alone in the universe. It had done so, I realized, since I was sixteen years old.

Angelo and Tonino came; Davide too. When Sonia turned up, she wasn't alone. A tall young man was holding the small of her back and with the other hand gripping a store-bought bottle of wine. His honey-colored hair was swept rather dramatically to one side, as if he'd just come from a stroll along the waterfront. He wore a stylish corduroy jacket, the same color as his hair but a size too small. His smile revealed slightly crooked teeth, a flaw that only drew attention to his overall attractiveness.

"This is Carlo."

"Ah, so you're the 'boys' I've heard so much about?"

Sonia was beaming. I watched her move around him, measuring how relaxed her gestures were, how broad her smile, in an effort to figure out how long they'd been together. My disappointment that she hadn't said a word to me about Carlo was dulled by the selfish relief that I hadn't left her to the wolves after all.

I observed Carlo closely, wanting to like him. He quickly mingled, holding his glass of wine loosely, as though it were a cocktail, an attractive accessory that he could have done without. I overheard his exchanges with the others enough to tell that he had that clear and airy accent, with its warm and rounded vowels, that placed him in the upper reaches of the city—and of society.

Soon we served dinner, which included an often-requested potato dish that frankly I'd made up. The wine broke everyone loose like the hours off a clockface, until once more it seemed, in spite of Luca's glaring absence, that tomorrow would never come.

At one point Carlo, an engineering student, told us about the construction of the Brooklyn Bridge, which I only vaguely remembered from junior high school. He wove a tale of ferry crashes and deaths from decompression sickness, and of the chief engineer himself, Washington Roebling, who ended up having to supervise the bridge's construction from a wheelchair in his apartment overlooking the East River. It was a captivating story that he'd undoubtedly rehearsed many times, given the well-timed pauses, the overdone American pronunciation, the theatrical inflexion.

"Incredible, it sounds like a film noir," said Sonia.

"Yes, well, it does make quite an impression . . ."

"Roebling's true passion, though, was for rocks and minerals," said Pietro, not in the deferential and subtle way he'd added to Luca's story some time back, but as if to contradict the storyteller, maybe even humiliate him. It surprised me even more when he added, "In fact, if you ever go to Washington you'll see that almost an entire floor of the Natural History Museum is dedicated to his collection."

Carlo forged an amused smile before looking away.

Angelo said, "How awesome would it be to go to Brooklyn one day and hang out with the Hells Angels."

"Hang out? Are you off your fucking rocker?" said Tonino. "Yeah sure, you go there and tell them your name is Angel, then you'll see how they welcome you with open arms. And spread-open legs."

"For fuck's sake, Tonino."

"Actually, I believe they're based in Manhattan," said Carlo, shaking the honey mop off his forehead with a skillful jerk of the head. "Right, Eddie?"

"Me? I'm not sure."

I'd hoped to stay out of the discussion, which highlighted my ignorance of my own country whereas the others seemed to know it so very well. Especially Pietro. And it wasn't just his historical knowledge that astonished me but the fierce pride he'd pulled out like a rabbit out of a hat.

I felt him caress me under the table. Later in bed, we would lie awake exchanging impressions of Sonia's new love interest. Charming, I would say, perhaps trying a bit too hard. I could hardly wait to hear what Pietro thought: he could pick apart any character better than a screenplay critic.

Afterward, I hoped, we'd make love before falling asleep in the gap between the mattresses, which caved in so easily under our weight that Pietro had named it "the crevasse."

I noticed his glass was empty, as was the bottle, so I nudged my still full glass toward his. Pietro said, "Ah, thank god for you. You're like my own private stock of wine. My wine bank."

"Wine bank?" echoed Davide. "Where can I get me one of those?" He pulled out two joints and gave one to Angelo.

Just then came Gabriele up onto the roof, flushed in the face and mad as hell—he was cursing under his breath—about the aerobic workout that those six flights of stairs always forced on him. Even short of breath, he managed to cut through the sticky air of the night to say, "Now just look at you all dining under the stars! If I hadn't known better, I would have thought you were enjoying the stuffed pepper festival in Monte San Rocco."

"Monte what?" asked Carlo.

I slid onto Pietro's lap to give my chair to Gabriele, who took it without a word, scissoring his legs and pulling out a handkerchief to wipe his brow. Only then did he seem to take notice of Carlo and remember his manners. He leaned across the table to shake his hand, though with a clumsy and over-the-top grip that made it clear that, despite his flawless use of the third conditional tense, he was completely trashed.

"It's a pleasure. Gabriele. Despite having been born in Schaffhausen, I have the misfortune of hailing from a tribe of Neanderthals in a site known as San Rocco Mountain."

For Pietro's sake, I rose in defense of the village, praising its beauty. But from the corner of my eye I saw Sonia looking at me perplexed. I should have told her earlier that I'd gone to meet Pietro's parents, that things were getting that serious. For her to find out like that, in front of everyone, would only have proved to her that it was too late for sharing secrets, perhaps on both sides.

Gabriele wasn't looking at me at all but at his brother, with eyes like two red-hot needles. It was surely the alcohol, I thought. Through clenched teeth Gabriele said, "I told you not to take her to the farm."

"Your brother's right, Pie'," said Davide, who also was from the Avellino area. "Why would you want to take her there? It's boring as hell."

"No, he means my mother can sometimes be hard work, that's all," Pietro spelled out in what sounded like a sincere admission. So then why had he told me his mother was harmless? He hadn't warned me and thus I'd turned up there completely ill-equipped.

"Ah, southern Italian mothers," cut in Carlo as if remembering the organoleptic qualities of a fine wine. "They're just hopeless."

"How so?" I asked.

Carlo explained, as engagingly as before, that the vice, or perhaps the duty, of any good southern Italian mamma was to put her son's girlfriend to the test. He compared it to a rite of passage. But in the end, she was genetically programmed to be a mother hen and would inevitably take the girl under her wing as if she were her own daughter.

"Mother hens?" said Sonia, laughing joyfully. "Is that what you're calling women now?"

"And how about for us dudes?" Tonino chimed in. "The test is even tougher with your girlfriend's dad. He drills you so bad—do you have a job, what intentions do you have with my daughter?—that you hardly even feel like screwing anymore. And then he bores into you with that look, like he's got x-ray vision and he's trying to see how much money you have in your pocket or how big your balls are."

"You're better off not having any balls at all," said Davide.

"Who do you think you're kidding, Tonino?" Angelo shot back. "As if a girl had ever taken *you* home!"

There was a peal of laughter as I leaned back against Pietro's warm body. A rite of passage, so that's all it had been. Not genuine dislike on his mother's part (she barely even knew me) but a necessary trial, a time-honored tradition, which, now seen within the context of my anthropological studies, seemed simply a matter of course.

"Meeting the parents already? Well, you guys don't waste any time, do you?" said Angelo.

They all began good-naturedly making a fuss over us, demanding to be shown engagement rings, urging us not to have babies out of wedlock, and insisting they be given a date for the wedding so that they could start thinking about the most seasonally appropriate suit and tie to wear.

Every now and then Pietro's leg lifted affectionately underneath me. He was unexpectedly submitting to the public banter, and even apparently enjoying it, something that gave me such intense pleasure that I had to lower my gaze. I hoped to avoid making eye contact just then not only with Sonia but with any of our friends, who were celebrating our love with as much noise and profanity as possible. I was afraid they would read in my eyes how happy I was about the turn my life had taken, wildly happy to the point of seeming ridiculous, and how fulfilled I was, so deeply fulfilled that our status as poor students and the uncertainty of our living situations just washed over me. My happiness was a betrayal and thus advertising it, I believed, would cause them pain, for if they looked at it for too long, if they saw it for what it truly was, in all its dazzling light, it would blind them. That's how in love I was.

"And for you, comrade, a nice army-green suit," Angelo suggested, at which Tonino sneered.

Gabriele said, "For all I know, our beloved parents would probably turn up in black."

"Gabrie'," Pietro warned him under his breath. "Go make yourself a coffee."

"C'mon, let's be honest, weddings are such pains in the ass," said Davide. "Listening to cheesy music and pigging out all day long—"

A loud popping stopped Davide from finishing his sentence; the rest of us stopped breathing. For a moment, the only thing moving in the air was the smoke of several cigarettes and joints uncoiling like charmed cobras toward the sky. Then there was another pop, followed by a scream.

"It's a shooting!" Angelo yelled.

We sprang into action at the call of the Sicilian, who had to know a thing or two, shoving aside our chairs in a mad dash for the roof's edge. Far below, the streets encircled our building like a moat. Jaundiced in the streetlights, they appeared empty and even uneventful, for once. Yet we could hear a swarm of motorbikes, the roar of their urgent departure, their skidding tires fading into the distance—surely a getaway. Maybe it had been a hit on a Camorra boss, or a kneecapping done to someone who'd overstepped his boundaries. Like the news journalists, we'd probably never find out. But, whatever the truth was, there was an undeniable thrill in being so very close to violence yet so safely removed from it at the same time.

"Let them kill each other," said Tonino. "It's the best form of natural selection."

It seemed the drama was done and gone. For a while the boys stayed leaning over the wall chatting, with Carlo beside Pietro, who was pointing at something across the gulf. I turned back to the table to sit beside Sonia, who was watching them with a somewhat forlorn look.

I said, "Well, Carlo is quite a catch. He's friendly, outgoing."

"Yeah," she replied with a sigh, "he's really something."

It was strange, but at that angle I wasn't so sure that Sonia was looking at Carlo and not at the lean silhouette that Pietro cut against the glow of the city. But it was a thought destined to remain formless, for in that very moment the divine lights of police helicopters came sweeping over us and the surrounding rooftops, but somewhat randomly and half-heartedly, as if they, too, knew there was going to be nothing to see.

I was increasingly fascinated and perturbed by Madeleine, who, not unlike my adoptive city, eluded my every attempt to pin her down, to put her in a box. She didn't spend much time at home, but sometimes walking in through the door she would join the rest of us, laughing and smoking merrily, while other times she would slam the door behind her and go straight to her room without so much as a hello. She was always willing to discuss architecture or politics with Gabriele, and in fact she could get quite fired up, whereas with me she would only engage in meaningless chitchat, looking at me all the while with an expression that was either curious, hostile, or maternal. With the summer finally here, Madeleine seemed to overheat easily, dressing more and more provocatively: however, some mornings, complaining of an imaginary cold spell, she'd put on a man's oversize sweater and furiously ruffle her hair that was already disheveled from sleep, as if attempting to scribble all over her own image and make herself ugly. But she never managed to: no one in the world would have been able to resist Madeleine's beauty and allure. Soon I learned to prepare for her mood swings according to the presence or absence of her boyfriend's crash helmet. If Saverio's helmet was sitting on the couch in the morning, that meant he'd slept over. If it was missing, that meant they'd had a fight and Madeleine would be sure to wake up in a foul mood.

One morning when the helmet wasn't there, I found Madeleine alert, her cigarette a straw to suck life through, her legs crossed skin on skin, a Japanese flip-flop kicking the void under the table. "Well, well, what do we have here?" she said in a voice that was at once mocking and seductive. "Miss America with her long hair so good-looking even in the morning. Or should we call you Miss Napoli?"

That day she seemed consumed by a discontent that went beyond Saverio's absence. I offered to make her a coffee. She accepted, becoming suddenly generous. She promised me that one day in return she would make me French liver and onions.

"I look forward to it." There was something about Madeleine that made you want to lie to her, even lie *for* her.

I busied myself in the kitchen, but by the time I came back to the table with the steaming coffee, the tic of her flip-flop had stopped and Madeleine was covering her eyes with one hand, as though struck by a migraine.

"Are you not feeling well?"

"I'm fine. Really fine," she said, but her voice had shattered into a thousand pieces.

I stepped toward her the way one might approach an injured animal. Instinctively she lifted her hand to wave me away, and as she did so I could see that her eyes were bloodshot with the effort not to cry. That wild look on the brink of tears terrified me. I feared that behind it lay something deeply disturbing and unstoppable, a chaos I couldn't handle. I tried to distract her, with coffee, with idle chatter. It worked.

I wanted to understand Madeleine, perhaps even help her, but honestly I didn't have the time. I needed to study. The summer session had just started and the first exam I had scheduled was in semiotics. Semiotics, the science of how we make meaning, was my favorite class; I'd even made it my minor. There was only a handful of us devoted to the subject, and in fact on the day of my final exam there were only two of us: me and my professor.

It was obvious at first sight that Professor Benedetti was a genius—not from his politically inspired uniform of blue sneakers, blue jeans, and blue sweatshirt, but from his eyes, of the kind found only in comic books, two huge and possibly mad orbs that bulged dangerously and were held at bay only by thick lenses reinforced with black frames. Not only that, but he would often go off on a tangent, in a staccato Milanese accent, saying things like, "And it is in the number three that we find the magical power of human cognition, the audacity to put forward ideas that revolutionize our way of seeing the world!" This is more or less what he said during my exam, an instant before slapping the desk with rapture, making the pens jump and bursting into resounding laughter that made his two front teeth stick out.

It was my exam and I was meant to be the one speaking. I *wanted* to speak. I wanted to clear out my head, voice my tangled ideas regarding the nature of man, and speak in such a way that there was no longer disparity between my thoughts and my words. I wanted to feel brilliant, a genius like Benedetti or Signorelli, to possess their unshakable faith in academic knowledge. But I just couldn't. These were not questions to answer but a flood of words in which I struggled to stay afloat.

It was only when Benedetti came out with the term "thirdness" that I managed to get a word in edgewise. Although it was clear that it took a concerted effort on my professor's part to not interrupt me, he didn't. From thirdness, I shifted easily into the concepts of secondness and firstness, adding that I'd read somewhere that philosopher Charles Sanders Peirce had extended his idea of the triad to the first, second, and third personal pronouns: I, thou, and it.

"Are we still drawn to proper linguistics, *signorina*?" he said with malicious pleasure, his eyes protruding.

"Well, pronouns are simply fascinating. There's no power game quite like dialogue."

Benedetti dove into another convoluted speech, cutting it short only when he caught a glimpse of the clock—he commuted from Milan and no doubt had a train to catch. He simply asked me if I'd thought about what subject I wanted to do my thesis in. "I'd imagine you have an inclination toward the field of semiotics. Why don't you think about it over the summer and get back to me?" I stood to take my professor's outstretched hand, and he pumped mine with indelicate vigor. Only then did he remember my blue exam booklet, signing it with a mad flourish. "Ah, so many formalities! But one must still follow procedure even while preparing the revolution!"

No, I wasn't a genius, but I had just received a full score. I walked in a happy daze back home, where I found the icing on the cake: a letter from America. Barbara was suggesting we meet at the end of the summer in the Cyclades, but before booking their flights she and my dad wanted to know what dates best suited me—actually, best suited the two of us.

14

S TRAIGHT AFTER my semiotics exam, I began preparing for my history of the theater exam. One thing was becoming increasingly clear: the importance of getting a degree. I realized that a degree wasn't the castle in the sky I'd always imagined it to be but, as Luca had so unexpectedly described it that time in the study hall, a very real parchment of great value to society. Once again Luca had proven himself right. That degree was the key to all our dreams. And I was becoming aware of just how sound and gratifying the steps required to achieve it might be— collecting signatures in my exam booklet, choosing a professor and a topic for my thesis, writing it, presenting it—basically, the *procedure* that Benedetti had referred to.

So then why was it that the city seemed to thwart my efforts to follow procedure? The more peace and quiet I needed, the more fits my neighborhood threw, and these weren't limited to the lewd daily arguments in the courtyard, which appeared to have something to do with water. For the residents of the Spanish Quarter, shouting *was* speaking. The auditory intimacy was constant. Even in that little death of the siesta, you could hear forks pecking at plates and soap opera actors divulging to all the neighbors the awful truth about a will, a gun, an identical twin— melodramatic laments that could hardly be distinguished from the real ones coming from Madeleine's room, whenever she locked herself in there to cry.

The garbage collectors went on strike yet again. The piled-up bags were promptly disemboweled and our neighbors' deepest secrets dragged across the cobblestones. Sanitary pads, chicken bones, overdue bills. The alleyways of the Quartieri were clogged with trash and the streets of the city center with cars. The traffic lights were often out of order, but even when they were working, people would drive through red lights all the same. It was as if Naples were spitting on my semiological studies, as if it had grasped well before Peirce and de Saussure, perhaps way back in ancient times, that the rules of the game were essentially arbitrary and therefore entirely unworthy of respect.

In stark contrast to all that chaos was the quiet, dignified homeless man on Via Roma. Once when I came by to bring him breakfast, I didn't see him but a crowd gathered around. Squeezing through, I could see what the attraction was. Two puppies, probably only days old, were wriggling on the soiled blanket spread out on the ground. I hadn't even realized his mutt was a female, let alone pregnant.

A little girl grabbed one of the puppies, who squirmed in her arms, showing its swollen, hairless belly. "This one got a name?"

"This one boy," replied the man. "This one girl."

His face had gone scrunched like paper from all the smiling. People were handing him money, and plenty of it, which he simply clutched between his grimy fingers as though not sure what to do with it. I crouched to stroke the other pup, picking up its sweet-and-sour smell of milk and urine. I gave the proud owner my last few coins before leaving him to his adoring crowd.

We had just turned off the lights one night in bed when I asked Pietro if he wanted to adopt a dog. Perhaps more than a dog, I longed for another being on which to unload some of the emotion overflowing from the two of us, to distribute it more equally and thus make bearable a love that at times seemed unbearable in its intensity.

"I already have a dog," answered Pietro. "In Monte San Rocco." Apparently, Gesualdo slept in the tractor shed and was often gone, sometimes for days at a time: that's why I'd missed him. "But I'd like a real dog," he confessed. "One we can let sleep on the bed, take for walks in the forest. Or in the rain forest in Costa Rica."

"Or on a beach in Thailand." I let out a resigned sigh. "I know, I know. It would be too hard to have a dog in Naples."

"Not hard, baby. Impossible. Everything about Naples is impossible."

We were running the risk of slipping into that same old discussion about the lawlessness of the city, with the same old adjectives. And yet that night, as the neighbors yelled themselves hoarse even in the dark, I couldn't muster the will to side with Naples, to jump to its defense and save it yet again. Let them sling mud at it, I thought for an instant.

"Anyway, I have to go back to Monte San Rocco soon. For almost a month this time."

"For the olives, for the harvest?" I questioned him anxiously. "You harvest crops in the summer, right?"

But that wasn't it, not exactly. He explained to me that, in order to pass his hydrogeology exam, he had to carry out surveys of the underground water sources—and the best place to do it was his hometown because he could get easy access to the locals' land. "I know practically every man, woman, and donkey in the place. And I'm distantly related to half of them. Not the donkeys, though."

I was heartbroken but I tried to laugh—and to be reasonable. Summer took away all my friends. Tonino had already left, without attempting a single exam. Usually I would leave too, for DC, to work in a coffee shop or restaurant and save up for my ticket back to Naples. An open ticket, a ticket of unknown return. But this time my dad and Barbara had already booked their flights to Athens for the end of July: all Pietro and I had to do was book our own passage. I had no doubt that we'd find room on the ferry as soon as Pietro raised the subject with his parents.

My apprehension, however, only eased when Pietro slid farther under the covers to tell me in a gravelly voice, "It's only a month separating us . . . and it's only a few little hills. But for you I would cross mountains, on foot if I had to. I'd cross them barefoot in the snow; I'd eat jackrabbits and crows to survive."

"Don't stop," I whispered.

"I'd cross oceans for you, even clinging to a raft. I'd use my T-shirt as a sail; I'd eat mussels and other shit like that." We started laughing. "Seriously . . . I'd happily do it, even if it took me five years, as long as I knew you'd be waiting for me on the other side."

Before he left, we were able to fit in an excursion, starting from Mamma Rita's house. She treated Pietro just as I'd expected, like another stray to feed. She didn't give us the usual parental advice—her own turbulent love life offered a roller coaster of emotions but no pearls of wisdom— yet I could tell that it gave her peace of mind to see me finally settled with a nice young man. Besides, Rita had already advised me so wisely in most other areas of life. She'd taught me as a teenager how to iron a man's shirt, how to clean a boiled octopus, how to fake the samba in a Sorrento piano bar. She was used to my disappearing acts, tolerating them philo-sophically like my mom did, so she didn't appear disappointed that we stayed only one night, continuing farther down the Sorrento peninsula the next morning.

I took Pietro to a beach I'd been introduced to, way back when by the Castellammare gang, a gem known by the locals as la Regina Giovanna. Sonia and Carlo met us at the local train station in Sorrento. From there we walked a long distance before passing through an olive grove, which later in the season would turn into an unsightly parking lot. But for now our only companions were the birds. Now and then out of the corner of my eye I would look over at Naples. A brown layer of smog rose off it, as though seeing us in such a faraway and idyllic spot made it choke with envy. This gave me an unanticipated twinge of remorse.

"Once I ate an olive straight off a tree," I said. "It was so bitter I had to spit it out."

"I bet you did," said Pietro, giving my ponytail a tug.

A dirt path began our descent toward the beach. The shade ended, the air became laced with salt. We walked in single file under the high sun until we came to the ruins of the Roman villa the beach was named after.

"There's hardly anything left of it," said Carlo. "It looks like just a pile of rocks. I have my doubts about the whole Roman claim . . ."

"Well, if you don't know, Carlo," said Pietro, "and you're supposed to be the engineer."

Pietro enjoyed taking little stabs at Carlo. He took offense at his upper-crust, know-it-all attitude. He would say, "All that guy's missing is the French *r*." And even I had to admit that when Carlo teased Sonia about her origins, as he was doing now by saying that Sardinia's entire cultural patrimony was a few megalithic mounds of boulders, it wasn't done with the same light touch as Angelo's.

"*Nuraghi* and sheep. Is that all you have?"

Sonia's reaction was to hit him with her rolled-up towel. "Watch out, mister, or I won't be taking you there this summer."

"Actually, the ferry will be taking me there, not you."

"Very funny!"

She hit him again and they both ran ahead of us, laughing. Pietro and I looked at each other in shock. Obviously I wasn't the only one putting myself through the rite of "going to the village." However, it seemed that for Sonia and Carlo it was no big deal. I didn't know whether to envy their flippant attitude because I would have liked to have it myself, or frown upon it because it made light of my difficult experience or suggested that their relationship came close to ours in intensity or commitment. Either way, I became suddenly afraid of how we might stack up against them.

Soon we were at the beach, a layered cake of dark rock tipping into the sea. Avoiding the cracks, we chose a smooth spot and changed into our bathing suits under our clothes. The stone, having gorged on sun all morning, quickly warmed up our flattened towels. Carlo was dressed first and dove into the sea with a showy splash. Resurfacing, he howled. The water was freezing, he warned us, shaking the hair off his forehead with a flick of the head. Sonia, on the other hand, sat down on the edge of the rock gingerly dipping her feet in.

"Should we go in too?"

"Let me have a smoke first," Pietro answered. "You know, warm up a bit."

There was something about the solemn way Pietro lit up, cradling his pale knees and staring skeptically at the sea, that made me think I'd made a mistake to drag him there. What *was* the point of making this trek? But he immediately settled my fears, stroking my tanned feet (he called me his Cherokee princess) and telling me it was a beautiful spot. Then he turned back to the water, squinting into the sun.

"Look at the two of them playing," he said.

Sonia was in the water now, squealing joyfully as she swam away from Carlo the great white, who was splashing and frothing the water all around them.

"They look happy."

"I'm telling you, Heddi, it's not going to last."

"How can you tell if a relationship is going to last?"

"You and me, baby. That's the standard I go by."

In the end he'd been the one to make the comparison, and they hadn't stood a chance. I pulled out my Minolta and focused in on the salt crystals, remnants of a stormier season, threading through the black grooves all the way down to the sea. I took a picture of Pietro in profile with a cigarette pressed between his lips, the Marlboro man in the flesh. It was a face I could never really get used to. As I looked at him, though, a doubt began to nag me. Wasn't that tone of voice, which I'd thought sounded so

142

reassuring—*it won't last*—actually one of paternal sternness? He'd used an authoritative and contemptuous tone that was ill-suited to him and that now, combined with that somber smoker's expression, all at once unsettled me.

Sonia came back toward us, breathless. "It's so cold, but it's lovely and clean."

Her long braids dripping with seawater, she lay down on her towel, followed shortly by Carlo, who flopped himself down beside her. I called them by name. The moment they spun around, I snapped their picture, their faces glowing with the pleasurable shock of being captured. Lying again on her back, Sonia gladly subjected herself to Carlo's tickles, though he did go a bit overboard. Surely Pietro was wrong about them.

"What are you guys waiting for?" said Carlo. "Scared of the cold? If it's not cold, it's not the first swim of the summer."

"And probably my last, with my luck," Pietro muttered as he put out his cigarette on the rock. Ashes to ashes, dust to dust.

I looked at him, puzzled. What did he mean by his *last swim?*

"Well, there are no beaches in Monte San Rocco," he said and, as if to make amends, he kissed me almost passionately, in a place that was almost public, behind the back of a couple that was almost—but nothing—like us.

"What, you're not going to go to the beach later on, in Greece?" I asked him.

"I sure am. In my mind, it's a done deal." His parents' consent, he believed, was a given.

I jumped to my feet from joy. Greece would most certainly justify our three long weeks apart; Greece would remedy everything. The black slab burned my feet as I dragged Pietro toward the sea.

"The water's fantastic . . . if you don't have a heart condition!" shouted Carlo behind us.

I did have a heart condition, I thought to myself, but if there was a cure I didn't want it. Just as Sonia had, I sat on the rock to test my feet,

143

white and foreign in the icy water, so cold in fact it took all my courage to jump in.

"Can you touch the bottom?" Pietro called out to me from the edge.

I was so breathless from the thermal shock that I could only shake my head in response.

"Looks like the Arctic Sea. No, thanks, I'll stay right here."

I dived under the water and came up near him. "It feels warmer now."

"Don't insist, please. I'm not coming in." He didn't say anything more until I clambered up the rocks and, back on my towel, the molten lava of my blood spread all through my veins. "Listen, baby," he said in a whisper that could barely be heard over the gently lapping waves. "I've lived my whole life landlocked. I was born in the mountains. I grew up in the hills. A couple of times me and Gabriele splashed around in a creek when we were little. That's all."

"Very picturesque."

"You don't get it." His voice was so faint against the sucking sound of the retreating sea that I almost had to lip-read when he finally said, "I can't swim, Heddi. If I jump in there, I'll sink to the bottom. Like a rock."

After Pietro left, I had a dream. I dreamed that I was standing on the very top of the island of Ischia, a peak as pointy as the ones in cartoons and just as risk-free. The view of the Gulf of Naples wrapped itself around me, a silk scarf textured in sunlight and ruffled by the wind. There were boats off shore and, farther in the distance, the islands of Capri and Procida.

I lifted my camera to trap all that beauty into a square. It was through the viewfinder that I saw the volcano. How had I not seen it before? Maybe I'd forgotten it was there. I lowered my camera to see the sky boiling with clouds. No, not clouds. Vesuvius was spewing out billows of charcoal that were rubbing out the sky, in the rough way that an eraser smudged in lead smears, rips, and ruins a masterpiece.

I realized the spot I was in was far too exposed. I had to get down, but my feet wouldn't move. I could do nothing but rationalize my inertia: I told myself that I was in a safe place, on the other side of the bay, with a camera shielding me from reality. But deep down I knew that staying up there, frozen in awe, was the worst thing I could do, and that watching that destruction was neither safe nor smart nor logical but driven only by a lack of willpower. Because that act of the volcano, cruel but also undeniably fascinating, was a spectacle my eyes wanted so badly to watch, and I just couldn't say no.

From: heddi@yahoo.com
To: tectonic@tin.it
Sent: April 12

Dear Pietro,

*I haven't thrown your words in the trash. Actually, I've reread them again
and again: they move me, confuse me, intrigue me. Now, if you feel like it,
I'll tell you a story too . . .*

*Do you really want to know why I came to New Zealand? It was because
of you, because of that phone call. The reception was poor and your voice
sounded metallic, almost robotic, as you said those unthinkable, unbearable
words. It was like something out of a nightmare. I don't remember how I
answered. Did I plead with you? No, I don't want to know.*

*Afterward I thought I was dying. I wanted to die: not to take my life but just
disappear so that I no longer had a body capable of such physical suffering.
The pain in my stomach was excruciating; I got my period for the second
time in the same month and two cold sores around my mouth. My tears were
so hot they burned, and they never ran dry. In fact, they carved grooves
to create a free flow for all the tears I'd saved up over those many years of
happiness in my life.*

*My dad thought I was going to starve to death, so one afternoon he knocked
on the door holding one of those fruit shakes he used to make me when I
was little: "tiger milk" he called it. I took a sip only because I was afraid to
disappoint him. I hadn't wanted to tell you till now, but my dad no longer
even wants to hear your name mentioned.*

*I was ashamed of the state I was in, and the compassion of my family and
old friends only made things worse. So I did what I've always been so good
at: I packed my bags. I made a list of three countries I could escape to—far
from you, but also far from me. The first two were Korea and Japan, places
where I knew I could find a job as a native English speaker. Number three*

was New Zealand. (Maybe I didn't tell you that Snežana's brother, Ivan, had moved to Auckland some time back.) This time I didn't need Snežana's advice to cross off my first two choices and go with the least sensible of them all.

Other than Ivan, I didn't know anyone here. All the better, because that way I didn't have to talk about myself or about what was ultimately, in this great wide world, just a minor personal tragedy. Plus, every word required great effort: I'd used up my last strength just to make the never-ending flight, get to Ivan's house, and put my meager suitcase in a corner. From then on I just let things happen to me, without putting up the least resistance. That's how I found myself being shipped off, only two days later, on a trip around the North Island with three perfect strangers (just one of them was a friend of Ivan's), who had planned a road trip complete with bungee jumping, white-water rafting, and rock climbing, the real kind with ropes and carabiners.

Among them, I felt like a complete klutz, but these three weren't just extreme sport enthusiasts but instructors, so they were used to people not knowing what to do and lacking confidence. They made me do all their insane activities and they taught me, of all things, wilderness survival skills. How to dry your wet clothes in the bottom of your sleeping bag. How to cook, in a single tin cup over a little gas stove, a complete and nutritious meal. I discovered that hiking makes you hungry, ravenously hungry, and that the body wants to live even if the soul doesn't. It was the beginning of a passion for camping and the wilderness that I've since been able to share with my parents and brother when they've come to visit me (twice now, the second time with my brother's girlfriend, a girl from Trieste). It was also the moment in which I began rediscovering some of life's small pleasures (or rather, small satisfactions). I'll always be grateful to those three crackpots.

I don't know why I'm going on like this at this hour of the night. I guess maybe I'm just talking to you like I used to. But I realize you're on the other side of the world and I'm even in a different hemisphere, a different season.

Is it night there as you read these lines? Is Gabriele there with you? I'd love to hear from him again. I've lost touch with almost everyone. The only one I've been in contact with over the years is Luca, right after his mother died. I could write to him now, just to say hi. I'm not sure why I haven't.

h.

15

THAT MORNING when the bus pulled into Borgo Alto with an exhalation of relief, Pietro was already waiting for me with his hands shoved into his pockets, trying to bury a smile. Neither of us could speak, and all we could do as we made our way to the car was clutch each other's hands, making a single tight fist to contain the surge of emotion. I couldn't keep my eyes off him as he carried my bag over his shoulder, but when I finally managed to look away, I could feel him stealing glances at me, his eyes boring into me.

"Hop in, baby. Today I'm going to take you to see everything."

I remembered that car, whose door he was now opening for me, the white car he'd swapped with the tractor the day of the Great Flood. As soon as he started it up, I reached out to stroke the back of his neck: it was on the verge of sweating. We followed the creases of the land until they flattened into a highway.

"I don't remember going this way."

"No, you wouldn't," was all he said.

There was a factory up ahead. We took the exit and turned off into a parking lot in the shadow of three or four chimney stacks. He turned off the engine. There wasn't a soul, only weeds breaking through the concrete. Pietro told me that at one time the factory had produced steel;

it used to provide a lot of jobs but it had been abandoned some time ago now.

We got out and followed a path lined with dry grass that prickled my ankles. When we reached a thicket, Pietro stopped and held my face like a cup to drink from. He kissed me gently, with the confident patience of a classic first kiss that was so unlike our own. How sweet it was to finally be alone with him. In the lacy shade, the smell of fir trees blended with his aftershave, the lattice of branches with his dark curls.

"You're the air I breathe," he whispered, "the water I drink."

He led me by the hand to a clearing. The cicadas were wound up by the heat; every now and then a bird let out a frantic little cry. I hadn't left the narrow streets of Naples in weeks so I didn't mind that this strip of parched land that passed itself off as wilderness bordered a derelict factory.

"Watch out for the vipers." I came to a sudden stop and spun around, to Pietro's great amusement. "Don't worry, I'll protect you. I know every boulder and tussock in this area." It was here, he explained, that he'd been coming to carry out his surveys. He would dig, observe, measure, and then sit down with a cigarette to sketch the data onto a map. "That tree over there gives particularly good shade. Come on."

Under the "good tree" I soon forgot about the snakes and let myself be carried away by Pietro's enthusiasm. As he talked about the fractured aquifers of the Apennines, I studied his tanned face, sparkling eyes, and hair lightened by the sun just like in the childhood picture he'd given me. Seeing him in such good form was electrifying. I said, "Thank goodness your assignment hasn't been a pain after all."

"Well, maybe it has a little, but what I like is getting out in the countryside—on my own, away from our land, from my parents. Out here I feel like Tarzan." He pounded his chest. "Actually, I'm thinking of doing my thesis in hydrogeology."

"But you're passionate about oil. Or have you changed your mind?"

"No way. I can still get into the oil industry later. Who's to say I won't be the next JR?" he said, laughing soundlessly. "But, unlike you linguists, to do our thesis we have to get out in the field, get our hands dirty. If I did a thesis in petroleum geology, it could take me anywhere. But if I do it in hydrogeology, I could easily do all the surveys in and around Monte San Rocco."

With a pebble I began scratching the baked earth. How was it possible for a thesis in hydrogeology to lead to a career in petroleum geology, for water to turn into oil? And how could a little town in the middle of Irpinia be the springboard for the great wide world awaiting us? I scratched and scratched, and still it seemed as illogical as a math riddle.

"I just don't know if I can stand being away from you any longer, Pietro. I'll lose my mind."

"And I won't?" He missed me, he said, from the instant his mother woke him up in the morning barking his name, till the night when he fell bone-tired onto the bed. A couple of times he'd found a strand of my hair stuck on his clothes and saved it between the pages of a book or in an empty cigarette packet. As he told me this, I could tell the confession cost him some dignity. "That's why I want to get my thesis over with as quickly as possible. Then all I'll have left to figure out is what the hell to do about the military service."

That statement was a slap that pushed me backward onto the brittle grass. More than ever, the military seemed criminal, an invention devised solely for human suffering. If a couple weeks of separation had been this painful, then what was a year meant to feel like? There had to be a way out. There just had to.

We discussed it at length; Pietro went through three straight cigarettes. We left no stone unturned, taking into consideration any solution. Applying for a passport and fleeing abroad before they drafted him. Pretending to be gay and therefore exempt. Faking a sickness, perhaps a mental illness. And, for a while, manic depression did seem like the answer to all our problems. But it didn't take us long to realize that all our ideas would have serious consequences for future job opportunities, even legal consequences. We were both incurably law-abiding and grimly in the best of health, physically and psychologically.

"Or I could do the civilian service."

"But what's the point of that?" I objected. "You'd only be doing more time."

"OK, but," Pietro said, not in the least discouraged, "you could come visit me more easily than in the barracks. I could request to be stationed nearby, maybe in the province of Naples. That way it would only take a short drive or a train ride to see each other every weekend." Without faltering, he'd come out with a plan that couldn't be argued with, and in such detail that I could see it wasn't the first time he'd entertained the idea. Perhaps it was that secretive scheming that wounded me more than the suggestion itself. He said with the same peppy resolve that in the meantime we could start getting organized properly: résumés, flights, job research, and so on. "Then, I swear, the very day I'm discharged, it's *sayonara, goodbye, fancul'!*"

Again I took up my useless calculations in the dust. I was drained, my mouth was dry; I could practically taste the aridness of that vast land, which reduced us to two tiny dots in a clearing. Tucking my hair behind my ears, Pietro began kissing me and murmuring "baby, baby," before singing the chorus from "Wild Horses," with a touch of embarrassment.

I let out a sigh. He understood those lyrics perfectly well—and he was right. Nothing could keep us apart: not wild horses, not even time itself. What was a year and a half for us? Nothing. I felt his hand under my dress, a vine tightening around my bare thigh and climbing its way up. I said, "What are you waiting for?"

"What, here?"

"No one's around."

"We can't . . . the vipers." He pulled me up. "Come with me."

We went back to the car, parked on the border between a wasteland and so-called civilization. We made love in the front passenger's seat, the breathing and the creaking masked by the hum of the highway. We were a little afraid. Afraid of being seen, perhaps by a poor unemployed soul who'd decided to go for a tearful walk around his former workplace. Afraid of making a mess of his parents' car, of breaking something. But we didn't stop our lovemaking as we gripped each other in that tight space full of hard edges. In fact, our fears only increased our pleasure, for, though we were already adults, we were experiencing a moment of teenage desperation that soon we wouldn't have to have—or get to have—ever again.

Pietro drove up and down hills that might have looked familiar had their greens not been repainted in duller, earthier tones, fields plagued by the sun and yanked this way and that way by the wind. Pietro was a man on a mission. He pulled up casually beside a fig tree, perhaps another good tree of his, and had me sit in its fat shade. From there we had a good view of the surrounding countryside.

Pietro was organized. He'd slipped two sandwiches into his backpack, evidently knowing all along that we weren't going to make it to his parents' by lunchtime. He handed me one before uncorking a bottle of his family's wine. Pietro always said that real wine was red (and that it kept the doctor away), but in this heat even he admitted that white was the only thing to drink. Indeed, it was light and, paired with the spicy salami and tough bread, it tasted like rotten fruit and wood.

"This land," he said, "belongs to my family."

I scanned the fields (wheat, I presumed), unsure how far to zoom out. And that wasn't all, he said. There was another piece of land a half an hour's drive from there, and then of course the land in Puglia, plus an olive grove, a vineyard, a pasture near the house . . . So it was true, I realized, that his family had hoarded random bits of land, but then why did he feel the need to list them all to me? I thought I understood why only when Pietro told me that one was in his name.

"Geologist, cook, and now landowner," I joked, but he remained serious.

When he finished his degree, he explained, the fields before us too would be his. Eventually all the family land would go to him.

"What, doesn't Gabriele count?"

"Don't you worry, Gabriele will get a big pile of cash, when and if he decides to graduate. But he doesn't want anything to do with the land." As for Vittorio, he'd given up every claim years ago when he made his escape.

We both sat there looking out over the wheat, gnawing at the bread that may even have come from it. I began to ponder this puzzling new concept, inheritance, struggling to see the equity in how it would be shared out among the three sons. One would get a lump sum, another nothing, and the last *a place*.

"But what are you going to do with all this land?"

"Well, if I kept the farm running, it would be quite profitable. But obviously that's not going to happen. There's no chance in hell." He took a swig, then a bite. "Do you know how much this land is worth altogether? Hundreds of millions of lire, maybe a billion."

"So . . . I don't get it, your parents are well off?"

"On paper they are. But in their heads they're as poor as the day they came into this world. They're still living the life of hardship they led fifty years ago. They grow their own vegetables, make their own pasta. Nothing's wasted. When their clothes get old, heaven forbid they throw them away: no, they patch them up and keep on wearing them until they're hanging off them like rags." Though he'd said all this with contempt, he now turned to me with a mischievous smile. "No, you know what I'm going to do with the land?"

"No, what?"

"Sell it."

I gazed at the squares of crops swelling and deflating in the wind, as endless and restless as a patchwork blanket tossed over a sleeping giant. "And what are your parents going to say?"

"What can they say?" According to Pietro, the land was never meant for them but for their children, to give them a better life. The world was a different place; these days there were many more ways to earn a living other than working the land. "What do they think Gabriele and I are getting an education for anyway?"

"For the heck of it," I said dryly, handing him the rest of my sandwich. It was too hot to eat much.

"It's peasant food, I know . . . One day I'll be able to take you out to dinner as often as you like. I'll order you Montepulciano wine, ostrich steaks, caviar—whatever the hell that is anyway. You won't want for anything."

"Don't give me ostrich and caviar. Just give me you."

Money had never made an impression on me. Growing up I'd proudly worn my brother's hand-me-downs and gladly ridden in that rusty car of ours with the broken heater. Although we'd traveled to Jamaica and Mexico, it was always on a shoestring, sleeping not in hotel beds but on mattresses thrown on the floor in locals' homes. And yet, upon discovering that my lover—a boy from the provinces who owned only five shirts and a prospecting pick—was, as it turns out, a rich man, a great burden was lifted off me, one that I wasn't even aware I'd been carrying since I was a child. The burden of precariousness: the many new rental homes and new schools, the many failed businesses and failed marriages. Pietro and I, on the other hand, wouldn't have to pay the price for all that freedom. We could have our cake and eat it too. Yes, I had to admit to myself, not without shame, that I was happy that money had come into play. Incredibly happy.

"Well then, you can afford a trip to Greece," I said with a smile that held nothing back.

Pietro smiled, too, a wide smile showing all his teeth. "My father has already agreed: we'll have your parents as chaperones, after all. So it's just a matter of time before my mother gives in."

I was on cloud nine. I had the sensation of being so unencumbered, in fact, that I could glide across those fields roasting in the sun to the spot Pietro was pointing to in the distance, a little white building with a tile roof. That, he said, was the church his grandfather had built, along with the rest of the community, using stones from the river below that they hauled up the hill with wheelbarrows. And their bare hands.

"I'll take you there now," he said, standing up.

All afternoon we doodled the hills with that little car, taking the most roundabout route possible toward Monte San Rocco. Now and again I asked him to pull over so I could shoot close-ups of the stalks of wheat lit like flaming torches by the low sun. Pietro drove me to the town where, as a teenager, he'd hung out with the wrong crowd. He showed me the field where years before Gabriele had thrown a snowball at him. The snow had begun to melt in the center of that well-compressed sphere so that by the time the ball hit him it had become a chunk of ice—but as Pietro's blood stained the snow like red wine christens a Sunday table-cloth, it was Gabriele who cried. Pietro pointed to a village teetering on a hilltop, a place thought to bring such misfortune that it couldn't even be named. Just hearing the name would set off among the locals a super-stitious sequence of ball-scratching and horn gestures. Once in the town, he told me, your footsteps echoed in the deserted streets, an unexpected pitter-patter that brought silent, ancient women to their doorways like the way rain brings out the worms.

But then finally Pietro took his hand off the steering wheel to wave to an old man, and I recognized the spot: the road leading up to the center of Monte San Rocco. A defiant lump rose up in my throat. I wasn't at all ready to face his mother; I hadn't even thought about what I was going to say or do. The only thing I'd done to prepare for the encounter had been getting her a gift: a silk shawl, in subtle creams fading into brown, as delicate as a moth's wing, which I'd bought on impulse in a street market in Naples. Pietro had suggested giving it to her nonchalantly, so as not to embarrass her. But now it seemed so absurd to give his mother something I knew she would never wear.

Pietro, so good at reading my mind, placed a reassuring hand on my thigh. "Don't worry, we're not going home yet. I want to take you to the town café. Are you up for it?"

I nodded vigorously.

"To be honest," he said, parking the car, "I can't wait to walk in there with you looking so tan and gorgeous in that dress, and show them once and for all what losers they are. I hope they die of envy."

Pietro nodded at the pudgy man at the entrance to the café, a secret code that slipped us into its cavelike interior. I felt the man's sweaty gaze trail over me with approval as Pietro ordered us coffees in dialect, gripping hands with the barista. All around, men were scrummed over tables, smoking, drinking, playing *scopa*. Other than the Virgin Mary, I was the only female. As we drank our coffee, black eyes pierced the veil of smoke to grope me, making no effort to turn away, no attempt to behave, no comment. Those men not only wanted me, they wanted to be Pietro. More tangibly than ever I grasped the abyss there was between him and his fellow villagers. Philosophically, emotionally, mentally—in every way, Pietro didn't belong. He wasn't even born there.

It was obvious from Pietro's expression that we'd achieved the desired result, and I shared in his satisfaction. Setting his cup down on the bar, he turned to me to say, "It's getting late. We should get going."

"Already?" The place was a wolf lair but still my heart sank.

"Otherwise my mother will think we've gone to Las Vegas to elope."

Elope? His parents still didn't even know we were living together.

16

As we pulled up to Pietro's house, I tried to hold on to the lightness of being our afternoon had given me. But it was like holding on to a new spiritual resolve once you've exited a church: it trickled out of me with every step I took toward the house, until at the front door there was nothing left.

"Gabriele," I almost sang out. He was standing there in the doorway like a copy and paste in the middle of nowhere, and I could have fallen into his arms with gratitude.

"Hey, Gabrie'," Pietro said, stepping inside, with a voice as flat as the TV in the background. "Where's Mamma?"

She materialized from the dark of the corridor, wiping her hands on her apron. I kissed her. *"Buonasera, signora."* Her first name was Lidia.

"Was your bus late?"

Fortunately Pietro answered for me. "Mamma, after picking her up I ran a few errands." I had to suppress a smile thinking of our errand in the passenger seat of her car. It was a memory I jealously guarded in the rawness under my dress.

When Pietro's father, Ernesto, called him outside, I fished into my bag for the shawl. Lidia took the gift listlessly, mumbling, "What, for your head?"

Gabriele rolled his eyes. She's just depressed, I tried to remind myself. Through the window I spotted Pietro maneuvering the tractor to park it in the shed. Overlapping the thunder of the machine was the growl of a dog, dressed in an old brown coat like a hermit. It had to be Gesualdo, the dog who wasn't a real dog.

Turning back around, I noticed that I'd been left on my own in the kitchen. I felt at a loss, no longer capable of relishing my solitude. I didn't know what to do with myself: wait for Pietro or join Gabriele, who had withdrawn into the darkest room of the house, his stark yet refined profile sketched by the light of the TV. He was right there, only a few steps away, but I didn't go to him.

However, at dinner that evening everything felt different, despite the television forever switched on. The sun was a candle that refused to burn out. It was almost warm. But the most remarkable difference was the presence of a conversation—a political debate no less, initiated by Gabriele.

"Whoever goes to live abroad soon realizes that the rest of the world sees us as such," he said in a big voice, his face flushed as he neglected his plate of fusilli. "We're all just doggone Italians. Those subtle cultural differences that we debate within the country mean nothing to everybody else, yet still we carry on about Padania, Sicily, Sardinia . . . Have we forgotten that Italy has been unified since 1871?"

"Gabrie', you're always going on about culture and history. But what does that have to do with anything here?" replied Pietro. "There's only one factor: money. It's a purely economic issue. In the north they don't want to cough up the cash if Rome is just going to pocket it. Period."

"Up there in Switzerland I once met this Friulian," interjected their father through a mouthful, adding something that sounded like, "I couldn't understand a darn thing."

"Papà, he probably didn't understand a word in your dialect either," said Gabriele in slow motion before turning back to Pietro. "I'm not much of a nationalist, as you are well aware. But how can we sit by and watch a harebrained secessionist like Bossi become no less than a senator claiming to be a spokesperson for the entire northern population?"

Their mother got up from the table. "Who wants more pasta?"

It was more of an accusation than an offer, but it was just the breach in the discussion I was looking for to say—given my exasperating tendency toward decorum—that the pasta was delicious. Gabriele waved his mother's ladle away with irritation, while Pietro and his father let her refill their plates without even looking up. Upon seeing mine, still full with the inhuman portion I'd been given, his mother knit her brow and sat back down with a flicker of impatience. How long was this initiation meant to last?

"But, etymologically speaking, Padania is a very recent term," Gabriele began again. "Invented, I dare say."

I watched as Lidia, with that hankie on her head, ate her own pasta joylessly, staring into her plate as though to block out all that carrying-on of the men. Of the youth. I stole a glance at her as she wiped her lips with the shriveled skin on the back of her hand. There was something in that gesture that triggered a wave of compassion in me. Were we really about to take away much of the land she'd grown old for?

I nudged my nearly intact glass of wine toward Pietro and he gave me a private wink for being his wine bank. I could tell he was starting to lose patience with his brother, who was displaying a moral indignance modeled on the high-brow parlance of Posillipo and intensified by the alcohol. In fact, Pietro's replies had dwindled to a series of snorts and terse phrases in a mixture of Italian and dialect, perhaps out of respect for their father, who, however, hadn't put forward any further comment and was now picking food out of his teeth with a finger.

And yet, how good it was to be in that house when Gabriele was around. Not only with him did the young outnumber the old, but Gabriele behaved just as he did with Madeleine and their other architect friends around our sloping table at Via De Deo. I loved how he got worked up over a political issue that had little to do with us, that he enunciated every word and became argumentative. I loved how he pulled opinions out of Pietro that I'd never heard and forced him to fervently take sides. Even with the curse words watered down out of politeness, Gabriele not only filled the silence of that country house, he spat at it. And every time I met his eyes, I thought I could see the glint of our secret, condensed like a tiny diamond under a pleasant sort of pressure, that all three of us lived together in Naples.

I felt even more confident when, after dinner, Pietro spared me the disgrace of yet another attempt to help in the kitchen with one of his irresistible propositions: "Would you like to come meet my cousin Francesco?"

Aunt Gina's sitting room, where we settled into a soft couch, resembled a trinket shop, with all its knickknacks and porcelain milkmaids, windmills and chickens, each to its own doily. His aunt placed a box of assorted butter cookies on the inlaid coffee table before us. In that frilly space, her son Francesco, standing beside the fireplace, looked like an intruder with his patchy facial hair that struggled to form a beard, his buttoned-down shirt, and the beginnings of a potbelly. He might have been a decade older than us: his eyes, framed by crow's-feet even when he wasn't smiling, lent him a permanent expression of mild amusement.

"Go on, they're good," Francesco said to me, adding without even looking her way, "Mamma, maybe she'd like a chocolate instead." I tried to object but his mother had already leaped up, her slippers flapping away into the kitchen. As soon as she was gone, he said, "Thank goodness, Eddie, that you made it out to Monte San Rocco. I'd had enough of this boy here pining for you. He was moaning like a whipped dog." He winked at Pietro, then changed tone. "But I know what it's like, the long-distance thing. I was once with a girl from Germany, a few years back. Karin."

"What happened?"

"Well, it didn't . . . I didn't—"

Aunt Gina came back into the room, apologizing for having run out of praline. The coffee table became so crowded with sweets that there was barely room left for the coffee tray. She asked me how much sugar I took.

"One sugar for her and a big splash of milk too. Otherwise it's too hard on her stomach," replied Pietro, letting it be known just how habitual our relationship was, and perhaps inviting his aunt to dig further.

I watched Francesco as he sipped his coffee with an elbow leaning on the mantelpiece. All his mannerisms and the tone of voice he used with his mother seemed to underline the fact that he was no intruder at all, but perhaps the true master of the house. It was he, in fact, and not Aunt Gina, who began asking me questions about Washington, DC. I didn't mind. I didn't mind anything about that environment: the whimsical porcelain creatures watching over me, the chocolate melting in my mouth, Pietro's leg pressing meaningfully against mine. His aunt leaned in to listen to every platitude I offered about the capital, every now and then widening her eyes with genuine amazement or nudging the box of chocolates toward me, yet without once telling me I was skinny and ought to put on weight. In the end, Aunt Gina congratulated Pietro on having found "such a pretty girl, and smart too," but that compliment, instead of flattering me, gave me the sneaking suspicion there was something in Lidia's behavior that was culturally inappropriate—and deeply wrong.

Francesco placed his empty coffee cup on the mantelpiece. "Come on outside, you two. I have something I want to show you."

By now darkness had submerged the town: crickets were scratching the cool air, stars were piercing the sky. Without a sidewalk, the street was one long wall: almost all new homes, probably replacements for those destroyed in the 1980 earthquake. Few old buildings remained standing but they drew attention to themselves with their abject plaster, darkened windows, and weeds sprouting from the gutters. Francesco led us to one of these, a kind of a storeroom at street level. He removed the lock and spread open the wooden doors like opening a stage curtain onto an unlit stage.

Pietro exclaimed, "Wow, you finally got it!"

"She's a beauty," said his cousin, stepping inside the garage. "Turbo engine, dark blue body, built-in CD stacker with removable face."

"When the hell were you going to tell me? You haven't even started your thesis yet, you lucky bastard."

The two men discussed horsepower and transmission, running their fingers over the station wagon like it was a time machine. Francesco unlocked it with a remote and lifted the rear door for us to admire its capaciousness. That simple gesture reawakened in me a long-lost memory of my brother and me lying across the many bags in our station wagon. What a great view from back there: the white asphalt of the highway stretching out behind us like the wake of a boat, the big fat cars tailing us, America finding it hard to let us go. Who knows where our mom was taking us that time; it may well have been the move from Boston to Washington because on our right the sun was setting over New York City, melting the sky like one of those orange Popsicles full of artificial colors and preservatives that we weren't allowed to eat. And I felt no resentment about not having made a stop there, no sorrow in saying goodbye, just the pleasure of moving on.

Back at Pietro's parents' house, I found out what had happened with Francesco's German girlfriend. Things went sour, he told me in a whisper, when Francesco had left her in Hamburg to take care of his ailing father, and for one reason or another—his mother's state of mind, exams for his law degree, his father's death—he never seemed to be able to return. But that wasn't all. Francesco had a dark secret that not a soul in the village, other than Pietro, knew: in Germany he now had a daughter. He went to visit her, without telling his mother or the extended family . . . but only occasionally, when work and circumstance permitted. I promised Pietro, crossing my heart and hoping to die, that I wouldn't say a word about it the day after next when Francesco picked me up to take me back to Borgo Alto.

On the morning of my departure, I packed my things with a swirl of melancholy and relief that refused to amalgamate into a feeling I could name. Pietro poked his head in, going straight to his childhood desk tattooed in blue ink, a little museum of rocks. He grabbed something before turning back to me. "Since we haven't had time yet to look for Roman coins . . . Here."

His palm blossomed, revealing a sculpture in dark metal. The head and arms were gone, leaving an inflated, athletic chest. A cloth curled around the torso and knotted at the waist before draping between the legs. Muscular, slightly parted and bent at the knees, they appeared frozen in the act of running, as in a race . . . or an escape. The figure was small enough to be a child's toy but too anatomically proportional, and far too heavy—probably lead. Perhaps it was a god or an effigy that once sat on a family altar, a reminder of a loved one who was no longer there.

"I can't, Pietro. It's too precious." But he'd already put it in my hand; I could feel its cold weight sink into my palm.

"It's just a bit of ancient litter. I found it lying in the pasture. Besides, what's mine is yours, right? Unless you change your mind."

"About what?"

"That you want to be with someone else."

"Seriously, Pietro? I'll keep this with me every moment we're apart. I promise."

As Pietro left the room, I placed the Roman sculpture on the bed. Before leaving I would slip it into my pocket: out of a long-standing and healthy fear of bag snatchers, I didn't trust my bag to safeguard the treasure all the way to the Spanish Quarter.

When Francesco arrived, with time to spare, Pietro leaped at the chance to examine the station wagon in the light of day. A spin would have to wait, though, since his cousin, who was already positioning my bag in the trunk, was scheduled to stay all day in Borgo Alto, where he worked on and off in a law firm. Now all that was left to do was to say my goodbyes. Their father wasn't around, but Gabriele was. Standing at the front door, coffee in hand, he shouted, "Mamma! Eddie's leaving."

Lidia appeared on the terrace. I went up to her, reached for her hands, still moist from her chores, and brushed my lips against those permanently chapped cheeks. "Thank you for everything, *signora*."

"It was nothing," she said woefully.

I kissed Gabriele goodbye. He was demonstrative as always, then headed back inside. The car was already whirring, fumigating the chickens. I got in next to Francesco. Pietro leaned through my rolled-down window and, with his mother right behind us, gave me a peck on the lips, a brief but no less extravagant kiss. "Have a safe trip, baby," he called out as the car backed down the driveway. "See you at home!"

For a moment I didn't pay much mind to those natural, rather ordinary words. *See you at home.* It took me a few seconds to truly assimilate them. If the tension between our three gazes could have been etched with a knife, it would have formed a triangle. I had my eyes on Lidia on the terrace wearing the usual mask; she, on the other hand, was staring at Pietro, who had brought a hand to his lips as if hoping to suck back his words; he in turn was looking at me with big speechless eyes. I could see him less and less from the moving car: he was getting smaller, or maybe it was the driveway that was stretching like a rubber band, so taut as to snap at any moment. It was clear that Pietro hadn't said it on purpose, that this was no act of heroism. Had his mother heard? If so, then the truth was out, as were the lies and deceit which I only now became aware of, and it was in plain sight of everyone, with the exception of Francesco, who hadn't noticed a thing so focused was he on looking at the rearview mirror to avoid running over the rooster.

I saw Lidia turn toward the front door, hunching over and wiping her hands on her apron as if begrudgingly going back to her chores. Maybe she hadn't heard, or maybe she had heard but hadn't put two and two to-gether. The chickens were all alive. The tires were now treading asphalt and Pietro disappeared behind the corner.

I could finally breathe again. Francesco's car was a well-oiled bullet that slipped fat and slick through those tight streets, practically filling them up but without making a sound—windows up, air-conditioning on. Viewed like that, the town seemed unreal.

"Isn't she quiet?" Francesco asked.

"She is."

But what was so bad, I reasoned, about letting the truth slip out? It wasn't as if we'd committed a crime. Besides, Pietro was going to tell her anyway, sooner or later. And sooner or later his mother was going to have to acknowledge my presence. It was about time. Maybe in the end Pietro's lapse was a good thing. With that moment of distraction, fate had been trying to lend us a hand, hustle us along. I felt rather refreshed now, but it wasn't the air-conditioning.

"All the comforts you could wish for."

"It's very comfortable."

The sensation didn't last but a few seconds. For some reason I suddenly felt uneasy and patted my pocket. I started. I'd left the Roman effigy on top of the bedspread in Pietro's bedroom. I felt like a liar, incapable of keeping the most basic lover's promise. I apologized to Francesco, ask-ing him if he minded turning around; he obliged with a "No problem, *Fräulein*." Actually, he seemed quite happy to demonstrate a U-turn with power steering.

The car was a whisper along the road back, until the tires began grind-ing the gravel in front of the house. The driveway had been emptied of humanity and poultry. I jumped out and sprinted toward the front door. It was open and I went in. No one was in the kitchen. I pushed on, call-ing, "Pietro? Gabriele?"

The television jabbered on without an audience. I kept going down the hallway. Still nobody. At this point I thought I would simply run upstairs, take the sculpture, and sneak off. Like a thief. At least that way I would avoid Lidia and another round of goodbyes, I would avoid any drama. But still, my heart was hammering inside my chest as I made my way up the first few steps. All at once voices from the basement stopped me in my tracks.

"Mamma, what's the big deal anyway? It's not like we're in 1962." It was Pietro, his voice low and tense.

"You're right," came his mother's voice, but with an assertiveness I didn't think she had in her. "Go on, go! Go back to Naples with that girl. Go get on a ferry to Greece or wherever. I don't care. You're my worst son."

I grabbed the Roman figure and lurched out of that house like a moth blinded by the daylight. No one had seen me.

From: tectonic@tin.it
To: heddi@yahoo.com
Sent: May 16

Dear Heddi,

Again I find myself writing to you not sure where to start. After rereading your last email three, four, five times, I've had thousands of things to tell you, fragments of thoughts.

I won't deny that I'm building castles in the air. I think about myself. I think about the moment in which I'll be so sick and tired of it all that I won't be able to put up with anything around me. Then I will be free. Free to leave without a destination, without a time limit. Then maybe I'll have the courage to call you and get your address and maybe come and see you, even just for a day, to look into your eyes again, to hear your voice again . . .

I would like to be the boy I was five years ago. Or at least something like that. Now I'm a grown-up (at least I try to convince myself that I am); I don't have any money problems, though I'm no Bill Gates, but everything else is missing from my life. I still dream of working in my field. I've sent my résumé to an Australian firm, you never know.

Every now and then I try to fall in love but I soon realize I'm just lying to myself. I read Coelho but it didn't change my life, I used drugs with the same result. Then I decided to just tough it out, trying to convince myself that everything I did, all my actions, were dictated by my free will, by an instantaneous desire that came over me. The real problem is my loss of historical memory: I can't remember what it was that I desired in the instant I acted, though I'm sure I wanted something. Now I find it hard to trust any gut feeling, even the one telling me to give up my job or hop on a plane. Will I find the courage? And even if I do, will you still be there?

A hug,

p.

17

WAS I DREAMING? Were Pietro and I really traveling together to Athens? Athens, Greece, and not Athens, Ohio? The ferry was rocking north to south, south to north, causing the open-air swimming pool to slosh its salt water out onto the deck. And circling that little square sea were twentysomething Norwegians, Spaniards, and Germans in Birkenstocks and pastel bandannas, drinking and strumming guitars as they settled in for the long night that awaited us. This was just the setting that befitted Luca, I thought to myself, if it was indeed like this when he crossed the Adriatic. I wanted us to blend in, and at least we did look the part. Like the others, our skin was already kissed by the sun and our backpacks-cum-pillows already blotted with vessel grease and weighed down by our provisions bought at a supermarket in Brindisi: a whole salami, two French loaves, water, and wine. And like the others, we resisted sleep, drinking straight from the bottle and chatting in English with our bedfellows.

Yet, although the scene wasn't new to me, I realized Pietro and I didn't really fit into it. For the others, Greece was merely a stop along an itinerary, one of the many knots on a long and well-secured rope with which they would dip down to Turkey, or Egypt at the farthest, before swinging back up to the long light of the north, to civilization, to normality. But we were not that free—or that normal. After Greece, we would be heading back to that tangle of streets known as Naples, for some of them another thrilling knot on their "third-world" itineraries but to us merely *home*. And each time a new travel companion asked us, flashing lovely white teeth, "So where do you come from?" I would feel at once pride and shame, a mixed-up emotion that Neapolitans had probably been experiencing for a thousand years and that succeeded in turning my stomach. Then again, it may just have been the strong smell of burning fuel mixed with the cold air and the rough sea that was becoming blacker and blacker.

Still, I couldn't contain my excitement. It was overflowing like the water from the pool, and if I could have, I would have clambered up that ship to shout it from the smokestacks. I was excited not just about the mind-blowing fact that Pietro had been allowed to leave flat in the midst of wheat threshing. And not just about the little adventure that awaited us and the beloved faces I would soon see. I was as excited as though I were about to receive an important recognition. Within a few hours, my mathematician dad and psychotherapist stepmom were going to have the chance to observe the two of us together and do what no one so far had been able to do—not our friends and certainly not his parents, but not even Pietro and I in an entire night spent pledging our love. The two of them, I was sure, would be able to identify that thing that was consuming us but that we could no longer live without; they would be able to find a name for it. "Love" and "passion" were mundane. And that name, whatever it was, would finally give our relationship a form, a concreteness of the likes of basalt, alexandrite, a black diamond. For otherwise who could have said for sure that it wasn't all a dream, a star that goes out as soon as the sun hatches from the Ionian Sea?

We arrived at the prearranged hotel before my folks, who still had to land, retrieve their luggage, and get through customs. Pietro and I could finally shower, and Pietro came out of the bathroom with his hair wet, a towel around his waist, and his bare chest traced by a thread of light allowed in by the closed shutters. We could have made love, too, for they had booked us a room all to ourselves.

"But what if your parents turn up? I'd screw it up big-time. I can't afford to be the worst son *and* the worst son-in-law."

I was too flattered by his semantics to be weighed down by his mother, not one but two seas away. As for my own family, Pietro needn't have worried: they announced their arrival knocking tentatively at the door.

Barbara enveloped me in an embrace jingling with earrings, sequins, auburn curls, and freckles. We laughed in amazement, as if we'd just happened to run into each other by chance in Athens. But hadn't we done this last summer in Turkey? And the summer before that in Sardinia? We were collecting a succession of summers like charms on a bracelet, starting from the first in Jamaica when I was four.

I had missed the very first exchange between Pietro and my father, who were now both looking around the room with their hands shoved into their pockets. My dad gave me a long hug that concluded, as he did with the cats, with a series of rhythmic pats on the back. I gathered my wits and introduced everybody. Barbara hugged Pietro like an old friend.

"Do you guys want to go have a shower?" I asked, before translating for Pietro.

"No, I got it," he murmured back without taking his eyes off them, like he was afraid to miss something.

"First a coffee, please!" cried Barbara with intentional drama.

"I'd like to pay for it but first I have to get some drachma," Pietro said to me, but Barbara was already dangling her purse before us, stretched to capacity and half-gutted, showing us her many scrunched purple and red banknotes, not to mention a necklace with a broken clasp, their passports, a collection of poetry by Odysseas Elytis, and a single orange sock.

Outside, the shop names and street signs were written in a pleasantly unfamiliar alphabet. A silky heat padded the little streets. I could sense Pietro's tension but it was well buried, and in any case I was too happy to pay it much mind. We found a café dripping with ivy and outdoor tables wobbling on the street stones. As we sipped that grainy, sweet coffee, Barbara asked Pietro questions about him, his study, his brothers. Her questions were respectful but fueled by the caffeine and that insatiable curiosity typical of not only her profession but also her temperament.

I translated back and forth, but the more he got used to Barbara's speech, the less he needed my help. It must have been hard work: his brow furrowed and his eyes sparkled like when he was studying his sedimentology textbook, but I was astonished how well he could manipulate the language, how he could handle it like a snake charmer. I'd never heard him speak in English for such a long stretch and with such risk-taking, and I listened to him utterly entranced.

"OK if I smoke?" he asked at one point.

Barbara nodded, saying that she and my dad had smoked for half their lives. "Camels," she said, venturing, too, the Italian for "twenty-five years" and checking with Pietro that she'd pronounced it correctly: she had a real gift for making anyone feel relaxed enough to pour out their secrets. Pietro was too much of a gentleman to correct her; he lit a cigarette with a tightly sealed but visibly pleased grin.

All the while, my dad sat there before his empty coffee cup, nodding at times at us and other times at the passersby, with the same rhythm tapping his foot as though counting the beats of his favorite Bach composition. He was already deeply tanned: the American Indian blood was on his side of the family. He'd hardly spoken, not even to pass judgment on the coffee, but he had that contented look of a man who, with an entire vacation still ahead of him and his family reunited, is soaking up the sultry air so like Longview, Texas. What part Pietro's presence may or may not have played in that peaceful equation was still an unknown.

It was Pietro who managed to get him to speak. He pointed to the street stones under our table and asked if he thought they were volcanic. My dad's foot stopped beating its fugue and his gaze dropped to the ground, but he didn't answer right away. Barbara's approval was a given at this point, and now all three of us were on the edge of our seats waiting for my father, as if his answer wasn't going to be a simple reply to a question but the final sentence of a judge. Knitting his brow, he said with the utmost gravity, "Marble, I reckon."

Now that a geological discussion was on the table, with all the Latin names, there was truly no longer need for my interpreting services. They fell deep into conversation, like colleagues. Pietro never ceased to amaze me: he'd instinctively known, without any suggestion on my part, what the key to my dad's heart was. And it had immediately unlocked something.

Barbara rested her chin on her hand and let out a satisfied sigh. "You know, Heddi, it's obvious that you and Pietro have a special connection. It feels very deep to me, very honest . . ."

"Oh really?" Here it comes, I thought to myself, the name—the *noun*—that would express the inexpressible. But she added nothing more, and I had to quickly come to grips with the fact that if Barbara, who lived off words and devoured books, couldn't find a word for it, then maybe there wasn't one.

She asked if anybody wanted another Greek coffee. "*'Na ciofeca*," Pietro said in Neapolitan, though he almost never spoke to me in dialect. A terrible brew, he'd ruled, and my dad too wore the very same expression of disgust and dread.

I settled my dad's fears with the news that we'd brought him a big bag of his favorite coffee, purchased just before leaving from the café tucked behind the Piazza Garibaldi train station. The place was unpopular and seedy: it had no windows and a single bare lightbulb, a fake-wood bar that was chipped, and a barista that had only one eye, but they roasted coffee beans that would have been the envy even of Gambrinus.

I'd ruined the surprise but my dad and stepmom were overjoyed nonetheless, letting out a little cheer for the city that had managed to save the day all the way in Athens. In fact, seeing Naples now through their eyes, I was willing to forgive it for everything. Removed from its context, even the grunty dialect of the Quartieri Spagnoli could be transformed into something delightful: a secret code, a lovers' game. Still, from that geographical distance I understood that what I felt for the city wasn't the love I once had but something akin to gratitude, for having given me Pietro. Naples was no longer a protagonist but a backdrop.

We headed back toward the hotel like two couples on a Sunday stroll, Pietro and I holding hands and Barbara and my dad walking a bit ahead of us. She snuggled in close to him, draping herself over his shoulder as she often did, and I thought I could hear them, and indeed the entire world, sighing with relief.

"So . . . ?" I asked Pietro. Undoubtedly he would be overwhelmed with impressions, but any one would do.

"Jesus, Heddi, what a family you have," he said with emotion. "And your dad . . . I'm just speechless."

For ten days we hopped from one island to the next, arid rocks plonked down in the middle of the sea and tortured by the wind but unbelievably inhabited by people—in houses all painted, as if by law, in white with blue doors and blue shutters. The summer wind in the Cyclades, the *meltemi*, was a tireless push from the north, apparently from the Eurasian steppe. It lifted the sand and frayed the waves; it upended umbrellas and overturned water bottles. We found the wind's single-mindedness quite comical, like that of a dog ramming his head into your leg throughout your entire dinner, in the hopes that sooner or later you'll give in. Ferries were often canceled, as should have probably been the ferry we took from Paros to Ios. The wind pushed hard against us for the entire journey, like it was trying to force-feed us to a sea that was already full. A little girl vomited. The benches, the floor, indeed everything, was turned on an angle, and we couldn't walk on the deck without grabbing on to something. This too made us laugh. The wind actually whistled.

I'm not sure how in all that wind at the highest point of Paros there was a valley of butterflies, so still in the trees they seemed asleep. We took a trip to Delos, the birthplace of Apollo, uninhabited except for the miniature dinosaurs, lizards scrambling across mosaics and over the faces of statues. Whenever I felt the urge, I'd pull out my Minolta. We ate plums and yogurt and (as a welcome break from the coffee) Milko chocolate milk, a local favorite served in every town café, where we'd sit leafing through Barbara's guidebook. From there I would watch shriveled old women in black cross the squares, reminding me of Lidia. I wondered if they, too, despite looking so feeble on the outside, were churning inside with bitterness toward the life that had bent them in half. On Mykonos it was pelicans that crossed the squares. As the island's mascot, those enormous birds had free rein to wobble through the streets like lame emperors, with Donald Duck feet and over-the-top beaks. When they walked past, the locals stroked them or even gave them a pretend kick for good luck. Although I was sure I didn't need any more good fortune than I already had, I brushed my fingers against one as it walked by. Its neck was rubbery and pale pink like strawberry gum that has lost its flavor.

Efharisto, petra. Thank you, pelican: that was the extent of my Greek. It turned out that we didn't need it because the wind carried with it from the north not only cool air but also English. The Dutch and Australian tourists spoke it, we spoke it. We used it to ask for hotel rooms—always separate, except on Mykonos. Pietro was collecting words like pebbles, lining them up in ever-new configurations, especially with my dad. The two of them examined all that exposed rock like it was a conundrum it was their job to solve. On those empty beaches, they inspected the sand with the same rigor. A few times I overheard my dad accidentally calling Pietro by my brother's name.

Such was the geological connection between my dad and Pietro that when one day on the beach Pietro pulled me up off my towel to show me something, I was sure it was going to be a rock. Instead he led me into the water until it was up to his waist, and then he lay on his back lifting his legs. In that bracing entrance into the sea, it took me a few seconds to understand what he was doing.

"You're floating, Pietro! You're floating!"

He grinned awkwardly and came back up. "Not so loud, baby. I don't want them to know I can't swim."

"Well, you nearly are. Anyway, hadn't you noticed that my dad can't swim either? That's why he never goes in the water."

This appeared to have an exponential effect on the esteem Pietro held my father in, and he glanced back at the beach. "Do you think he likes me?"

"Are you kidding? Yes."

"How can you tell?"

"It's obvious."

"I sure hope you're right."

I could tell from his tone that he craved the type of acceptance that up until not long ago I had hoped to earn from his mother. And yet I'd had the impression that Pietro, unlike me, had a handle on the situation.

The water was a kaleidoscope of blues and greens that blossomed around our stirring hands, our swiveling bodies. Doing away with modesty, we pressed hard against each other, entangling our legs and sinking deeper and deeper into the sea. We gave ourselves over to it, letting the salt water relieve us of gravity and seep into the warm grotto of our mouths. There was the visceral taste of salt and the clean sea, free of flaws or secrets, the lightness of our bodies and the love like a wave carrying us, and on the horizon the knowledge that we had our whole lives ahead of us. All this came together to create such perfect, crystalline happiness that I didn't think I could bear it, and in fact it was spoiled as soon as I became afraid it would end.

We got goose bumps and got out. My wet feet wore slippers of sand as I took a seat on the towel beside my dad. Like Pietro, he was an excellent judge of character, and I was so confident that he liked my boyfriend that I would have wagered everything on it. But still there was a trace of doubt.

Without prompting, he said, "Pietro's a real nice boy."

"You think so?"

My dad nodded toward the sea, his lips making a little line of satisfaction.

"What if we wanted to get married?"

My dad put his sun-warmed hand on my wet knee. "Then we'll have everyone around for a big barbecue."

I burst into giddy laughter. I glanced over at Pietro, who was sitting next to Barbara asking about her novel, and I tried to catch hold of his gaze. I wanted to communicate to him with my eyes that there was nothing to worry about anymore, that the moral support I'd enjoyed since I was a child, in my every wise and every foolish undertaking, was now his too.

From: heddi@yahoo.com
To: tectonic@tin.it
Sent: May 27

Dearest Pietro,

Again I find myself worrying about you, about your state of mind. You were born to accomplish great things, to climb and study the world's mountains. But instead you're still there, surrounded by material goods that don't give you any form of happiness.

I've often wondered what this fleeting thing is that people call "happiness." I don't know. I've meditated, done yoga, listened to CDs on Buddhism, and all these things teach you that true happiness is balance. *Maybe it is. But I have to say that I don't remember the happiest moments of my life being like that.*

I've tried falling in love too. The relationship started not long after I got here, and it lasted as long as it needed to. Ivan introduced me to him, perhaps thinking that a romance would be just the thing to bring me to my senses, and I just let it happen to me. And, objectively speaking, he was gorgeous. A half-Samoan surfer with browned skin, tall and muscly, a real head-turner that no one (man or woman) could help take notice of on the streets, but on me his beauty was wasted. He was very good to me. He took me out on the sea to kayak, to the mountains to snowboard; he even took me to Samoa for about five weeks to visit all the beaches and all his aunts and uncles. I took some nice photographs there, of the floral lavalavas and the pineapples peeled in a spiral.

He led a healthy lifestyle, all yoga and sushi, no alcohol or cigarettes: just the kind of guy my mom would have picked for me. But together we were like two recovering alcoholics, each consumed by our shameful misery and unable to really trust each other.

He was the one who taught me how to drive. Are you proud of me? I'm the delighted owner of a golden wreck of a car, manual no less. You made it look so easy when you drove your parents' car up and down the hills, steering with one hand and changing gears without even needing to look. But it actually does take a while to learn.

I almost forgot my real reason for writing. I have good news. My brother and his girlfriend are getting married! I think I already told you that she's originally from Trieste, even though she's lived in America since she was little. They're planning an initial celebration in Washington, but the actual ceremony will be in Trieste in August. I'll be the maid of honor. Of course I can't possibly miss the chance to go down to Naples. Will you be there? I hope you won't have taken a job with some Australian firm by then or we'll be like two planes passing in the night.

h.

18

BY THE END OF SUMMER, with the exodus of the out-of-town students (including Pietro and Gabriele), Naples resembled a ghost town. In reality millions of locals stayed put, but they only made their presence felt after the sun had rolled like a marble behind upper Naples, the hour in which all that humanity came trickling out of the buildings, freshly showered and voraciously awake. Yet for many hours of the day the inhabitants were battened down in their homes, hiding from the heat.

That clammy heat—*afa* they called it—was not just hot air but a *thing*. A touchable, almost corporeal entity that exhaled sulfur through the streets and dug its sticky fingers into the garbage to then stroke the nape of your neck, fondle your breasts, grope your inner thighs. There was no outrunning it. It would slip into the ground-floor *vasci* and would crawl just as effortlessly through the window of your seventh-story bedroom, where it would slide into bed with you, on top of the origami of your sheets. In the delirious siesta, the *afa* panted on your neck and licked your hair and wouldn't let you sleep.

I tried to study, but all I really wanted to do was go to the beach. Fat chance. The Gulf of Naples, whose water was good only for feeding mussels, sat there sparkling like fool's gold, winking and laughing at those of us who were left behind in the city.

I decided to bide the remaining heat at Rita's house. But sometimes when we went out at night, along the promenade in Castellammare or Sorrento, I'd look out at the bay, black as tar except for cardiograms of yellow lights on its surface, and on the other side Naples would be glaring at me. Enveloped in an orange haze, it seemed to be slowly burning away in the embers of an old fire. I knew I had to get back to the city. I had to be there, for better or for worse.

As soon as Pietro came back to Naples, he took his sedimentology exam and failed. It had little to do with our two-week vacation and more to do with the farmwork and his hydrogeology assignment. But there was no opportunity to present these justifications to his mother when she phoned him.

"Hello?" he said. "Have you eaten?"

His mother didn't answer but simply asked, "Did you pass your exam?"

"No."

She hung up.

Pietro sat there on the couch with the receiver bleating in his hand. We left the apartment in the direction of the city center, mostly in silence. I was sifting through my memories for a similar anecdote from my dad's geology years to console him with. But I couldn't think of anything.

The streets around the university were already being deconstructed with discussions of Descartes and Derrida. The students had once again taken over the city. And this meant business not only for the second-hand bookshops but also for our favorite haunt, La Campagnola restaurant, where we were meeting Sonia and the boys for lunch and where every day the menu was a surprise scribbled on a blackboard and the bill an approximation scribbled on butcher paper. The place was a hole-in-the-wall that sizzled with people joking and squid frying; the stench of hot oil democratically permeated the tweed jackets of professors, the plaster-spattered smocks of builders, and the retro shirts of students.

"Let's order some red wine for the table," Pietro said, adding in English, "Even if their red wine sucks."

True, it was no longer the season for white wine. And now that we were back to our abnormal normality, the dialect could no longer be our secret code.

Pietro motioned to the owner to bring us two whole jugs of wine. "Might as well blow my last cash," he said, reverting back to Italian, "seeing as how I'll probably get disowned."

"It's just one exam. You can take it again next session."

"Either way, I'll still be the worst son."

"Oh, that."

Somehow I'd managed to convince myself that those words, attached as they were to me, *that girl*, had hurt me more than they'd hurt him. In any case hadn't they freed us, absolving him of all responsibility and allowing us to go on vacation together? But now it occurred to me that maybe we hadn't left so much carefreely as carelessly. Wasn't it really for Greece, and not for the exam, that his mother had hung up the phone on him, to make him pay for it? *You're my worst son.* I'd been foolish to brush off those words, pronounced in Italian as though he were the foreigner, for hearing them again they still shocked me.

"I'm sure she didn't really mean it, Pietro," I said. "It was probably just the heat of the moment. Or maybe that's just her way of saying you have bad taste in girlfriends. You know, that skinny American girl."

Lidia sure did have a gift for conciseness. *She's too skinny.* I recalled how those three tidy little words had been able to sum me up, isolate me, and reject me all in one quick slap. And much of their power, I realized, lay in the pronoun *edda*, the third person singular in their dialect . . . And, just like that, I thought I might have found a topic for my thesis.

"She doesn't understand the first thing about you, Heddi. I don't know what I did to deserve you. Maybe some heroic act in a previous life."

Without much ceremony, the wine and glasses came clanking down on our plastic tablecloth. Pietro filled our glasses and drank greedily, wiping his lips with those long fingers. He let them stay there, covering his mouth in thought, or perhaps in self-imposed silence.

"But I'm right about your mother, aren't I? She can't stand the sight of me." Openly associating his mother with contempt I found somewhat exhilarating: it felt almost transgressive crossing that line, the line of politeness.

"Nothing slips by you, baby." Pietro lit a cigarette as if to collect his thoughts. "So what are you going to do about it?"

"Me?" Was he reproaching me for the fact that, unlike him, I hadn't been able to win over any hearts?

"Then who?"

"You, Pietro. What are *you* going to do about it?" My face felt flushed though I hadn't yet touched my wine. Now I was indignant.

He answered that he was already doing everything possible to put his foot down, that he'd told his parents he would return to the farm only once between now and Christmas. "They can have my slave labor for the olive harvest and that's it. They can sow the wheat themselves. But, baby, I really need you to do your part too."

"What more can I do, Pietro? Offer for the hundredth time to do the dishes?"

"Forget the dishes." He crushed out a perfectly good Marlboro Light and pressed my hand with purpose, like a lump of clay. "Look, my folks have figured out what's what. They know it won't be long before I graduate and so they're shortening the leash. I need your help getting them off my back a bit."

I slipped my hand from his grip. "Wait a second. I'm supposed to save you from your own family?"

I was smiling, fully expecting him to contradict me. But he didn't. He pointed his eyes on me so hard it nearly hurt, a look that lasted far too long and was broken only by Angelo coming through the door of La Campagnola.

"Man, you guys look great!"

Peruvian saddlebag over his shoulder, Angelo weaved like a skateboarder through the restaurant crowd to hug us in the indelicate way of the strong and healthy. Plopping himself on a chair and pouring himself some wine, he told us the disjointed story of his summer: the outdoor concerts in Catania; hooking up with a hot Israeli chick on the island of Filicudi; learning how to spearfish, unfortunately for him in a marine reserve and at a heavy penalty. The thought of fishing seemed to whet his appetite, and he suggested we order at least an antipasto. There was no point waiting for Tonino, who was still packing up his books, he explained going off on a tangent, but I only truly lost the thread of the conversation when he started talking about beams.

"I admit it does look a bit Frankenstein," he went on, rearing back in his chair. "But when they cover up the beams with the floor, you won't notice a thing. The only difference will be that the kitchen floor will be a half a meter higher, but who the hell cares with those high ceilings. And as soon as they put the new tiles on we can move back in."

Only then did it register, but I didn't even get the chance to apologize, for Angelo was already saying they were planning to ask Davide to move into the old place. The new place. How was it possible that in my heart I couldn't find the slightest trace of nostalgia for that apartment I'd so loved but merely a childish feeling of hurt that they hadn't asked me to move back in with them?

Sonia turned up. Flowing behind her like bat wings were her flared sleeves and raven hair, yet with that golden skin you would never have known she was a goth. As we ate, she told us about the picture-perfect

Sardinian beaches she'd visited with Carlo. I didn't dare ask if Carlo had been allowed to sleep in her room or been spoken to at the dinner table. When the question came around to our side of the table, our amazing adventure abroad, all *meltemi* and temples and tame pelicans, allowed us to leave out the fact that we'd actually spent most of the summer apart.

When Pietro finally stood up, no doubt to surreptitiously pay the entire bill, Angelo began gutting his bag in search of lord knows what. In that gap Sonia leaned toward me to ask how it had gone with Pietro's parents. She would have been right to expect some sort of improvement, but instead we now had a *situation*, the mere thought of which suddenly triggered a tiny dull ache inside me. I wasn't able to lie, not to Sonia.

"C'mon, Eddie. How could his mother possibly hate *you?*" was her reaction. "Well, even so, you're still the luckiest girl in the world."

"How so?"

"Pietro loves you madly: you'd have to be blind not to see it," she said lowering her voice. "Isn't that what everybody wants, to be loved like that?"

I couldn't say I agreed with her on that score. My experience had taught me that the real thrill was loving. Being loved was secondary.

That Pietro and I had had the closest thing we'd ever had to a lovers' quarrel didn't upset me in the least. Some truths had surfaced and we were all the closer for it, or so it seemed. Our lovemaking received a new burst of life, as if we'd tapped into a previously unknown and gushing underground spring. In any case, after our so-called fight his mother pleasantly evaporated from our conversations. We had other things on our minds.

The new academic year was a whirl of activity, amid exams, meetings with Benedetti (as the supervisor of my thesis), seminars, and lessons. Nevertheless, after those encounters I didn't feel like wandering the streets with my head in the clouds as I used to, bowled over by the notions that the various academics had exposed me to. Instead I walked head down, picking apart their arguments and noticing where they'd fallen prey to hypocrisy, vagueness, or arrogance. I even found it hard to get excited about the debates led by Tonino, Gabriele, or Madeleine regarding the difference between socialism and communism or the advantages and disadvantages of public housing. I wanted to pass my exams. Do research for my thesis. Graduate.

I ran to and fro buzzing with an impatient sort of energy, especially in the city center, home to the vast majority of university students—often in awful shared rooms at inflated prices. I felt comfortable in that part of Naples, where the strong out-of-town element, not to mention the presence of African street hawkers known as *vuccumprà*, watered down the Neapolitan element. Besides, its tangled paths had an immediate antidote: Spaccanapoli, the Greco-Roman street dissecting the whole of ancient Neapolis from east to west, from one sun to the other, as straight and deep as a scalpel incision performed by a steady hand and cold heart, without a moment's hesitation or a single deviation. All the alleyways around the university, among the narrowest and darkest in the entire city, sooner or later flowed into it, and suddenly you'd find that your claustrophobia was gone, for Spaccanapoli offered the closest thing the historic center had to a panorama. But it wasn't a view of the gulf or the castles or even the sky. It was a glimpse penetrating the *heart of Naples*, as far as the eye could see, and yet it was as dizzying as a skyscraper. Looking into Spaccanapoli made your head spin because you could stare at it as hard as you wished, until your eyes went blurry, and still you could never see where it ended. The end, if there was one, always slipped out of sight, blending with the shadows and hiding behind the laundry, the motorbikes, the multitude.

It was on Spaccanapoli one day that I noticed a hand-painted sign hanging above a bolted door. *Napoli sotterranea*, Underground Naples. I'd never seen it before: perhaps it was new. Was this an access point to the underground caves Gabriele had told me about? I resolved to mention it to him. Maybe we could make a "field trip" out of it, but for what purpose was not clear in my mind. I only knew that I could reignite my passion for Naples if I treated it like the temporary stop that it was.

And yet that detachment didn't come entirely natural to me: it was like an act I hadn't yet mastered. Because, no matter where I went in the city, I was accompanied by that melancholy I'd known since the first day I'd set foot in it, a sadness that remained insensitive to the positive signs of an urban regeneration we were coming to trust more and more. It didn't make any sense for me to still be suffering from it. I was fulfilled with my life, or nearly, and happier than I'd ever been—in love, strong, maybe even unconquerable. Perhaps then it wasn't a melancholy related to my inner reality but rather an external malaise that was there long before my arrival and simply took me over, like the way the winter gives you its blues. It was a sorrow too deep, too ancient, to be mine: it had to belong to the city.

Melancholy lived in the Ospedale delle Bambole, the Doll Hospital, on Spaccanapoli, an old buildup of broken dolls, of unfinished work, so eruptive as to practically swallow up the worktable and chair used by the overworked "doctor." It was in their limp bodies, heavy makeup, and clumped hair; it was in their arms outstretched in an unreciprocated hug. Lolita dolls with faces as beautiful and unreadable as Madeleine's.

Melancholy lived in every alleyway, locked between the arms of two best friends strolling in sexy miniskirts while sucking on lollipops: it was in their lost childhood. Melancholy was with the unemployed men outside a café discussing the latest soccer results, and with the coffee grinder grumbling about having to repeat the same old routine day in and day out without ever getting to the bottom of anything. It was in the middle-aged woman peddling children's books on the filthy steps of a church, struggling to sound out the words to *The Three Little Pigs* in plain sight of everyone. There was sadness in her lack of privacy and in her lack of shame. It was in the midmorning drizzle, drops as light and disoriented as snowflakes, and in the way the cobblestones would then become coated in a slick layer of grease for the sea snail vendor to plow his cart through. The melancholy would ring out in his street cry (*Maruzziell'! Maruzziell'!* Come get them fresh *maruzziell'!*), a chant as mournful as a call to prayer from a minaret. It was in the way that, after he'd passed through, the street smelled like fish and candy, ignorance and good intentions, sewage and frankincense.

But most of all, melancholy was in the volcano, slices of which from the city center could only be glimpsed at the end of certain streets: flat, meaningless pieces of a much larger puzzle. Vesuvius didn't come to us. It sat there biding its time, and it could wait tens or even hundreds of thousands of years. Our ambitions, our fears, our tremendous love—all that meant nothing to it. Was this a kind of wisdom as deep as its magma chamber, or was it simply indifference? It was hard to tell. But now I wondered if what truly unsettled me was not that the volcano might be indifferent to all of us, but that it might be indifferent to *me*. Its silence was personal.

Century after century nothing in Naples ever really changed. And I was beginning to sense that the strange sadness that was perhaps uniquely Neapolitan might just be the knowledge that, no matter what, life goes on.

Life in fact went on without Luca. During the summer his absence wasn't anything out of the ordinary, but now with all the students back it was obvious he'd gone and taken his magic with him. It was in the Spanish Quarter that I missed him the most. Luca had been able to take the neighborhood in his stride, as though he could see its inner workings— just as he could see the inner workings of humankind itself. But without his higher perspective, the quarter was just all too real and its ugly side impossible to ignore. Rabbit skins hanging outside the butchers'. Rats in broad daylight surgically opening the garbage bags. The hopeless darkness of the side streets, the doors opening onto prostitution and drug deals. And in one of those streets, who knows where, was that enormous dog guarding his walls underneath the scaffolding, king of a small territory that interrupted the grid pattern of the neighborhood like a metal parenthesis. And everywhere motorbikes growling, people hollering, car alarms hooting, shoes clicking up and down the streets, hundreds of them all together as if in a collective tap dance. But this was no musical.

More than ever I adhered to my memorized paths, but one time my feet betrayed me and took me in the direction of the old house. On the way I bumped into Tonino, who had popped in to check how the renovation was progressing. Abruptly I pulled him toward me and held him so tight I was scratched by his stubble and infused with his smell of too much coffee and too many cigarettes.

Tonino admitted he'd been up all night cramming for an exam. "Sanskrit, finally. We'll see how it goes."

"Good luck."

"No, this time I don't think luck is going to cut it."

"Then I'll go to church," I said in jest, "and say a prayer for you."

"Yeah, go on. Go straight to the top, to the patron saint of Naples, San Gennaro, and tell him I need a fucking miracle."

"All right, I'll see what I can do . . ."

"And while you're at it, ask him if he'll make my cock the size of the Incredible Hulk's."

How good it was to be laughing stupidly as always.

Then Tonino said, in a more sober tone, "And if I don't pass, I might just leave this black hole of a university and get a job like Luca."

"What do you mean *a job?*"

"What, didn't you know, gorgeous? That bastard got himself a job in the army, as an *officer*," Tonino explained. "In a way, Falcone is a genius. All the others just let themselves get fucked in the ass, a year in the military for a daily allowance that won't buy you a pack of smokes. But our Luca, he knows how to work the system, getting them to pay him a shitload just to boss all those dickheads around."

A Vespa swerved skillfully around us, leaving us in its nauseating wake. How could someone like Luca Falcone, surely a bona fide conscientious objector, voluntarily join the army? Luca with the wild hair, Luca the metalhead, the calligrapher, the tarot reader, the mind reader? And anyway, none of this was meant to begin until after graduation, right?

"Did he tell you all this himself?"

"I heard it straight from the falcon's mouth." At his pun on Luca's last name, Tonino burst into hoarse laughter, but I must have looked humorless, if not distressed, because before leaving he pulled from his wallet a slip of paper with Luca's phone number in Varese.

Afterward I stood there steeping in that smog, still holding on to that pointless series of numbers. First his escape to Greece, and now this. How vain I was to have thought I reserved a special relationship with Luca, to think I could possibly interpret his hypnotic glances. In the end, I didn't know who the real Luca Falcone really was. Maybe none of us did.

The only certainty was that Luca was outrageously independent. He challenged people's expectations of him by doing the exact opposite. After his parents had run for their lives up north, Luca returned south. While all of us were studying for exams, he was teaching himself to read the runic alphabet. After the ceiling had collapsed and we were all looking for a new home, he was ferrying off to Greece. And while Pietro and I were in Greece, as if merely chasing his shadow, Luca was already off getting a job. Now there was someone who knew how to break the mold and when to move on; he had the courage to make a clean break—with places, with people, with *me*.

And there I was, still in the Spanish Quarter.

19

OUT OF SHEER PRACTICE we became masters of time. Time obeyed us, stretching out upon request and shortening when necessary. The trip Pietro had to make to Monte San Rocco flew by, whereas the afternoons spent studying broke themselves down into minutes packed with valuable facts. We were obsessively collecting signatures in our exam booklets like stamps in an album. Yet we still had time left over: for dinners with our friends, often mixed with Gabriele and Madeleine's crowd; for film festivals with heavily discounted student tickets; for open-air concerts organized by the students' association. We were especially masters of the night, at least in the city center. Piazza Bellini, with its mood lighting, exotic music, and risqué conversations, put the darkness in time-out like a child who has pushed their limits and hasn't earned the right to stay up with the grown-ups. It was too snobby, though, for Pietro, who preferred Piazza San Domenico Maggiore, where a bar had recently opened with hours suited to those who could choose whether to get up early or not get up at all.

I had so much time, in fact, that I willingly handed it out to the homeless man on Via Roma. A couple times a week I'd bring him breakfast, for which he always thanked me with great courtesy and humility. One day I found him in the usual spot not in the morning but in the afternoon.

I crossed the boulevard on purpose to say hello, although out of pure habit I said *buongiorno*. A broad smile splintered his face, revealing teeth I no longer found upsetting. But still there was something different about him that day, at that late hour . . .

"Would you like a coffee or something to eat?"

"Already eat. Thank you, thank you."

My eyes darted to the blanket spread out beside him. His dog was digging into her belly with her teeth—fleas or maybe mange. A moth-eaten sweater had slunk off her back, for the cold weather was just around the corner. Then it registered. "Where are her puppies?"

"Away, away!" I could tell he wanted to say something else but the language was a barbed-wire fence he couldn't cross. When I asked him if they'd found good homes, he didn't answer but simply wiped his grubby forehead with a trembling hand.

"Are you cold?" I asked, addressing him for the first time with the informal "you," as I would a friend.

"Fine, fine. At evening I go center. Give food. Sometimes shower."

There are times when the body acts and the mind just sits back and watches. Thus, as if suddenly overcome with exhaustion, I sat on the ground beside the man's wheelchair, right on top of an offensive accumulation of urban grime. From that angle it was impossible to ignore the fact that he was half a man. His legs had been lopped off just above the knee as brutally as a sword cut. They scared me. And all the while, whooshing past us without a care in the world were pants, skirts, shoes.

"*Signore*, I hope you don't mind me asking, but what happened to you?"

He turned to me with a paternal expression, or maybe it only seemed that way because I was looking up at him instead of the other way around. "I?"

"Yes, you. Why are you here?"

The man made a sweeping motion over his legs with both hands, like a magician about to make an object reappear. "Come Italy long, long time.

From Germany. I priest. Understand?" He thrust a finger into his chest, like he was accusing himself of something.

"You were a priest before?"

He didn't reply, burying his gaze once more in the pedestrian traffic. That seemed to be the extent of his story; it was up to me now to fill in the gaps. But I didn't know how. What kind of priest leaves his vocation? One that, for some unknown reason, stops believing in that miracle he thought he could bask in, like a cat in the sun, until the day he died and even afterward?

I was just about to get back up when the man directed his blue, blue eyes back to me, a purifying rather than an icy stare. "Then *catastrof*. Big *catastrof*!"

"What happened, an accident?"

"*Catastrof*!" he repeated, a frightening howl of desperation. But it wasn't madness. The homeless man said nothing more and, having no coins left to give him, I stood up and headed home.

There was not a single tree in the Spanish Quarter, nor much sunlight, with which to judge the change of seasons. To see the transformation taking place you had to look at the fruit stands: at the melons magically changing into pumpkins, the plums into persimmons. You could see it in the housewives inside their *vasci*: no longer wooden clogs and light, pastel dresses but lined slippers and formless cardigans in earth tones. You could see it in the resigned expression on people's faces, ancient features built to grin and bear it. You could see it in the way that, no sooner had the siesta ended, the night sky was a lid closing you in a catacomb. A cold dampness would then seep into your bones. But at 33 Via De Deo, Pietro and I didn't really feel the cold. Not only did we have a gas heater in the living room, but between the sheets we created more heat than a copper bed warmer. From there, the lights of the port looked like distant bonfires slowly burning away in the night.

Nobody ended up moving back into the old house, forever fossilizing the sweet memories I had of the place. The repairs were taking too long and the owners had meanwhile upped the rent, for, never ones to miss a get-rich-quick opportunity, they reasoned that with those shiny new tiles the house was sure to make a fine impression now. So it was that the boys decided to find a new place with Davide in the Sanità district. And so it was that, just before Christmas, they invited me and Pietro over for a Sunday meal. I had no doubt, indeed I hoped, that they would serve nothing fancier than spaghetti with puttanesca sauce.

It was a long way on foot and the weather was unseasonably warm. Via San Gregorio Armenio was packed with miniature nativity scenes for sale, and from the other narrow streets of the historic center came wafts of roasted chestnuts and blizzards of light from enormous snowflakes strung between balconies. There were even a few women in fur coats, probably rabbit fur dyed to look like mink, because if a lady couldn't wear hers at Christmastime, then when would she ever be able to wear it? And in the midst of all that overheated humanity slipped a cool and silent car, a mobster's no doubt. The masses split as they would for a coffin, and as the car drove through the only thing they were able to see in its darkened windows were their own expressions of awe and deference at that brush with death.

"Now that's a car," said Pietro.

"Paid for in blood, though."

"Look, baby, today I'd settle for one like Francesco's. My legs are killing me walking around like a gypsy."

I didn't say anything. It was hard to say what sickened me more: that black stallion pumped with steroids or Francesco's blue station wagon, which on the outside looked like a practical family car but on the inside had that bitter smell of brand-new things that overpowers the sweet smell of dreams. That car was reparation for a life unlived, but I knew Pietro didn't see it like that.

Once inside the Sanità, we nearly got lost. Passersby eyed us suspiciously, even in the deli where we stopped to buy bread and wine moments before it closed. Pietro didn't stoop to asking the way, instead muttering the boys' directions under his breath. Finally we spotted the landmark we'd been told to look for, the skeleton of a burned-out Vespa. And there in fact beside it was the right building number, 17, unlucky since Greek times and slapped onto the stone in red paint as if to mark it with a cross.

There were no names, no intercom. Our doubts as to whether we'd found the right place disappeared only on the fifth floor, where a semi-open door released the feral odor of marijuana and the feedback from an amplifier. "Hey, boys," said Pietro, walking in, "did someone mistake your intercom for a laptop and run off with it?"

Davide turned off the amplifier and Angelo put down the electric guitar to greet us. Tonino came out from behind the stove, his glasses fogged up from cooking. "It's better to be anonymous around these parts."

"Alcoholics Anonymous," said Davide, and we all laughed.

"But the intercom's not the biggest pain in the butt," said Angelo, serious now as he tweaked his nose ring. "The real problem is the phone. Telecom won't connect it."

"Why not?" I said. "You're model citizens."

"Because you know what our delightful neighbors do? They get on the phone and call their uncle, their cousin, their grandfather, their mother-in-law's sister in Argentina; they talk for four hours and then conveniently forget to pay the bill. And in these dark and winding streets, who's going to ever track them down?"

"Leeches," muttered Tonino. "We were better off in the Quartieri."

After a quick tour of the house, it was lunchtime. Much of my relationship with the boys played itself out around the table. Davide fit easily into that scene, so this meal too felt just like old times: Angelo stealing olives off my plate; Tonino cursing about politics; the conversation turning, in accordance with male tradition, to digestion and then inevitably to sex; the wine spilling on the tablecloth and the bread mopping it up. I didn't ask them about their classes or even Tonino's Sanskrit exam. It was obvious that in that household studying was a low priority, and I didn't feel like spurring them on, not even for fun.

After a coffee we all sank into a comfortable, well-worn silence. Davide got up somewhat lethargically to tune the electric guitar. Tonino lit a cigarette, as did Pietro as he pulled my feet up onto his lap and undid my shoelaces. Angelo started rolling a joint, but with that blond mop of hair and that face it all looked very innocent. Outside the open balcony it was a beautiful sunny day. But the city showed few vital signs, and even that apartment was at risk of falling into the Sunday coma. It was like a second hand that's stuck and goes *tick tock* but without moving forward, an immobility that made me itchy. I could hardly remember: Had it been like this in the old house too? All that wasted sunshine. Now I craved only to be outside, to shake off that contagious drowsiness and go for a walk.

"Where are you guys spending Christmas?" Angelo asked, lighting up.

It was a topic the two of us had been able to avoid so far, but Pietro answered, "Well, Monte San Rocco, of course. You pretty much have to spend it with the old folks, don't you?"

"Fuck me," said Tonino, "the most traditional event of the year with your future in-laws. Maybe they'll take you to midnight mass too. What a bowl of cherries that'll be."

I heard Davide from the other side of the room say, "It'll make you want to slit your wrists."

"Heddi's tough, though," Pietro hastened to say. "She'll get through it."

It was at once an invitation and a compliment, but it gave me a start. I said under my breath, "No, not Christmas, Pietro. I really don't think it's a good idea."

Pietro looked hurt. "Where were you thinking of spending it then?"

"It's just a couple of days. I'll stay in Naples and study or something. Or I'll go to Castellammare. Yeah, that's what I'll do."

"C'mon, baby, it's Christmas. We have to be together. It'll be fun, you'll see."

When I looked up, I could see the boys had discreetly removed themselves, Angelo to the couch to nurse his joint and Tonino to the kitchen to noisily pile up plates as if to test their resistance. I stood up to give him a hand.

"Sit down, gorgeous. You're a guest," said Tonino, heading back my way. He too hurled his weight onto the couch, deflating the cushions and sullying them further with his shoes. "Besides, Angelo does the chores around here."

Angelo groaned with annoyance. A curl of smoke uncoiled toward the ceiling before spreading into a mushroom cloud that remained trapped in the room. I stared at the joint he held so delicately between his fingers like a fountain pen.

"Can I try?"

Everyone, even Davide, turned to look at me, dumfounded. Tonino sat up straight on the couch.

"What?" said Angelo. "You mean this?"

"Yeah, I've never tried it before."

"I know!" Angelo grew a pleasantly stupefied smile as he handed me the joint.

I took it, trying to hold it as he had, pressed lightly between my thumb and forefinger and using my pinkie as a counterweight. Before me the smoke slithered in slow motion, creating vivid, oily shapes. Eels in the sea, dragons in the air. The moment had an oneiric quality to it, but it was a lucid dream and it was up to me to make the next move.

"What do I do?"

Angelo infused his voice with the warm patience of a schoolteacher. "Take a breath in, just a little one. Then hold it there for a bit before breathing it out."

I glanced over at Pietro, who looked at me full of wonder and nodded in encouragement. Why had I asked for the joint? Was I suddenly curious after all these years? I didn't feel curious. Or afraid. I felt nothing at all. In any case it was too late to go back now: the roll, as fragile as rice paper, was already pressed between my lips.

I drew in a breath. The smoke slid into my mouth like a liquid, tepid and so delicate that I feared it might melt into nothing. I held it there for as long as I could before sending it out with a kiss like I'd seen the boys do. Then a stench accosted my nostrils: that odor of burnt rubber and wet henna.

"How was it?" asked Angelo.

"I don't know. I don't feel anything."

"You probably didn't inhale," said Tonino, lying back down.

Angelo suggested I give it another go, but I shook my head and passed him back the joint. For one exhilarating second when I'd been able to capture the smoke in my mouth, swirling inside me was my entire past with the boys: our hourless parties and empty hours, our hot teas and dirty jokes, our conspiracy theories and B movies. But the smoke was an elusive pleasure that faded behind my lips, and I just couldn't hold on to it. There was no point trying to pretend. An era was over.

Perhaps seeing a side to me he'd never seen before, Pietro looked at me with fascination and mouthed the words *Come ti voglio bene*, in Naples the only real way to say "I love you." Words you would say not merely to your lover but to your best friend, to your father or daughter, to those who felt like part of your flesh.

Christmas was only days away when the phone rang. Pietro picked up and asked in a monotone, "Have you eaten?"

It wasn't a real question but a greeting with a deep stratification of meanings, a custom used perhaps throughout Irpinia or maybe just within the walls of the Iannace household. For me, those first words to his mother were my cue to leave the room. I fiddled in the kitchen until I thought enough time had elapsed before going back to the living room. Pietro had already put down the receiver but was still sitting there on the couch with his mouth in an unfamiliar contortion.

"Something wrong?"

He combed the floor with his eyes as if he hoped to spot a gold nugget. In the end he said, "It's about Christmas."

"What about it?"

"She wants it to be, you know, just a family deal."

"You mean I'm not invited."

"I'm sorry. I assumed it would be OK."

I sank into the couch beside him. The vinyl screeched, my stomach churned. It wasn't simply the effect of the bad news: it was the inexplicable feeling that something terrible was about to happen, in the same way that I knew that a cold sore was about to erupt on my lower lip.

"And what did you say?"

"What was I supposed to say? I didn't say anything. But, baby, this holiday is just one big act. A bunch of best wishes here, best wishes there, visiting people you see only once a year because in real life you don't have a thing in common with them. Zilch. And then, not because they genuinely like you but only because they feel obligated to, they offer you something to drink, something to eat—and if you refuse, woe to you and your entire family. All this deep-fried, sickeningly sweet stuff. At Christmas they stuff themselves like it's postwar famine, I swear. They eat like if they don't gobble it down fast enough the wolves are going to come down from the mountains and snatch it straight out of their mouths. Believe me, I would much rather stay here with you."

For a moment that flood of resentment toward his hometown left me speechless. Then I said, "If it's going to be so awful, then don't go."

"If I don't go," Pietro answered gravely, "we're both in deep shit. My mother could actually decide to disown me. So even if she pisses me off, I bite my tongue for the sake of peace and quiet. I have to appease her for a little while longer."

I went quiet, stunned by the amount of anger he was now spewing at his mother. Was he simply venting or was he trying to get me to intervene in some way? But on such short notice, just three days before Christmas Eve, I struggled to find the oomph for a rebellion. I already had a more intimate battle on my hands, a battle against a loathsome self-pity I'd known since I was a little girl. A negative trait of Cancerians, I told myself in an attempt to fend it off, further reasoning that I hadn't even wanted to spend Christmas in Monte San Rocco in the first place. Nonetheless, I couldn't deny the fact that Lidia had gladly and openly rejected me, in no uncertain terms, during the holiday period when I didn't have any family around, something I experienced not as an insult but as a wound in my chest that was becoming more and more painful. My throat went tight and it was all I could do to fight back tears.

Pietro again apologized, hesitantly brushing a strand of hair off my face. He'd done a deal with his parents, he said, that he would spend Christmas there but return to Naples for New Year's. "This one last sacrifice and we'll be celebrating the beginning of our lives together."

Why was it that he was always talking about us in the future tense? And yet I was guilty of it too. Because all our plans, all our dreams—the castles we were building—were as vital to us as the air they were built in.

Madeleine was the last to leave. She was in a bubbly mood, no doubt due partly to the fact that Saverio was waiting for her in the street below on the restless horse of his motorcycle, poised to whisk her away. At the door she wished me a merry Christmas, adding with a small voice and big eyes, "But what a shame to leave you here all lonely. Poor you. I will save for you some panettone!" I tightened Madeleine's rainbow-striped scarf around her neck, wishing she would just hurry up and go. Madeleine, full of pity for *me*? Oh please.

But as soon as the lock clicked behind me, the house seemed suddenly drained of life, as though the electrons of every object in it had stopped spinning. The only light on, the desk lamp, was a flat reflection in the windows, and the festive sounds from the courtyard came through muffled: the bubbling and the frying, the grating and the arguing in preparation for the big Christmas Eve dinner.

I didn't have to be there, in the Quartieri. I had chosen not to go to Castellammare only out of pride, so as to avoid explaining myself to Rita, who thought I was with Pietro in his hometown. And anyway, what was Christmas once the magic of childhood was removed? A mere convention, nice and colorful but ultimately devoid of intrinsic value, a tradition that could be broken as easily as drinking a cappuccino after midday.

Why wait till morning then, I argued, to open the presents according to my own American tradition? I pulled out the package my dad and Barbara had sent, cutting through the masking tape. Inside were, among other thoughtful items, a bag of New Mexico chili peppers and a silk shirt for Pietro. I brought them to my face and breathed in their unfaded scent of the house in DC. But now was not the time to give in to missing my family. Not tonight.

My cold sore by now had aggressively taken over and my lip was throbbing with heat. I opened up the box of a new antiviral I was willing to try since lemon juice and the other natural remedies had failed to work, swallowing down the first two pills at the kitchen sink. The water in Naples always tasted like chalk. I sat at Pietro's desk and pulled the gas heater close enough to warm my hands. I figured I might as well study.

I began browsing through my index cards with quotes that would potentially be of value to my thesis. I lingered on one in particular where I'd jotted down: "The third person is historically the weakest form . . . [undergoing] a fierce decline."

He, she, it, they . . . These were all destined, not just in Italian but in many other languages, to evolve, become simplified, or even fall into disuse. Spoken Mandarin didn't distinguish between *he* and *she*. English speakers were more and more inclined to opt for the genderless *they* instead of the burdensome *he or she*—thus, at least in language there was gender equality. However, I grasped a certain naïveté in that quotation that brushed off the third person singular: it underestimated how powerful it was, deviously so, but maybe that's why it was still alive and kicking after thousands and thousands of years. Because referring to an individual as *he* or *she* was an unavoidable form of othering. They were saying, authoritatively and nonnegotiably, that that other person was unlike them, an outsider to their community and their family, such an outsider in fact as to appear invisible despite standing right there before them in the very same kitchen.

I let my mind stray to where it had wanted to go from the very beginning. To Pietro's mother. *Edda*, that's what she'd reduced me to. That very first morning she could have said nothing, but if she really couldn't keep it to herself she could have at least told me to my face, *You're a skinny little thing, aren't you?* That pronoun *edda* wasn't even a grammatical necessity (the conjugated verb and the feminine form of the adjective would have sufficed)—but no, Lidia had deliberately chosen to use it: she'd meant to underline my irrelevance in that room; she'd meant to negate me.

Now in the stillness of that house I tried to pronounce it faithfully, but my tongue struggled to reproduce that double *d*, reminiscent of Sicilian and subtle enough to sound like an *r*. *Edda, erda, erra*. No, I couldn't quite get it. It was one of those unreachable, mountainous sounds of the dialect. *Edda*. Now that I thought about it, it actually sounded like a woman's first name, an old, black-clad, bent-over widow like those dotting the streets everywhere. Certainly not a name suited to my character, my age, or my love of life. So then why was it that it had taken me this long to realize the name was almost exactly like mine as it was usually mispronounced?

The night was gradually pervading the apartment, but under the lightbulb I could clearly see that pronoun for what it is; I could interrogate it, dissect it. Everything was coming into focus now. Had I really thought, even for a second, that his mother was simply going to welcome me with open arms into their home for a traditional family Christmas, a Catholic holiday no less? The scene so implausible it could have been lifted from a bad Hollywood movie, a cheesy and even nauseating resolution. As if on cue, a wave of nausea thrust its way up my throat, but then again it could have just been the antiviral, which I'd taken without having read the contraindications.

Yes, it had been uncouth of Lidia to exclude her son's girlfriend right at Christmastime, given that our relationship was now official . . . in more ways than one. So in a certain sense, her rejection was actually a rejection of the expectations society put on her, a refusal to go along with that masquerade requiring her to use good manners and all the niceties. She was tired of pretending—and actually I was too. The absolute frankness of her gesture ended up giving me a strange sense of peace.

The nausea again: I hadn't imagined it. I ran up the stairs toward the bathroom, making it to the toilet bowl just in time. There must have been something in the pills I was intolerant to. Or was I meant to have taken them with food? I drank from the faucet before lowering myself onto the chilly tiles, trembling but relieved.

Out of sight, out of mind. Lidia was probably feeling quite pleased with herself right now that at their table decked with food there was just my ghost. But she was delusional if she thought this meant I would simply give up on her son and fly back to America. Again I had to lean over the toilet to expel nothing but the water I'd drunk. My throat was burning, my stomach was empty. I had nothing left to lose.

Surely it was a pitiful scene, me all alone on Christmas Eve vomiting my guts out. But instead of feeling sorry for myself as the zodiac expected me to, I felt almost happy. I'd relieved myself of a burden and now I was light, ready to start over. With or without a name, what Pietro and I had was unbreakable, a bond stronger than blood or bones. Together we were not merely the sum of one plus one but an exponential multiplication, a force greater than the two of us and mightier certainly than some third person who was tired and depressed and trying to get in the way.

As if the universe were confirming as much, in that very moment the phone rang. "It's hell here without you, baby," said Pietro, pierced with guilt at what he called his "weakness." No, I replied, he hadn't been weak. He had been right all along: his battle was mine, too, and we were going to fight it together. In fact, together we had an almost unfair advantage.

From: tectonic@tin.it
To: heddi@yahoo.com
Sent: June 16

Dear Heddi,

That really is great news. I'll be there in Naples, don't you worry. I'll come pick you up, whatever you need. Give me your dates as soon as you have them.

Getting your email did me a world of good, and I apologize that it's taken me this long to write back. Recently my life has been consumed by health problems. I haven't worked over the last few weeks: I've swapped one shithole (the Adriatic) for another (Monte San Rocco). I sustained a knee injury, the kind athletes are supposed to get, but the accident I had you see more often in old men. I won't go into it: it's too embarrassing.

Anyway, my knee kept on bothering me, or maybe it was just an excuse to get out of laboring in the middle of the sea and have some time to think about life . . . I'm always looking for excuses. So I decided to get myself seen by a doctor, hoping he'd write me a note saying I needed some time off . . . but no! He said I needed a "tiny little" operation. But from the very beginning I knew that something was amiss: I probably ended up in the wrong hands, in the hands of two characters who call themselves doctors but actually would be more suited to selling chestnuts on the street corners . . .

In any case I'm alive and kicking, despite the sweat trickling out from underneath the bandage. The warm weather makes me want to sleep all day long. Not exactly the period of reflection I thought it would be: it's more like moments of boredom alternating with moments of chilling out or feeling comfortably numb.

Today the big boss called me and, putting on a charming voice, asked me what my plans were for the near future. I said that slaving away out at sea is not for me, that I have (or at least I had) other ambitions, and he—

sounding now like a kid standing before an ice cream vendor—told me that it was never his intention to work me to death (a watery death!) and that he had other plans for me which he wanted to discuss with me personally. But I won't fall for it, I know his type: he called me only because he's in shit up to his neck and wants to convince me to stay on . . . but I'm not willing to sell myself for money. I'm happy doing nothing, at least for the time being, and anyway c'mon, man! I'm still young and I can come up with something better! I still have too much of the world to see.

Don't I?

p.

20

NEW YEAR'S EVE was a breach in time that didn't belong to the old year or the new one, a no-man's-land that wasn't subject to the usual laws. The house filled once more with pirates—from France, Sardinia, Sicily, Irpinia, America—who since the night before Christmas had been cutting notches into the wood of the dinner table, counting down hour by hour to this moment, this neighborhood. Thirty-three Via De Deo thus became a port, a melting pot, a night without a nation, without a history. Again everything became possible.

We went on a last-minute shopping quest, and we weren't alone. The stores stacked up our street were crammed with people stocking up as if for an air raid. To make better time, we split up. Sonia and Carlo went to the seafood shop; Angelo, Davide, and sister Silvia to the delicatessen; Madeleine and Gabriele to the bakery; while Pietro and I went to the fruit and vegetable grocer, the one who always managed to slip in a rotten apple or squashed tomato for good measure. He was constantly trying to pull a fast one on us, but we just let him because he looked like he could use the money.

"It's gonna be a good night for them fireworks," said the vendor, looking up at the fracture of clear sky between the buildings and handing me a bag of rather apologetic-looking escarole.

Apart from the escarole, I was pleased. That night in Piazza Plebiscito, across from the mountain of salt that had been installed with wooden horses poking out of it ("art" they called it), the city was putting on a free concert followed by a fireworks display. Why watch from the rooftops when we finally had a reason to get out into the streets?

"Careful, kids," the fruit vendor added. "After eleven o'clock it's nuts out there."

It was already eight thirty by the time we started preparing the big New Year's Eve meal. Even within our rebellion, there was an allegiance to the traditional southern Italian recipes. Tradition was alive in the mere fact that we had to eat in order to have a good time. But without food, how could we celebrate anything or disagree about anything or show one another our affection?

There was a great deal of slicing, sautéing, setting out plates and silverware. I'd been entrusted with the important job of making the lentils with pork cotechino, the consumption of which was apparently key to a good financial year. But because we were broke we had to forgo the meat, making up for it by adding a sprig of rosemary according to the recipe from Davide and Silvia's hometown. Through the open French doors I could see the terrace stretching out like a cold sigh, and beyond the protective wall the lights of houses clinging optimistically to the volcano. Gabriele came in from outside, a glass of red wine in hand, and sat down a bit unsteadily on the step to watch me cook.

"I might just put forward the idea we stay here all night talking. What do you say, Eddie, would I have your support?"

"And miss the fireworks?" Somewhere in the Quartieri a cheap firecracker, one of the many being let off over the last few days, made a well-timed entrance, a sizzle followed by an undignified death. "C'mon, it'll be fun to go out."

"All right," said Gabriele. "Whatever you wish, my dear sister-in-law."

From anyone else it would have sounded like mockery. But Gabriele wasn't just anyone, and that *dear sister-in-law* moved me. I felt certain in that instant that long, long after all the other noises had died out—the firecrackers popping, our friends laughing, their mother grumbling with discontent—there would still be the three of us. Him, Pietro, and me.

"Give me a kiss," he said.

I obeyed, leaning over to press my lips against Gabriele's cheek, sandpapery like Pietro's especially against the tender spot my cold sore had left behind. It was a big kiss, with my eyes closed, as if to forever seal that bond.

"Not that kind of kiss."

I pulled back as if burned by his words. For the very fragile instant that I was able to bear the weight of his gaze, in his eyes I saw the same rage I'd already seen aimed at Pietro, anger mixed with an almost unbearable love. But now that furious passion was directed at me, and god how it hurt, it burned much more than the steam rising off the pot of lentils that my eyes would very soon have to turn back to. Was I still trying to tell myself it was just the alcohol?

Alcohol or not, I was sure I was to blame. With that request for a kiss—a *real* kiss, there was no room for doubt—was he reproaching me for those intimate and fleeting instances of weakness where I'd nearly taken him for his brother? Was he trying to show me in my true light or question my decisions in love? I'd never wanted more than in that moment of accusation to finally tell Gabriele how much I cared about him. But there's no point in saying certain things. We cared for each other not like two friends but like two individuals thrown haplessly into the same family; ours was the naked and urgent affection of two castaways washed up on the same beach. I had a vague sense that it wasn't truly a kiss Gabriele wanted from me but an act that was just as real, just as risky. He wanted me to go deeper, perhaps to see something I wasn't seeing or do something I wasn't doing. *Stop fooling yourself*, I almost read in his eyes reddened with frustration and wine and sulfur that was coloring the night.

But before I could put my finger on what exactly it all may have meant, let alone reply, Silvia squeezed into the tiny kitchen to clean the fish and Gabriele stood up to go.

It was ten thirty by the time we finished dinner. The frequency of firecrackers was increasing, but to our ears it was just a lot of noise: popcorn, whistles, and occasionally thunder that made the glass jiggle in the window frames. The sky was a low ceiling as yellow as imitation sunlight in a zoo. Pietro lit a cigarette. He suggested we all stay put and watch the show from the safety of the terrace. Angelo and Silvia were fervently opposed, and Pietro was visibly irritated that it was Carlo who agreed with him the most.

"I've heard some stories, I tell you," Carlo said. "Third-degree burns, lost limbs, you name it."

The table went quiet.

But I must have won Gabriele over to my side, for he was the one who insisted, "Tall tales, no doubt, Carlo; the newspapers make a living off such stories. But in any case it would pay to make it to Piazza Plebiscito early so we get a decent view of the stage."

When we finally pulled the door behind us, our coat pockets hard with liquor, I was afraid to look at my watch. The stairs were abnormally dark. Perhaps our neighbors had gone out earlier or turned out their lights to better view the show. But there was nothing to see. The sky above our courtyard was a rectangle of flickering light as smoky as a forest fire pressing its way down toward us from the gardens of the monastery. It was not a display of fireworks but rather a concert of fireworks, with melodramatic rumblings, panicky falsetto, suspenseful silences. No wonder in Naples fireworks were called *botte*, "bangs" or "blows": they weren't dazzling sunflowers but punches, deafening slaps that rocked your head like a soccer ball and stung your eyes; they made you eat gunpowder and burnt plastic and made you sorry you'd ever left the house.

Gabriele was the first to step through the gate, with a sure and sober foot. I followed behind him, right away stepping on broken glass. A dinner plate. Covering our mouths with scarves or coat collars to keep from inhaling the malignant air, we began navigating toward Via Roma. It was an obstacle course of smoldering trash, gutted comforters, smashed furniture. Mysteries like green feathers or the jack of clubs stuck to our shoes. To move forward I looked for the black street slabs underneath it all.

It was the beginning of a fast, a detox. While we'd been eating dinner, the neighborhood was cleansing itself of all its broken and useless items with the fury that the undesirable deserved. Everything out over the balconies in an ecstatic collective regurgitation. Part of me wanted to stop and scavenge to uncover the slum's dirty secrets, but then a sudden peal of thunder shook the street and all its debris and us, too, as we were now an inextricable part of it. We were inside a snow globe that was being shaken with malicious delight; who knew what else might come falling down now. A series of firecrackers let off in our direction, sparks and all, sounded like a warning.

We quickened our pace. I looked up to see that our group had split up. I could no longer see Gabriele—or maybe that was him a few steps ahead of me, but it was hard to tell through my watering eyes. And yet I felt it was important for us not to lose each other. Pietro grabbed my hand; there was no talking, or even thinking, with the air hissing and splitting all around us.

Something landed in my hair, dissolving like ash between my fingers. Pietro yanked me hard to the other side of the street just as we heard what sounded like a car crash behind us. We spun on our heels to see a washing machine lying twisted on the street, still trembling after its brutal fall from a balcony. I could feel my eardrums ringing with that metallic thunder and Pietro's long, slender fingers seizing mine to the bone as we ran for cover under a first-floor balcony.

More items rained down, some in a great hurry, pieces of crockery perhaps, and others with an angelic serenity, like the pages of a notebook containing who knows what confessions. Pietro and I stood there in our shelter watching that perverse rain, erratic like all things Neapolitan. We were waiting it out, but it was a storm whose next move we couldn't predict. Our backs pressed against the damp, crumbling tuff of the building, I tried to remove the washing powder from my hair. Pietro said in my ear, "I understand 'out with the old, in with the new,' but these people are out of their minds!"

We spotted the others. Madeleine, Davide, Silvia, and Angelo were huddled under a balcony across the way. A bit farther ahead of us, hugging our very same building, were Gabriele, Sonia, and Carlo. Pietro and I tacitly decided to join them. We advanced along the building flattened and unarmed like war correspondents, our jackets rubbing against peeling posters and the barricaded door of an evacuated *vascio*. One foot before the other, we managed to reach them in one piece. Under their balcony Sonia was somewhat hunched over as though her height might make her particularly vulnerable.

"Let's turn back, guys!" Carlo's voice joined the cacophony.

Now, I thought, after we'd come this far? I turned to look behind me. In reality we'd only progressed *one block*, and now the building protecting us came abruptly to an end in a cross street.

"At this point we should just keep going, don't you think?" said Sonia.

Carlo was scanning our faces for consensus. "What, you guys want to cross this?" he yelled.

The alleyway was reverberating and trembling with explosions, with fiery droplets ricocheting between the buildings, a cross fire we'd have to get through if we ever wanted to get out of the Spanish Quarter and into the piazza. I wasn't so sure I wanted to anymore.

Pietro said, "We don't have a choice. Let's turn around."

I looked over at Gabriele, his chest heaving and his back pressed hard against the plaster, and yet he had a smile on his face and a glint in his eyes. Was he excited by our foolhardiness or was he still feeling the wine? Then there was a moment of relative quiet and in that lull Gabriele barked, "Let's go!," a strict order that tolerated no dissension or hesitation or even contemplation, a call to an instinct that we'd assumed was long forgotten.

We ran for it. We ran under the open sky covering our heads with our bare hands, losing sight of one another. I ran and I couldn't see anyone in front of me or behind me; I could only see my own feet pounding the devastated yet still traceable cobblestones. Pietro's grip had come undone: I'd lost his hand, I'd lost him. But the blasts wiped away all emotion and I ran as if my life depended on it.

At the other side we all gathered under another balcony, thrilled and breathless. If we could make it across that side street, then we could make it the three or four remaining blocks to the relative safety of Via Roma. Across from us Angelo, Madeleine, Davide, and his sister had made it, too: in fact they were already running up ahead. So again we darted, running individually, blindly, euphorically, street after street until the broken dishes and charred garbage gave way to dead firecrackers and bottles of Heineken, signs of a younger, tamer party.

"I told you we should have left earlier," said Carlo, putting Sonia into an affectionate headlock. "Those barbarians nearly got us killed."

"It was actually kind of cool," she said.

"Cool? It was awesome!" shouted Angelo, and Davide howled.

Silvia was laughing, everyone was laughing, even Carlo. Our cheeks were rosy from the adrenaline: the only one who'd lost his color was Pietro. He lifted up the collar of his jacket and shoved his hands into its pockets. He called the whole expedition "training for the Secret Service" and pulled out a Marlboro Light before turning his back to us and heading in the direction of the piazza.

His seriousness struck me. Pietro suddenly seemed like the only responsible adult among us, the only one aware of danger and loss. He had real obligations—he was a landowner, for goodness' sake—and to him this was no game. I quit laughing. Thunderstorms and vipers had already well earned my respect. Funny then how I'd never really considered the possibility that Naples, too, by just trying to scare the pants off us, might end up harming us. I may have been naïve.

The concert in Piazza Plebiscito was in full swing, but no one appeared to be listening to the pop music blasting them from the stage: the audience was buzzing with laughter, cell phones, beer, joints, and plenty of dialect. It was as packed as a wardrobe, and as we squeezed through the wool coats and sheepskin jackets we inadvertently brushed against gelled hair and costume jewelry. If this too was part of the urban renewal, well then maybe it was having a bit too much success. We found a spot under one of the equestrian statues.

"King Charles III of Spain," Gabriele illuminated us.

Pietro asked, "Is he the guy you're named after?" but Carlo didn't hear him.

Angelo and Silvia were deep in conversation. Madeleine smoked solemnly as she looked off into the crowd: perhaps she and Saverio had fought again. She didn't notice Davide staring at her as if dumbstruck by her beauty, or maybe she did notice but she'd become numb to those looks. Pietro took a bottle of whiskey from his pocket and passed it around. Carlo had Sonia locked in his arms as though he was afraid to lose her in the crowd, but she didn't seem to mind: she smiled her moon smile, her night-black hair parted down the middle.

The lead singer announced it was nearly midnight.

"About time," Carlo said, his breath hanging in the air. "Who brought the Moët et Chandon?"

"Yeah, right!" said Angelo, pulling out a cheap bottle of bubbly. "Let's toast to our survival!"

Gabriele, on the other hand, was uncorking a bottle of the family's wine, muttering something about old habits. The band members had quit playing, and behind them you could once more hear the Spanish Quarter in its mad rush to self-destruct. The crowd in the square began counting down, lighting sparklers and firecrackers, opening bottles. *Eight, seven, six* . . . Angelo was grappling with the "fucking wire cage" around the cork and in the meantime the crowd had made it to *one*, at which a triumphant roar muffled a string of Sicilian curses and the already blazing sky swelled with color.

New Year's usually put me in low spirits. I couldn't understand why everyone was so eager to celebrate the death of an entire year of life: Didn't it deserve to be remembered, to be mourned? But I didn't feel that way now. The piazza was being showered with sparks and best wishes and disposable champagne, and I had the sense I was at the epicenter of it all, surrounded by some of the people I loved most on the planet.

Pietro came close, pressing his stubble against my forehead and warming my face with his distilled breath. I wrapped my arms around his neck, and together we created a hot and humid space all our own, a tropical island far from the popping and the whooping.

"This is the happiest New Year of my life, Pietro."

"This is going to be our year, my love. We'll finish our studies and then we'll leave. We'll hop from one country to the next until we find a place we want to put down roots."

"Yes, roots. I want to do it with you."

I felt Pietro's fingers under my coat, creeping up my back and clinging to my ribs. "I let you down at Christmas," he said. "I didn't stand up for you, I betrayed your trust. I was such an idiot. I even asked *you* to save *me*. Can you ever forgive me?"

"I was weak, too, Pietro. Never again. From now on we're going to face every obstacle together."

"It's an understatement to say that I love you. You're pure oxygen to me." He squeezed his eyes shut. "I was miserable when we were apart over Christmas. And the whole time I had the strangest feeling, like I was under water just holding my breath and looking up toward the light. But I was comforted by the fact that soon I would be able to see you again, to come up for air. Do you know what I mean?" He looked me square in the eyes. "Heddi, I promise that from now on I won't let other people walk all over me. I'm going to stand up for our love, whatever the cost."

What do you need stars for when the sky is twinkling with emeralds and rubies? Pietro and I kissed like only lovers do on New Year's. His whiskey warmed my mouth with its candid, full-bodied heat, a liquid sunrise that spread out through my chest and between my legs, on its way down loosening the bolts of my knees and thawing my feet. So much love. Did we really have to walk all the way back along that ravaged road to be finally wrapped around each other in bed?

A cold bottle pressed against my arm. "Stop snogging, you two," said Angelo, passing me the champagne with a smile. "It's New Year's. You have to kiss everyone, remember?"

I took a swig and wished everyone a happy new year. I purposely left Gabriele last: I just didn't feel ready, with Pietro's kiss a candy still melting in my mouth. Gabriele, however, grabbed me the way he usually did, like an uncle I hadn't seen in years, an embrace without undertones or ambiguity of any kind. He seemed to have sobered up and forgotten all about what had happened in the kitchen, if anything had actually happened at all.

We broke apart. Gabriele began telling Madeleine about the church before us that was reminiscent of the Pantheon in Rome. I felt like having a chat with Sonia: we'd had so little time together that evening. And there she was, freed from Carlo's hold and standing more elongated now, proud as a ballerina. Pietro was at her side, laughing in that soundless way of his, a silence I recognized even amid the commotion in the square. He looked so relaxed, so lighthearted, no longer a grown-up landowner but a carefree boy. I wished I'd been the one to make him laugh like that, with such spontaneity and transparency. That I'd been the one to have come out with a pun, a witty saying, or an astute observation about the humanity around us. The one to have lifted a weight off him and made his face light up.

I was on the verge of formulating some sort of New Year's resolution, but then I thought the better of it. We already had several new promises to keep and those alone, without counting our exams and theses, would sap most of our energy.

The bubbly was all gone, the whiskey too. As we headed back toward the Quartieri, Angelo's eyelids were heavy and Madeleine was singing to herself in French, teetering like a drunken sailor. Only Pietro looked as sober as morning.

The last few firecrackers were like the sputtering of an old car taking its final breaths, and this time when we turned up Via De Deo there was no need to take shelter. Our neighborhood looked like it had been through a war, and it wasn't clear yet if it had come out the victor or the loser. We might as well have been the sole survivors as we stepped through the rubble in a ghostly calm. A dog scuttled past us, limping.

"Poor thing," I said. "He looks injured."

"A stray, I bet."

I noticed Pietro's Marlboro quiver between his fingers, the streetlights of the Spanish Quarter lending him an unusual pallor. As soon as we walked back into our apartment, he flew up the stairs two at a time. I heard him cough and raced after him. I found him in the bathroom in the exact same position I'd been not long ago, kneeling on the tiles, hands clutching the toilet seat and dark curls falling over his face. He hadn't betrayed even an instant of drunkenness all night. But still, how could I not have noticed how much alcohol he'd been putting back?

He retched again and then let out a little moan, his forearms shaking from the effort of grasping the rim. It shook me to see him so vulnerable. Kneeling beside him, I placed my hand under his forehead. I wasn't sure why I did this except that it might somehow keep his head up, and through his heavy breathing I did feel that he rested some of the weight of his forehead into my palm. Again he vomited.

"It's OK," I tried to reassure him.

He shook his head and found the strength to say in an echoey voice, "Leave me." Again he coughed. "Go. I don't want you to see me like this. Go!"

I pulled my hand away, hot with his shame. I too was ashamed, of trying to help when he didn't need me. I walked out but lingered in the hallway, in case he fell. I heard a flush, followed by running water. Shortly thereafter Pietro came staggering out and crumpled onto our bed fully clothed. He probably would have slept like that till morning had I not removed his shoes and jeans.

21

I STOPPED TO ROLL UP my pant legs; my boots, I could see, were coated in the finest dust. There were no trees, no shade at all; the sky was a piece of blue construction paper with the occasional scribble of a cloud. The dry air was odorless, but it brought that dust with it, that taste of the volcano. Maybe it was summer, it was hard to say: although the sun was beating down, nearly blinding me, I couldn't feel its heat.

It felt like I'd been walking for hours and hours, yet the top was still far from my reach. I was on a geological expedition (I had to be: I was carrying a prospecting pick), but I had no idea what I was looking for. All I knew was that I had to keep going onward and upward, higher and higher, until I could stand on the edge of that giant bowl carved by the giants, or by the gods, and look into its depths. I was determined to reach it even if it took me all night. As if I were heading there to meet my beloved, the passing hours and the grueling hike didn't weigh on me. So then why was my immense desire tainted with an unspeakable fear?

Step after step the details came back. I remembered that earlier I hadn't been alone: I'd been hiking up the volcano with other people, a team of anthropologists and linguists. It had become a geological mission only after the others had decided to turn back. They'd learned that Vesuvius was about to blow, for the first time since that minor eruption during the Second World War, but this time it was going to be a big one, the one everyone had been fearing—and secretly hoping for. And yet I still kept making my way toward the top because, I figured, what could possibly go wrong on such a beautiful day?

All at once the sky went dark and the wind picked up, so strong it seized the pick out of my hand. The bad weather was here: the blue sky was a sham, the sun a big fat lie. And I'd fallen for it. I started back down the path. Little rocks at my feet began hopping about like they too were trying to hurry down the mountain, even though by now it was clear to us all how very futile it was. I could already feel the warm breath of the ash behind me as I raced down the incline, but I was too afraid to turn around and look straight at that heartless cloud swelling and thundering toward me and about to swallow me whole. It was nothing personal, though: I was just collateral damage, a random victim, a minor personal tragedy.

Like hands on my shoulders, the cloud gave me a shove that detached my feet from the steep terrain. I closed my eyes and fell into the void. I was falling for such a long time in such complete darkness that I even had time to cry. I had no fear of dying, only the certainty of it. The only thing that scared me, actually it terrified me, was the moment of physical pain I would feel on impact with the ground. So as I plunged through the abyss, whose bottom I would soon hit, I twisted my body, struggling not against death but against the inevitability of pain.

The pain awoke me with a jolt. My back was arched like a bridge, the muscles seized up: it hadn't happened since I was little. Pietro was asleep by my side, his shirt badly wrinkled. Relaxing my spine, I propped myself up on my elbows to look out the window.

It must have rained overnight. The buildings tumbling down to the port were a shade darker, the color of drenched stone. The sky was quilted in clouds so laden they might douse us again any minute. And against that dark background the volcano lay dormant and clad in snow.

It wasn't just a sprinkling: Vesuvius was covered in snow as I'd rarely seen it in all my years in and around Naples. The rough features of its peak were wrapped in a dazzling-white royal cloak, perhaps the true source of the soft winter light suffusing the city. Within that dim landscape it was in fact the only sun, the only god. I couldn't keep my eyes off it. It looked like a painting of Mount Fuji, like the one printed on a handkerchief I'd once owned, but in the flesh our volcano was far more impressive. It was majestic and fearsome. The more I looked at it, the more I realized it might only be pretending to sleep.

A chill snaked down my spine. I got back under the covers, moving in close to Pietro. I was hoping to wake him, but he was out cold and—I could see now catching a glimpse of the radio alarm clock—it was sinfully early to wake him on the first day of the year. I got up, put on a sweater, and went downstairs.

Madeleine looked like she'd been waiting for me. In skimpy pajamas, she sat as if in a trance before the chaos of the abandoned table; her legs crossed, she was kicking her Japanese flip-flop to a song only she could hear. In the semidarkness her face resembled an old photograph, blurred further by the smoke of a neglected cigarette.

"This is the part I hate," she said.

"What part?"

Madeleine remembered her cigarette and inhaled through it meaningfully. "The next day."

I asked her why she was up so early. Apparently the neighbors had woken her up again. I hadn't heard a thing, just as she hadn't seen the snow on Vesuvius. Her reaction was, "Snow, *merde*. Wasn't Naples supposed to be sunshine, sea, and pizza?" She let out a forced laugh before turning on the radio.

The kitchen was a hideous sight of crusty plates and fish tails on oily newspaper, and all I could cope with was salvaging the coffee machine. Making coffee was a ritual I found comforting. I used the hard water from the tap, said to be the secret to Neapolitan coffee, and pressed down delicately on the grinds while listening distractedly to the Luca Carboni song over the radio. For a long time I stood there watching the hissing blue flame. I couldn't see Madeleine from there but I could feel her heavy presence, her bad start to the day, her desire to say more—much more.

"Last night was crazy," came her voice from the living room.

"Was it?" I opened the fridge. We were out of milk.

"We were big idiots, Eddie. It was like a war out there."

I came in, adding our steaming coffees to the clutter of the table, where Madeleine proceeded to pierce me with her gaze until the guilt set in, as though it had been my idea to go out into the streets. Yet I wasn't sure she was really talking about last night. I sensed that a little game had started between us, a game that wasn't new to me but to which I didn't know the rules, or even the purpose.

"It's just another one of those silly things not to tell your parents about, Madeleine. Nothing bad happened in the end."

"It was chance. We won at the roulette. But it could have been a catastrophe."

I wished she would just drop it. I didn't want to be forced to think about the homeless priest and the mysterious *catastrof* that had cut him in half. Nevertheless, Madeleine's words started to dig into me like that coffee on an empty stomach. Could it really all be just a gamble, simply a matter of good or bad luck? But not wanting to concede anything to her, I said, "Well, once the garbage collectors have gone through, the neighborhood will go back to the way it was before."

"But even before it sucked. A sucking fucking labyrinth."

"It's not a labyrinth, Madeleine. The Spanish Quarter has a predictable, mathematical layout," I said, not wanting so much to contradict her at this point as to engage her in any sort of academic discussion. "It's just a grid. Isn't that what it's called in urban planning?"

"Grid. A network of streets crossing one another at right angles according to the urban planimetry typical of Roman cities and some eighteenth-century settlements," she said dryly. "Thirty points *cum laude*." Her cup came to rest with a clunk. "So really, Eddie, you have never got lost in the Spanish Quarter?"

"No."

She drew another cigarette from her pack. I couldn't tell if, by accepting my half lie, she'd let me win or not. I finished my coffee, too, grasping that the game we were playing had something, if not everything, to do with my own pride.

Madeleine smoked, the house slept, the radio filled the silence. I was trying to remember the legend of the classical labyrinth, in Knossos, that my Greek professor had taught me during my first year of high school in Castellammare. If I remembered correctly, King Minos of Crete demanded of the Athenian king a yearly tribute of fourteen youths, seven young women and seven young men, to be let loose in a maze so intricate it had imprisoned its own architect, Daedalus. It was a warren of passageways that twisted and turned, forking off into multiple choices, leading to dead ends—all through almost pitch blackness. At the heart of the labyrinth lived the bloodthirsty Minotaur, half man and half bull, who devoured the youths one by one as they became lost. It was the stuff of nightmares. Finally, the monster was slain by Theseus, son of the king of Athens, whom Minos's daughter had fallen hopelessly in love with. Ariadne, that was her name, had given him a ball of string to roll out so that he could feel his way back out of the maze. Afterward, despite her act of love, Theseus didn't take the princess back to Athens with him, abandoning her instead on an island where they'd stopped to rest during the return voyage. He lifted anchor while she was sleeping.

Maybe Madeleine too was lost in such thoughts, for she said, as if to settle the matter once and for all, "Better a labyrinth than a grid."

"Really?"

"Yes, really. Because in a grid all the streets look the same. So you think you're on the right path and then you suddenly understand that, oh shit, you are lost."

That foot started kicking again, completely out of sync with the new song playing on the radio, and with more vigor than ever. Rage was becoming on Madeleine: it wiped the slate clean, revealing her breathtaking, primordial beauty that made me feel, if not ugly, decidedly average. With that cigarette she seemed to be sucking back unutterable thoughts.

"Eddie, tell me. Why are you here in Naples, in this shithole?"

"It's a long story, Madeleine."

"To learn about a few stupid buildings? To meet some boy and then go back home?"

It took me a moment to understand she was talking about herself. I said, "You can always come back."

"Sure I can," said Madeleine with a mocking grimace, threatening then to wake the entire household by belting out half the chorus to "Torna a Surriento." But maybe it was a mistake to fish out from Naples's deep past such an emotionally charged song, for her sarcasm turned against her, twisting the corners of her mouth and wetting her eyes. "No, no," she said, shaking her head. "It was always supposed to be a short time. Just a parenthesis and then I go back to my life. And back to my French boyfriend."

I'd lived in Naples too long to be shocked by infidelity. However, I'd always considered it an ill of the older generations, and the fact that a young intellectual woman, a foreigner no less, could cheat on or alternate lovers further complicated the picture I had of Madeleine.

"Soon I have to leave," she struggled to say. "But what will I do? I don't know who I am anymore. I even don't remember how to speak French."

Everything about her moved me, against my will—her defeated tone, her glistening eyes—but all I could offer her were a few measly words. "It's not the end, Madeleine . . ."

"Don't you get it, Eddie? I have lost myself!"

I thought she was angry with me, but then the tears broke loose, big and shiny like drops of mercury. She seemed oblivious to them and unashamed, as though they were not her tears at all but raindrops fallen from the sky. She didn't even try to dry them. The game was over, and she'd won. And yet all she could say over and over again was how *lost* she was.

I wasn't involved enough in her Neapolitan life or her relationship with Saverio to understand exactly what she was referring to with that Gallicism *I have lost myself*. To my ear, it sounded like nothing more than the rambling of someone who was hungover, overtired, or hypothermic. At the same time I sensed that that phrase, purified by the tears and the cheap champagne, was the truest of truths and thus made perfect sense and that I was the one who failed to understand it because of its simplicity, because there was no ulterior motive behind it other than to be whispered like a mantra. She was sobbing and I was just sitting there watching her, unable to sympathize or act in any way.

"Wait one moment!" said Madeleine all at once, cranking up the volume on the radio. "Yes, it's that song! Remember it?" She sprung up, her flip-flops smacking the floor, her hips swaying to a samba. It was "Joe Le Taxi" and Madeleine was singing it in a voice no less captivating than that of Vanessa Paradis eternally stuck at fourteen, raising her arms to the ceiling and twirling them like a belly dancer. I was mesmerized as I listened to her sing in her mother tongue, which made her more sensual than ever, until she reached those arms out to pull me up. "Come, dance with me!"

I danced half-heartedly and ungracefully, my body suddenly heavy with sleep deprivation. But I couldn't let her dance alone, not the first day of the year with tears drying like fresh paint on her cheeks. When the song faded out, Madeleine flashed me a smile that felt like a personal compliment. She draped her arms around my neck, enveloping me in her scent (she didn't smell of alcohol at all but milk), and saying, "One day you must come visit me. Me and you in Marseilles!"

For a moment I was deeply flattered, but I resisted the temptation. Only in theory were we alike—both the same age, far from home, with an academic streak—but the similarities ended there. I wasn't endowed with her magnetic beauty, like that of a falling star, nor her fickleness, and for the rest of my life I wouldn't be able to love another man. Maybe these were shortcomings, maybe they weren't. So if I squeezed her tight right then, it was only to rush the embrace to its natural conclusion. I was going back to bed, I told her, adding that she ought to put on a sweater because with that T-shirt and this cold she could easily catch something.

"Joe Le Taxi" hadn't had the least effect on Pietro, who was still asleep half-dressed in the fetal position. I slipped under the blankets and cuddled up to him. This time he woke up, telling me to bring my cold feet closer. I told him about the snow on the volcano, although he didn't feel like turning around to see it for himself, and I told him about my dream, feelings so sharp I began to wonder in my sleepiness whether the eruption of Vesuvius had been real after all and the strange, chimerical conversation with Madeleine was just something I'd dreamed up.

"Do you believe in prophetic dreams?" I asked him.

"Look, baby, when that pimple blows, we'll be long gone from this squalor, I guarantee you that. It was just a dream, that's all."

Feeling reassured, I said, "Then let's play the numbers." It was a joke, of course: we wouldn't have been caught dead with a copy of *La Smorfia*, the traditional Neapolitan book associating dream events with lucky numbers to be played in the lottery.

"Yeah, right. Feeling afraid, number ninety."

"A disaster, seventeen."

"We're going to get rich." He brought my hand to his lips and kissed my fingers. "Anyway, apparently we're all good for the time being, since San Gennaro's congealed blood melted again recently. It's a miracle, a miracle!"

His dry tone filled me with shame: in truth, that dark religious rite fascinated me. "And what happens if one time it doesn't melt?"

"A calamity, according to these troglodytes. Every time it didn't liquefy when it was meant to and then afterward some sort of disaster occurred, they used hindsight to connect the two events. And they call it science."

"Like what kind of disaster?"

"Like the earthquake in Irpinia."

I pressed my face into the chain of his spine. Suddenly overcome by an unbearable adoration, I closed my eyes to breathe in his smell of forest and sweat. That was when I experienced something of an out-of-body experience. As in a bird's-eye—or a pigeon's-eye—view, I could see myself and Pietro from above.

I could see us lying curled up on a mattress on the floor. It wasn't a room we were in after all but a glorified closet, and it wasn't a real house we lived in but an illegal floor, one of the many in an infinity of illegal floors building a tower of Babel as they raced each other up to Saint Elmo's Castle, if not to the low-lying clouds themselves. And seeing it from above, our neighborhood indeed proved itself to be a labyrinth, a series of identical alleyways and dead ends, many one-way streets and only one way out, all buried by last night's festive violence, which, even if it did get swept up, would return sooner or later. The volcano could see all this from its throne but would neither confirm nor deny. I was amazed to discover from that great height that the land encircling the bay resembled an enormous mouth, a Pac-Man trying to gobble up the islands, and from higher up still I could see the basin of the Mediterranean and all Eurasia and then the entire Earth that only looked like a stationary globe but in reality was at the mercy of a dizzying logic.

For Pietro and me it was now the first of January, but elsewhere in the world, in Sydney or Beijing or Hong Kong, people were already welcoming the first few hours of the second day of the year, the first few hours of tomorrow. I wondered what was happening in this place called tomorrow. Great things for sure, I thought, wonderful and modern and important especially in their vagueness. Whatever these great things were, in that moment I realized that I was missing out on them and in fact I'd missed out on them for years. Hundreds and thousands of lost tomorrows, of wasted opportunities. I felt a stab of misery, a sensation of intolerable immobility, a sense of loss there was no remedy for. In Naples we were always a step behind, incurably trapped in yesterday with its old magic and blood science. What the hell was I still doing there?

I recognized that my pride was the very reason why I would never win that confusing chess game with Madeleine, whose moves were glances and double entendres. She was rubbing in the fact that after that first exchange year I'd decided to stay on in Naples, this *shithole* that made people lose their bearings and overwhelmed them with conflicting emotions. For her Naples was an unlucky roll of the dice, an unsuccessful spin of the roulette wheel. She was thus forcing me to defend my choice, to justify my entire adolescence and young adulthood spent there, *a third of my life*, and the fact that I couldn't give her a good answer made me resentful. Because now, from above, I could see Naples for how the rest of the world saw it. Not dangerous, inappropriate, or maddeningly beautiful, but simply fallen behind, left in the dust. Gone. Forgotten.

I opened my eyes with a start. I'd been teetering on the razor's edge between wakefulness and the daily delirium of sleep. Pietro asked me if I was still awake: he wanted to know if I felt like making another trip to Monte San Rocco. The cold weather had arrived and soon it would be time to kill the pig.

From: heddi@yahoo.com
To: tectonic@tin.it
Sent: June 21

Dear Pietro,

Sorry to hear about your knee (although I enjoyed your colorful descriptions of the characters in your story). I hope you'll have more or less recovered by August, physically but also to some degree psychologically. I don't know what to expect when I see you, I don't want to have expectations: maybe it's a good thing that lately I've been too busy to think about it . . .

I leave for the States on July 22nd and then I fly to Milan on August 6th. I've already been in touch with Luca and we've arranged to meet at Lago Maggiore, where he's restoring an old farmhouse he bought. After the wedding, I'm meeting up with a Kiwi friend of mine who moved to London a year ago: we'll do some traveling around Italy together. I should be in Naples by August 18th. So you and I can see each other on the 20th, if that works for you. Could you come pick me up at Rita's house, maybe in the morning? That way we could have the whole day together. In case you don't remember it, here's the address: 47 Traversa Fondo D'Orto, at the far end of Castellammare, near Pompeii.

I hope the date won't mess things up for you at work, but it would be good to see you. In all honesty, I'll be terribly disappointed if we don't manage to catch up. Would you mind telling Gabriele, too, wherever he is? Or maybe you could just give him my email address. It would be good to see him again if possible.

Sorry for the short email. I'm juggling a lot of things these days; plus, it's late and I still have homework to check . . .

Hugs,

h.

22

W HEN WE ARRIVED, the pig had already been slaughtered. It was the quiet after the storm. As we pulled our bags out of Francesco's car and waved him goodbye, the animal came into sight, cut in half lengthwise and hanging from its foot on the terrace. More than a pig, it was a cross section, a sawn-off slice for a biology class, not a real pig but an abstract one. Nevertheless, I felt ashamed for that animal that I had never known alive but that now hung before me in such an immodest position, legs spread wide and its most intimate details on display.

The sun came through the skeletal trees, dappling and striping the exterior of the house in a colorless, but not joyless, light. Standing around a worktable was a gathering of elderly men and women dressed in burly sweaters, sleeves rolled up. They were chopping. Their hands were huge and reddened, with cracked nails and calluses, the hands of the giant who chased Jack back down his beanstalk. As the old folks talked and laughed in the cold, steam came out of their toothless mouths and off the flesh of the animal still warm on the table. It was the picture of village life that I had always imagined, the place that Monte San Rocco should have been and might still be, as hectic and picturesque as one of those miniature nativity scenes you could purchase in Naples.

They spotted Pietro and called him to them, big smiles making apples of their cheeks. As we passed them on our way to the front door, Pietro nodded respectfully several times. I had the impression that he knew each and every one of them; he was probably even related to a few. Then they went back to work, lowering their large butcher knives and tossing filaments of fat like socks into a laundry pile.

Inside, the house smelled of burnt wood. Goose bumps traveled along my arms and over my breasts, not only from the damp and chalky cold seeping out of the walls, but also from the gall of showing up uninvited in Lidia's kitchen. But no one was there to greet us: the kitchen was for once empty. The fireplace was a box of ashes; two coffee cups sat discarded in the sink. His parents were most likely somewhere outside, also, too busy butchering to have even noticed us arrive.

"This is great," I said. "Everybody working together like one big family."

"You see?" Pietro broke an edge off a block of hard cheese on the table and ate it. "They'll be working till evening to finish making the capocollo, the sausages, all that stuff. It all has to be done in one day, otherwise the meat will go bad."

I sat down and rested my feet, almost comfortably, on the slate of that fireplace I'd gotten to know so well. I let out a sigh of gratitude. The volunteer butchers would be there till sundown, drowning out the silence and making it easier to say what we needed to say to Lidia. Besides, there would now be an entire driveway of witnesses to the fact that Pietro and I were a couple. It would become public throughout the whole town and his mother wouldn't be able to deny it anymore. She would be defeated by all the life going on around her, in spite of her.

Settling down beside me, Pietro peeled off his jacket. "I hope it wasn't too bad for you, seeing the pig like that."

"I didn't even know his name."

"It didn't have a name. It was just Pig."

He broke off another piece of cheese and fed it to me. I was hungry, and eating that aged cheese, which tasted of a quiet patience that gradually intensified until it burst with flavor, was almost as enjoyable as

Pietro's loving gesture. He told me we were lucky to have arrived after they'd killed the beast, not because of the bloody mess it made but rather because of the noise. The pig, he explained, knows when it's about to be killed, even before any axes or shotguns have been readied, and it starts to yelp, to cry like a child, and it doesn't stop until the very end. Many locals slaughtered their pigs on the same day, so all throughout the village bloodcurdling screams could be heard from dawn. "You wake up to that, you never forget it," he concluded, visibly amused by the effect his story was having on me. Again he brought a piece of cheese to my lips.

How could a pig know when it was going to die? It was a true mystery. Maybe all pigs of all times carried that knowledge, like some kind of ancestral memory, in their blood.

"*Buongiorno*," came a feeble voice behind us.

We stood to attention. Pietro's mother forged a smile as she held out her hand, a lackluster invitation for me to come closer. It found this odd: I'd expected Lidia to greet me with open hostility. After what had happened at Christmas, what point was there in continuing to pretend? Yet there she was, extending a hand with the same polite ceremony as always. I took it and drew in close, hoping that my barefaced, flesh-and-blood presence there in Monte San Rocco would catch her off guard and that my kiss would be brazen enough to mark her exterior with an *x*, like you do with chestnuts in order to shell them.

That forced smile sank as she turned to Pietro. "Boy, go get some more wood, it's cold in here for her," she said in their dialect, adding that lunch would be ready in an hour. I acknowledged her dogged use of the third person singular, but this time it was merely a semiological observation that might come in handy for my thesis.

His mother left. Pietro went to the woodpile outside the front door and returned cradling logs and small branches. I gave him a hand with the kindling. Silently absorbed in that domestic chore, now and then Pietro and I exchanged a smile of complicity. We lit the fire and I leaned in close to the newborn flames, their little but energetic heat spreading pleasantly over my face. Pietro had stood up but not gone far: I could feel the warmth of his tall body standing behind my chair, an olive tree watching over me.

After a while he asked if I wanted to go outside to see how the meat was prepared. The fire had warmed me to the bone, and outside I couldn't feel the cold. Now at the head of the long wooden table pink with blood was Pietro's father, who was laughing at full volume and inspecting through thick lenses the various slabs of flesh arranged into puzzling piles. The air was rich with the creamy smell of raw meat and the dull thuds of knives, which the old folks seemed to have a longtime friendship with. They lowered the blades with blind faith, moving their fingers away just in the nick of time.

I followed Pietro as he made his way around the table. He was gregarious and courteous with everyone. At one point he stopped to talk with an elderly woman whose hair was still jet-black. He asked her questions I couldn't understand, about bones and entrails, before introducing us. I liked her straightaway for her name alone: Aunt Libertà.

"Hello, darling," she said, "I'd kiss you but I'm a mess." There was indeed a streak of pig blood across her temple. Nonetheless, she was a very attractive woman with that impossibly black hair, lily-white skin, and rosebud mouth. "Bring her with you to my house tomorrow, you hear, Pie'?" she added to Pietro in dialect, while looking at me with eyes that shone with an instinctive hospitality.

"We'll see if there's time, *ʒia*. We'll see," he said continuing around the table.

I spotted Lidia alone in the ground-floor apartment, which opened up onto the driveway. She was stirring something inside a huge pot placed directly on top of sticks burning away on the concrete floor. I found it baffling that she would choose to cook in such a makeshift way when she had not only an old range beside her but also a perfectly functional gas stove upstairs. She didn't seem to be cooking so much as punishing herself. Surrounded by jars of pickled vegetables, sacks of potatoes, sticks and ashes, she wore a gloomy expression as she carried out the work she'd probably had to do her whole life.

Feeling bold after Libertà's kind words, I stepped a few feet over the gravel until I was standing in the open doorway. "Hello, *signora*. What are you making?"

"A dish we make when we kill the pig," replied Lidia without looking up from the simmering pot.

"What's in it?" I asked. It was a hard habit to break, trying to ingratiate myself, to show her I was capable and eager to learn, to prove to her in that old-school way that I deserved her son.

"It's nothing much. Pork, potatoes, peppers. It's made with a part of the pig that people today don't like so much."

"What part is it?"

"I don't know," she said, surely meaning she didn't know the word for it in Italian but didn't wish to say it in dialect. "We eat it because we don't waste anything. It's not that nice meat you find in the butcher shops in Naples."

"Well, it smells great."

"It's nothing special." As if to signal it was time for me to go, she set down her wooden spoon and dried her hands in the worn folds of her apron. I heard a couple of branches snap underneath the pot as I walked away.

It wasn't long before lunch was served. The old folks came inside, into the formal dining room I'd never eaten in. The television was off. Heading the table was Pietro's father, and on one side sat the men, caps still on, and on the other side sat the women in their kerchiefs. Everybody was starving, so without further ado Lidia's stew was dished out. The women's gold earrings swung to the rhythm of their jaws as they chewed their way through the mysterious meat. The men, too, ate with gusto and noise, eagerly accepting another helping and, with just as much gusto and noise, discussing farm equipment and money. That cheerful ruckus, exclusively in dialect, was loud enough to shake the crystal glasses in the display cabinets, and the butchers' thirst great enough to empty four or five bottles of wine in no time.

Pietro's mother sat across from me, ostensibly focused on passing bread or wine around the table but with a watchful eye on my bowl, measuring my progress. It was the same sour look as always, only now amid the merrymaking it seemed to lose its strength, and in fact it reminded me of the weary supervision of a card dealer during a long and rowdy poker game. Despite not having worked alongside the others, I felt a part of something. Now and then Pietro's ebony-haired aunt would smile my way, while his father was nearly in stitches with laughter. Incredibly, under the tablecloth Pietro's hand came to rest on my leg. Just as I'd thought, the joy toned down the hostess's discontent.

One of the men, with an unshaven white chin, asked Pietro a question that I didn't catch. Pietro answered, something about his thesis, and then I distinctly heard him say that he would be graduating soon. A few of the others overheard those magic words and cheered: a son of their village was going to be a *dottore*! Someone asked about Gabriele, and Pietro filled him in in a few brief words, sighing with paternal disappointment and for some reason tightening his grip on my thigh.

"What about this pretty little thing here?" asked a heavyset woman, indicating me with a flick of the chin.

"She's majoring in languages and I guarantee you she'll finish before me," replied Pietro, winking at me and adding, for my benefit in Italian, "She's extraordinarily intelligent."

The man with the white stubble asked him, I think, when we were heading back to the city, and Pietro's answer was "the day after tomorrow." When an old woman then asked how many hours it took to drive to Naples, Pietro seemed ashamed to admit that we would be taking the bus.

"But it's faster by car," the lady insisted, clearly not understanding that Pietro didn't own a car. When she finally figured it out, she said, "Doesn't matter, Pie', when you get that degree they'll go give you one."

For no apparent reason, the old folks all started laughing. I recalled how astonished and envious Pietro looked when he first saw that Francesco, who hadn't even graduated yet, had been given a brand-new car. Was buying sons a car upon graduation, or close enough, some sort of modern-day village tradition?

One of the men asked him what kind of car he was eyeing up.

"A Ferrari!" replied another to the whole table, which was looking for any old reason to laugh and toast.

"No."

The laughter stopped dead, even the wine in the glasses stopped rippling.

"No," Lidia repeated, adding in Italian as if handing out a warning, "It's obvious Pietro doesn't want a car anymore."

"What are you talking about, Ma'?" said Pietro. "Of course I want a car."

"Don't you worry," bellowed his father. Whatever he said next, it did the trick, for the table reverted back to its natural state of hilarity. His father raised his glass, in a toast dedicated either to his unexpectedly academic son or to the successfully sacrificed pig, before skulling the contents.

It was back to work again. Pietro and I were left at the table sown with mandarin seeds. As I'd learned to do during my summers as a waitress in DC, I scrambled to clear the table. And I was not the only one desperate to wash the dishes before his mother came back: Pietro too seemed to have grasped that this was our one and only chance. Into the fire went the paper napkins, triggering a contagion of flames; tangerine peels wilted and blackened. Then we filled the sink and, encouraged by Lidia's exceptionally long absence, I thrust my hands into the gratifyingly hot water.

I scrubbed while Pietro rinsed. We worked silently with the concentration of athletes in the zone, now and then looking across at each other in disbelief. Could it really be that, with Pietro's help, I was washing the dishes in Lidia's house? I dared to hope that leaving them had been not so much an oversight on her part as a concession. That all that loud, oblivious affection, openly shown toward me, too, may well have undermined her defense. That today she just might be starting to cave.

Pietro rinsed the last plate. He stole a glance over his shoulder before kissing me then and there in the kitchen, topping if off by saying, "We did it, baby."

Just then his mother came in hauling an enormous pot. Pietro lurched forward.

"Mamma, give it here."

Lidia didn't say a word, nor did she accept his help. She heaved the pot up onto the counter, its bottom black with soot. In the process, the lid went sliding off and steam came billowing out. It was boiled water. Without even glancing at the dishes drip-drying next to the sink, his mother said in an Italian devoid of emotion, "So I see no one will be needing this anymore."

"We could use it to wash down the table," said Pietro, undoubtedly referring to the butcher table outside.

His mother mumbled something in dialect, waved her hands as if lost for words, and shuffled out.

Pietro shrugged. "Never mind her."

So Lidia had had every intention of doing the dishes herself but was simply waiting for the dishwater to come to a boil over the embers of her cooking fire. Pietro and I had managed to beat her to it thanks to nothing more than a hot-water heater. It was modernity that had won out over the old ways of her primitive kitchen, the old ways that couldn't bear to waste the last heat off the day's fire and insisted on doing things the slow, hard way.

Pietro led me out onto the front terrace. It wrapped around the house, allowing us to watch the butchers happily working away while at the same time to stay clear of the hanging carcass of the pig, which from that angle gave the kind illusion of still being whole. The faraway hills were spotted with old snow and the air was laced with sweet memories of hearths I'd never actually experienced.

Pietro lit a cigarette and exhaled with deep relief. His damp hand took mine to wedge it under his arm. As he smoked he touched my pruned fingertips one by one as though they were places on a topographical map of an unknown land. "We're having pork again tonight. Can you handle it, baby?"

"I don't mind. How about you?"

"Me? I'm used to it." He took a puff. "You know, nowadays it's illegal to slaughter your own pig like this, without any sort of regulation. If the authorities find out, there's hell to pay. But the people here keep doing it anyway."

I scanned the terra-cotta tiles of the nearby houses, trying to identify which one belonged to the uncle they were all forbidden to even say hi to, and which one belonged to the girl his mother fooled herself into believing Pietro would take as his wife. But to me the houses all looked the same.

"So, what's this car thing?" I asked, but Pietro shook his head, puzzled. "That lady said you'll get one when you graduate. Unless I misunderstood."

"Oh yeah, *that* car." Pietro confirmed that the gift was a given since the day he started university.

"Wouldn't it be cool, though, if you and me saved up and bought a used car of our own?" That idea, which I'd thrown out without much thought, had a romantic ring to it that I ended up liking. I wound my arm around his. "You know, an old beat-up melon."

"You mean a lemon."

I hid my embarrassment by looking out into the distance. With that error, which may have been more than simply semantic, I had the feeling that something was slipping through my fingers.

"I need a car now anyway. How else will I be able to visit you when I start my civilian service?" As if to make up for the painful reminder, Pietro pulled a roasted chestnut out of his jacket pocket and placed it in my hand.

Automatically I peeled back its mahogany outer shell. "When are we going to talk to your mother, Pietro?"

"About what?"

"About our plans. About the future." It had to be today, with the place pleasantly humming like an anthill, on the crest of that tiny but significant triumph.

"Actions speak louder than words, don't you think?" He smoothed my hair. "Heddi, what we're doing now—being here together in front of half the population of Monte San Rocco—is no small feat. It took real balls for us to show up here, and it will pave the way for everything else."

He was probably right. I bit into the chestnut. I could never decide if I liked the taste of chestnuts. How could something so beautiful and so sweet leave such a bitter aftertaste?

"But right now, baby, let me lie down," Pietro said, turning into the house. "Please, I'm dying for a nap."

With Pietro succumbing to the couch in the dining room, I sat by the dying fire, occasionally prodding the charred logs with the prongs. They burst into ephemeral flames that gave out little warmth. In the stillness of the house I could hear the ticking of the clock, syncopated to the sound of chopping that was coming not from outside but from inside the house. It had to be Lidia in her downstairs kitchen.

I was seized by the urge to go down and speak to her. Did I really need to wait for Pietro? The truth was that his mother had forgiven him for his deception about our living arrangement and had gotten over our trip to Greece. She didn't have a score to settle with him, but with me. And today, when I was no longer feeling like a victim, was a fine strong day to discuss things openly and honestly.

I made my way to the stairs, without pausing to consider if I should always be so trusting of my impulses and without any idea of what I might say to Lidia once we were face-to-face. Only a few steps down and I could already see her woolen stockings stuffed like butcher paper into her chunky black shoes and a bowl of pork meat on the floor next to the little table where she sat. It was too late to turn back now.

"Hello again, *signora*," I said, feeling self-possessed and shivering only because of the sudden drop in temperature.

His mother greeted me in a limp voice without looking up from the chopping board where she was dicing meat.

"What are you making?"

"Soppressata."

That took me back. I remembered how during that first dinner party at my place Pietro had brought homemade soppressata to share. Now I realized that, on that electrifying night that had changed the course of my life, I had savored and ingested something made by Lidia's bare hands. In that hand-to-mouth exchange there was an involuntary but undeniable physical closeness, almost a bond that couldn't be severed.

"Delicious," I said as I eased myself down, since there were no other chairs, on a sack of flour against the wall.

"That's our wheat."

I felt the sting of that subtle scolding and looked out through the glass door at the friends and family in the driveway, a festive, faraway world. Lidia's kitchen was now garlanded in fresh salami that clogged the air with the sickening smell of meat, and I could already feel my resolve begin to weaken. What had I really thought to accomplish by coming down here, on her turf? I made to get up.

"The wheat that comes from our land," Lidia went on. "The land that's going to be Pietro's one day."

She seemed talkative as never before. I sat back down in my irreverent seat, hazarding the question I already knew the answer to, "And what about Gabriele and Vittorio?"

"Vittorio? Eeeiihhh . . ." It was a high-pitched wail, like the screech of a crow, all I'd ever heard her utter about her eldest son. Then, as if struck by a toothache, she let out a moan in which she named Gabriele. "Who knows when that boy will ever finish his studies. He's always asking for more and more money. And to think he was always the good one at school."

"He is very good, *signora*. I've seen his drawings."

"Drawings? After all these years all he has is a bunch of drawings . . ."

"Degrees take time."

"What would I know?" she said, throwing cubes of fat into the bowl on the floor. "I only got to do four years of schooling."

I was impressed. Here was a woman who hadn't even finished elementary school and yet she was quite well spoken, despite her habit of pronouncing each word the same way she did her chores, in a sort of sluggish and calculated way. And I was amazed that, although she kept on staring into that bowl of meat, Lidia had just shared a piece of her childhood with me. Had Pietro been right all along, that doing the dishes was actually the key to wrench open her heart?

Dolefully she continued, "I had to work on my father's land, to put food on the table. Those were hard times, not the life of luxury young people have today."

"Where's your family's farm?"

"Doesn't matter. I got married off and never stepped foot on it again." Her face twisted briefly as if she'd smelled something foul. "I was old by then, almost thirty. I didn't have a choice. It's not like these days, with people living together and whatnot." I held my breath, convinced that our talk was about to take a turn for the worse. But it didn't. "My husband didn't own any land," she carried on. "We already had our first boy and still we had nothing to our names. So we went abroad . . . as laborers, working six days a week, for fifteen years."

"That must have been hard."

Pietro's mother stood up without a word. It occurred to me that she might not actually want to have a conversation with me: she only wished to speak. I would gladly settle for that. She went to the far corner of the room to fumble among some jars and burlap bags. I stole glances at her as she bent over to grab a handful of something from a sack on the ground, another handful from a jar, movements that caused her to let out little huffs of exertion and her kerchief to fall forward over her forehead. I tried to picture Lidia as a young woman, newly betrothed, to conjure up her smooth but plain face. Yet I could only really see her as she was now, old and frustratingly fragile.

"Can I help?"

My rhetorical question fell on deaf ears. Lidia came back to the table, pulling from her apron pocket a fistful of rock salt and peppercorns that she then scattered over the meat and fat. The mixture went the same pale pink as her hands kneading it. "We sent the money home to buy land," she picked up her story. "We've worked our whole lives for this land, this house."

This time I had the wisdom not to comment. I mentally sewed together the various stories Pietro had told me. Two years after they came back from Switzerland, one cold Sunday in November of 1980 during a televised soccer match between Juventus and Inter, the earthquake hit. A violent movement of the fault that would later be described as "extensional" or even "normal," but for the peasants who experienced it the land had turned into water. One minute and thirty seconds, an infinity, in which the land rolled like the sea and howled like a storm and swallowed up houses, churches, hospitals, entire villages. Almost three thousand dead, nine thousand injured, three hundred thousand displaced. The province of Avellino was the worst hit, with the so-called earthquake capital, Sant'Angelo dei Lombardi, located only a few kilometers from Monte San Rocco. The earthquake spared their newly built house but many others didn't survive.

"All those sacrifices. It was all for them, for those boys." Lidia shook her head, her gold earrings shaking. "But they don't care a thing about the land."

"Pietro often comes to lend a hand."

She lifted her eyebrows derisively. "When he feels like it. But when we die, God's will be done, there won't be anyone left to look after the land. No one at all."

I nervously readjusted my weight on the sack where I sat, on the heart of the land. Had his mother already figured out that Pietro was going to sell off the plots one by one? To preempt a possible attack on my lover's moral character, I replied feebly, "Pietro's doing the best he can."

"Eeeiihhh . . ." she uttered again, a sound I'd assumed was reserved for Vittorio alone. "If he was doing his best," she said, "*si sposasse quella brava ragazza.*"

He would marry that nice girl. My chest ignited with fear, despite the fact that his mother had just exposed her education in all its provinciality by mangling her conditional tense—*si sposarebbe quella brava ragazza* was the correct form—a mistake that could have given me a false sense of superiority, and despite the near certainty that she was merely referring to their neighbor, the girl who was as much of a marriage prospect as a mollusk.

"Right now that boy's not thinking straight," Lidia mumbled as if talking to herself, "but it's just a phase . . . it'll pass."

I looked down at the concrete floor. *It'll pass.* I was the phase that would eventually pass, like the way a fever passes or a wound heals. She'd said it without malice, in the same crestfallen way she'd spoken about her own life. Still, the phrase was as concise and final as a prophecy, almost a curse.

The time had come for me to say something. Something that summed up our love in a few unassailable words and made it clear that nothing and no one could make me walk away from him. A phrase uttered in a firm voice, in clear Italian with a smattering of Neapolitan to lend it a devil-may-care attitude. But nothing like that came out of my mouth. I quickly made up an excuse—dishes to dry or something like that—and climbed back up the stairs without looking behind me.

The fire was dead as I collapsed on the couch at Pietro's feet. He was sleeping like a rock. I gently laid my hand on his chest, not to wake him but simply to remind myself of my incredible good fortune. In sync with his breathing, my hand rose and fell in the same hypnotic way we rose and fell driving over the hills around Monte San Rocco. It lulled me. How nice it would be to fall asleep, I thought, to surrender to it, to just let go. Let go of everything.

And I really was tired. Tired of the effort of continually seeking Lidia's approval, and tired already of trying to keep the noble promises we'd made at New Year's. It was obvious to me now that not only would his mother never warm to me, but she would even actively oppose our future plans. She'd taken the time to tell me her tale of famine and arranged marriages not because she wanted to let me in or even vent her own grief, but for the sole purpose of showing me that her dislike for me was entirely justified. We'd been acting under an illusion. In reality there was no heroic battle to win because Pietro and I didn't stand a chance. There was only one thing left to do: walk away.

I was struck by an idea that was astonishing in its simplicity. I could simply leave, go back to Naples. I didn't know why I hadn't thought of it before—perhaps my optimism, or my masochism, was to blame. I could leave that very evening, even in the dark, the bus rocking me to sleep, the window my starry cushion. The mere thought filled me with a colossal, even final, sense of freedom, as though if I left Monte San Rocco now I'd never ever have to come back for the rest of my life.

When Pietro stirred, I whispered his name.

"Hi, baby," he said through a stretch.

"Did you sleep well?"

"Sure did. The sleep of the just."

He was already reaching for his cigarettes and lighter so I quickly added, "Pietro, listen. I know we have another couple days here but I'm thinking of leaving earlier."

"When?"

"This evening. Tomorrow morning."

"OK," he said, not looking at all surprised: if anything, he looked relieved. "There's a bus from Borgo Alto at noon tomorrow." His readiness perplexed me. Wasn't he even going to entertain the idea of leaving with me? He turned to me then with something like nostalgia in his eyes and said, "Look, Heddi, if only one of us can be free, I want it to be you."

Later in the afternoon the hanging carcass was gone. The only traces of the pig were scraps lying across the bloodied table. Many of the villagers had gone home; those who remained scraped bones to salvage every last thread of flesh. The sun, too, was hanging by a thread, and the driveway was growing heavy once more with the chill of winter and the fear of being wasteful. On the terrace I lifted my scarf over my mouth, whispering into it the warm secret of my departure. I stepped on a fallen branch and it let out a satisfying snap.

Pietro, wearing that black wool hat, called out to me from the driveway. "You still want to go for a tractor ride?"

"I'd love to."

He spread open the metal doors of the shed. Gesualdo the dog wasn't there: maybe he was off on one of his escapades or gnawing a pork bone somewhere more private. Pietro took a seat and started up the tractor with a roar that sounded like an act of rebellion. He was using farm equipment in an entirely unproductive way and he didn't give a damn. He reached out his hand, saying, "Watch your step."

On top of the tractor I felt tall and exposed to the elements. The lingering butchers waved up at us as we rolled down the steep lane. It was hard to keep my balance; I kept slipping forward on the metal seat toward Pietro, and the effort to stay put made me laugh. "I'm going to fall!" I shouted, but my voice could barely be heard over the engine and my breath escaping from my scarf melted into the air.

"You won't fall," Pietro turned to me to say with the same heartfelt and confident voice he'd used the very first time we were driving to Monte San Rocco—when, like a pool player sinking the eight ball, he moved the black gear knob smoothly into place without even having to look at it—and he told me that we weren't in the eye of the storm, that there was no storm at all.

The sun had almost completely burned out and the air smelled of snow as we drove past windows, vegetable gardens, doors. An old man saw us and waved. I waved back the ecstatic way you do when you're passing by in a parade and you never have to stop or see that person ever again. It was odd, though, that little old man waving mutely and our big beast needlessly growling past him.

I looked at Pietro, who was waving too. He looked slightly amused but tired, like he was listening to a favorite joke for the hundredth time.

23

I GENUINELY DIDN'T THINK I'd ever see Luca Falcone again. So when I saw him standing before me one night at a free concert in Piazza San Domenico, I thought I was seeing a mirage. Everything around me was swaying to the rhythm of reggae—braids and dreads, hemp bags and Peroni bottles—and I just stood there in the middle like a statue. I blamed Tonino, who'd planned the surprise by pulling me and Angelo by the hand to a spot whose dismal view of the stage only made sense now.

"Heddi," Luca said with that off-center smile.

So absorbed was I in the unique asymmetry of his face that I didn't at first notice his arms were open wide. I fell into them in what was not so much an embrace as a wrinkle in time, a scrunch of worn leather I'd perhaps always known, a familiar infusion of dried lavender and loose tobacco, and yet when we broke apart I was astonished by his changed appearance. It was his hair. Gone was the unkempt ponytail (Angelo was ruffling his cropped hair) and along with it had gone his wise old look. Had I never really grasped that Luca was only twenty-six years old? His youth was startling.

The boys too were looking at him with admiration, asking how long he was in town. He was only staying for a few days with his aunt in

Barra, Luca told us with a particularly melodic accent, his voice having lost any hint of Neapolitan gloominess it may have once had.

"Go on," Angelo said, "give us some stories from the barracks. Do you have to shine your boots before roll call?"

"Bunk bed plastered with Monica Bellucci pinups, I bet," said Tonino. "Naked, obviously."

Luca smiled as if to humor them. He didn't live in the barracks, he told us, but most nights made it home for dinner with his parents. Much of his work consisted of pushing paper at a desk. He'd even put on a bit of weight, he admitted. He was an officer, after all, and well paid at that, a role of responsibility and respect only the well educated had access to.

I was only half listening. I was trying to fix in my mind everything about him: his gestures, the way he talked. Who knew when I'd see Luca again. I knew that I had no right to expect another visit from him, that I wasn't a close enough friend. And yet I couldn't stop thinking about the fact that he'd conspired with Tonino to plan this little surprise, conceivably for me.

A blond girl hugged Tonino and Angelo and handed them beers. In that break I asked Luca how his mother was doing, a question I instantly regretted when he answered, "She has cancer."

Of all the words in the world that was, and perhaps always has been, the most terrifying. It's the ogre in the dictionary, the loathsome but very real possibility that none of us will be rewarded for our talent or kindness or healthy lifestyle, and that maybe death gets a kick out of taking the most talented, the kindest, the healthiest of all. But in the end death can weasel its way out of any responsibility for it, it washes its hands of it, because a tumor is not just any illness but the betrayal of one's own body, which turns out to be capable of harboring evil within, to live with it for a long time without ever knowing, to destroy itself in all innocence.

I muttered some sort of condolence, which Luca accepted with dignity, silently reaching in his jacket for his tobacco and rolling paper. A beer bottle shattered somewhere in the square. For a while I pretended to listen to the music but I was all too aware of Luca's larger-than-life presence, a colossus by my side. I was afraid to say anything else, to break the spell and make him vanish.

It was Luca who bridged the distance by stepping closer and pressing his shoulder against mine with pretend casualness. "I have something to tell you. I might be sent on a mission."

"What kind of mission?"

"I'm not sure exactly. They won't give out the details unless I agree to take part. Even the country is classified information."

"You're leaving Italy then," I said, as if resigned to living perpetually in his shadow, and it was only when he said, to the increasingly frenetic beat of the congas, the fatal words "the Middle East" that it occurred to me to protest. "No, Luca, not into combat . . ."

"I wouldn't be going as a soldier. It's my knowledge of Arabic they want."

The rolled cigarette was balanced between his lips, a tiny papyrus that he hadn't lit yet and maybe had no intention of lighting at all; he might even decide to put it back in his pocket and simply walk off into the night. It was impossible to predict Luca Falcone's next move, for regardless of where he was living, near or far, he never ceased to amaze. He'd been able to find a use for his abstruse academic knowledge, but well outside the university environment. He was going into a war zone, but as an intellectual. And here we were among all those swaying dreadlocks and lip piercings, *his* tribe in the first place, and there was Luca standing out from the crowd with his crew cut, all cleaned up and respectable, making the straight and narrow path at this young age the only true rebellion. Never had I been more confused—and fascinated—by Luca Falcone.

"It would pay very well," he added, "and there would be no expenses."

"It sounds like you're going then." If it came out sounding more detached than I'd meant it to, it was only because I thought I'd already lost Luca—and how could you lose a person twice?

"I haven't decided." Luca finally burned his creation. "I'd like to know what you think."

"Me?" Something in me instantly melted, just like the time he'd asked me for help with the song lyrics. I felt privileged, maybe even chosen. "I think you . . . should follow your gut," I replied somewhat giddily, although I knew my advice couldn't possibly help, but I had no other answer, even for my own life.

Luca reached out with his free hand to tousle my hair like an older brother would, hard enough for me to tell that his fingers were calloused despite the paperwork. I felt little and important at the same time as he smiled and fixed his magnetic gaze on me, which as always tried to capture me and expose me in all my ignorance.

But this time I summoned the courage to lift my eyes to his and hold them there for as long as need be. There was nothing easy about this, as anyone who'd ever met Luca Falcone could attest to, because he was never the one to let go first, and in fact I battled indecision and embarrassment as I stared back at him in an almost romantic way in a place full of people. But the longer I matched his gaze, the less it seemed to intimidate me, because I understood now that with that look Luca didn't actually want to communicate or teach me anything at all. He was simply looking at me the way the moon looks at you. That light that makes you feel, for a moment, that you're not merely a human being but part of something eternal, maybe even divine. That enigmatic smile that reminds you there's no need to ask so many questions, for you already have the answers within.

All at once, I could see our friendship with almost painful crispness: all its shared passion—for knowledge, for life, for people, for *each other*—compressed into a nearly invisible dot, a speck of saffron with the potential to burst with inexhaustible color.

"Hey, who wants some of this soup?" Tonino cut in, pushing a beer into Luca's hand. "It's warm as piss but I took it anyway. I'm not one to offend a lady, am I?"

Their friend was gone and it was the four of us again, just like old times: only Sonia was missing. Luca took a swig of beer and handed me the bottle. I didn't refuse. Nothing, not even alcohol, could have tainted my high spirits or my clarity of mind.

"This band's not too bad," said Angelo.

Tonino adjusted his glasses in the direction of the stage, giving them the benefit of a moment's doubt. "Are you deaf, blondie? An attack of diarrhea has more rhythm than these guys."

After my Italian literature exam, there was only one blank space left in my blue booklet, for Russian literature. But that would have to wait until my professor had recovered from an unusual case of amnesia. Word had it that, shocked by the infidelity of her husband, who coincidentally was my Russian language professor, she had lost the memory of the last thirty years of her life. She was regaining her memories bit by bit, in chronological order—the first being how to speak Russian again, which she'd learned as a young woman—but she was still far from remembering any of her students' names, and so for the time being she was at home recovering. Either way, I'd lost any passion I might have once had for that useless language with its sounds that stuck to the palate like boiled potatoes. Russian had only ever been a vague interest dating back to a short-lived Dostoyevskian phase as a moody teenager. Therefore, with or without my professor's amnesia, in that overcrowded classroom I was never going to be anything but a nameless face.

The scirocco came back. It blew with wild determination through the streets like tropical stormwater racing toward the gutter. As it passed through, it tore open jackets and amused itself with skirts. It wrestled with fishermen pushing out to sea and table umbrellas outside Caffè Gambrinus. It ripped off my wool hat to play with it across the cobblestones like a cat with a hapless sparrow. It blew chalk through my hair, caressing the nape of my neck, and panting into my ear, *Remember me? Remember when we were in Greece together and we capsized ferries and then afterward we'd go back to the hotel and screw?* It was all just hot air. The scirocco embellished the truth so as not to have to admit that it had never actually been to Greece, that it came from the Sahara, from Africa, where many said the city should piss off to anyway. Bunch of Moroccans, they said up north.

The wind whirled, time flew, and the only thing that thankfully didn't change was Pietro. Every detail about him reassured me. His glasses reflecting the computer screen, his hand curled thoughtfully over his mouth when he was reading *National Geographic* or the Italian translation of Krakauer's *Into Thin Air*, about the disastrous ascent of Everest. The courteous way he always put down grocery bags, like he was afraid to bruise the pears. How, when he talked about physics or was nervous for some other reason, it almost sounded like he had a lisp, a stress-induced speech impediment. The blurry yin-yang tattoo he'd needled into his own forearm with the same steady hand he'd cut his name into the handle of his pick. The pearly buttons leading down his shirt, the little plunge his chest made in the center. His broad hands, the salt on his skin.

We made love as though he was about to be sent to war: in the morning, in the evening, sometimes in the deep of the night when we were awakened by an accidental caress or the moon snowing onto our covers. We called each other by those private names that make single people cringe. But mostly I loved calling him simply *Pietro*. Pronouncing it was like breaking into a broad, sunny smile before blowing a kiss, one that went unreciprocated and ended in that closed *o*, a beautiful though somewhat sorrowful conclusion.

With the arrival of the scirocco, Sonia and Carlo broke up and Madeleine went back to Marseilles. In the days leading up to her departure, I strictly avoided looking her in the eye, afraid to see tears or an invitation to play one of our little games. But in the end, the day of her departure arrived without incident, her last moments in that apartment abruptly announced by Saverio pressing the buzzer three times.

At the door Gabriele took her in his arms, saying, "Please don't, Madeleine, you'll make me cry too. We'll see each other again. One day I'll come visit you in Marseilles, I promise. It will be a good opportunity to practice my French, *mon petit chou.*"

"I'll miss you too," she said, now turning to Pietro, who hugged her with the usual suspicious affection he had for her before making his second rhetorical offer to walk her downstairs.

With that heavy suitcase, Madeleine appeared to falter on the threshold, like she was wavering. I pulled her toward me, as hard as ever: she was so petite, so fragile, that I suddenly feared I might crush her. A cacophony of goodbyes and she was gone, just like that, sucked down by the stairwell.

"What a shame she's left," said Pietro. "I sure will miss the way she kicked that hot-water heater."

"A shame? It's devastating," replied Gabriele. "I abhor it when people go out of your life like that."

As soon as he went upstairs to his room, I turned to Pietro. "When we leave for good, we have to take him with us."

"Who?"

"Gabriele."

"As if. Can you imagine you, me, and Gabriele traveling the world? What a threesome. Where did you get such an idea?"

The phone rang and Pietro picked up. Rolling his eyes, he collapsed onto the couch. "Have you eaten?" I was already starting toward the kitchen to give him his privacy when I overheard him say, "Easter? Of course I'll be there."

Outside the sky was colorless and the air odorless, yet the scirocco had its days in Naples numbered. As did we. But leaving the city didn't seem like a choice to me anymore: we *had* to go. Because among the thousand tired old reasons to drag the city through the mud—heard up north and down south, uttered among Neapolitans and among us—the most serious was its geographical birth defect of being only one hundred and two kilometers from Monte San Rocco.

From: tectonic@tin.it
To: heddi@yahoo.com
Sent: July 15

Dear Heddi,

*I'm sorry for my usual silence, by now you know what I'm like . . . Today
I was out in the countryside. I cut willow branches to use as string for the
grapevines. I planted some trees, one with your name.*

*I have to confess that I think about you all the time, and I'm ashamed of
it. I believe I'm suffering from a sort of double personality or even a triple
one, I'm not sure . . . I only know that when I think of you I see myself as
a different person, completely different from who I am and who I represent
myself as being in my everyday life. I love thinking about that person that
I once was, or maybe it's only my imagination. Sometimes I fantasize that
when I see you again it will be just like when we left off. I can't imagine that
you've changed at all, and you've hardly changed on the outside judging
from the picture you sent me . . . I remember you well and I will never be
able to forget you. And I really mean it: I will never forget you or who I was
or everything you taught me or how I sacrificed you . . . and you aren't even
capable of hating me.*

*I'm useless, I know, but I'm horribly human. I hurt you, I lied to you . . .
even during that fateful phone call. There was no other woman: that was
really just an excuse to leave you. I'm a coward. I have never been, nor will
I ever be, good at picking the right way when put in front of a crossroads.
Often I've thought that the secret is not to choose, not to think at all about
the consequences, everything is meant or not meant to be. But destiny is the
excuse of fools and the weak . . .*

*I'm blathering on and on, I know, but I would like to be able to share
all my thoughts with you. And I'd like to be optimistic: according to my*

horoscope, this year everything will be resolved! And why not believe in it just a little?

You're leaving in a few days, so I wish you a safe trip. I'll see you on the morning of August 20th at Rita's. Wait for me . . .

p.

24

I SPENT EASTER in Castellammare with Rita, a quick visit because I needed to keep chipping away at my thesis. When Pietro and Gabriele returned to the city, loaded down with hydrogeological surveys and peasant food (a misnomer, I now knew), my excitement was such that I invited them both to come with me to the so-called Underground Naples. Pietro's justification for not going was that he was only interested in natural caves, not the man-made kind. "Besides, they're probably full of crickets," he added.

It seemed appropriate, in any case, that Gabriele would be the one accompanying me into the bowels of the city. As soon as we hit Via Roma he locked his arm in mine and didn't let go the whole way there. Gabriele was like that: he showed his affection through old-fashioned, chivalrous mannerisms, unlike his brother, who, as though afraid to spoil a secret by broadcasting it to all of Naples, was becoming more and more jealous of our privacy. As we walked arm in arm, Gabriele told me how lucky I was not to have spent the holiday with them. "Easter in Monte was nothing more than a feeding frenzy," he explained, "from which I barely escaped alive." *Easter in Monte*. I loved how Gabriele, not in the least intimidated by the village, shortened its name. The Mount sounded like a ski resort.

We found the hand-painted sign; the bolt was undone. It was almost lunchtime and the yawning doorway let out a blast of warm, earthy air that made the notices and brochures in the tiny entranceway flutter. A bearded young man on duty lifted his eyes from a book and told us to hurry if we wanted to catch up with the last tour group of the day. He added, in a welcome instance of the Neapolitan art of rule bending, that we could pay another time. He showed us the way by pointing to a stairwell that descended into the very throat of the earth.

"So should we go then, Eddie?"

"A guided tour? I don't know . . ."

I would have preferred to go adventuring like always; however, Gabriele wasn't referring to the tour but to the dark descent before us. As if to muster all his will, he ran a hand vigorously over the fresh stubble on his head, freshly shaven to tackle his creeping baldness.

"Wait. Take these," said the man, handing us a couple of lit candles, the long white ones usually used in religious processions.

We started down the stairwell. With one hand I shed quivering light onto the uneven steps that had been yanked forcefully out of the rock, while with the other I steadied myself against the damp and grainy wall. I kept my eyes on Gabriele's shape ahead of me and on his flickering shadow, sometimes statuesque and sometimes grotesque, cast onto the wall that was coming off on my hand.

"Tuff?"

"Exactly."

At the bottom of the stairs all we had to do was follow the voices. A woman with a well-to-do Neapolitan accent, like Carlo's, was saying, "And then in World War Two they were used as air-raid shelters. Come in closer. Do you see these?"

Our passageway ended in a small room carved into the rock, where five or six candles were gathered round to light up a wall that resembled a Neolithic cave painting.

"Take a look at this," Gabriele whispered. He brought his candle up to a drawing etched into the volcanic tuff, a fighter plane with clouds of destruction beneath it. It was signed "Enzo" and dated August 6, 1943.

"The bombing from the Allied forces must have seemed to the people of Naples like endless, gratuitous violence," said the guide, her face a mere sketch in the dancing light. According to her, during the air raids—which lasted days, weeks, and sometimes months at a time—the civilians who had sought refuge in the underground caves had nothing to do but "fill the time with prayers and express their fear through art."

"Graffiti, in other words," said a man with a Tuscan accent. "Naples sure does have a long tradition of that."

"As you wish," was the guide's retort, "but remember that Naples was the most bombed of all Italian cities."

"Show some respect," another man joined in.

"People were married down here," the guide went on. "Children played, babies were born." Records stated that a certain Carmela Montagna gave birth to a baby girl, who within months died of pneumonia brought on by the cold and damp conditions. "A life cut short without a single caress from the sun."

Her words affected me, although I couldn't decide if they were simply scripted for the tour. Authentic or not, they brought to mind the child-size coffin I'd seen at the Fontanelle Cemetery. A bead of water fell out of nowhere and landed on my cheek. I wiped it away.

After the war, the guide told us, the city was buried in debris but life must go on—and people of Naples always rise up again. Nonetheless, with all means of transport destroyed the only way for the inhabitants to clear the city was to dump the rubble of their fallen homes into the underground caves, filling them in. "Perhaps they were also attempting to bury the memories of what they'd endured down here. And in fact from the 1960s onward no one talked about these caves anymore."

"So why wasn't this one filled in?" asked a girl.

"You have to keep in mind that there were over four hundred of such bomb shelters all over Naples. Actually, most buildings had internal access to one. And besides, a single generation couldn't have possibly undone the great architectural and engineering feats begun in Greek times. Please come this way."

Gabriele and I tagged along as the guide led us to an adjoining square cave. Almost the entire floor space was taken up by a pool of water, which straightened our group into a row of candles along the edge. A bare lightbulb hung over the pool, coloring it a chemical green that bloomed with circles every time a drop of water fell from the ceiling. They went *plip plop* like the pattering of keys on an untuned piano.

"This is a cistern, an example of what the Greeks excavated first, around 470 BC," said the guide. "The first cisterns collected rainwater, but the network of cisterns and tunnels was subsequently expanded by the Romans with the introduction of the aqueduct." She went on to talk about the close connection between the water supply system belowground and the city aboveground. In the not-so-distant past, most buildings in Naples had a well in the courtyard, which the residents used to draw their household water directly from the ancient underground cisterns, like this one. "Hence the local superstition of the *munaciello*, who comes into one's house up through the well system."

"Excuse me, what's a *munaciello*?" asked the girl from before.

"According to an ancient myth, it's an ancient little spirit wearing a monk's cape who sneaks into your house at night to wreak havoc: he breaks dishes, jumps on the bed, rings the doorbell, hides things, and so on. That's why even today Neapolitans believe that when you move into a new house you must always leave some money out for the *munaciello*, so that he brings you good luck and not tragedy."

She pronounced this last word with foreboding measure, perhaps intentionally. She was standing on the edge of the cistern, the rippling water creating a play of light on her otherwise indiscernible face. "The well was also an access point to the tuff underground to be used as construction material," she continued, "and indeed few buildings would have been built at all without a well, which allowed the locals to pull up the tuff block by block, with their bare hands."

"Just like you were saying," I said excitedly to Gabriele, who showed no sign of remembering our distant conversation. He too seemed absorbed by the tour that only a short time ago I'd been reluctant to take part in.

"Since ancient times Naples hasn't felt the need to borrow from elsewhere—neither construction material nor fashion nor philosophy of life," added our guide. "You could say that Naples was born of itself and therefore doesn't owe anybody anything. This autonomy, this self-referentiality, is intrinsic to its origins and inevitably binds Neapolitans to the land under their feet." I struggled to follow her line of reasoning, but it did seem to me that she was speaking off the cuff, something I became even more convinced of when she added, in a low voice as if speaking to herself, "It's that intimate relationship between the sunshine outside and the darkness below, between what is out in the open and what is hidden beneath the surface . . . between what is spoken and what is left unsaid."

She left no room for questions as she ducked her head, exiting the cistern through the small opening. We followed her out, deferentially stepping through the slender passageway. Where it widened, the guide stopped to raise her candle above her, instructing us to follow suit, but the ceiling was lost to the darkness regardless. "This here is the first access point we had to this part of the underground city. But it was filled with debris and garbage. It took us months just to clear it all."

"You mean *you* did it?" someone asked.

"With the Association, of course. Someone had to do it. If we just sit around waiting for the city politicians, we'll be waiting till kingdom come," she said impatiently half in dialect, proving she wasn't one to be messed with.

"So the steps went all the way down here?"

"Steps? Not on your life. We lowered ourselves down here with ropes, harnesses, picks."

Judging from the ensuing silence that fell over the tunnel, this gave the guide more than just poetic authority. As we followed her through the buried Greek marketplace, we took delicate, padded steps over the rounded stone slabs. After a while she halted before a narrow shaft to conclude rather formulaically, "There is still a great deal of work to be done to reclaim the underground city and make it accessible to the public. This site is of incalculable value both for furthering our archaeological knowledge of Naples as well as for fostering a greater appreciation of the city among Neapolitans themselves. Thank you for your contribution. This is the way out. But I have to ask: Is anyone here claustrophobic?"

"I'm a hypochondriac," Gabriele whispered to me. "Close enough."

"Don't lose sight of each other," were the guide's last words as she dipped back into the shadows from whence she'd come.

The tour was over. I had learned some fascinating facts, yet I realized I was disappointed. I'd squeezed through one of the city's ancient veins, which through an intricate circuit fed the very heart of Naples, but I was none the wiser. If anything, I was more of an outsider than ever. A tourist.

Gabriele and I were the last to step into the shaft, which by its very nature thinned the group into a broken line. In front of me Gabriele's form pulsated to the rhythm of the flame as the yellow tuff tightened harder and harder around us, scraping our clothes. The stone walls, chiseled but smooth to the touch, shot upward until they disappeared in a blackness so thick my eyes ached trying to penetrate it. I hoped Pietro was wrong about the crickets.

At one point the walls narrowed to such a degree that we had to walk sideways. We inched along like that, with awkward little steps, the rock rubbing itself against us in a sort of opportunistic embrace that reminded me of the scirocco. Yet I found it fitting somehow that I was being forced to walk like a crab, to bend myself to the will of the rock.

All of a sudden, like the tide abruptly pulling away, I felt my blood pressure plummet from head to toe, the way I imagined it might feel to be drunk and not realize it until you've stood up and it hits you like a sledgehammer. I was sure I was about to fall, or was already falling, and the walls seemed to have come to life; they were moving and between them I was nothing, just an empty shell.

An earthquake?

Gabriele had stopped too. "Damn, what an idiot!" he yelled, looking down at his hand.

"Did you hurt yourself?"

"Not badly," he answered, but there was blood on his knuckles speckled with yellow stone. He'd scratched his hand, he explained, while trying to keep his candle from falling. "I'm all right. Let's keep going. We shouldn't fall behind the others."

"You're bleeding, Gabriele. Let's clean it up first."

He protested as a matter of politeness, for he was already reaching his hand toward me. The tightness of the tunnel made it impossible to move naturally, and I had to maneuver to pass my candle into Gabriele's decent hand so that I could pull a paper tissue from my pocket. It was a good scrape and I tried to blot the wound without rubbing the sand in further. Then I took out a fresh tissue to wrap around his knuckles.

"Give it here," he said, pointing with noticeable shame to the used tissue soaked in blood.

"It doesn't gross me out, Gabriele. Your blood, Pietro's blood, there's not much difference really."

He turned to look at me, the rock a pillow against his cheek. He said, "I understand why my brother is so in love with you."

We looked into each other's eyes. The unstable light from our candles accentuated Gabriele's aquiline features that he shared with Pietro. We were shoulder to shoulder as though together we had to bear the weight of the rock, and my breathing and his seemed to synchronize as we inhaled the uncensored, unadorned smell of the earth. I thought I'd repressed the memory of him asking me for a kiss, *a real kiss*, but no, I remembered it perfectly and so did he. I was struck by an incredibly vivid thought, almost a premonition, that Gabriele was going to reach his bleeding hand behind my neck and press his mouth to mine. I was seized by an intoxicating fear.

It was Gabriele who broke the tension by letting out a little sigh and lowering his gaze. "My brother has always been lucky in life."

"And you haven't?"

"I don't know, Eddie. I have a lot of friends, a lot of books . . . all the wine I could possibly wish for. In Naples I've finally found a place where I can belong. I should be happy, but something important is missing from my life."

"What's missing?"

"Someone who loves me."

His confession pained me somehow, and all I managed to say, a bit inanely, was, "At least here you're spoiled for choice. Naples is full of beautiful, intelligent girls."

"And boys . . ."

I looked at him perplexed.

"I've never said this to anyone, Eddie. The men I've loved, from a distance so far, partly I wanted to be with them and partly I wanted to be *like* them: handsome, sophisticated . . . I don't even know if there's a difference, I haven't really gotten my head around it yet . . . I've also fallen in love with women, always hopelessly, always ending in utter solitude."

"I'm so sorry."

"You see why a place like Monte San Rocco just isn't for someone like me?" He laughed bitterly. "And I owe it all to Pietro that I was able to escape from that horrific place. I'll always be grateful to him for that."

"Grateful to Pietro?" Surely he meant the opposite: after all, Gabriele had been the one to coerce their parents into allowing his younger brother to study. The grateful one should have been Pietro.

"What, he never told you this story?"

"No," I lied. "Tell me."

According to his account, Gabriele had come to the realization that the only way to rescue oneself from that small-town mentality was to earn a degree. Pietro, on the other hand, had no desire whatsoever to continue his studies after getting his diploma: he really dug his heels in. But Gabriele couldn't tolerate the idea of letting him rot in Monte San Rocco, so he announced to their parents, who'd been more than happy for their middle son to be out of the picture, that he wasn't going anywhere without his little brother. Knowing how much it meant to Gabriele, Pietro finally gave in and enrolled at the university too. "He sacrificed himself for me, for my dream," Gabriele concluded.

It was the same story I'd been told, but distorted like in one of those fun-house mirrors. Gabriele had made himself into the lead character, completely editing out Pietro's passion for geology, not to mention his determination that had pushed him all the way to Rome. According to his story then, if it hadn't been for his stubborn older brother, Pietro would have ended up like one of those card players in that smoky bar or, in the very best scenario, like his cousin Francesco.

I refused to believe it. Maybe it was selective memory on Gabriele's part, or perhaps an amalgamation of the two brothers, a narrative fusion of their dreams, desires, and destinies to the point where they couldn't be told apart. I also considered the malicious possibility that his story was fueled by resentment toward Pietro as the favorite son (or at least he used to be) who was graduating before him even though they'd started at the same time. Yet in the candlelight as Gabriele recalled that shared past with his brother, he didn't betray even a shadow of bitterness but only an immense and painful love.

"I'm pleased I didn't give up on him. Look how incredibly well he's done." Gabriele handed me back my candle, adding, "We should keep moving. Otherwise they'll lock us in here."

"Good idea. Let's go."

The truth was I couldn't wait to walk away from all the stories whispered in the darkness of those caves—and to shake off the quiver of excitement I still felt from the kiss that never was and could never be.

Because, yes, I had to admit to myself that I'd wanted my future brother-in-law to kiss me, but I didn't know if that desire, wrong in every way and frightening in its clarity, was really due to Gabriele's similarities with Pietro and not to all the qualities that made him different—his independence that bordered on marginalization, his pigheadedness in being true to himself at all costs, his fire burning inside that would sooner consume him than surrender to dying out.

Fortunately, it wasn't long before the passageway released us from its grip and we climbed the stairs back up to the light.

Later on I overheard on the evening news that our neighbor was watching (it was hard to miss it at that volume) that there had been a minor earthquake in the Campania region. When I mentioned this to Pietro, he downplayed it as a minor tremor: the epicenter was near Benevento and claimed only one victim. "Some old guy who dropped dead from a heart attack," he said, blowing smoke out through our porthole window.

"Can you maybe feel an earthquake more if you're belowground?"

He said it was the opposite, that the effect of an earthquake underground is one-half to one-third of the effect felt on the surface. Seismic waves, he explained, are like radio frequencies that become amplified as they travel their way up through the rock layers. Hence the sensation, and the damage, is always greater aboveground.

Clearly what I'd experienced in Underground Naples wasn't an earthquake. I was strangely disappointed. Disappointed that I didn't know what an earthquake was like, and thus couldn't even recognize one, just like I didn't know and would never know bombings and other similar disasters except through other people's stories. It wasn't that I wanted to suffer, because I didn't. I simply had the impression that happiness and true knowledge were mutually exclusive.

Pietro must have interpreted my furrowed brow as worry because he hastened to say, "Relax, baby. The next time an earthquake hits Naples, we won't be around. The news won't even reach us where we are in the Outback counting kangaroos." He drew in thirstily from his Marlboro Light. "But if there's ever an earthquake, you know what to do, don't you?" I shook my head. "Go stand under a doorway. If it's built in a structural wall, the doorway is the strongest part of a building. You should have seen some of the houses destroyed in Monte San Rocco in 1980. Often all that was left was a doorframe."

As usual, his science managed to comfort me. "You know about so many things. You're a natural-born scientist," I said, not noticing immediately that in reality it wasn't a compliment but a subtle prod. I wanted him to reconfirm his stubborn old propensity for geology; I wanted him to disprove Gabriele's story.

"I'm not what you think," he said instead, putting out his cigarette to take me in his arms. "Without you, I'm a moon with no sun. I have no light of my own."

When Pietro kissed my neck, once and then again, I knew how the evening would turn out. As I kissed him back, through the window I caught a glimpse of the volcano encrusted in lights: the illegal houses tempting fate on a daily basis. Everyone knew that Vesuvius would sooner or later lose its patience and blow its lid. So then could those people on its flanks truly be said to be living in fear of a terrible disaster and not in anticipation of a spectacular show? Perhaps the events we fear the most, I mused, are paradoxically those that deep down we want to happen. It was as if the most primitive and unmentionable part of us— maybe the amygdala, that impulsive and preverbal almond nestled in our brain—was trying to preempt tragedy by saying, *Just do it. Go ahead and get it over with.*

From: heddi@yahoo.com
To: tectonic@tin.it
Sent: August 27

Dear Pietro,

I'm back in New Zealand safe and sound. You see, there was no need to worry about the flight in the end? I just curled up with a novel, with my thoughts and fantasies . . .

I realize now that I wasn't psychologically prepared at all to see you again. My attempt to defend myself with Zen was an abysmal failure. But how could I be expected to remain indifferent to the sound of your voice calling up to me from the street? When I looked over the balcony, it was like falling not from the second floor but from a great, great height. And then when I saw that flash of silver, the ring on your finger, let's just say that I was the one who felt like a traitor for having sent you back your sun years ago, for having lost all trust in fate. But maybe there are some things I shouldn't admit to you.

The day we spent together wasn't a day but a week, a month, a lifetime. So many unexpected confessions, so many old, and new, feelings . . . It's not a day I can easily erase from my memory, and I don't even know if I want to. I'm attaching the snapshot we took of ourselves down on the beach at Puolo. Sorry that the colors came out looking a bit unnatural, or maybe we actually did get a bit sunburned. I forgot to tell you that from there it's only a short distance to la Regina Giovanna, at least by sea. Do you remember when we went there with Sonia and Carlo?

As you know, the next day I met up with Gabriele in Naples. Now I wonder if you two arranged it like that on purpose so that your paths wouldn't cross at all: you driving away in your flashy car (sorry to be so resentful) and him getting off the train all disheveled. I was already missing you and so

268

straightaway I started talking your brother's head off, about you. Gabriele must have thought I was crazy, though he didn't say so. He seemed to understand my need to let it all out. I talked about you in the little streets around the city center, I talked about you at La Campagnola restaurant. The food was amazing, I even drank a bit, and finally I got to the end of all that latent energy that had me so fired up. Gabriele didn't talk much about himself: Am I wrong or is he more disheartened than before? But even you may not know the answer to that . . .

Naples hasn't changed. Maybe it's true that the city always stays the same and we're the ones who change. But what's wrong with not changing, with being consistent with one's nature till the very end? (Even if, in the case of Naples, being consistent also means sometimes being inconsistent, unpredictable, and barking mad?) In order to be true to yourself, you first have to know who you really are, to be able to look in the mirror and recognize yourself . . .

Anyway, our old place hasn't changed, either, at least from the outside. Gabriele told me that he couldn't handle seeing our building again and that he'd wait for me at the café at the bottom of the street. So I walked up Via De Deo by myself: funny, I hadn't remembered it quite that steep. Did you know that the vegetable grocer who was always trying to rip us off is still there? And did you know that 33 is still my lucky number? Maybe it was a good thing that the gate was locked. I didn't want to get emotional, I wanted to be strong for Gabriele.

We stayed the night on Corso Umberto, in the apartment of a friend of his who'd gone on vacation. It was stinking hot even at night, so we turned out all the lights and opened the balcony to let in some fresh (though polluted) air. We sat there in the dark watching an old movie on TV while Gabriele drank whiskey. The scene was so familiar that suddenly all the painful memories came flooding back and I just couldn't hold them back anymore. Now I understand why you used to say your eyes stung every time you came back to Naples, although for me it's not because of the smog.

I have to go. I keep thinking of you, but the pictures I keep seeing in my mind's eye are no longer past-tense images but the present-tense ones from only a few days ago. So you're not just some ghost after all, but a man in flesh and blood . . .

A big hug,

h.

25

THE SPRING FLEW BY between writing the first draft of my thesis and hanging out with our friends. One evening when I went out with Angelo and Tonino, we were walking along Via Costantinopoli in the direction of Piazza Bellini when a moped rode up close to me, much closer than necessary given how empty the street was at that hour. The Vespa slowed to a crawl and, with the muscle control of a skilled classical dancer, edged in close enough to caress me with its breath but without so much as brushing against me. Then the driver reached a hand out to slide it like a letter opener between my legs. Just like that. Then he revved up and sped away, with the boys chasing after him hurling abuse at his wake. When I got home I didn't mention the incident to Pietro. It would have only fueled his anti-Naples fire, which was already raging with polluted air and potholed roads, unemployment and corruption. And even I was starting to suspect that the urban regeneration we'd gradually come to believe in might simply be a gift that could be taken back at any given moment.

It was in just such a climate of distrust that the day arrived when I was scheduled to discuss and defend my thesis. As though it were any old morning, I first stopped by the homeless man, the priest, to give him breakfast. As I left, I told him to take care, reverting back to the formal "you" that his true social position deserved. He waved back at me joyously: he'd never done so before and I took it as a good sign.

The truth was that I was in a mild state of panic and searching for signs: any one would do. I'd begged Pietro not to come with me to the deconsecrated church across from Palazzo Giusso, so as to not make me nervous. However, Mamma Rita hadn't taken no for an answer. Her bleached blond hair was easy to spot among the other parents and relatives dressed in their Sunday best. I squeezed through to sit in the pew next to Rita, who smelled of Fendi and roasted eggplant and fresh nail polish, wishing we weren't there but in her kitchen cooking and gossiping. All the more so when she pointed her candy-red nail at the photographer she'd hired to take pictures of the big moment.

"Don't look at me like that, sweetheart," she said, pretending to be cross as she often did. "What, you think the pictures are for you? They're for your dad and Barbara." Then she loosened my hair from its messy bun, blending in some dialect to say, "But, for heaven's sake, you could've at least brushed your hair. You look like a wet cat, just like the first day I met you at the train station in Castellammare, remember?"

"How could I forget?" I said, waiting excitedly for the story she loved to tell again and again.

"It was drizzling and your hair was plastered onto your scalp just like it is now. And there was Tanya coming off the train along with you, and without even having seen a picture of you I recognized you straight off the bat. I said to myself, I did, 'That's my Eddie.' Remember? And Santina was still being such a pain in the ass, going on and on like a broken record, 'C'mon, Rita, why don't you take Tanya home with you instead? She won't be happy at Giusi's house. I'll just swap the forms for AFSAI and it's done. One American girl is as good as another.' And I went, 'Forget it, Santina, for the last time! Tell AFSAI that I don't want no girl called Tanya. Eddie's coming to live with me, end of story.'"

Rita giggled like a schoolgirl, heedless of the seriousness and pride surrounding us. A few audience members turned to look at her, while others preferred to simply eavesdrop.

"And you remember how my sister Italia couldn't ever remember your name so she decided to call you Candy Candy, like the doll?" She was laughing contagiously, infecting me only to then reinfect herself and making her long earrings jingle, a pair I'd given her years before. "And now look at you, all grown up. Nearly a university graduate."

The anxiety came back with a vengeance, worse than ever when a procession of professors walked in to reign over a long table decked with bound theses and microphones. A sacred silence fell over the audience when the first candidate was invited to take a seat before the panel. I tried to focus more on what the girl was saying than on my heart hammering inside my chest, but her words—mangled by the microphone and echoed in the vault of the church—seemed unreal. Compounding my stupor were the camera flashes from the professional doing ninja moves around her.

I came back down to earth only when the poor girl was asked a question by none other than Signorelli, my glottology professor who had kept me glued to my seat morning after morning at the Astra Cinema. I was relieved to see that my supervisor, Benedetti, was seated beside him looking positively amused by the excess of formality. At the far end of the table sat my Russian language professor, the unfaithful husband of my amnesiac literature professor, wearing the expression of a death mask, his eyes pointing downward and cheeks drooping earthward as if tugged down by the gravitational pull. Was it boredom or rather regret?

A round of flashes and a round of applause and the student wasn't a *studentessa* anymore but a *dottoressa* and they were already calling my name. Rita gave me several encouraging, snappy pats on my thigh.

I stood up and walked toward the panel professors as if in a dream. Everything sounded faraway and was moving in slow motion. I had enough time to straighten my pant legs and survey the crowd of relatives, the statue of Saint Mark taming the lion, and even the photographer inserting a new roll of film into his camera. And still I hadn't reached the committee table. My feet were leaden; I had to drag them.

When I finally did reach my seat, the real world flooded back to me in all its speed and coarseness. Someone in the audience cleared phlegm from their throat. The fat microphone shoved into my hand was sticky with the previous candidate's cold sweat. "*Buongiorno*," I heard myself say in an amplified, foreign voice.

When Benedetti lifted up my thesis—its blue cover and gold lettering— summarizing it with excessive praise, I landed firmly in the present. I was in fact so rooted in the moment, maybe even bogged down, as to be certain I wouldn't retain a single memory of any nonsense that came out of my mouth. I spoke about pronouns and political correctness. I pulled out dazzling terminology, I gesticulated liberally. I even made an ironic joke that caused Benedetti to guffaw and whack the table—and the pens to go flying. I faltered only when my Russian professor asked me a question in Russian. As I stammered out an answer, kneading and shaping those impure vowels with my tongue, I hoped with every ounce of my being that I'd never be forced to use Russian again, every sound of which was a painful reminder that I'd made a terrible mistake. Nevertheless, my Russian professor nodded his approval and I found myself on my feet along with the committee, showered in flashes. Benedetti cranked my hand up and down, saying over the applause in his booming, northern voice, "One hundred and ten points with honors! Excellent job, *dottoressa!*"

I had pulled off my last disguise.

One more candidate and the morning session was over. We all flowed out of the church like a river into the sea. Outside, the stagnant, early-summer air embraced me. My relief was so enormous as to appear fatal, and I was suddenly overcome with the sleep deprivation accumulated over the previous few months of obsessive rewrites. Rita held me against her—she was laughing or perhaps shaking with emotion, I'm not sure—and I collapsed into her large chest, brittle hair, and red sugar-coated kisses. She said, "Listen, sweetheart, this Saturday night we'll all be waiting for you in Castellammare to celebrate. Bring something sexy to wear because afterward I'm taking you out dancing in Sorrento."

I was still waving her goodbye when Benedetti sidled up beside me and leaned against the low stone wall. I noticed that, true to his principles to the very end, even today he was wearing blue jeans. Fixing his outrageous eyes on me from behind his thick lenses, he flashed me a mischievous smile. He told me there was a small publishing house he'd already published with that might be interested in putting out my thesis. I was watching his lips move but I couldn't make sense of his words. It was only when he mentioned a doctorate that I gathered my wits.

"I have connections at the University of Bari," he was saying. "You'd have a good chance of being offered one for the next academic year." With that, he gave me a comrade's pat on the back so hard it nearly took my breath away.

I was flattered, but no. The last thing I wanted was to keep on studying until I turned into Benedetti, somewhere even deeper in the boot than Naples.

To celebrate my graduation, we partied into the night. People I hadn't seen in a while turned up, as did others I didn't know at all—Tonino's or Gabriele's friends or perhaps friends of friends—who seemed unaware of the occasion. All the better. I drank a beer and half a glass of wine, I was cheerful and outgoing. But eventually I became nauseated and irritated by the music turned up too loud and the smoke saturating my clothes and hair. I thought about seeing if Pietro wanted to sneak away from it all, upstairs to our bedroom, but I couldn't find him. I scoured the living room and the kitchen, squeezing through the guests to make my way out to the little terrace. And there he was, in a poorly lit corner of the roof talking with Sonia.

He was leaning against the protective wall, his legs slightly parted. Smoking a joint, he was listening to her carefully, nodding and grinning. Sonia looked agitated: she was talking with her hands, laughing nervously. It was crazy but seeing them like that, just the two of them on the roof with the city ablaze behind them and the surprise of the marijuana—the pure secrecy of the scene—I felt as if I were burning inside with a little blue flame, a cold hissing heat.

"Oh, hi, Eddie," said Sonia as soon as she saw me in that rapid-fire way of hers. Pietro turned to look at me, letting out a soundless, self-conscious laugh. Sonia, quickly saying that it was late and she needed to get going, left us alone on the black bitumen, hot under my feet as if it had absorbed all the sun beating down on it throughout that long summer's day.

"Are you all right?" he asked.

"It's nothing . . . maybe I had too much to drink."

"You could afford a hangover, you know."

I took it as a criticism—always the one who didn't know how to drop her defenses, let loose, chill. But evidently that's not what Pietro meant.

"You don't have class tomorrow morning," he clarified with a mixture of admiration and envy. "Not tomorrow or ever again. You're free, now you can do whatever the hell you feel like."

That's when it finally hit me, the extraordinary reality that after two decades of continuous study I was free. And that the only thing now anchoring me to Naples was Pietro.

As soon as the sun came up, a humid heat would start rising off the Spanish Quarter like sweat evaporating with the first rays of light. The *afa* was back, that bad breath released from the street slabs which first snuck into the street-level homes to then move on to the first-floor apartments. By eight thirty in the morning the *afa* would already be slithering up the crumbling plaster of our courtyard, stopping off at every balcony— on the second, third, and then fourth floors. It took its sweet time, drying itself off with the laundry on the line and licking the garlic braids and maybe even dropping in for a coffee. Then it would make its way to the upper floors, hauling up with it, as though personally delivering us a full *paniere*, all the smells and sounds of our building's residents as they dragged themselves out of bed: the first smokers' coughs, the first showers, the first altercations.

The *afa* got under people's skin. Our neighbors at 33 Via De Deo bickered more and more often, at more and more indecent hours. Two voices in particular stood out from the rest: a female voice all fire and brimstone (and yet she was always referring to that other element, water) and a male voice claiming innocence, even ignorance. But if he wasn't able to mollify that fire alarm by playing Mr. Nice Guy, then it would get ugly fast, with him screaming back at her in the most graphic language. Had they not been separated by the courtyard, they surely would have come to blows. The uproar would wake me up for good, if it wasn't the heat that got to me first. Especially now that I had no lessons to run to, the *afa* poked fun at me first thing in the morning; it seemed to enjoy watching me toss half-naked on the sheets and laughing at my freedom.

One morning I cajoled Pietro away from the computer to come out with me for breakfast. Knowing Gambrinus made him feel on edge since it was "only for a certain class of people," I suggested the humble little café on Via Roma. "Plus, there's a man there I'd like you to meet."

But amid the morning mob—people heading to work or window shopping—I couldn't see the priest's wheelchair. Pietro and I went in the café and ordered coffees and a croissant to share. Once outside, I again scanned the bare patch of sidewalk. Maybe he was spending the day at the shelter, in spite of the fine weather.

"So who was the guy you wanted me to meet?"

"Oh, maybe another time."

"Should I be jealous?"

To stretch our legs, we cut behind the old bank building to reach Piazza Municipio. Overlooking the square was Maschio Angioino Castle; the sea was reduced to a dotted line behind the ships docked at the port. The sky was that chalky blue that signaled a sweltering day was on its way, and in fact the stray dogs in the piazza were already gasping for breath in the paltry shade of the umbrella pines. Emaciated, they lay there with their titties stretched out beside them like IV bags barely keeping them alive. Nothing moved in the still air.

"Cigarette break? Take pity on me," Pietro said, dropping onto a bench. "It's stinking hot today. I can't wait to get out of this city, to run for the hills. Even if I have to do my civilian service to do it."

"Well, you've asked to be stationed in or around Naples, so just wait and see."

Pietro said nothing as he pulled out a cigarette. Although there wasn't even a hope of wind, perhaps out of habit he cupped his hands around the flame to light up.

"You've put in a request, haven't you?"

His lips pressed around his Marlboro, Pietro mumbled something that was neither a yes or a no but managed to devastate me all the same. "They would have never given it to me anyway, baby. That's not the way it works in Italy. They try to send all the peasant boys to the north and the factory boys to the south. That way, at least in theory, the two learn to not beat the crap out of each other. And so it will have taken *only* two hundred years to achieve the unification of Italy. *Here we either make Italy, or we die!*"

I tied up my hair, damp with sweat. He'd quoted General Garibaldi in an unpleasantly cheerful military voice, as if he took pleasure in following orders. "And that's OK with you?"

"Hell no. I'm just saying that's their plan and we're just pawns in it." Pietro blew smoke toward the sea; the ash crawled noiselessly up his cigarette, and beyond it the traffic moved smoothly along the road flanking the port.

"Don't you want to be near me?"

"Is that what you think? It's not about you." He crushed his half-smoked Marlboro under his shoe to look me square in the eye. "I don't come from money, like Carlo, and I'm not well connected so I can forget about getting stationed in the province of Naples. But even if I wanted to try my luck by requesting it, it would be like shooting myself in the foot."

"Why?"

"Because staying here would mean another year and a half with my parents breathing down my neck. It makes no difference to them whether I'm in Naples studying geology or playing bingo with paraplegics. They'll still want me to make the trek all the way to Monte San Rocco every goddamn weekend to work my butt off."

"You could say no once in a while."

"Easy for you to say. Don't you see how hard it is to say no when they're just a stone's throw away? I need physical space from them, that's what I need. Monumental space, topographical space! Is that too much to ask, for fuck's sake?"

It shocked me to see him so short-tempered; I almost thought I'd done something wrong. I wrapped my bare arm around his, creating a silk of perspiration between us. "OK, let's talk about topography then," I said, listing each and every one of our dreams around a world that was a ball in our hands.

My words seemed to lighten his mood because he squeezed his eyes shut, saying, "It doesn't matter where we are, baby, as long as we're together. I'd live with you in a suitcase, in the trunk of a car, in the hold of a ship . . . a tepee in the desert . . ."

". . . an igloo in the Arctic . . ."

It was a testament to just how inhospitable Monte San Rocco was that we would find it more feasible to live out of a car or sleep on the bare ice. Ignoring the heat and the public place, we kissed. A Vespa came sputtering up a nearby street, and as soon as the young driver had reached our height he mimicked a sloppy kiss, with sucking sounds and all, at the nasty end of which he shouted in dialect, "Get her to do you a blow job too!"

"Swear to god, I can't take it no more," said Pietro, resorting to another cigarette as well as his own dialect.

It wasn't just a dark mood, I could see that now, but rather a discontent with roots that went frighteningly deeper than I'd thought. But whatever it was that was undermining him, I had to help him snap out of it. I changed tactics, talking about the practical steps we needed to take in order to get our plans off the ground. The more details I came up with, the more momentum they gained.

I suggested that while he was completing his civilian service I could get an odd job and start saving up for our plane tickets. In the meantime Pietro could work on his résumé and research jobs in oil, starting with his petroleum geology professor. As for my own future career (a dauntingly adult word), the truth was I'd never thought seriously about what I could do with a degree that was as elegant and flimsy as the parchment it was printed on. Even in this respect I was waiting for fate to show me the way, to assign me a new dot for starters, and then like a chameleon I would blend into that new scenario. I was good at that.

However, it was difficult to say at which point my destiny, work-wise and location-wise, had become so entirely, and probably unfairly, pinned on Pietro. I realized that as much as he needed me to get him out of Naples, to the same degree I needed him to get me out—to tear me away from the city, help me battle my fears, and tell me not to look back. I was sitting there on a bench gesticulating and confidently itemizing the concrete details of our great adventure, but inside I was afraid of being full of baloney, of ultimately being all talk and no action. Hot air. I wasn't quite sure how, but somewhere along the line I'd become just another dreamer in a city already teeming with them.

"Then we'll be free," I wrapped it up rather overdramatically.

"Free . . ."

Liberi . . . Indeed it was a lovely word even just to pronounce, the tongue arching toward the palate as if about to take flight. But it didn't seem to make any impression on Pietro. "Isn't that what you want?"

"I'm just tired, baby, that's all. I'm a prisoner of my family. And sometimes I feel like a prisoner of the university too."

Out of the blue I was reminded of that evening when Pietro had dismissed the notion that I'd experienced an earthquake in the underground city. Undoubtedly he was right, but hadn't I felt *something*, a sensation of bewilderment and loss as if every cell in my body had forgotten its purpose? Now I had the same intuitive feeling of loss that I couldn't deny and yet its source was a geological impossibility.

"Pietro, do you still love me?"

"Don't you know the answer to that?"

After Pietro went home to keep on typing up his thesis, I stopped in a local market and bought him the heaviest band of silver (from Mexico, or so said the vendor) that I could find. I bought it on impulse, and only afterward did I think to give it to him on his graduation day. I wasn't sure, though, if I'd gotten the right size because, even though Pietro had large hands, they were, in the words of Sonia, *the hands of a gentleman*.

From: tectonic@tin.it
To: heddi@yahoo.com
Sent: September 7

Dearest Heddi,

I was waiting for your email. I was anxious but I knew it was coming. What can I say? Every time I read your words I feel the distance between us grow smaller. I always read your letters with a smile, for the way you write. It was wonderful to see you again, unforgettable; it will be a chapter of its own in the book I'll write when I'm an old man. You haven't changed a bit, at least not on the outside and, as far as I could tell, not on the inside either.

I'll try to be honest. I expected you to tell me that you'd found love again, that you'd moved on . . . maybe I even hoped so. It would have mortified me a little, made me feel like a dog with its tail between its legs and reminded me of what an idiot I was to leave you . . . basically I wanted, and perhaps I still want, the extra dose of suffering I deserve. But instead I came back home with a much stronger feeling: I feel I have to do something. That something is to leave everything behind and escape, to come to New Zealand.

But obviously there's a wide gap—an ocean—between words and deeds, especially when it comes to me. I won't deny that I'm in a very confused state of mind. I spend a lot of time imagining the scene, the places, your house, your friends, and I try to paste myself into those pictures. I like what I see. But I'm also well aware that I might be misunderstanding, or at least it might be easy to misunderstand, what I feel for you and my desire to live a life that's different from the one I have, the one that is probably my lot. What do I feel for you? An affection that knows no bounds: such a large part of me belongs to you, was created and shaped by you, from the way I dress to the way I think, to my craving to see the world . . . I want to come see you "down under" if for nothing else than to see what possibilities I still have and what is left to salvage of what we once were or what we could have been. I don't know if I can make it . . . I will certainly try.

I know it's difficult to understand my behavior, but every which way I look at my situation it's hard to see a way out. It's that terrible combination of my character, my matriarchal-patriarchal upbringing, the ball and chain of my possessions and attachments, as well as laziness and fear. It seems that whatever I do I have to give something up, and giving up means losing out . . . I haven't figured it out yet, you'll have noticed . . . I'm confused and afraid but I don't want to make the same mistake again. I don't want you to wait for me. I want to surprise you . . .

I'm holding you close,

p.

26

A ND THEN it was Pietro's turn, a much less formal affair compared to the discussion of my thesis. Unsurprisingly, Lidia and Ernesto showed up that day at the Department of Geological Sciences, accompanied by Gabriele. Although the cloister was a peaceful spot, the urban commotion banging at the door made their parents look overheated and overwhelmed, like peasants fresh off the transalpine train. Their mother in particular, deprived of her kerchief and her dialect, looked out of her depth, and I was again nagged by that insidious compassion that came back whenever I was finally feeling strong.

Afterward I gathered them under an arcade for a family portrait. I clicked once. Twice. Three times. From one frame to the next there was no change in their expressions or postures, like they were painfully posing for a daguerreotype. All four had their arms crossed and were, despite me urging them to move in closer, remarkably disconnected, as though they were magnets with matching poles and therefore repelled each other by their very nature. I hoped in any case that this memento of Pietro's graduation day, nicely framed, would be worthy of a second glance, unlike that ludicrously feminine shawl. I was well past trying to win his parents over, but I recognized that giving them such a gift on such an occasion was the proper thing to do. One last show of goodwill before taking their son away.

I waited until they'd gone to give him the silver ring, which Pietro slid onto the ring finger of his right hand. "I love it, baby," he said. "I'll never take it off."

I was just in time to give him that private symbol of love, which very conveniently advertised publicly that he was taken, for soon he was called to carry out his civilian service in the province of Rome and I got an under-the-table job in the café in Piazza San Domenico. It was the kind of frantic and servile work I was used to in DC, but I also had to clean the bathrooms, which resembled crime scenes after those free concerts. The irony was not lost on me that my highbrow degree had led me to soil my hands in such a humiliating way, whereas Pietro's degree, which practically required him to, had led him to work, albeit without pay, in a library.

Like an out-of-shape runner, the bus struggled up the hills of the Castelli Romani, which from the window looked like a set of postcards. On the phone Pietro had told me it was like that. *Jewels* he'd called them. I listened to my fellow passengers as they chatted away using those lazy consonants, that laid-back accent the Romans had every right to have after so many centuries of extraordinary and strenuous endeavors. Except for the background sounds, the journey was much like the one to Borgo Alto. A hilly land possessive of its clusters of houses, the road that wandered and lost its train of thought and never seemed to get to the point.

When the bus finally arrived at the edge of the town, Pietro was waiting for me along with four or five others, his hands jammed into his pockets and barely restraining a smile. It was that inner battle he always fought in the name of discretion, but it moved me nonetheless.

He kissed me and grabbed my bag. "Welcome to Monte Porzio Catone, population 1,227."

"Is that all?"

"Well, plus one. Today, plus two," he said, starting off. "Monte Porzio Catone, population 1,229." He seemed to like repeating the name; it rolled off his tongue with a Roman drawl he'd clearly been practicing since he'd left. I noticed too that he looked refreshed—his eyes were bright, his skin glowing—and I suddenly understood the toll it had taken on him to complete his thesis in such a short time.

"You look great. The fresh air must be doing you good."

"Fresh air is a God-given right."

The way to his place was a freshly swept pedestrian lane. It was like walking into a tourist brochure: bicycles leaning up against buildings that were only two or three stories high, hot-pink geraniums oozing from balconies that had nobody leaning over them, nobody screaming their head off, and an ambiguous light that could have been either morning or afternoon sun, as you pleased. It looked like a movie set. It was the siesta and the only sounds were our footsteps over cobblestones, a series of little pillows that rounded the soles of my sandals. I had the crazy thought of moving to that sleepy town just to be near him.

"Remember," he said, taking out a set of keys, "if anybody asks, you're just stopping by for a coffee. If my supervisor finds out I have an overnight guest, I'm in deep shit."

We stopped at the door of a new structure, "the summer villa," as he called it. Beside it was a soccer field littered with banners and foldout tables and chairs, and beyond that was the wall encircling the village. We'd walked straight through the town in a matter of minutes.

"This weekend they're putting on a dog show," he explained. "Cani e Castelli. It's the biggest event on the Monte Porzio summer calendar."

"A dog show? Let's go!"

"Sure, if you feel like it."

His apartment, on the ground floor, resembled a motel room. Newly tiled and painted, it had an electric burner, a bathroom, a single bed, and a single window. Pietro opened it up, letting in the pleasant scent of freshly cut grass from the sports field.

"So what do you think?"

"Well, it's hardly what I imagined. It's very comfortable."

"I know. I lucked out, didn't I," he said with satisfaction. "I'm always on my own and there's nothing to do in the evenings, but it won't be for long. In two or three weeks another poor soul will be joining me to liven things up. Some guy from Calabria."

"The unification of the nation, right?" I put on a lighthearted tone but deep down I was troubled by his semantics. *Lucked out?* This town, his apartment, in fact this entire situation, was only temporary, a minor, calculated deviation in our plans. So then why was Pietro talking like it was the final destination?

I handed him the latest issue of *National Geographic*; he suggested we go for a walk. Preparations were in full swing on the soccer field, where dogs of all sizes and colors were weaving through the people, sniffing each other, rolling on the grass, and chasing tennis balls. As soon as they saw us strolling past, they leaped up to greet us with senseless joy. Pietro looked at ease, ruffling a few coats and letting the dogs play-bite his hand.

He took me along the wall that signaled the end of the old town. We leaned over it, our elbows on the rough stone, and gazed out over the valley, which was barely visible in the summer haze.

"Up here I have the illusion of being—how the hell does it go?—master of my fate, captain of my soul . . ."

"It's a pretty spot."

We continued down the dirt path that followed the wall. The cicadas were scratching at the tree bark and the dusty heat was a veil we had to move out of the way with our hands. I asked Pietro if we could have a look around the town center, but he wanted to wait till evening. "I'd like to take you out to dinner. There's this little restaurant that looks promising. I've been wanting to try it out since I got here but I don't have the bucks to live the high life anymore."

"I have some money," I offered, but it was the wrong thing to say to Pietro, who always wanted to be the man.

"Keep your money," he said sullenly, looking down at his shoes, which were the same ones he wore when we first met but which suddenly didn't seem so practical in this heat. "Anyway, I was waiting for a special occasion to go. I've invited Giuliano and his girlfriend to join us. They're driving in from Rome." The same Giuliano who used to be his classmate, the one who'd saved him from possibly spiraling out of control.

They had ventured all the way to the capital and were living together, so I expected Pietro's friends to be two alternative students, even more alternative than us. Yet Giuliano wasn't a boy at all but a soft couch of a man. He was tall with square shoulders and square glasses like little televisions reflecting the fluorescent light of the restaurant, and the beginnings of a potbelly. He worked part-time although he hadn't yet finished his degree. As they talked about felsic and ultramafic rock, Pietro watched his old friend with an admiration I could almost touch.

His girlfriend, Rosaria, dark-haired and olive-skinned and native as well to the province of Avellino, had fertile hips and a warm, nononsense voice. From across the checkered tablecloth, every now and then she widened her eyes at me with implied exasperation before finally announcing, "Boys, we like rocks too—well, sort of—but enough is enough. Why don't you pour us some more wine?" I let Giuliano fill my glass, too, but only so I could be Pietro's wine bank. Rosaria said, "There, that's better. Now let's talk about something we can all join in on. For example, the wedding."

Pietro blushed, curling his fingers over his mouth.

"Not yours, you poor pup," she clarified. "Ours."

Pietro nodded with approval, congratulating them both. Rosaria accepted his best wishes, pretending to be in a huff and saying it was about time, after seven years together.

"Now we can finally tell our parents we're living together," said Giuliano.

"No, sir, not before the wedding!"

As if to celebrate the good news, the waiter arrived just then with a steaming plate of *coda alla vaccinara* and roasted artichokes. We all dug into the oxtail stew—"a country recipe," as Pietro and Giuliano praised it—as we discussed the dress, the church, the reception. They had "only" ten months to get ready.

Talking about these topics made Giuliano grumble, but I think it was only out of embarrassment. Like Pietro, he was humble and unaffected, and most certainly he didn't like the prospect of spending an entire day in the center of attention. To make light of it, he turned toward me to say, "Eddie, do you see what women are like in our neck of the woods? They're high-powered planners. Rosaria would make a great manager of a multinational company, don't you think?"

"Well, what can you say?" she said, punctuating the air with her fork. "You know the old proverb: Choose wives and oxen from your hometown." *Mogli e buoi dai paesi tuoi.*

We burst out laughing, and Pietro proposed a toast. "To the best couple I've ever met."

We drank. Giuliano told us we were obviously invited to the wedding. "And don't you dare bring an envelope full of cash. We would never accept it from you. All you need to do is turn up, eat, and dance."

"Like total boors?" said Pietro cheerfully. "It would be an honor. I wouldn't miss it for the world."

When the men started up again with rocks, I took the opportunity to ask Rosaria more about their Irpinia wedding, which she seemed more than happy to answer. The music, the party favors, the honeymoon: she had in fact worked it out down to the last detail. The concept of a wedding as a lavish party had never entered my mind, yet our conversation still managed to make me feel that they were the real adults and not Pietro and I—regardless of our degrees, our titles as *dottori*, our great potential . . . and our great expectations. They had their feet firmly planted on the ground, and next to them we were nothing but fluid and elongated shadows at their backs, slender and prolonged forms of youth.

Toward the end of dinner, I nudged my wine toward Pietro, but he made what almost seemed like a gesture of annoyance. "I'm good," he said.

Afterward we went back to Pietro's hygienic apartment. Through the window, the soccer field was filling with the silhouettes of four-legged friends and their chaperones. There was talking, barking, laughter, music. The sky was split in two: on top the night pressing down, and below a sunset the color of a bitten-off plum.

There was nowhere to sit in that bare space but the single bed. I sat on the edge, while Pietro leaned back comfortably against the wall. "I really enjoyed meeting Giuliano and Rosaria," I said. "They're lovely people."

"And now they're settling down too."

"Did you know that in English people say 'to tie the knot'? As if marriage was a knot that can't be undone."

"More like a ball and chain."

My heart sank violently.

"It's just a figure of speech, baby. They make a great couple."

"Right, they're the best couple you've ever met."

At my involuntarily bitter tone, Pietro hastened to say, "You and me, we're like spaghetti and sauce. There's no contest." He rested his head back against the wall and closed his eyes. "Jesus, I'm tired. I could almost go to sleep right now."

"What about the dog show?"

Pietro seemed not to have heard me. How could he possibly be sleepy now, when we hadn't seen each other in sixteen days? Forty-eight hours was all we had, and I'd already squandered three of them on the bus.

Admittedly, he'd done all the right things from the moment I'd arrived—carried my bag, paid for my dinner; he'd reassured me, kissed me—but all those gestures felt slightly off, like the notes of a familiar tune played off-key. I called him by name, but still there was no reaction: he was dead to the world. Could he be pretending to sleep?

"Pietro," I said again, louder his time. "Is there something wrong?"

"No. Nothing." He opened his eyes and reached over to the bedside table for his fresh pack of Marlboro Lights, hitting it again and again to push down the tobacco and repeating again and again that there was nothing wrong. The more he said it, the more I sensed that that something that wasn't there was even more wrong than I'd imagined.

"It's just that you don't seem like yourself anymore."

"Of course I'm not myself anymore, baby. Do you realize what my situation is?" He tore off the cellophane and snatched out a cigarette. "I'm being forced to live in a town in the middle of nowhere, all by myself, working my ass off every day—boxes full of books that weigh a ton, *put that one here*, *put that one there*—and they don't pay me a dime. Is this what I did five years of university for, to be someone's lackey? Goddamn it, this is called slavery, or am I wrong? Castelli Romani—peaceful oasis, my ass. Let's just hope this Calabrian is my kind of guy because the only way to deal with these conditions is to be high as a kite. Otherwise, I swear, it'll be *Escape from Alcatraz*."

I couldn't argue with that, and in fact I remembered Pietro once saying he'd rather die than go back to Rome. And I was relieved to discover that we shared the same attitude toward his placement after all. So then maybe with the expression *lucked out* he'd merely been referring to his accommodation, so very different from the buildings we were used to in the Quartieri. It was a modern structure without a history, a place he was simply passing through, not a home but a way station whose floor he could sleep on until the train turned up.

But it still didn't add up. The future seemed to be of no consolation to

Pietro, as if his geological fatalism had morphed into personal defeatism. Besides, he was far too irritated for a weekend of leisure. I would have almost said he was annoyed not so much with the inevitability of the civilian service as with *me*, as if the location and the solitude and the degrading work were somehow my fault. Was he blaming me for the decision we'd made together for him to avoid the military?

The night was dropping lower and lower upon us, leaking into the room. I could hardly see Pietro's face anymore, until his lighter flicked, lighting up a scowl. It was no use looking for excuses: he truly had changed. But was this mutation just from today? I remembered how quick-tempered he was that morning in Piazza Municipio—and the *afa*, I knew, had little to do with it: that sticky heat was merely the salt on an unspeakable wound. And before that there was New Year's, when, with his head over the toilet bowl, he'd sent me away with an echoey voice. *Go!* That's exactly what he said, plain and simple.

"Are you angry with me?"

"Give me a break," he muttered with his cigarette sticking out the corner of his mouth like a cowboy.

"That's what I'm talking about! I ask you a question and you just snap. What have I ever done to you? Just fucking tell me!"

I put my hand over my mouth. I grasped that we'd never actually had a real fight until now and that I'd uttered something irrevocable, tiny but ruinous words like hairline cracks in a porcelain vase. I stood there in shock, covering my mouth with my hand that, I realized now, was trembling uncontrollably.

"You're cold? In this heat?"

"No." I folded my arms. "I just want to know why you're mad at me."

"Let me say it again, I'm not angry with you, baby. Why should I be?"

Outside a love song came blasting through the speakers; the dogs started yapping, the humans started laughing. All together it was deafening. I felt unreasonably cold, my mind fogged by a baseless emotion that wouldn't allow me to think straight, to connect the causes with the effects, to follow a logical thread through the narrative of our relationship. Those words, I sensed, had set me out on a perilous but hazy journey, without a map and without footholds, and in fact Pietro's cigarette smoke was filling the sealed room and the only thing able to punch through it was his fury, like the way a mountaintop tears the clouds.

"I don't know," I said once the volume was adjusted. "I actually don't know why you should be angry." The shaking eased a bit; even the dogs had begun to settle down.

"So you see that you and me have nothing to fight about? Let's just go to sleep." He got up and began unbuttoning his shirt, adding, "The night's gotta pass, as they say in dialect." *Adda passa' 'a nuttata*, Naples's somewhat darker version of "Tomorrow's another day."

I turned away so that I didn't have to see his naked chest, silver with sweat in the late light. I didn't want to desire him: I wanted to order my thoughts. Had his anger really crept up on us at New Year's in the Spanish Quarter and not before, at Christmas, when Pietro had had to go to Monte San Rocco without me? No, earlier still. His was a hot rage, one in fact that had reared its ugly head in the summer . . . All at once I thought I knew what the trigger was. *You're my worst son.* That heinous statement had troubled him then, two weeks before our trip to Greece, and had continued to eat away at him in silence. To consume him.

I glanced over at Pietro unbuckling his belt and went hot with a sudden rush of daring. I was either about to rip his jeans off, kiss him in every corner of his body, and make him mine again, or I was about to set upon him with the most outrageous words, the most scandalous thoughts. It was the rise in body temperature that hits a second before facing something head-on, the red fever of a torero. All trembling ceased at once, and I said with a steady voice, "No, Pietro. There *is* something to fight about, but not with me. It's been staring you in the face for over a year now. But you don't want to rock the boat."

"Exactly. I don't want to make trouble, not with you or anybody else. I want to live in peace. Why do you think I'm doing my civilian service instead of learning how to load a semiautomatic?"

"You know, you should actually make some trouble once in a while. Make a fuss, ruffle some feathers. Lose your temper!"

"You want me to get pissed off, is that what you want? And who do you want me to pick a fight with, huh? With Gabriele?" he said, bulging his eyes like a Maori warrior as if pushing me to confess sins I'd only committed with my mind, for all at once I saw my very presence as an outsider in that sacred bond between brothers as something unforgivable. But then Pietro went on, "For always making me feel, since we were little, like a piece of shit stuck to the bottom of his shoe? Or should I pick a fight with Luca? Because, I swear, just hearing his name makes my blood boil over how close you two are!"

I was disarmed. I didn't think Pietro had a drop of jealousy in him, and yet something as ancient and black as crude oil had just gushed out from his depths. And if he was jealous, did that mean that he was more in love with me, or angrier with me, than I'd thought?

"With who then?" he was pressing me. "Who?"

"Your mother, Pietro, don't you get it? You should be pissed off with your mother!"

He yanked the cigarette from his mouth as if it had burned his lips. "You don't get the situation, Heddi."

"What is there not to get? She's doing everything she can to make sure we break up."

It was dark by now, and Pietro bent over to flick on the bedside lamp. "C'mon now, my mother's four foot eight. She's old, and ignorant at that. What sway could she possibly have over us?"

I wished he hadn't turned on the light, which instantly defused the drama. Plus, at the dog show everyone was having a blast. But I could no longer bear to hear that old refrain of his and I said, "And yet you let her boss you around."

"All right, I'll give you that. I pretty much do what she asks. But, believe it or not, there's something in it for me. Every time I bend over backward for my parents, it works to my advantage. Otherwise, there's no way in hell I'm getting a car." Pietro showed no signs of wanting to sit back down on the bed. He was restless, drawing greedily from his cigarette in the direction of the closed window. "It's disgustingly hot in here, but the mosquitoes . . ."

"But of course you want a car," I kept at him with undisguised irony. "A brand-new one like Francesco's."

"Yes, baby, I do. Do you see how hard it is to live in a place like this without a car? It's like being in exile. But look at Giuliano: even with that rusty piece of junk he owns, if he feels like it, he can leave Rome for a fun night out."

Hearing him associate with such superficiality the vacuous concept of a fun night out with a concrete symbol of aborted dreams, I lost it. I started ranting about how Francesco had given up everything, even his daughter, just to avoid displeasing his mother, that the car wasn't a car but a trap. *Trap*, I used that very word. But I no longer felt hot or cold or afraid of saying the wrong thing because it was the words fueling me and not the other way around. I didn't care how Pietro took it, and in fact he reacted with weak excuses, such as that I was making too big a deal about it, that his parents were just countryfolk intellectually incapable of plotting and scheming, and that they would eventually give him a car. His refusal to incriminate his mother—his generalization, his *pluralization*, of the problem—pushed me to the end of my tether, and I cut him short with the same sarcastic tone. "Never mind, the car is nothing. What's worth much, much more are those wheat fields . . . those sure do make a great bait."

"It's not like you think," he said through clenched teeth. "I have to play my cards right. I can't afford to start acting up at the wrong time." Pietro ran a hand through his hair, the Mexican ring a flash of light among his dark waves. He was smoking nervously and, if before I feared his anger, I now discovered I wanted to feed it.

"When is the right time, Pietro? You have your degree now, so where the hell are those plots of land they promised you? Have they even brought up the matter since your graduation day?"

"Fucking hell, it's like a Turkish bath in here." He started pacing back and forth like a caged animal. "I've sweated blood and tears on that land, too many to throw it all to the wind. I've made a lot of sacrifices! And have I ever complained to my parents? No!"

Just as I'd hoped, he'd raised his voice. Then with a maliciousness I didn't think I had in me, I laid it on even thicker. "Don't you see that you've taken the bait and they've got you in the palm of their hands? They think you'll want that land so bad that you'll do anything to have it. Leave your girlfriend, marry a mussel, whatever they want!"

He came to an abrupt stop, crushing his cigarette to a pulp in the ashtray. "I'm not some fucking puppet!"

I'd done it. Pietro was seeing red. Outside a dog let out a long, primal growl. I'd spoken so recklessly that sooner or later I would regret some of my riskier statements. I'd said offensive things and I hadn't spared anyone. But it had felt good to vent my feelings, and in the satisfaction of the moment I had only the compulsion to keep going. I was almost giddy, drunk on truth, a sort of *in vino veritas* without alcohol that had already made me spill so much red wine onto those hideously white tiles, so why not go all the way, why not tip out the whole bottle?

I stood to face him, warning myself not to—*don't do it*—but still the words came pouring forth. "Don't you see, Pietro? Your parents are taking advantage of the fact that you're so eager to please. What do they care—no, what does your *mother* care—about you finding a career, personal fulfillment, true love or happiness in your life? Compared to postwar famine, these things are self-indulgent luxuries that don't fit into her way of thinking because in Lidia Iannace's world the only things that matter are working hard, saving up, and making sacrifices, all the way to the grave! And she'll give you her support, and maybe even her affection, only when you've thrown your life away like she has!"

Pietro's eyes went wide; he looked stunned by what I'd had the nerve to say. I could hardly believe I'd said it myself, but this time I didn't even remotely want to take it back. I felt I was in the right, safeguarded by the facts. I looked him straight in the eye until he looked away. Then, still bare-chested, he leaned back against the wall; he seemed to go limp and then his knees buckled and, like a raindrop on a window, he slid down to the floor. Curled up in a ball, Pietro buried his face in his hands. "No, you're wrong," came his muffled voice. "No, no . . ."

It was one of those scenes I thought only happened in the movies: the moment of truth, a gut-wrenching epiphany. All at once my bitterness was gone, and I crouched down beside him. I loved and desired him more than ever and I had the familiar impulse to stroke him and make him feel safe. But I didn't. My love for him was no longer a drug, no longer a need to satisfy. It was the beginning of everything; it was the god I'd never believed in.

I lowered my voice. "You need to understand, Pietro, that being with me means you might get cut out of the inheritance." The risk was very real. Wasn't his brother Vittorio, who had received neither land nor money nor even a mention, as good as disowned? And his only sin was setting up a life far from Monte San Rocco, against Lidia's wishes, and marrying a foreign girl.

Pietro didn't say a word. He was just shaking his head, kneading his temples like dough. Maybe it was a good thing that I couldn't see his face. I needed him to fully explore his pain but I wasn't sure I was strong enough to watch it.

"And anyway, what do you need that land for if you're only going to sell it?" I said in a gentler tone. "We're graduates now; we can earn our own money. We'll be poor but happy."

He uncovered his face, reddened though devoid of tears, before looking away toward the wall. For some reason the dogs started howling, just like they did at night in Monte San Rocco. They sounded like wolves. We listened to them for a while without talking; then Pietro went back to

297

working his temples even more furiously. But there could be no resolution without a conclusion.

"In the end the choice is yours. What's worth more to you: your family's money or your freedom?"

It was a very simple question, maybe even idiotic, the correct answer to which was based on not only our own values but the value system of our entire generation. But Pietro didn't answer. Instead he kept digging his fingers into his perspiring forehead as if hell-bent on skinning himself alive.

The only light left in the sky was a fresh green glint on the horizon, as pale as sea glass. The first stars were coming out of hiding. Pietro and I sat on the damp grass, far from the floodlights and people on the incomprehensibly festive field.

There was laughing, singing, and clapping for several dogs standing haphazardly at a starting line, held back by their owners. So it wasn't just a dog show but a dog *race*. "Three, two . . ." came a voice through the microphone, but there was a false start, followed by more laughter and clumsy attempts to pull the animals back in line. The presenter, amused by the disorder, began the countdown again and finished with a loud, "Get set . . . Go!" at which the contestants dashed down the grassy track chasing, it seemed, only the air.

I thought of turning to Pietro to say something about the dogs but I didn't know what to say. We'd come to a kind of no-man's-land beyond words, even beyond feelings. So I said nothing at all, and we both sat there as drained and bare as a bathtub.

But the race, though an amateur and lighthearted event, wasn't over, and the fastest eight dogs were chosen for a second round. Once again toenails tore across the already mauled grass; ears flapped about comically. I almost laughed out loud, a surge of joy that was immediately killed by the memory of our argument. It weighed on my heart like a boulder.

The competition was halved. Among the four remaining, I spotted one dog in particular. Skin and bones and gray as a ghost, she looked like a miniature greyhound. Female no doubt, judging from her showy collar. Most certainly she was shaking like a leaf, and like a leaf she was about to be outrun, if not trampled. Poor thing. I almost turned away so as not to witness her downfall, but in any case I immediately lost sight of her, only gathering from all the fuss at the finishing line that she'd come in first. The applause grew in intensity: the last race, between the two finalists, was about to take place.

The owners restrained their dogs by wrapping their arms around their protruding chests. The little greyhound was champing at the bit, leaping forward to catch, I could see now, a bait that was quivering tauntingly before the two dogs. Then "Go!" and they were let loose. The tiny dog was a shooting dart, but the bait was jerked left and right as if pulled by an impatient fisherman. Her adversary didn't fall for it, but she did . . . and she slipped. Her skeletal hind legs seemed on the verge of detaching from her torso as she twisted herself into an inconceivable posture and grass and clumps of dirt went flying. But in a flash she was back on her feet to continue the contest, which more than a race seemed like a desperate flight, a run for her life.

She won. Everything was over in an instant, among applause and shredded terrain and barks that could even be called happy. Pietro and I went back to the apartment and made love, without sheets and without a word, the whole time looking at each other defiantly in the eyes.

From: heddi@yahoo.com
To: tectonic@tin.it
Sent: September 13

Dearest Pietro,

I read your email this morning at work. I probably shouldn't have, though, because it made me very pleasantly agitated and then only a few minutes later I had to teach a lesson, on conditional sentences no less. Then in the afternoon during a staff meeting, I found out that they're going to have to lay off a few teachers because the number of enrollments has dropped again. Even more surprising was my impulse (though I didn't go through with it) to put my hand up, to be the first one to leave.

I keep thinking about a trip I made a couple years ago with my German roommate to a place about an hour's drive from Auckland, a beach called Pakiri, where you can do horse trekking in small groups. Our instructor got us to saddle up and ride along a path that weaved through the forest until it came to a fork. She asked which of us wanted to keep on going through the woods, an easy ride for beginners, and which of us more experienced riders wanted to canter on the beach. The sea was right there; you could see the stretch of dazzling white sand. My friend, who had much more experience than me with horses, opted for the beach, while I chose the forest. But my horse wouldn't budge, he wouldn't follow the single file ducking under the trees no matter how hard I kicked him in the sides: he was just standing there, still but tense. Then without warning, he spun around and started running toward the sea. I grabbed the reins but I was practically suspended in midair above the saddle; I could feel his muscles taut with his frightening strength, his hooves crushing the scrub and wrecking the sand dunes, his mane flapping against my face. He was actually galloping, just like they do in Westerns, and it was a miracle that I didn't fall off. He slowed down only when he got to the water's edge, once he was side by side with my friend's horse. I only found out later that he was in love with that horse and couldn't stand to be away from her.

New Zealand has helped me find pleasure again in being by myself and finally trust my abilities. But, in a certain way, everyone who passes through here does so without leaving a trace—they're footprints in the sand. New immigrants are always coming in, while those born here sooner or later leave to explore the world, including many of my friends. I've always accepted their departures gracefully and welcomed with open arms those newly arrived to take their places. Will this junction end up being the place where I can finally rest my itchy feet? But then what am I meant to do with this Neapolitan heart of mine?

I have to tell you that I'm afraid, too—of the thoughts we're confessing to each other, the daydreams that we're having . . . I won't deny that I often imagine the two of us here together, walking up volcanoes with our backpacks or having dinner with my friends, who have that funny accent you'd have trouble understanding at first. I imagine you finally working as a geologist, and you and me in Italy two months a year, in the summer there, and the others saying "Lucky them" because we will have found a way to spin the earth like a globe between our hands and make it so that for us winter and bad weather no longer exist.

I hope you can imagine how difficult it is for me to write these words to you. I know that this way I run the risk of making the same mistakes too. But we have only one life to live . . . or maybe not. I hope you'll have it in you to bet on this hand (bet it all?) and come see me at the ends of the earth, even if it's just for a short vacation. And then we'll see.

I'm hugging you back,

h.

27

I FELT LIGHT. My feet seemed to float above the path and my body was wrapped in the finest sheet of mist. For once I was on an excursion without my camera, so I wouldn't even carry a memory of this hike that left no footprints. My bag didn't weigh me down, either, for I'd left it behind, nor was I burdened by the awareness of not knowing where I was or where the dirt path was taking me. All I had in my hand were a few crinkled sheets of paper.

I looked down at them. They were scribbled with frantic peaks like electrocardiograms. They seemed like important graphs but they weren't mine and I couldn't decipher them. Suddenly, I remembered I'd been handed them by the professor in the observatory. *It's the writing on the wall*, he'd said. And there was the observatory down there, a little square painted, like the Capodimonte Museum, in a shade of red that was neither here nor there, and built in a secluded spot high up enough to stay clear of the lava flows. It was a historic building that knew its place and that's why after so many centuries it was still standing. *Don't go to the crater*, the professor had warned me. *Take my advice.*

But in the meanwhile I had nearly made it to the crater. I could tell from the sharp tilt of the path, which was crumbling more and more beneath my feet, and from the sudden difficulty I was having gaining ground. I could tell from the mist that wasn't mist after all but a cloud, and I was inside of it standing right before the shrouded mouth of the volcano as if I'd stepped into the path of a Chimera. I could tell from the feeling of being trapped in a nightmare.

The wind began to blow, ripping the papers from my clenched fist and releasing them into the void. They flapped about like seagulls before a storm and then disappeared. I was truly on my own now. The wind blew away the cloud, too, revealing the jagged, desertlike crater in all its terrible greatness. Under the blinding sun I could see with almost painful clarity every single rock, big and small, each one halted in its own inexorable roll toward the bottom. And below merely debris, pulverized rock, a wasteland. Is this it? I thought to myself.

The crater that I'd so longed to reach wasn't a thing and it wasn't even a place. It was simply *nothing*, an emptiness I didn't think our planet was capable of—it was like a crater on the moon, a void without any hope of redemption or hope of life. I grasped that there is something infinitely worse than an eruption.

But I had no intention of giving in to the sense of betrayal, and even less to vertigo, and I quickly turned to begin my descent. As if toying with me, the volcano started moving, shimmying this way and that, until I tripped. I ended up facedown on the path, my mouth dry with that reddish earth that tasted like nothing. I closed my eyes tight to block out my reality, but underneath me the mountain kept on rolling like a water mattress. So this was what an earthquake was like?

I struggled to get back on my feet, to save myself, but my legs felt like they'd been set in plaster casts. I begged the painfully bright sky to give me a reason to get back up, something to believe in so as to prevail over my weak body, my tired spirit. But the sky did nothing. It was the dreadful knowledge that I was all alone but somehow had to find the strength anyway.

The sun in my eyes woke me up. We'd neglected to lower the blinds, so the morning rays came freely through the window from the sports field.

It was a tight fit in that single bed, and I'd been keeping my legs unnaturally straight in the unconscious attempt to give Pietro space. Only half-awake, I rolled the other way, pulling the sheet with me. I distractedly fingered my silver pendant, hoping to fall back asleep.

But soon details from the night before resurfaced: the pacing back and forth, the extreme words, the drops of sweat, and my final, unanswered question, *The money or your freedom?* Memories that now, in the light of day, devastated me.

"Could you pass me my cigarettes?" came Pietro's voice. "On the bedside table."

"Sure."

He straightened up, hunching his back against the bare wall. He took the pack listlessly and squeezed his eyes shut, as though it had just dawned on him, too, what juncture he was at. I almost expected him to announce that he was going to speak to his mother this very day. Instead he said, "My back hurts."

"Where?"

"In the middle, maybe a little bit over to the left."

"A cramp?"

"No, it's more like a dull pain."

"You probably slept funny."

"Could be. This bed must have been built for one of the seven dwarfs." He lit a cigarette. "I'm not used to sharing a bed this small."

I lowered my bare feet to the tiles without leaning over to kiss him first. It was the only way I could get back at him for his selective memory. How could he not remember the countless times we'd slept in that tiny bed of his before the ceiling collapsed? I was already halfway to the electric burner when Pietro said there was no coffee or anything at all to eat. He suggested we go out for breakfast.

"A café in town?"

"No, we'll just go to the hotel up the hill."

We got dressed and headed out. It was a Sunday and the village was still sleeping. After a few minutes, Pietro stopped in that crooked stance and scrunched up his face.

"My back," he said.

"Maybe your muscles have seized up. If you want, we can turn back and I'll try to massage it out." When he declined, I told him the knot would probably work itself out as the day went on—unless he'd pulled a muscle.

Pietro nodded. Maybe he wasn't listening, and I, too, had the impression I was talking nonsense. Either way, I made no further mention of it. Fumbling in his pockets for another cigarette, he said, "Just give me a minute to catch my breath."

The road wasn't that steep and his sluggishness, indeed his lethargy in *everything*, was sorely testing my patience. Or perhaps it was just the heat. The cicadas were sounding their incessant alarm to warn us of the scorcher on its way. Even though it was only just after eight o'clock, a hot humid haze was already back blanketing the valley, which was still indiscernible but must have been truly beautiful if it had made Pietro feel, if only for a moment, like the master of his fate.

"That's the hotel up there," he said, pointing to the top of the street. He took a few drags from his Marlboro Light, deeply as if breathing from an oxygen mask, before making another series of steps forward. "Let's keep going. I can make it."

We were no more than twenty meters from our destination, but from the way Pietro was talking you would have thought we weren't walking to a hotel but tackling a summit at high altitude, conquering Everest like they did in books.

Our conversation was further reduced, to the point where over breakfast we exchanged only pleasantries. Afterward Pietro took me to see the library where he would be slaving away for an eternity yet.

"Here it is," was all he said.

The library was closed, so we stood in the shade of a tree looking at it from the outside. I didn't know what to say. If only there was a breeze, I was thinking, to make a little choir of those leaves above us—any noise to shatter this fake calm! But there wasn't even a breath of air.

Pietro smoked, inspecting the cobblestones. "It's hot today."

"It is . . ."

In reality, though mild compared to the Neapolitan *afa*, the heat was sucking every last drop of vitality from me too. It was as though a battle had ended and I couldn't tell, nor did I have the strength to figure out, whether I'd come out of it defeated or not. I was confused and exhausted.

We kept on walking through the little streets. Maybe he thought he was simply doing his duty, given that yesterday afternoon I'd asked him to show me around the town center. But yesterday afternoon seemed to belong to the distant past, and the stroll felt forced. There were no signs of life, the stores were closed, and every now and then Pietro had to stop to catch his breath. The healthy glow he had yesterday had vanished and he was chain-smoking. Had my arrival done this to him?

"This is the piazza."

"It's nice."

More than a piazza, it was a statue, a bench, and a phone booth randomly thrown together. Pietro crushed his cigarette butt underfoot, saying, "So do you like it?"

"Like what?"

"Monte Porzio Catone."

Hearing him once again pronounce the name of his prison so very faithfully and lovingly, I was gripped by a mute fury and said, "Why, do you like it?"

He didn't answer, reaching into his pocket to take out yet another cigarette. All at once I found I could no longer tolerate either his Marlboro Lights, and light they most certainly were not, or these meager dialogues, which were nothing but commonplace strategies to avoid the heart of the matter. *The money or your freedom?* I felt like shouting it, but how could I repeat a question that was essentially rhetorical, a question to which there was only one possible—only one conceivable—answer?

"Do you really think you should still be smoking?"

"Why not?"

"Well, you don't look in very good shape today."

"It's the last," he said, adding derisively, "May I?"

He lit the flame with an expert flick of his lighter. As I watched him burn his cigarette to ashes, it suddenly occurred to me that I may have misunderstood the heart of the matter. Perhaps the choice he had to make was not the rather abstract and open-ended one between the money and his *freedom*, but rather the more concrete and immediate choice between the money and his *girlfriend*. Pietro must have been aware of it, too: that's why he was avoiding my eyes. But if that was the real question, I reasoned, wasn't it even easier to answer? No one in their right mind would choose money over the person they professed to love. So then why put off answering, why make small talk and smoke like a chimney? It was an extravagant waste of time that I was simply not going to put up with anymore.

I glared at the cigarette that gave him such comfort. He'd said very little all morning, but now I saw him make a move that was much more eloquent than any word he could have uttered: he turned his back to me and crossed the square by himself. At first I just stood there watching Pietro, who was a gentleman by nature, leave me in the lurch and walk away with the cavalier strut I recognized from the Spanish Quarter. Then I started thinking crazy thoughts. That he wouldn't stop at all, that he'd walk on without a backward glance till he got to the far edge of the town, that he'd climb over the wall and disappear, covering his tracks. That I'd never see him again.

I got scared. I ran after him, not without a hearty dose of self-contempt, chasing his toxic wake through the winding street. Pietro must have heard me coming because he stopped for me to catch up. Interpreting this as an olive branch, I became hopeful, yet when I reached him he wasn't extending that or his apologies or even his hand, which he brought instead to his chest, digging in his fingers with an afflicted expression. I fell back into my funk.

We started walking again, together this time but god knows where, and after a while he stopped again, and then again, with a shortness of breath that wasn't improving even now that the street was going downhill. It was getting hotter and hotter, and I realized it wasn't a normal heat, not simply a new summer's day on its way, but a stagnant, threatening heat like a storm cloud that hadn't burst. Not even Pietro's backache was what it seemed, since his chest apparently hurt now too. But my bitterness was such as to make me think he was merely exaggerating the discomfort in order to stir my compassion and throw not only me off the track but also the issue tailing us everywhere we went.

Before long we were back at the widening in the main road where the bus had dropped me off the day before. There wasn't a single car and Pietro crossed the road without even looking. He leaned against the stone wall beyond which the town wasn't authorized to go——nor he. I followed him.

"There's more air here," he said. "Before I felt like I was suffocating."

I took the hint—that I was smothering him—and grew indignant. "Who do you think I am, Pietro? I'm not one of those classic uptight girlfriends, the jealous ones that hassle you and won't let you go out with your friends and then demand an engagement ring and a house and a wedding, just for appearances' sake. I am not a ball and chain around your ankle."

"I wouldn't be with you if you were like all the other girls."

"So then let's get this straight: Are you with me or not?"

"What's that supposed to mean?"

"I want to know at the end of the day what your decision is going to be."

Pietro turned his back to me. Leaning forward over the wall, he looked through the veil of haze to admire the hills, somewhere beyond which was Rome. Then he inhaled deeply from his cigarette before saying, "What decision?"

"What decision," I mumbled, pressing my hand against my forehead in exasperation. Pietro just kept on pretending nothing was wrong, forcing me to voice a vulgar alternative that made me sick to my soul, a choice that cheapened and debased our relationship. Love for sale. Yet, willing to do just about anything to get past this crisis, I said crudely, "It's either me or the money."

Silence. The mere fact that Pietro didn't refute it was devastating confirmation that I had in fact found, within that tangled ball of wool, the end of the yarn, the bottom line. Finally he muttered, "What can I say, baby? Everything hurts."

"If you have to think twice before answering that question, then . . ."

Pietro spun around. "Then *what*?"

"Then . . ." Why was I always the one having to say what he didn't have the guts to? Why was I always the one dirtying myself with words? "Then that means you've already made up your mind. You've chosen the money. OK. Are you happy?"

I'd said it without believing a word of it. It was simply a false accusation aimed at shaking him out of his apathy. I wanted a reaction. I wanted us to argue, make up, make love. But Pietro replied matter-of-factly, "The fact is, Heddi, I can't afford to . . . burn bridges with my family and end up on the street."

The thick air pushed me backward. Oh god. Not only had he known the real question all along, he already knew the answer too. Thus not answering, since last night, was him simply stalling for time: he was waiting for a more favorable moment to destroy me. It had been a conscious, deceitful silence. And now as I took one step backward, then two and three, everything seemed to be crumbling down around me, a landslide tumbling on top of me and turning my strappy sandals into rubber boots that quickly filled with mud and debris.

"All that, in Greece," I said, meaning by *all that* traveling together, being part of a real family, being so ridiculously happy, "did it mean nothing to you?"

"Ah, Greece . . ." Pietro said with a painful exhalation of smoke, as if recalling a moment that, far from representing the beginning of something big and wonderful in our lives, had regrettably concluded. A beautiful parenthesis.

"All those plans . . . to get married, travel the world . . . did you really want to do them?"

"I don't know what the hell I want anymore."

I took another step backward, dragging my feet. I knew this nightmarish feeling: refusing to accept the terrifying reality but being utterly physically powerless to change it—or even wake up. "I have to leave," I said with a feeble voice and unsteady gait. I reached out to keep my balance but the wall wasn't there and my hand cut through the air.

I must have stumbled because Pietro tossed away his cigarette and stood to attention, though with a slightly curved back. "Where are you going?"

"I can't stay here with you if you don't want me anymore."

He didn't contradict me, merely repeating, "Where are you going?"

I didn't know myself. I kept walking backward on the open road, the most convenient escape route. Pietro was getting smaller. Out of the corner of my eye I could see, on one side, the phony landscape of the Castelli Romani, and on the other side the ghostly calm of the bus stop. I'd hop on the first bus, that's what I'd do, without my belongings or even money for a ticket. I would leave as a stowaway and a gypsy, whatever it took to avoid remaining a second longer before a man who didn't love me and maybe even despised me. I had the same sense of definitive freedom as when I'd left Monte San Rocco by myself after the slaughtering of the pig. Now I understood it wasn't freedom at all but a chasm opening up. It was the earth being ripped right out from under my feet.

"Where are you going?" I heard his voice as if in the distance. "What are you doing?"

"I'm going . . . I'm going away."

"Away where?"

"Naples, Rome, I don't know."

"My god," he said, not in his usual baritone. "Are you . . . leaving me?"

I stopped to put Pietro into focus. The blood had drained from his face and he just stood there, palms facing upward toward the sky as if waiting for something to rain down on them. My heart went wild like a little bird in a cage as I stared at the face of the man who wanted to sell our love: his was like the face of a stranger and yet my lips knew its every hill and valley. I looked hard at him, trying to recognize him, to peel off the contrasting emotional layers from his face, to tear off the petals of his affection. He loves me, he loves me not, *he loves me*. Yes, without a shadow of a doubt Pietro was shocked and afraid; I could see in his eyes that he was on the verge of desperation at the thought of losing me. How could I leave him?

And so, despite knowing that the only way to come out of the situation with moral integrity and a positive outcome was to see my action through—keep on walking, backward like a lobster if need be, and then catch a bus or hitch a ride somewhere—and despite my intuition telling me *Go back and you'll die*, just as I'd dreamed the first time we made love and Vesuvius erupted and I had the only boat, despite all this and despite the almost absolute certainty that I would ruin everything forever, I went back to him. I went back.

"I couldn't do it," I said in disgrace.

Pietro hugged me, leaning into me and sinking his face into my hair. I could feel the heat of his breath, the heat of tears buried just beneath the surface. "Don't leave me, please," he whispered. "I'm alone in the world without you."

Maybe we were both alone in the world. During that long embrace practically in the middle of the road, not a single car drove past, not a soul. Pietro was trembling, as was I, shaken by how close I'd been to the edge but also horrified by the failings in my character. When we pulled apart he didn't stand up straight but remained hunched, nearly bent in half.

"Is your back that bad?"

"It's like a knife . . . that goes from one side . . . to the other."

"From your back to where?"

"To my heart. Heddi, I can . . . barely breathe."

The distance from the edge of town to the center seemed to have grown. Pietro struggled up the incline, pausing every few steps and no longer even attempting to smoke. It took an eternity to get to the piazza, which was still inexplicably empty. Maybe the crowds we'd seen at the dog show were people driving in from other towns; maybe the inhabitants of Monte Porzio had all gone to the seaside for the summer, or maybe the place really was just a postcard. Pietro collapsed onto the bench. Bent over his knees, he smothered his face with those long, slender fingers.

"Maybe we should get a medical opinion," I said. "There must be a pharmacy somewhere around here."

"There is . . . but it's probably closed," he said, pointing down a side street.

"You never know." I headed down the little lane at a normal pace. But as soon as I was out of his line of vision, I broke into a run, stopping only when it became obvious that the shutters were locked down. Panic began to set in, but I went back to Pietro instilling my voice with a realistic casualness. "It doesn't matter. We might be able to find a doctor instead."

We took the few steps toward the phone booth. By now Pietro had lost his pride: every step was accompanied by a grimace. It was clear that this was more than just a bad night's sleep. The inside of the booth was damp and intimate, and as I flipped through the white pages I noticed up close how very difficult it was for him to breathe and how the pain made him bite his lip. There was only one doctor in town, and as I inserted the shiny coin as if into a slot machine I prayed that that particular Sunday the doctor wasn't away on vacation or sleeping off a Fernet-Branca hangover and that he would pick up straightaway. But the phone rang five, six, seven, eight agonizing times. I hung up.

"No problem," I said with a composure that was clearly unraveling now. "Let's try calling a doctor in one of the surrounding villages. What's the name of the nearest town?"

Pietro shook his head, reminding me that we'd have no way to get there anyway. He said, "I'll call Giuliano." Flinching, he twisted around to pull from his wallet the piece of paper that had all his important numbers written on it. I inserted the coins for him. It must have been Giuliano who picked up, and not Rosaria, because he spoke without ceremony, in dialect and in a deep, monosyllabic voice, putting the receiver down without so much as a goodbye. "He's coming to get us," he said.

"That's good. He can drive us to the next town over."

"We're going . . . to Rome."

"Good idea. There will be lots of doctors on call there."

"No, he's taking me to the hospital."

"The hospital?" I said with a start, instantly betraying every secret of my anxiety for him. For us.

Pietro seemed to sense this, for he said as justification, "I feel like . . . I'm drowning. But the sea is miles away."

28

WE TOOK THE HIGHWAY, as straight and inevitable as every road that leads to Rome. And all the while Rosaria, beside me in the back seat, was pressing him, "Are you sure, Pie'? Maybe you ran into something without realizing it."

"How the hell do you run into something without realizing it?" Giuliano spat back, hunched over the steering wheel of the Fiat Uno that made a giant of him.

"It's a broken rib, I'm telling you."

Pietro wasn't even making the effort to protest: his eyes like two slits, he just sat there in the front passenger seat scratching his shirt. Every now and then I placed my hand on his shoulder from behind, and he gave it a lifeless squeeze. I looked out the window searching for a sign of good luck, a nod from the universe that everything was going to turn out all right, and in fact I spotted a red car with the number thirty-three in its license plate and a billboard with a smiling child giving two thumbs up to Mulino Bianco cookies. I knew fully well I was clutching at straws and by doing so making each and every propitious sign I'd ever been given meaningless.

Finally we pulled off the highway, piercing through Rome's outer layer until we came to a ramshackle hospital. Once Giuliano parked under a pine tree and turned off the air-conditioning, the midday heat overwhelmed us. Like in Monte Porzio, the only inhabitants seemed to be cicadas, as though even the sick were away on vacation. The nurses idly waiting outside the emergency department pounced upon Pietro as soon as Giuliano opened the passenger door. They helped him to the hospital entrance, telling us tersely to wait outside.

"I bet it's a pinched nerve," said Rosaria, hands on her hips in the jagged shade of the pine. "Or maybe a slipped disk . . ."

I didn't argue with her. I was mulling over in my mind the drama that had turned our lives inside out within the course of a single day. When I'd arrived, Pietro was perfectly healthy. Did I have to be so hard on him? I felt that somehow I'd broken him.

After a while Pietro came out supported by nurses. I knew it was serious even before they made him lie on the stretcher and began preparing the ambulance. I could tell from his blank stare and stiff body that was well past trembling now. "Heddi," he said on his back, that *H* costing him dear, "they have to operate on me."

"Operate? Why?"

"I have a pneumo . . . pneumothorax."

"A pneumo what?"

"One of my lungs . . . collapsed." Now that his eyes were present again, it was worse. In them I saw a sense of injustice over how he'd been wronged and a helplessness that I couldn't bear to look at.

I tried asking the nurses a question, but they were too busy. The only information I managed to wrangle out of them was that they were taking him to Carlo Forlanini Hospital. But no, only medical staff were allowed to ride in the ambulance with him.

I grabbed his hand. Pietro squeezed mine back so hard his knuckles went white. It wasn't hard enough for me. I wanted to feel his level of pain, make it mine and take it from him. I leaned down to kiss his cheek. "Don't worry, Pietro, it's going to be OK," I said. "They're going to take good care of you."

"Fuck, baby . . . I'm scared." He strained to remove his wallet, keys, and watch and handed them to me: he'd been told to take everything off before the operation.

"What about your ring?"

"No, I already told you," Pietro said. "I'm never taking it off."

The next time I saw him, he lay propped up against several white pillows, his chest bare except for a square dressing with a long, slender tube jutting out from underneath.

"Hey, buddy," said Giuliano. "Everything went beautifully. Except they also had to perform a tiny little emasculation procedure while they were at it."

"You'll be the one shooting blanks," Pietro shot back, letting out an involuntary smile.

I took heart. I hadn't seen him smile in twenty-four hours, let alone make a joke. But Rosaria said, "My god, look at you. You look totally stoned."

"Sedatives are pretty good drugs, aren't they?" said Giuliano.

"This is one hell of a party."

We were all standing around his bed, our healthy bodies the only partition in that greenish room he shared with ten or so other patients. Relatives were camped around them, holding containers of pasta, crossword puzzles, cards. Only the smell of disinfectant managed to cut through the air that was fat with meat sauce, latex gloves, rotten flowers.

"Well, I think you look good," I said, smoothing his sheet, careful not to touch him.

"But every breath . . . still hurts."

"That's just the chest tube exiting the wound," the nurse said at our backs. I didn't get the chance to ask her what the chest tube was for, or how long his recovery would take, for she was already clapping her hands and announcing that visiting hours were up. The visitors packed up their picnics, and I went back to Giuliano and Rosaria's tiny apartment in the outskirts of Rome.

The two of them performed enviably well under stress. Rosaria pulled out a fresh set of pajamas for Pietro, one of Giuliano's T-shirts as a nightgown for me, and two toothbrushes still in their packaging—basic supplies until Giuliano had time to drive back to Monte Porzio Catone, possibly Tuesday after work, to pick up our things. I hadn't even realized we wouldn't be going back there.

Giuliano splayed a map across the table, tracing his finger over the veins and capillaries of the capital. To get to Forlanini tomorrow, I would first have to cut through the city center by tram and bus, swooshing past the aqueduct and the Colosseum and people dressed in the latest fashions and gleaming cars, all under a spotless sky. It pained me to think of making a journey that would start out like a field trip but end at the hospital.

They had me make a long-distance call to Gabriele to tell him what had happened. He was about to leave for Monte San Rocco and didn't even hint at the possibility of him coming up to Rome: it wasn't an option. Everyone had charged me with Pietro's care. It was what I wanted, and it was also a public acknowledgment of just how serious our relationship was. How ironic then that the recognition I'd so longed for had come only hours after Pietro and I were about to throw it all to the wind.

That evening Rosaria made meatballs. My stomach was in knots, but she insisted, "You have to taste them, Eddie. It's a recipe from back home."

Despite the meandering journey and the warren-like hospital complex, I arrived well in advance of the morning visiting hours and found the door to his room locked. I walked back outside. Straight across from his ward was a shady park with concrete benches. I hadn't brought a book or anything to distract myself with, so I simply sat there staring up at the façade of the building wondering which of those windows was his. The cicadas announced the start of the mating season from the pine trees, where they too sat in wait.

I went in forty-five minutes later. It was a Monday, drastically culling the number of visitors in the room. The sick were all lying in bed, their faces lined and beards unkempt. Those who weren't asleep acknowledged my arrival with lackluster interest. Pietro wasn't in the same bed as yesterday but in one beside the open balcony.

"A room with a view," I said in the sunniest voice I could muster.

He cracked a smile. "You're here, baby."

"Where else would I be?" I sat on the arthritic bed, kissing him lightly on the mouth. He had chapped lips and gave off an antiseptic smell that reminded me of the cleaning products I used to scour the bathrooms at the end of the night in the Piazza San Domenico café. "I'm staying here as long as necessary. I'll quit if my boss isn't happy about it."

"I hate the fact that you took that job. You should, I don't know, work as an English teacher, for example . . . you'd be really good at that."

As he spoke, he caught me stealing glimpses at his chest tube and hastened to demystify it for me: its job was simply to release the air. With a pneumothorax, air had slipped in between the pleura and the lung, deflating it. As an emergency procedure, they'd inserted a needle into his chest cavity, replacing it afterward with the tube.

A needle in the chest. I could practically feel the pinch myself, the long, drawn-out assault of it. And, whatever a pleura was, I grasped that yesterday in Monte Porzio he'd had only one good lung. He'd gotten by on half the oxygen he needed and he'd hardly complained.

It took all my goodwill to face the ugliness of the tube. It gave the impression of coming straight from his heart, to then slither off the bed until it reached a glass bottle on the floor. It was like a cider bottle or the kind used for bottling oil (and in fact it contained a layer of yellowish liquid), not a piece of medical equipment but something scrounged from an old hut in the mountains. I didn't know what disturbed me more: the thread of rubber keeping him alive or that crude thing weighing him down to the bed.

"So once the air is gone, you can go?"

"I dunno," he said reflexively in his dialect. "They'll discharge me when there's no more 'pleural space.'" He clarified, "Space in the pleural cavity."

Plural space? More than ever, glottology struck me as pitiful preparation for real life. I didn't have the lexical or psychological means to comfort him, especially when he added with visible concern that if this treatment didn't work he would require a more serious operation. "It'll work," was all I could come up with. "It has to work."

"I swear, why does everything always have to happen to me? As if I didn't already have enough to worry about, I had to get a fucking spontaneous tension pneumothorax."

Spontaneous instantly lost any fun connotation it may have once had. Based on what the surgeon had told him, a small air pocket formed on Pietro's lung; it might have been there for years just biding its time. Then for some reason, it popped, puncturing his lung.

"Apparently, the pneumothorax I had was a major one: there was the risk of going into shock . . . cardiac arrest." All of a sudden his eyes went glossy and his voice splintered. "Do you realize, Heddi? If we'd waited any longer, I could have died."

I pressed my cheek against his, not only to console Pietro, who was now shedding hot tears and trying to stifle his sobs, but also to console myself. He'd never shed a tear in front of me, and now seeing him cry with such despair, like a child, hurt me deeply. I was beating myself up. If Pietro was in that bed with his life hanging by a thread, it was my fault and no medical opinion—no *science*—could have convinced me otherwise. For the first time I felt I hated words, my *own* cutting words, my big fat mouth. I'd attacked him verbally and unrelentingly, expecting him to be far more heroic than I could ever be and thus putting everything on the line. Everything. And once more, just like during the years they'd spent together in Rome, Giuliano had been the one to come to the rescue, not me.

That clumsy embrace was the closest I could get to him without touching his fragile chest. Afterward his red eyes seemed to burn with humiliation. *Go!* I almost expected him to say, *I don't want you to see me like this.* But he said nothing.

"I'm here for you . . . I won't leave you," I said. "I love you."

Pietro turned toward the balcony, wiping his eyes and nose. "You love this? This broken man?"

He kept on looking outside, so I followed his gaze. Beyond the little asphalted road melting in the sun was the park I'd sat in earlier. From above, it was impossible not to notice that all the benches faced the hospital. They sat there in front of the ward counting down the hours, serving their time. It was their only purpose.

One of the benches soon became mine: between visits I would go straight to it. The odd thing was I never read. I would sit cross-legged like a monk in prayer, staring at Pietro's balcony window and taking deep breaths that sounded like those embarrassing *Om*s I would hear my mom make years ago whenever I'd catch her meditating. I was trying to summon for Pietro the healing of the body, for me fortitude of spirit. And still I suffered. I grasped that true unhappiness is not being far from the person you love but being so very close, almost within your grasp, without being able to reach them.

Naples seemed very far away, in space and in time. From this distance, it was hard to believe that somewhere in the world there existed a place so unruly, so consuming and so *excessive*—always overdoing it with its ferocious beauty and unforgivable ugliness. I looked around the deserted park, wondering where the other friends and relatives went during the breaks between visiting hours. Home, undoubtedly, for that's what Rome was to them.

Home, *casa*. The word still made my head spin, tangled my hair into knots. Is home, I mused, the place where you were born or where others speak your language? Or is it simply the place where you choose to put down roots, or the place that's assigned to you? How could it be that after all these years in Naples I still couldn't understand the true meaning of the word? Once I had loved the city so much I thought I could die, until something greater had taken ownership of my heart . . . Perhaps the reason why I found it so hard to get my head around the concept of home, I considered one afternoon, was because I was constantly trying to dissect it, to analyze it academically. Yes, it was true. I'd been shortsighted; I could only see trees, trees, trees and not the forest. And it wasn't until that moment, alone on a park bench in an anonymous corner of the outskirts of Rome, that I finally got it.

Home wasn't a *place*. It never had been.

One time I couldn't find Pietro next to the balcony. I sat down on his bed, the springs groaning underneath me, and waited long enough to start worrying. Had they had to wheel him out to perform that other surgery? Finally he came shuffling back in, toting his bottle by its handle; his chest was particularly concave and his slenderness exaggerated by Giuliano's oversize pajamas. He'd been to the bathroom: for the first time the nurses had let him go by himself. It had taken him ages to make it there and back, though the bathroom was just around the corner.

"Well, one small step for man . . ." I said, hoping to make him laugh.

"A three-year-old can go to the bathroom by himself. What would your father think if he saw me now?"

It was tricky helping him back into bed without tangling up the chest tube. Afterward I pulled out the daily edition of *la Repubblica* and a selection of Giuliano's novels, planning to read to him as I'd seen other visitors do. But Pietro wasn't in the mood. He apologized, saying he'd slept badly, what with the medications administered in the middle of the night, the snoring, and the tossing and turning. He was tired.

When he closed his eyes, it was my chance to run my gaze over him for as long as I pleased. It was torture not being able to touch him. Those thick eyelashes, the strip of bare chest, the tanned muscles of his forearms, his hands . . . Compared to the other patients, Pietro was the very picture of health. If I blocked out the dressing and the chest tube, I could picture him as just another boy on vacation soaking up some rays. For an instant his condition didn't seem real at all but a hoax, one of those scams they pulled off on the streets of Naples. And last summer, I remembered, hadn't he toyed with the idea of doing just that, fabricating an illness to avoid the military service? Now we had a good enough excuse—a short-lived episode and not a true illness, but one that was on paper nonetheless—to ask the authorities for a period of leave for his so-called recovery. A month, two months. Was it too much to hope for?

I woke Pietro, who may not have been asleep anyway, to tell him my idea despite the fear of coming across as naïve or insulting him with yet another attempt to corrupt his morals by urging him to commit federal fraud.

"The moment I got sick," he replied without emotion, "my civilian service was over. I'll be discharged." Not only, but the doctors had given him a probable date of discharge from the hospital. Friday.

His words had a magical effect, a spell that turned the puke-green walls into vast meadows. My eyes went big. This meant we could get our lives rolling again—and not in a year and a half but *in three days*. Happiness swept over me like a breeze. I didn't know whom to thank: that scratch-and-win destiny I believed in only when it was magnanimous, or my lover, who in order to obtain this grace had had to sacrifice a lung. Either way, a thanks would have been in poor taste so all I said was, "That's incredible!"

Pietro didn't reply; he was looking with concerned familiarity at the tube sticking out of his chest.

"Aren't you happy?"

"Of course I am. But what a plot twist, don't you think? I'd love to have a word with whoever the hell it is that's directing my life and ask him why he decided to kill me off in such a pathetic way."

It was only three days, but they moved with sluggish stickiness. Rome, the eternal city. I spent most of my time not with Pietro but with my bench. It never occurred to me to sightsee between one visit and the next. I didn't want to stray far from the hospital, and if my legs became restless, I'd merely wander aimlessly in the immediate vicinity.

The chest drainage was working as expected: the pleural space was diminishing and the lung was reinflating. And yet Pietro himself was more and more deflated with each passing day. To compensate, I grew more and more cheerful, feeding him words of encouragement and celebrating every small sign of improvement. I was taking on the cheerleading role as I had with the boys in their studies, only now it wasn't a game but a serious task—one that in reality I had no real talent for. Often Pietro wouldn't answer at all: he'd simply rub his long stubble and look away. There was always something left unsaid in our conversations, but I didn't want to dig deeper. I was afraid that if he confessed to me what a week in the hospital really felt like I wouldn't be able to maintain the detachment necessary for my optimism. It was the fear of putting myself in his shoes, of staring into his abyss. It was also the somewhat childish fear that he'd burst into tears again.

One day I handed him one of his T-shirts, brought by Giuliano from Monte Porzio and laundered (and I think ironed, too) by Rosaria and ready to be worn on the day of his discharge.

"I need some air," he said. "Can you help me?"

I carried his bottle as we inched toward the balcony railing. Focusing on a spot on the road, Pietro asked if I'd seen "that guy." Not in the outside world, he added, but the one directly across from his bed. I cast a sidelong glance at the handsome young man asleep in his bed. His hair fanned out on the pillow was dark and wavy, like Pietro's but a bit longer. They'd brought him into the ward last night, Pietro told me, after operating on one of his lungs.

"A pneumothorax too?"

"No, a tumor." Pietro was still looking outside with undue concentration, as if trying to count the pine trees in my park. "But the surgery didn't go well. I know because I've been talking to him a little bit. He's a really nice kid. Only twenty. He never smoked a day in his life. He studied, didn't take drugs. He did everything right."

"That's terrible."

"It's unfair, that's what it is," Pietro said hotly, plowing his fingers through his hair. "His life had only just begun, and now he won't get a chance to live it. You tell me why such a nice guy deserves such a raw deal."

Having no answer to give, I superstitiously touched my pendant. If fate could be so cruel, wasn't I cruel, too, for believing in it, even only when it suited me? Out on the balcony, the heat was bandaging me from head to foot and I could feel the cicadas growing anxious and vibrating as if in my very throat. I could no longer run from the repulsive thought that for days I'd been refusing to confront. The thought of death. How many hours, how many *minutes*, had we had before Pietro suffered a heart attack? By how many millimeters had he dodged death? This time we'd had a lucky escape, but sooner or later death would have the last word. It always did. And in the face of it, we were nothing. Debris, ash, stardust.

Then one afternoon the tube was no longer snaking out from under his bandage. Pietro was untethered now, but he kept on moving with extreme caution. I assumed this was simply out of habit, or out of fear he'd rip open his fresh stitches. The true reason threw me. "I'm not out of danger yet."

"What do you mean? You're all better now."

"The hell I am," he nearly shouted. And now, though lowering the volume, Pietro began to purge all those thoughts he'd kept buried till now in an incandescent stream of words, skillfully shifting between medical terminology and lewd dialect. He reiterated that his pneumothorax wasn't triggered by a trauma, such as an explosion or a car accident, but by a piss-ass subpleural air pocket, a relatively rare event that occurs in victims who had the nerve to be tall, slim males under forty years of age. He said that there could be other fucked-up air pockets on his pulmonary apexes and that they, too, might decide to pop one day—maybe even the *next* day—perhaps this time involving not one but both lungs.

"Who told you this?"

"The surgeon."

Now I was the one fuming, though I kept it to myself. I was angry with the doctor whose flippant comments threatened to undermine all the confidence I was battling tooth and nail to instill in Pietro. I was angry with the statistics. I was even angry with the handsome boy who had the gall to die of cancer right before his eyes.

"Just my luck. I drew the wrong card, the one that says 'Go directly to jail, do not pass Go,'" Pietro went on. "I had only just begun, not exactly to travel, but at least to head out from my starting point and . . . wham! I got nailed straightaway. Jesus Christ, I only got as far as Rome. What a great world tour that was."

"Doesn't Greece count?"

"Do you realize, this could have happened over there. And who could have saved me in the Cyclades, the pelican vet? And can you imagine if it happens to me when we're in some Thai town in the middle of nowhere? Maybe the only surgeon with a bit of experience there is the guy who's a butcher by day."

Anxiety was starting to creep into his voice, I could hear it. I looked him straight in the eye and told him we could start all over and rethink our plans. It didn't matter where we went—I stressed this point—as long as we were together. I took his hand and held it tight, channeling all my strength into wiping from his memory that moment in Monte Porzio when I'd almost made him believe I could walk away from him. Now all our problems—his mother, the money—faded into the background. I wasn't even sure anymore that these were the real issues. I had the nagging feeling that, in pointing the finger at Lidia, at a little old lady, I'd missed something bigger. Something much bigger.

"And until we figure out what to do, until you're better," I said, "we could stay in the Spanish Quarter."

"No, I'm through with Naples."

"Me too."

It was a retort I'd blurted out thoughtlessly, a *me too* that felt at once like a betrayal and a liberation, an evil truth I'd been too much of a coward to put into a complete sentence. But now I was adrift. Where would we go if the world was, for the time being, no longer at our fingertips? Monte San Rocco was out of the question and, since Naples was now, too, what alternative did that leave us? Perhaps Pietro had been right all along, that America was the most sensible choice . . .

"I want nothing more than to spend the rest of my life with you, baby," he said. "But it's not that I don't want to travel, it's that I *can't*. The doctor said I have to avoid high altitudes or this will almost certainly happen again. How am I going to travel the world if I can't take an airplane?"

Enough, I'd had it. I resolved that before Pietro was discharged, I would demand to speak with the surgeon to clear up all the misunderstandings and expose him as the scaremonger that he was. I might even win him over to my side: I needed someone in a white coat, a male no less, who could back my conviction that Pietro would live his life to the fullest. Pietro told me he'd try asking, though he wasn't hopeful the surgeon would grant us a meeting because, being the chief physician, he was a very busy man.

———

We did get a meeting, but from the onset things did not go as I expected. The surgeon wasn't the coldhearted, tactless professor I'd imagined but a deeply tanned family man with a broad smile, loose tongue, and thick Roman accent. His office wasn't lined with books and skeletons after all but was airy and sparse (except for a framed picture of his wife and children), underlining its democratic nature as part of the public health system. He invited us to take a seat, starting off by asking Pietro if he liked Greco di Tufo wine.

"I prefer red," he answered self-consciously, no doubt so as not to admit that, despite its being a local wine, it was well beyond his means. "But I can see you have fine taste."

The head doctor praised the capocollo from the Avellino area before stepping forward to check Pietro's incision one last time. "Good," he said before moving on to Irpinia's chestnuts. It was clear that Pietro's case was neither rare nor one of particular interest. Most likely Pietro had taken an offhand comment and magnified it. Like a true scientist he'd done too much investigating and discovered one too many ifs. Undoubtedly, fear had blown everything out of proportion. And even I had to acknowledge that, although the surgeon was downplaying Pietro's illness and speaking to us like old friends, in the flesh he intimidated me too. Here was the man who'd opened up my lover's chest; here were the hands that had sewn it back together. He'd seen inside him. He'd saved his life.

Nonetheless, before the doctor could glance at his wristwatch and herd us out of his office, I had to find the chance to ask him the crucial questions that Pietro wouldn't venture as he sat there flipping through his discharge papers, freshly showered and dressed in street clothes, pen in hand and ready to sign.

"So is that all?" I asked. "He doesn't need to come back to the hospital for a checkup?"

"No, no." The surgeon explained that all he had to do was see his family doctor to change the dressing. The stitches would dissolve on their own. "In fact, I never want to see this young man again!"

327

"So you're saying that he shouldn't have another pneumothorax . . ."

"Well, you never know in life. But listen to me, don't think about it . . . You're young: go to the beach, eat, drink, and be merry. He got himself a good fright but look how well he is now. Healthy as a fish," he said, using that common expression, *sano come un pesce*, which struck me as particularly inappropriate in this instance. "He can continue doing all his normal activities; he can even go surfing if he wants to. The only thing that may reduce the risk of a reoccurrence is quitting smoking."

Pietro lifted his eyes from the documents as if startled from sleep. I was just as dazed. How could I have forgotten the symbiotic relationship between Pietro and his Marlboro Light, the meditative way he used to hold it wedged between his fingers? Therefore, for the entire week in the hospital Pietro had been battling not only pain and fear but also nicotine withdrawal. It all made sense now: the mood swings, the rage, and the desperation.

"Other than that, he can do anything . . . even fly in a plane, right?"

"Absolutely."

"What about the altitude?" asked Pietro, who was all ears now.

Making a little temple of his golden fingers, the surgeon confirmed that the chances of a recurrence increased at very high elevations insofar as they were oxygen poor. "So you wouldn't want to be climbing Mount Everest or doing other nonsense like that."

Taking the signed papers from Pietro, the doctor shook our hands with fondness and vigor, wishing us a good summer and recommending we try Greco di Tufo. All in all, the meeting had gone very well, but outside in the empty hallway Pietro appeared morose. I assumed it was the news about the cigarettes that had disheartened him so, and in a way I would miss them, too, so out of genuine sympathy I said, "What a bummer, though, about the cigarettes."

"It's not that. It's the Everest thing that's bothering me."

"You didn't seriously want to climb it, did you?"

"Who knows," he answered, looking down at his shoes. "Who knows what I might have done with my life."

As if at a sudden impasse, he stopped midway down the corridor to lean on one leg, that asymmetrical, biding stance that was so familiar to me—and yet for a moment I barely recognized him. Who was this man who was afraid to travel in a pressurized cabin with air-conditioning and pretzels but who wanted to ice-climb to the roof of the planet? Who was this man who was more concerned with what his girlfriend's father thought of him than what she did? Who was this man I loved?

From: tectonic@tin.it
To: heddi@yahoo.com
Sent: October 25

Dear Heddi,

Thank you for your wonderful email. I really needed some warmth and affection . . . The night before a weasel had slaughtered all the rabbits and some of the chickens. A terrible sight. My father cried like a child. And me too.

I haven't written in a while: I'll try to explain. You've said more than once that you like the way I write; I hope I won't disappoint you now. I'm not well. Do you remember that problem I had with my knee? It hasn't gone away: actually, it's gotten worse. Every twenty days the pain routinely comes back. Maybe it's an inflammation, maybe they cut something they shouldn't have. I don't know, it's a nightmare. When it flares up, I can't walk, I can't even really sit at the table, all I can do is lie on the couch. Heddi, I'm in deep shit, and I have the distinct feeling it's not the first time. Maybe it's my natural habitat and I splash around in it like a frog in a swamp. Maybe I like it. I don't know what to say.

I've booked a ticket for Auckland, February 19th, through Hong Kong, 1,250 euros, a reasonable price without taking into account how long it takes to get there (26 hours). But I feel I want to do it. For you. For your eyes. For your skin, your hair, your voice. For all the things you taught me. For your stories, your family, the warmth of your body. For everything that you know and that you haven't learned yet. We're so far from each other, in every way, and I can't forgive myself for my actions. But only a masochist would repeat the same mistakes.

Recently a girl read my cards. She saw you in the queen of cups and me in the fool of cups, separated by the seven of wands. What does it mean? I don't know, and the fortune-teller didn't know, either . . . I have few certainties

330

in my life, as you well know, but one thing I know for sure is that you're the only person who's made me feel like a man, in the fullest sense of the term. I've learned that you are and always will be the only woman I would have wanted to have children with . . . babies, a couple of little Pietros. I know I'm being stupid and cruel to tell you these things, but they are my deepest and most intimate thoughts . . . don't be mad at me.

I'm a stupid dreamer, even if I'm somewhat ashamed to be and I try to bury myself in work (when I'm well, at least). I've finished refurbishing the ground-floor apartment, even though my parents still insist on just using it as a storage room. The other two floors in theory should be mine. But all this space, all this effort, makes no sense—I'm alone, in spite of the fact that I know a lot of people. I'm missing a part of myself. And I think of you, I won't deny it, with me . . . spending a few months of the year here, in this shithole that has nothing to offer other than what you can grab with your bare hands, but these are my ineradicable roots . . . then spending Christmas with a real family like yours, in a fantastic place like the US, and traveling somewhere new every year. Well, these are my fantasies, I can't help it . . . I'm a lousy fatalist yet I'm always hoping there'll be an improvement.

I know, I deserve only for you to spit in my face, but I really did love you. And I still do. Even if deep down I hope you'll find the right man for you, I, Pietro Iannace, of cursed and hopeless stock, will never be able to live without you. At least in my dreams. I will always dream of being for you what you are for me . . . Maybe sometime in the future when I'm feeling scared and confused (it often happens when your health fails) I'll finally give in to some nice hearty girl. But no one will be able to replace what you've been for me, and what you'll always be for me, and the place you've embodied in my life . . . I can't explain it, but you are tattooed onto my heart. You just are, even if you don't want to be.

Maybe I'm able to open my heart to you now at this late hour of the night because I'm afraid . . . I keep thinking about pain and death and about leaving everything behind, even my beloved car. I'm well aware, even if I try to hide it, that I'm clutching at straws. I had my chance. I had my time when I could have done anything. I thought I could take on the world, bend it to my will (some would put this in the box labeled "errors of youth") . . . and now I'm limping around the house like an old man. Ironic, don't you think? It really is like a novel . . .

Well, I have to say goodbye for now. I need to get up early to go make chicken feed—with the tractor, of course—then to the hospital in search of a butcher willing to carve me up and explain how exactly he intends to cure me.

I'm holding you to me, closer than ever. You'll be with me, whether you like it or not, for as long as I live . . .

p.

29

I WALKED THROUGH the Spanish Quarter as if in a lucid dream. Though I'd only been gone a week, the neighborhood was nothing like I remembered it. Via De Deo in particular looked inconceivably narrow and dark, aggravated by an extraordinary quantity of sheets and tablecloths hanging from balconies and stealing the last pearls of opaque sky. Had the buildings always been this dizzyingly tall? To keep from losing my footing, I lowered my eyes to the ground and found the street slabs different too. They were more worn than I'd remembered them, and much blacker, black as night and oiled like skin. The *afa* was still there living it up, and it was uncannily quiet, as though all those who could had escaped.

"Where is everyone?" I asked Pietro as we stepped over the threshold into our courtyard.

"You know what it's like here at the end of summer. Half the city goes away. And those who can't, turn to food for comfort."

Indeed, it was lunchtime, and the residents of our building were among the poor souls who didn't have the means to run for the sea. Forced by the heat to leave their front doors wide open, they seemed to be challenging each other gastronomically by circulating the tantalizing smells coming from their kitchens—the second floor took the prize for the crispiest seafood fry-up, the third floor had the smokiest provola cheese and the arugula with the strongest bite, the fifth floor the richest eggplant parmesan. If cooking was a competition, eating was a prayer. The only sounds we could hear were the sizzling of oil and whining of children, a running faucet and a dramatic line from the *Bold and the Beautiful*, simply *Beautiful* in Italy. Perhaps it was these faraway, muffled noises, not to mention my complete lack of appetite, that made me feel that I was dreaming, that I could wake up whenever I wanted to and make it all disappear. I just had to decide when.

"I can feel it in my eyes already," echoed Pietro's voice as we stepped inside our apartment.

"Feel what?"

"The smog. My eyes are already stinging."

He gently set his backpack down on the tiles. I looked around the living room. Here was our undisputable reality—our books and CDs, the computer, an espresso cup left in the dip in the table—which lent the place a sort of sad coziness. The air was stuffy, so the first thing I did was open the windows and balcony doors. "Let me take a look at those eyes in the light," I said, turning back toward him. "You're right, they're a little red. But I predict a full recovery."

"Thank you, *dottoressa*."

Without another word, Pietro led me by the hand upstairs to the bedroom, where we made love with the blinds still lowered. It was all very delicate: the diamonds of light piercing through, the still neighborhood, the soft kisses. I made sure not to touch his wound, fearing he'd once more end up bent over in pain because of me. We fell asleep in utter exhaustion.

When I woke up, my hair was damp with sweat. Pietro was gone. I crept down the staircase still in my underwear—we were alone in the house after all—to find him sitting on the couch with the phone pressed against his ear. Legs crossed, he was jerking his leg to a nervous tempo, maybe dying for a cigarette. "All right, all right," he was saying in that curt way he always used with his brother, like he'd already had an earful. He put down the receiver. "Gabriele says hi."

"How's he doing?"

"Depressed as usual."

I sat beside him. "You know, my eyes are sore too. I don't know if it's the smog or the sleep."

"All this smog is definitely not good for my health. The surgeon said no smoking, but a day breathing in this lethal air is like smoking half a pack of cigarettes."

"Do you really think so?"

"And these stairs? After a week in bed, they're one hell of a workout." It seemed there was more to come, and in fact even before I could comment Pietro concluded, "Maybe I should go back to Monte San Rocco for a while."

So that's what he'd been discussing on the phone with Gabriele. Perhaps it was all organized already. "If the stairs are the problem, you don't need to worry about a thing. I'll go out to get the groceries. I'll cook for you. You can rest, you can read . . . you won't need to lift a finger."

"Baby, you're the sweetest nurse in the world, but it's not you. It's this building, this neighborhood, this madhouse they call a city! I can't handle it anymore. If I have to spend one more day here, I'll go out of my mind."

I sensed that his aversion to Naples, right or wrong, was only the tip of the iceberg of that unclear, unresolved crisis. Wishing only to smooth things over, I quickly replied, "OK, whatever you need." And how could I blame him, after what he'd been through? In his shoes I would probably have run home to my parents' too. And maybe a bit of mountain air would do him some good.

It wasn't until he said, "You can come visit me," that I let out a cynical laugh, knowing full well I would be willing to face anything, swallow any bitter pill, just to see him again. "Tomorrow morning Francesco's coming to pick me up, though I'm not so sure about him driving that

335

brand-spanking-new car all the way up our street. In any case, since I'm getting a ride I might as well take some of my stuff back. Books, other heavy items. There must be a few cardboard boxes around here somewhere . . ."

"OK," I repeated mechanically. "I'll help you."

I was saying one thing and thinking another. Inside I was completely at a loss. Pietro was packing up and leaving, and it was clear that he wouldn't be coming back to live in that apartment ever again. There was no need to spell it out. And he was leaving not because the Spanish Quarter had, within a few undramatic hours, pushed him to his limit, but because in his darkest hour I hadn't been able to truly support him and because now, on the spur of the moment, I hadn't been able to come up with a better solution than *Monte San Rocco*. But I didn't have any answers or any plans (not even for the immediate future, in which I'd be homeless); I had nothing to offer him but my useless love.

Pietro too appeared bewildered because out of the blue he said, "Without you, Heddi, I'm just a leaf swept away by the wind."

I didn't know what he meant.

When Francesco arrived at 33 Via De Deo, the curious and the lazy swarmed around the station wagon. It wasn't simply because it was a Sunday, for in the Spanish Quarter meddling was the first order of business. Kids with dirty fingernails asked, "You got a name, mister?" Men in undershirts and old women in dressing gowns leaned over the balconies to join in for the collective chorus that went, "Who is it? Who is it?" A few insulted residents glowered at the intruder: the woman living in the *vascio* that Francesco had parked his car in front of; the man on the motorbike who stopped right before its license plate, head-on as though about to gore it with his handlebars, murmuring abuse and pretending he didn't have the dexterity to weave his way past.

Everyone was checking out the shiny car as we loaded it up; some even groped it. And they looked at Francesco the lawyer with the same lack of modesty: at his polished shoes and showy watch, the starched shirt that hugged his belly and the unfashionable beard that aged him. In that sweltering scene of urban decay, Francesco stood out as the good-natured and well-fed man from the provinces who was about to get screwed over in some way. So provincial, in fact, he might as well have been from the suburbs.

"Let's get a move on," Pietro said anxiously as he handed Francesco the last bag, but his jumpiness eased as soon as he hopped in the car.

I gave him a quick peck through the rolled-down window and waved to Francesco. I said, surely in vain, "Don't drive too fast." The car inched up Via De Deo, whose gradient became so impractical a few meters ahead that it was forced to give in to a series of steps.

"You can't go that way!" I called out after them.

The residents turned to look at me: the clamorous lack of dialect had exposed me, threatening to make me a target like Francesco. Whether he heard me or not, he pulled off a three-point (or four- or five-point) turn to head down toward Via Roma. Several street kids ran after the glossy car as if scrambling for a single lollipop. With more restraint but with the same insatiable hunger, I followed it too. Then the street swallowed them all up and they were gone.

I no longer had a reason to be out in the streets, no lessons to go to or shifts at the café or visiting hours at the hospital. If I lingered in a state of waiting, it was purely out of habit, for the fact of the matter was I no longer had any deadlines or goals I was working toward. Nevertheless, my feet had a relationship all their own with the streets of Naples. I could have walked blindfolded and still my feet would have taken me to the place I didn't even know I was meant to be.

That's how I found myself only a few steps from the spot where the homeless man was always parked. So that was the reason I was there: to bring him a cappuccino and a croissant. I might even sit on the ground next to his wheelchair; this time his ghost legs wouldn't frighten me. And

337

maybe if I waited long enough, he would finish telling me the story of his *catastrof* and why in the world he'd stayed on in Naples afterward.

But the priest wasn't there. His spot was smudged and disturbingly empty, like a pencil drawing that's been hastily erased. I went into the café anyway and ordered a cappuccino. I asked the cashier, "Excuse me, do you remember the man that usually sits outside here with his dog? I think he's German."

"Do I remember him? How the heck can you forget a guy like that? You can smell him all the way from Piazza Plebiscito," she replied. The young barista joined in on the chuckling.

"He's actually a very decent person, you know," I said to that woman who wore on each finger, save her thumb, a golden ring mounted with a rainbow of gemstones. What did she know about living in the streets?

"I know, he's got a heart of gold. You can tell, even if you can't understand a darn thing when he opens his mouth."

"Has he been around lately?"

"What would I know, miss? I'm always in here working my butt off, even on a Sunday in the middle of August . . ."

I thanked her and placed my receipt on the counter with a two-hundred-lire coin. But of course, why hadn't I realized it earlier? Here things didn't work the way they did in Washington. There was no way a homeless person could have camped out next to the café every single morning begging (or waiting) for alms without the blessing of the owners. To get by in Naples you had to know the right people, and the same went for a disabled foreigner with broken Italian. It may well have been anarchy but it had its rules . . . and its humanity. I regretted having thought badly of the cashier, who in reality had helped him out without any personal gain.

The barista placed the coffee before me. "Anyway, that hobo hasn't been around for a while now. I think he's left for good. Who was he, though, somebody from your country?"

338

The arrival of new customers spared me from having to answer. The coffee took immediate and fierce effect. With every sip, my heart rapped faster and faster at my ribs. When was the last time I'd seen the priest? Maybe even the day of my graduation. That morning he'd waved me goodbye, an unusual gesture . . . maybe a farewell.

I wanted to believe that he had found a permanent place in the shelter or been taken in by the monks or, better yet, that someone from his past, a brother or a niece, someone who all these long years had searched for him high and low, had finally tracked him down. I wanted to believe he'd fled from Naples on a magic carpet.

But there was something phony, even hokey, about my optimism. Only Hollywood could guarantee a happy ending. In the real world, a fit nonsmoker could die of cancer at twenty, so I was kidding myself if I thought something sinister, like a heart attack or assault, couldn't happen to someone who was handicapped, malnourished, and elderly. I couldn't even rule out the possibility that, given the social isolation and the solitude he would have had to combat every day, he hadn't decided to end it all, regardless of the religious stigma. And who would remember him now that he was gone? He didn't even have a name.

I had a sudden flash of that communal grave at the Fontanelle Church—the unnamed femurs, ribs, skulls—and my stomach churned. What had I done to help that lovely man other than hand him my spare change and the occasional breakfast, when it fit into my schedule? I'd been no better than all the others who'd paid him attention only when the puppies were around, even though I was the one (and perhaps the only one) who knew who he really was—not some crazy wino but a man of god. But now it was too late.

He's gone. A deep sense of unrest washed over me, one whose source couldn't have been just the caffeine but may not have been simply the priest's disappearance either. I was hit by a wave of loss greater than the situation. I felt left behind, and deservedly so. Luca had been the first to leave Naples, then Madeleine. And now Pietro had left, with his rock-heavy books, his prospecting pick, his button-down shirts, everything that carried his incomparable scent. It was hot and the café was quickly filling up, the coffee grinder was growling, the steam wand was whistling. I had to get out of there, and fast.

Half the city may well have been away, but the other half held captive was enough to prevent me from finding an easy escape route. On Via Roma there was two-way foot traffic that overflowed from the sidewalk and engulfed me with its counterfeit perfumes and sweet Sunday pastries. The mob was dragging me and the shore seemed farther and farther away, and then panic grabbed me by the shirt, pulling me down with it. But finally the crowd seemed to have sensed my urgency, for it pushed me out into a side street of the Quartieri lined in death notices. I found shelter under a balcony and burst into the most pathetic tears.

But in Naples, even in the most insignificant and darkest alleyway, you're never alone. I'd shed only a few scalding tears when a gaggle of girls came up from behind. They were heavily made up with plunging necklines, set to prowl the piazza, yet they were the ones who looked at me judgmentally. I acted like nothing was wrong, drying my face and smudging my mascara, before heading, with no real purpose, back to Via De Deo.

From: heddi@yahoo.com
To: tectonic@tin.it
Sent: November 8

Dear Pietro,

I loved reading your thoughts and hearing your voice, even if it is from a
distance. I'm sorry though to hear about your health: Is there any way you
could see a specialist, or have you considered trying alternative medicine?

Did you know that I'm officially unemployed now? I quit my job two weeks
ago. I can get by for about two or three months on the money I have saved
up, and anyway I don't have many expenses or needs. I'm happy enough
having my freedom back, especially now that summer is on the way. Now,
whenever I feel like it, I can hop in the car and explore some new corner of
the rain forest, which is just outside the city limits. It's full of birds that make
beautiful, strange songs—some sound like hiccups or sneezes or laughter—
and it's so thick with trees that if it rains you don't even get wet. Anyway, I'd
like to take you there . . . but first you have to get better!

Once you asked me if I have a tattoo. I don't, but not because I'm afraid of
the pain. Tattoos are forever: What symbol, what concept could I believe in
forever? I don't know. Once I met a young Maori woman who came from
a little town called Tuai, in a very isolated part of the country on the shores
of Lake Waikaremoana. She said that if we were ever in the area to ask for
her uncle, who for a very good price would let us ride his horses through the
practically virgin forest. She told us the story of how when she was about
twelve years old her grandmother called her over and said simply Come with
me. She didn't know where her grandmother was taking her until a man had
her lie down on a bed and began tattooing her back. It was her entire family
tree, so that she'd never forget it. It took many sittings to tattoo the trunk
and all those branches. And every time she would cry beforehand but her
grandmother each time would hold her down. She didn't show us the tattoo
but told us it spanned her entire back, with a bit of skin left to complete the

family tree further down the line. But she had no intention of finishing it, and she'd since moved to Australia.

I'm going on and on, I know, but it's almost like through our letters I've remembered the language that you and I have always spoken, and I don't want to forget it again . . .

Yours,

h.

30

I TRIED TO KEEP MYSELF BUSY. I opened an electronic mail account and exchanged a few emails with Snežana. I started packing up my own books in order to ship them to Barbara and my dad's place, all the while trying to ignore the pandemonium that broke loose in the courtyard once or twice a day. In the evenings Pietro would call and we'd stay up so late talking that the couch would turn into a bed and the receiver into a shell that I pressed hard against my ear so I could hear it whisper like the sea.

There was no rest for him in Monte San Rocco. His father was always barking orders: to collect the firewood, drive him somewhere, move sacks of flour or cases of the family wine. Around the table, all anyone talked about was money, who owed whom what, a conversation that only the TV could interrupt. Having Gabriele there was of little solace because, due to either the heat or the wine, he seemed more fed up than usual. He didn't even want to talk politics: he'd simply get up from the table, glass in hand, and withdraw into the other room, legs crossed ("like a marquis," in Pietro's words), to read Proust or channel-surf.

"I swear, you'd think they were the sick ones," he said one night, followed by a long pause that sounded like a drag from a Marlboro.

"How's it going without cigarettes?"

"It's tough, baby, really tough. Maybe that's why I sometimes wish Gabriele would just piss off. He smokes like a Turk!"

"In the house, right in front of your parents?"

"Yeah, in the house . . ." But the real torture, he added, was being far from me. And, as if alleviating my loneliness could in some way alleviate his own, he suggested I get together with the boys and Sonia.

Sonia was meant to be in Sardinia. I had no news from Tonino, Angelo, and Davide: Telecom still hadn't granted them a landline and probably never would. But in a way, I didn't want company, other than Pietro's. The windows of the apartment were wide open, letting in at that late hour the monotonous swish of mopeds and the unshakable light of the streetlights. With that sallow halo that would be there till dawn, Naples was adept at keeping away not only the authorities, if the phone company could be considered such, but even the night itself. Tonight in particular that strange yellow light played tricks on my mind. It illuminated the alleyways and night owls in a radioactive, almost alien, glow that was neither light nor darkness. It was a color that, like the red safelight in a darkroom, washed out the ugliness and the beauty of everything it touched and created a certain suspense; however, unlike a darkroom session, that yellow night produced nothing magical.

"Baby?"

"I'm still here."

"I have a nice story to tell you."

"Go on then." I pried my eyes from the city, settling deeper into the creaking, sticky vinyl. I wanted to hear a nice story. I wanted a fairy tale.

He told me he'd found a puppy, a lump of skin and bones under a tree in the middle of the countryside. He looked like he hadn't eaten a meal since he was weaned and he was covered in fleas the size of ticks. Pietro had taken him home and bathed him in a bucket before giving him some milk and leftover pasta.

Suddenly no longer sleepy, I sat upright. "Are you sure he was abandoned? He may have just run away from home."

"I'm absolutely sure. People around these parts, you know what they do with animals they don't want around? They put them in a sack and throw them in the middle of nowhere, or more likely in a river." But this one, Pietro reassured me, had been rescued. In that very moment he was sleeping safe and sound in the tractor shed with Gesualdo for company; tomorrow he'd take him to the vet. "Start thinking about what we should name him," he said, "because he'll be our dog."

Our dog, a *real* dog, no longer the random recipient of our surplus passion but that third being which was beginning to seem more and more essential to the preservation of our relationship. I was mortified by my childish tears in that backstreet. Incredibly, and despite all the hassles and errands that could potentially have deteriorated Pietro's health, a change of scenery and fresh air had actually healed him and he was once again embracing life. And now, unexpectedly and somewhat prematurely, the two of us were the owners of a tiny dog with brown fur and a pink nose. It didn't matter that we didn't yet have a place to keep him. We were young and healthy and madly in love, and that was nothing but a logistical detail we could deal with later.

Pietro had been right: Sonia was back in Naples. She came to see me one roasting afternoon, hot enough to melt the bitumen on the rooftop. We sat outside under the savage sun to catch up on the events of the last month. Of the week in the hospital, I spared her the grittier details and vulnerable moments (not to mention the true cause of his ailment, our fight), partly so as not to relive them and partly so as not to tarnish the image Sonia had of Pietro. So as not to have to tell her that loving a man is loving him for, and not in spite of, his weaknesses.

"It must have been a nightmare," she said at the end with those big

345

eyes the size and color of chestnuts that seemed able not only to speak but to listen too. "So when is Pietro back in Naples?"

It seemed like a trick question, and I couldn't come up with a good answer.

"Well then, you'll have to say goodbye to him for me."

"Are you leaving again?"

"Oh, Eddie, I'm so glad you're in town because I really couldn't wait to tell you!" she burst out, with her bony hands stirring the soupy air of the Quartieri. "I'm going to Portugal! For a whole year. I won an Erasmus scholarship, can you believe it?" Sonia was shaking her head in disbelief and looking at the volcano as if she didn't see it at all, and in fact Vesuvius was barely visible behind the sheer veil of the *afa*.

An exchange program abroad. I was happy for her. I really was. So if I came across as a bit perturbed it was probably because of the car alarm that had gone off somewhere down in the streets and was now bleating bitterly.

She explained that she'd received the acceptance letter a while ago but was unsure whether to go ahead with it or not. "I'm not a fearless traveler like you. I'm one of those people who needs to think things through carefully before making a decision. Did you know I even asked Pietro what he thought I should do? I bugged him even during your graduation party! I didn't ask you, of course, I already knew what advice you'd give me . . ."

I wondered what Pietro had counseled her to do: stay or go? The fact that I couldn't honestly say how he might have answered made my head throb like that car alarm. *Stay or go?* And I had to admit to myself that that night, upon finding the two of them secluded on the rooftop, I'd experienced a moment of the most vulgar jealousy.

A deep memory resurfaced, one dating back to my first year with AFSAI. Among the foreigners hosted by Castellammare families was a Danish girl, sixteen years old like me. Her name was Inga, if I remembered correctly. She was the one who pointed out to me, once when she was putting on mascara in the mirror in Rita's bedroom, that the two of us could have passed for sisters. I looked at our reflections. It was entirely conceivable that I had some Viking blood in me, too, because in actual fact the resemblance was uncanny—same light-colored eyes and hard-angled eyebrows, same delicate nose and sharp cheekbones, same downward turning lips and squared-off jaw—with the big difference that she was much prettier than me. Not only that, but she was also more self-possessed, more extroverted, more independent. She didn't get frazzled or hung up, she didn't apologize for everything like I did. She was a charismatic but serene person. She didn't overthink things but neither did she trust every crazy impulse that came over her. Inga was the more successful version of me. At the end of that year in Castellammare, she filled her luggage with all her useful experiences and went back to Denmark. No one heard from her again.

What was special about me? Fearless traveler? It was just an illusion. I thought about the Scandinavian girls Pietro and I had met on the ferry to Athens, with their heavily stamped passports and their leather chokers and long tanned legs, and I was gripped by a sense of dire threat and primitive territoriality that I couldn't control. I grasped that true jealousy wasn't what I'd tasted a month ago on the roof. True jealousy was *this*, this terror and ruthlessness, sprung from nowhere and pointed not at a single woman but tens, hundreds, thousands, *millions* of women that I didn't know and that spoke languages I hadn't studied. It was the chilling truth that there was an entire planet of women, *real* women, all with sunnier dispositions and more bold and beautiful than me, who could make Pietro wild with desire and could run their hands down his chest and clutch his sex and steal the secrets of his mouth . . . and the secrets of his soul. It was the cold and excruciating injection of poison that was now spreading through every vein in my body and wouldn't let me breathe.

Finally the car alarm stopped. Gradually my dark thoughts faded, like a nightmare upon awakening, and I let myself be infected by Sonia's enthusiasm as she talked about getting ready for her trip. As it always did around that time of day, the smell of fresh bread rose from a nearby bakery up to our roof. The air was thus hot and inviting, practically edible, and yet it made me only want to make a run for the sea. And there it was, blue serrated pieces of it behind the TV antennae.

"I'll be back in Italy for Christmas," Sonia was saying. "I'll try to make it to Naples, too, we'll see. I haven't had a chance to say goodbye to the boys yet . . ." Tonino was still in Puglia, she told me, but apparently Angelo was back in town, having fallen hard for some girl from Mergellina, that strip of seaside that made Naples look like a resort, surely one of those girls that Pietro would have defined the "high and mighty."

"Sonia, what ever happened with Carlo?"

She sighed toward the unobtainable gulf. "I don't know . . . He became too possessive. Or maybe I just didn't really love him. Either way, as soon as I broke up with him he slept with my roommate . . . right in my own house." She added, in a deviation from her usual calm and collected self, "Nothing like a bit of revenge sex!" before standing up and wiping the dust off her pants.

"Are you going already?"

"Yeah, I need to move out and send all my things to my parents' house in Sardinia. But even if I weren't going to Portugal, I still wouldn't be able to go back to living in that house . . ."

All at once, I understood I had a bond with Sonia that I didn't have and would never have with any other friend, and she was already at the door when I became dreadfully afraid to lose her. Only my best intentions (that Pietro and I would go visit her in Portugal, and so on) prevented me from considering the possibility that I'd never see her again. I'd been a terrible friend, and I would have given anything for a chance to start all over again and relive with greater mindfulness all those days and all those nights spent eating and philosophizing and risking life and limb.

On the doorstep, instead of kissing each other's cheeks we hugged, and I held her longer and tighter than was culturally acceptable.

The next time we talked on the phone, Pietro lying in the little bed in his childhood bedroom and me on the couch, he entertained me with his many colorful stories. The hectic days, the bulls in the pasture, the late-summer food festivals (which he didn't go to), such as the *zenzifero* festival—and even he didn't know what food that was supposed to be.

"So, what about our puppy?" I asked him at one point. "What name should we give him?"

There was a stillness at the other end in which I could have sworn I heard an inhalation of smoke. "Baby, I meant to tell you . . . I'm sorry, I had to give him up. My mother found him in the shed."

I sat up. "But you were going to take him to the vet," I said, but my tongue had tied itself into a knot and the word *veterinario* came out all twisted. "Did you tell her that?"

It was like talking to a wall, according to Pietro. Besides, with a hole in his chest and an even bigger hole in his pocket, he wasn't in any position to put his foot down. After a while, though, he stopped justifying himself to ask for my forgiveness, thinning his voice until it was as inconsistent as the telephone cable connecting us. "I feel terrible, baby. Like a real jerk. I can't eat, I can't sleep . . ."

"Maybe not all is lost . . . maybe you could get him back. Who did you give him to?"

"It's too late."

I leaped to my feet. "Says who?!" I wanted to stay cool and pragmatic but even I could tell that my voice, amplified by the receiver and invaded by the dialect, was starting to unravel as I remembered how the locals got rid of unwanted animals. "Where, Pietro? Where did you take him?"

"Far from here. I put him in a box and then I put the box in the car. I drove a long way, far out into the countryside."

"And then what did you do?" I began pacing back and forth, as far as the telephone cord would let me. "Please tell me!"

"Fuck, I'm so sorry, baby. I can't even believe what I did . . ." He'd pulled over on the side of the road beside a wheat field and searched for a good tree. There in its shade he'd put down the cardboard box, one of the ones he'd used to bring his books back from Naples. There was a farmhouse nearby: that's why he'd chosen the spot, in the hopes that the puppy would find his way there or that the owners would come across him working the fields. "He's probably found a new home by now, I'm sure of it . . . No harm done then. Only cats get attached to places. For a dog, one house is as good as another."

"But that makes it worse."

"How so?"

"Because the puppy will have gotten attached to *you*."

There was another long silence. Pietro was smoking, I was certain of it. "Look, I know," he said finally. "And I hated myself as I did it. When I put him down and opened the box, he looked so cute . . . with his tongue hanging out, his little wet nose, eyes are big as saucers. He was even happy to see me, but I could also tell he was sort of confused as to why he was there, in the middle of nowhere. I couldn't even look at him I was so ashamed. Then I got back in the car and drove away as fast as I could, before I could change my mind."

"Do you remember what area the field is in? We could go back there and look for him. Do you remember the exact spot?"

Pietro let out a weary sigh, saying that it would be like looking for a needle in a haystack and that I should try to forget about him. That's when I decided that it couldn't be put off any longer, that before another sun spilled its red onto the horizon, I'd be on the bus to Borgo Alto for the fourth (and maybe the last) time, even if it meant making bad blood worse.

From: heddi@yahoo.com
To: tectonic@tin.it
Sent: December 22

Dear Pietro,

I'm writing you from a campground. They have a computer with internet access here, coin-operated no less. I was checking to see if you had replied to my email, but clearly not. Did you end up having that surgery in the end? I haven't heard from you in two months; your silence has gone on longer than usual. It seems you don't feel like talking much these days . . .

I printed out and saved the last email you wrote, as I've done with all the others. Maybe you can use them one day for that novel you want to write . . . But obviously you can't write it yet because you don't know how it ends.

Years ago, in Naples, I saw our relationship as perfect, destined to be, and it was inconceivable to me that we would ever part. I was afraid of losing you, of course, but to an accident or an illness. What a fool I was: I didn't understand that destiny (which in theory kept us together) and death (which had the potential to separate us) are the same damn thing. I was too caught up in cosmic matters, or maybe too in love, to take the human factor into account . . .

I'd love to listen to your voice till the sun comes up, to feel your arms tighten around me like a ribbon around a present. If you don't want the same thing, please tell me now. February is around the corner: it's the start of the first semester and I've found a new job, in a university. Not to mention that you have a flight booked for February . . . I'm not convinced at all that you'll get on that plane. In fact, I'm not waiting for you anymore, even if you asked me to (at least, I think you did). But if in the end you decide not to cross the ocean for me, I'll accept it and I'll finally come to see that destiny isn't written in the future but in history.

Affectionately,

h.

31

BUONASERA."

That one-word welcome stretched out of Lidia's small mouth like a particularly unpleasant household chore that unfortunately had to be done from time to time. And repeating that farce weighed on me, too, having to work my mouth into an unsuspecting smile and Lidia wishing me a good evening (for heaven's sake, it was only two in the afternoon!) as she peeled a hand from her middle and gave it to me like a gift she'd rather not hand over.

"It's lovely to see you again, *signora*."

I kissed her. I'd always assumed her cheeks were rosy thanks to a healthy exposure to the elements, but this time up close I realized they were blotchy with broken capillaries, yet another sign of old age. I'd thought I was immune by now to her subconscious attempts to stir my pity but, as I once more noticed how miserably human she was, my chest tightened. It probably had something to do with my growing suspicion that I'd exaggerated, in my head and in the war of words with Pietro, how large a role she'd played in the breakdown of our happiness. Whatever had triggered it, the sensation didn't last. It had been just a physical pain after all, a mere cramp.

"Mamma," said Pietro, setting my bag down on the kitchen floor and continuing, "go get them papers for the lawyer, wouldya?"

"You going now? They'll still be closed for lunch."

"You go get them and let me take care of it."

Only after his mother had left the kitchen did Pietro turn to say under his breath, "Don't worry. The errand is just an excuse to get out of here. We'll go for a drive. You up for it?"

It was what I'd hoped for. This time we'd done the dutiful thing and come straight home from the bus stop. But I hadn't traveled that entire distance to face Lidia in the kitchen but rather to pull Pietro close to me, embrace him in a clearing, make him mine. He gave me a quick kiss before saying that the errand itself was real: he had to go to the lawyer's (not Francesco's studio, though) to drop off some paperwork relating to a plot of land.

"Which plot?"

"The land down in Puglia, the one my father and I drove the tractor to, remember?" But before the slim hope could take hold that it was a transfer of ownership from Ernesto to Pietro Iannace, he added, "My folks want to make sure it's in our names."

"Don't you own it already?"

Pietro combed his fingers through his hair. "It's complicated. I'll explain later."

I didn't get the chance to ask where Gabriele was, for his mother was already making her way back to the kitchen with labored steps, document folder in hand. "Hurry back," she said, followed by a rush of dialect from which I only fished out the pronoun *edda*.

I waited till we were getting in the car to ask, "What did your mother say about me?"

"Nothing, she's just being stupid."

"C'mon, you can tell me. I have thick skin."

It was a blatant lie but it must have worked anyway because Pietro answered, "She said you have to go to bed early tonight, otherwise you'll sleep in again."

Involuntarily I rolled my eyes.

"Never mind her . . . That's just the way she is. As they say in these parts, first she opens her mouth and only afterward she remembers to turn her brain on."

It didn't seem so to me. But as the car reversed down the driveway, grounding the gravel underneath, I decided that on the subject of his mother it was best to bite my tongue. And maybe on other subjects too.

We drove aimlessly over the hills. It was as if the summer had stored up all its heat to go out with a bang. I leaned out of the window, letting the hot wind slip like a comforter through my hands. The landscape, yellow and thirsty, wielded an austere beauty.

Pietro pulled over and turned off the engine. Outside the car, the cicadas serenaded the heat in that strange language of theirs, all hisses and clicks. I wondered if it was true that cicadas spend seventeen years underground, waiting in silence to come out and spend just one season, one glorious season, on this Earth.

We leaned against the warm hood of the car. "My god, you're beautiful," Pietro said, handing me a bottle of water. It tasted like warm plastic but it was good. I asked to see his wound, motioning him to come closer. With a knowing smile, he began unbuttoning his shirt to show me his chest, the sweat barely there. How long did we have before we had to go to the lawyer's?

"It's healing up. I'll have a good old scar, though."

In fact, after having been forced to stay open for four days, the incision had left a thick line of pink skin, raised like a row in a vegetable patch. I reached out but it looked too tender to touch, so instead I took his hand, the one he wore the silver ring on. I brought it to my lips, turning it over to kiss his palm, an instinctual act of pure passion, of pure submission. It tasted like salt, dust . . . and something else.

"You've started smoking again."

"Just once in a while," he said, retracting his hand.

"But you went cold turkey in the hospital. They say that after the first week the physical dependence lessens."

"Doctors talk a lot of crap."

"Who knows if there's an acupuncturist in this area . . ."

Pietro ruled it out, but he lost his wry tone, sounding almost enthusiastic, when I suggested we buy him some nicotine patches. He stood to go, saying we could look for them in the pharmacy in Monte San Rocco. At the thought of already heading back to the village, my chest seized up again, just like it had when I'd kissed his mother, only this time there was no release. The next breath in gave me a tiny electric pang that made me dig my fingers into my skin.

"Are you all right?"

"Yeah. Can you take me for another drive?"

"Where do you want to go?"

"Anywhere," I said, changing my mind once we were back in the car. "You could take me to the field where you left the puppy."

Pietro placed a hand kindly on my shoulder. "Baby, I'm begging you, please let it go. Otherwise it's just too hard . . . on both of us."

I kept my breathing shallow along the winding road, flanked by stalks of wheat that were dry and ruffled like sun-lightened hair. The spasms in my chest kept coming, closer and closer together. I didn't even reach out, as I usually did, to caress the nape of Pietro's neck as he drove. I wondered if this was how he had felt when he woke up that morning in Monte Porzio Catone. How could I possibly be experiencing the same thing? I felt like a phony. Yet there was nothing fake about the very fine thread of pain that was being stitched through me with extreme precision.

I needed distraction, so I asked him, "What's the deal with the land in Puglia?"

Pietro dove into his story with gusto, his eyes glued to the road as it slipped beneath the car like a conveyor belt. It was a plot that his parents had bought in the '60s, he explained, when the government had put some schemes in place to promote agricultural development in southern Italy. Back then it was practically still postwar famine down south, so many people took advantage of those incentives to escape poverty. Lidia and Ernesto also seized the opportunity to purchase a plot of land, despite it being far from the town. As it turned out, however, the recipients hadn't won actual grants but co-owned the land with the government. "I guess my parents didn't read the fine print before signing."

With an *x*? I wondered. "So what are they going to do now, pay out the government?"

"Are you kidding me? Do you have any idea how much that would cost?"

"Why, is it a lot of hectares?" I asked, trying out that word that I didn't know the real meaning of.

Pietro laughed. "No way, that plot is only a small portion of all the land we own . . . basically, the government had no intention of ever exploiting the land in any way. So after all these years they've decided to give up their share of ownership. But they don't make it easy, you see: you've got to apply for it. A thousand forms to fill out, a thousand documents to get notarized, enough to make you want to pull your hair out. And of course, as they always do in Italy, they set the deadline right in the middle of the summer, when half the country is away on vacation."

"Let's hope your folks can make it in time."

"We'll make it. We have to," he said gravely. "Otherwise, some serious shit will go down at home."

Pietro had taken a bureaucratic matter regarding a small, faraway piece of land that wasn't even in his name very much to heart. Actually, he was funneling more energy into it than I'd seen in him in months. I was perplexed. What did it matter to him since—sooner or later, one way or another—he would be giving it all up, leaving scorched earth behind him? I said lightheartedly, "Some serious shit over such a little thing?"

"It's not a little thing, Heddi."

For a while I watched the landscape whoosh past. By now every breath was a stab in the heart. One particularly bad spasm made my face twist into a grimace and my fingertips burrow into my chest.

"What's wrong, baby?"

I brushed it off at first, but when I saw how truly concerned he was I ended up telling him the truth. Pietro, changing gear and then course, stated in a calm but resolute voice that he was taking me to the family doctor, just to be on the safe side. I was struck by the role reversal but tried not to compare my performance to his. In any case, I was in too much pain to think about it or even to protest. We'd already taken the turnoff toward Borgo Alto.

The doctor's appointment initially went as I'd expected. Sterile office, chilly stethoscope, elderly doctor with moisturized hands. He palpated me, lifted my arm. In a measured Italian well suited to a foreigner, he asked me questions about the pain and my breathing; he asked me how long Pietro and I had been together and whether I liked Naples. He seemed satisfied with my answers. "All right," he said. It was somewhat humiliating to be declared in perfect health and to sit there in my bra. The doctor then turned to Pietro to check his wound. "All right," he said again as I put my T-shirt back on, figuring that was the end of it.

But then the doctor did something that surprised me. He spun toward me to look me tenderly in the eyes. "Pietro suffered a pneumothorax, and you . . ."

"And I clearly haven't," I said to preempt him.

"Yes, but you are presenting some of the symptoms. Have you asked yourself why?"

"No." I cast a glance at Pietro; his brow furrowed.

"I believe that you're suffering from what is called a *somatization* of Pietro's sickness. Do you understand what that means? I'm talking about psychosomatic pain."

I was struck dumb. It was a New Age thing that Barbara would have said, not a backward doctor in an even more backward place. But I didn't like that diagnosis that put my physical pain down to a wild imagination. Not only that, but it exposed me as a liar in front of Pietro by letting him know that the inner strength I'd shown him in the hospital was all an act, that deep down for the entire week I'd been just as frightened and dispirited as him.

"I'll write you a prescription for painkillers," concluded the doctor, "because pain is pain, regardless of the cause."

"I still have plenty of Voltaren at home," Pietro said. "You prescribed me enough to medicate a horse."

"Oh, so this lovely girl's staying at your house? Good, all right then. Say hello to your father . . . and, Pietro, do try and rest a little. Technically you're still recuperating."

We got back in the car and, after popping in to the lawyer's in Vallata, drove straight back to Monte San Rocco.

It was the five of us for dinner. This time Gabriele's presence didn't lighten the mood at all. He picked at his food and drank plentifully, without engaging any of us in conversation but simply huffing every now and then at the television. More than an absence, Gabriele's silence was a presence that made itself felt. It was silence used as a protest; it was a hunger strike. Nonetheless, after dinner when Pietro went up to his room to get me his painkillers, I joined Gabriele on the couch in the lounge where he'd withdrawn to watch TV. He didn't say a word, merely acknowledging me with a nod.

I hadn't offered to do the dishes. Left on her own in the kitchen, their mother was washing them like she was trying to punish them for something they'd done to her. I watched her from behind: the gray hairs popping sheepishly from her kerchief; her compressed stature, as though she were crushed by an unfair dose of gravity; her back hunched by the lowliest tasks that give no gratification because they have to be done and undone every single day; her blind devotion to a world that was disappearing. It was a sorry sight: an old, unhappy woman pitifully alone even in her own house. All of a sudden, I understood that what I had interpreted as a manipulative tactic to make me feel sorry for her was in fact completely involuntary. Lidia was truly worthy of compassion. Therefore, seeing her in all her fragility wasn't a concession on my part but the most merciless way of disarming her. And just like that, she lost every hold she'd ever had on me, perhaps forever.

It was a hollow victory. Because if his mother was powerless, if in the end she *didn't matter*, then why was Pietro still there? I felt sore and useless. I hadn't achieved anything since my arrival. I hadn't managed to get the puppy back or restore hope in the man I loved or create an action plan for our future. Gabriele was distractedly changing channels and the television was doing the talking. Thank goodness. I was more convinced than ever that language doesn't help change the world for the better: words are either hot air or sticks and stones. I would be heading back to the city empty-handed, having only gained this worthless, delayed psychosomatic pain. My god, was I only capable of *feeling* and not *doing*?

Gabriele was sipping his whiskey and looking straight ahead, his face lit dimly by the screen, so it surprised me to feel his hand come to rest on top of mine in the darkness. He'd never done so before and his palm was tender but very hot, as though he'd held a hot coal tight in his fist for a long time and without a word of complaint.

The gesture injected me with such intense pleasure that I only managed to mumble, "It's almost like you have a fever."

He turned to look me square in the eye. "Mine is indeed a fever, and I would never dare give it to another person. Especially the person I love."

I didn't understand; he seemed angry with me and in fact he pulled his hand away. I asked, "Are you actually sick?"

"No, I'm not sick. In truth, I never have been. And neither has Pietro."

I still couldn't follow, and yet at the same time something inside me dropped, a cold awareness that was small but incredibly important, like a key sliding through a tear in my pocket.

He sighed, softening his voice. "It's not us, Eddie, it's the place. It's this land that makes people ill. And if you stay here, it'll end up making you ill too. Run away, if you care for me as much as I care for you . . . and you can't begin to imagine how much. Run and don't look back."

He turned back to the TV, and so did I. An image from that afternoon had flashed before me, the drive back from the doctor's. I remembered watching with relief as the town crumbled away and gave way to hills set aflame by the sun. Pietro was rubbing my thigh; he looked content—and more relaxed than I'd seen him in many months . . . or in many places. We flew by fields, thickets, dilapidated farmhouses, a couple of goats tied to the roadside. Through the open window came the smell of sage and the sound of cicadas, all of them together like bells jingling on a gypsy's anklet. I wished the road would never end, a road at the mercy of the rolling land, twisting and turning with it, crawling up and diving down with it. And inside the car, we too obeyed the land, which, because of the gear changes, frequently interrupted our stolen caresses in those last stolen moments as it rocked us to its lullaby. Up and down and up and down, the land swelled over those warm sunlit hills and sank into the cool shaded dips; it rose and fell just like inhalations and exhalations. Because of the pain, I wasn't taking deep breaths—the kind that Pietro had been completely deprived of not long ago—but the land was. The land was *breathing*.

From: tectonic@tin.it
To: heddi@yahoo.com
Sent: January 14

Dearest Heddi,

Sorry for my long silence: my computer caught a virus over a month ago and I've been cursing at it like a sailor. On top of that, over the last couple of days a Siberian snowstorm has buried us under a half a meter of snow.

I should consider myself lucky . . . the operation went well this time. They tell me that soon I'll be able to climb mountains, but obviously to climb mountains you need more than two good legs.

Everything you said in your email was true and irrefutable. What you wrote about our love is founded on the most absolute of truths. I loved you—no, it was more than that, I adored you, more than that, I worshipped you . . . and I still do . . .

But I no longer know if all those dreams, projects, and scenes I see in my head still belong to me. I wish I were a different person. I want to be happy but I'm not. I want to be free but I'm not. I want to be healthy as a fish but I'm not. I want to be with you but I live in Italy.

Sometimes (often) I fantasize for the briefest of moments about the day when I'll be on my own, for good, that is, when my folks will no longer be here. Then it seems that I can glimpse some brighter opportunities for myself. But it's a thought that repulses me and so I shake it off like one of those flashes you have while sitting on the bus in the middle of traffic, your eyes are wide open and as soon as you blink the image is gone . . .

Heddi, what can I say, how can I say it? I think of you all the time, even if I keep it to myself . . . but how can I break away from everything and everyone? That's the problem, because I've always been certain I would succeed in achieving anything I wanted, but in this case, no matter how I look at it,

I see nothing but obstacles. Every day I think about New Zealand and you and the summer while here it's cold. But I haven't paid for my ticket yet and I can't promise you anything. I can only hope in a lucky roll of the dice in February and hope that you're still there waiting for me . . . I'm even thinking of coming over there and taking you away with me. Will it work?

It would be totally different if you and I belonged to the same world, or at least if our focal points—our roots, our origins—were a bit closer together . . . because where I'm from people are not accustomed to moving around. Maybe you still carry the blood of some of your Cherokee ancestors who were used to packing up and moving from prairie to prairie, without a specific destination in mind . . .

I think of you often. I know this doesn't help you. But I can't help anyone.

A chilly kiss,

p.

From: heddi@yahoo.com
To: tectonic@tin.it
Sent: January 17

Dear Pietro,

Thanks again for opening up your heart to me. I understand that your situation is complicated, though not entirely new . . . Sometimes I think it would be easier if you had nothing to your name, if you lost everything. Then you could start all over.

I haven't told you about something that happened to me when I first went traveling with those three adrenaline junkies. They made me do a pretty extreme climb, a cliff over the sea with very few holds: I clung to the rock face literally by my fingertips. I was scared as hell and grasped that I might have a life worth saving.

Once I'd come down from the cliff, I sat on a boulder. The sea was sparkling. I hadn't noticed it before but it was a beautiful spot. I pulled out my Minolta to take a picture, but in doing so I knocked it into the sea. I fished it out of the salty water and unscrewed the lens to open it up: it was like emptying a full cup. It was brutal. I'd finally lost everything. I hardly had any clothes or any money, I had no job, no love, no future. And now I had no means of capturing all the small and beautiful things in the world, so in a way I'd lost my sight too. I knew I had to start all over, there was no going back. I grieved for that camera for months and months, even after my new friends generously pitched in to buy me a new one. For over two years I kept its salty, rusty corpse in a shoebox because I couldn't bring myself to throw it away.

I know, I'm probably trying to impose my life choices on you, and it's not fair. It's just that I would really love to see you again.

h.

32

THE QUARTIERI had come back to life. The locals had returned in hoards, and there was an electricity in the air similar to the pre-academic excitement that arrived like clockwork at the end of every summer. It was the beginning of a promising and productive new season, an almost biological reawakening that my body still hadn't quite kicked the habit of. But it failed to truly stir me.

Actually, now that the neighborhood was reanimated, it felt more surreal than ever. Theatrical even. Shop owners advertised their goods with oratorical tones and sweeping gestures. Children cried, on cue it seemed; housewives fanned themselves. The residents, increasingly distrusting of the intercom, lowered their breadbaskets and fired dialect at each other between the balconies and the street and the *vasci*—cryptic and often angry messages that, had they been visually tracked, would have created a grid of infrared lasers worthy of *Mission Impossible*. I thought I recognized a few criminals from the newspapers, beefed-up guys strutting around with gold chains and puffed-out chests. Everyone was moving like stage actors with utter disregard for their audience, like a flash mob of people carrying out the most unthinkable choreography in a public place for the pure pleasure of performing. The place was so bustling that I could walk right through it practically alone with my thoughts.

I thought often about that moment; it had, in fact, come back to haunt me. That moment I'd stood by the town wall in Monte Porzio and Pietro had said, *My god, are you leaving me?* That instant had been a turning point, a tiny breach in the laws of time and space that had made everything come to a standstill: the cicadas had stopped singing, my feet had stopped walking away. In that moment the power was in my hands, the power to change our destinies. But in the end I'd chosen the easy way, the way back to him. And here I was now, by myself, standing before our gate at 33 Via De Deo.

I started up the stairs. I'd only reached the first-floor landing when I heard a woman's screams in a murderous form of dialect reverberate through the funnel-like courtyard. They were followed by plaintive excuses delivered by a male voice that was meek now but might just blow up any second . . . they were the three dots before the exclamation mark. I recognized the voices: it was the same old bickering over water. I climbed the stairs softly, as if to get to my place I first had to walk past not a woman at all but a pit bull come off its leash. My heart was in my throat; every step brought me closer to that alarm that was raping my eardrums. And on the third-floor landing I found myself for the first time face-to-face with its source.

The woman looked so small, though less so in girth, as she stood there shouting at the air and brandishing a tomato-coated spoon. I had a violent flashback of a scolding I once got when I was eight or nine—an elderly immigrant all red in the face who was yelling god knows what in Italian from her doorway in our otherwise dead suburb—and only now did I realize she had to have been Neapolitan. The woman before me now, armed with a spoon, was ageless: she could have been just as easily in her fifties as in her twenties. The fluorescent light, a must in that dark kitchen even at noon, highlighted every groove of discontent on her face. Her fury was such that smoke was rising off her—no, it was just a pot steaming away behind her on the stove.

As soon as she saw me, she broke into an ingratiating smile. *"Buon-giorno, signori',"* she said in a sugary voice before collapsing her smile and knitting her thick black eyebrows. "You wanna see what that no-good excuse of a man has done? Come with me so you can see with your own eyes!"

There was no resisting her invitation, for the lady of the house had already curled her chunky, cracked fingers around my wrist and was pulling me through her kitchen. On my way through, I saw a baby girl in a high chair and the meat sauce cooking down on the burner for so many hours the oil had gone black. With that padded handcuff she dragged me farther, through the hallway lined with pictures of grandfathers and other saints, all the way to the bathroom. There she let go of my hand but not her spoon, which threatened to spatter red all over those sparkling white tiles.

"This bathroom is brand new, miss."

"It's . . . lovely."

It was the wrong thing to say. She went ballistic, painfully yelling in that tight space, "Lovely? Is that what you reckon? Look up!" She pointed her bloody spoon at the ceiling. There were black moisture stains and white paint bubbling and peeling off. "It's disgusting, mold everywhere, it's a mess. We just had it done up real nice. Cost us an arm and a leg. Now look how he's wrecked it!"

"Who's he?"

"Who do you think? That asshole that lives on the fourth floor! Every time he takes a shower, all the water comes down into our apartment. But he doesn't give a shit!"

"Maybe the pipes need replacing," I suggested.

My humble advice enraged her even more. She said that they'd put in a few pipes during the remodeling, thus the responsibility landed on her neighbor. But she and her husband couldn't afford to do the repairs. All at once she pulled out a mournful Pulcinella face to make a desperate confession. "We got nothing left, all our savings is gone. And we got these little ones to feed, but my husband is the only one bringing home the bacon. What are we gonna do?" Her voice broke, rising to an alarming falsetto. "I'll make him pay, swear to God I will!"

With the necessary solemnity, I took one last look at the ruined ceiling. "Very sorry, *signora*," I said, somehow managing to slip out of the bathroom and down the hallway. In that run for the landing, I made an effort not to laugh at the tragicomic side to Naples that I seemed only to have noticed now, after all these years. At the amount of rage, the amount of *passion*, wasted on what were actually surmountable, if not petty, obstacles. At the jarring contrast—not unlike the fluorescent light exaggerating my neighbor's coarse features—between sounding so very fierce and actually being so very small and so terribly, terribly human.

On the doorstep, wooden spoon still in hand, the woman smiled at me again, genuinely this time, as though she was seeing me for the first time. "You the American?"

I was already heading up the stairs when she asked me. I should have denied it, but then I changed my mind. "Yes, I'm American."

She looked me up and down with an expression that was at once tender and wary, before turning her back to me to go stir the sauce.

The bizarre encounter with our neighbor served as material for storytime on the phone that night with Pietro. He burst out laughing and said, "Unbelievable. Every single day for the last year or so, they got that pissed off over something that stupid? All they had to do was call a plumber . . ." He told me that he didn't miss Naples at all but that he missed me terribly. He said Gabriele would be coming back next week. Then he started telling me about the wheat they'd sold, for a good profit, and about the other farmwork and hoops he'd jumped through for his parents. This time he didn't complain much. He gave me the news that the application for the land in Puglia had been filed on time. "Thank god. Now all we have to do is wait."

Wait. Now that we were apart again, I had fallen back into a state of anticipation. And this time the distance made itself felt. I could physically feel each and every one of the one hundred and two kilometers between us: every step along Via Roma and the Rettifilo all the way to the central train station; every jerk of the bus as it passed through the netherworld of the industrial area before ducking behind the volcano; every grunt of effort for it to get over the first few hills. And I felt every plain and every crease of that vast velvet land separating us. We loved each other, I could no longer doubt that. Then why weren't we together?

"Pietro, when is your recovery going to be over?"

"I don't know. I'm doing pretty good for now, but who knows what might happen . . ."

There was a long pause in which I was certain I heard the crackling of cigarette ashes. "You're smoking in the house?"

"Yeah, but my folks don't know that."

"But I do. And I worry about you, Pietro . . . about your health. You should keep looking for those nicotine patches. Maybe they sell them in Avellino."

"Would you just stop it?" he said, but without anger. He was almost beseeching me.

"Stop what?"

"Stop trying to change what can't be changed."

Dinner sounds came rising up from the courtyard. How could anyone be enjoying a fatty, hearty meal at this late hour? I could hear Pietro's cigarette burning in the receiver and forks and knives clinking on plates, the heedless smoking and eating and the smug absence of dialogue; I could hear him and the city distancing themselves, detaching from me and sliding into the background, becoming the backdrop of my life. And what was left in the darkness was me, a still hazy and porous identity but one with a well-defined voice, that unique blend of Anglo-Saxon exactitude and southern Italian mellowness, which was now saying through the receiver, "I think I'll go back to Washington."

Pietro stopped blowing smoke; he may even have stopped breathing. He asked me to say it again, he asked me why. I didn't know myself, but I infused my voice with common sense to tell him that tomorrow morning I would call United to see about availability. I went overboard, becoming chatty and inappropriately cheerful. I told him that my open ticket would expire if I didn't use it soon. That I wanted to see my family. That I'd nearly run out of money and needed to get a job, a legal one this time. That I wanted to rewrite my thesis in case there was really a chance of getting it published. All these things were true but meaningless to me. Yet the more I talked about them, the more my impulse became a plan, and the plan became reality.

"I get that you need to see your family. I mean, it's the right thing to do. But do you have to leave right now? I'll go crazy without you."

"You could always leave with me, you know."

"Just like that, with a hole in my lung? With an unresolved legal issue?"

"I don't know what to tell you . . ."

Only then did I grasp what I was really doing. I was trying to recreate that moment in Monte Porzio Catone: I was walking away from him, backing away blindly, not to leave him but simply to shake him out of it, to make him reexamine his priorities. Love and money, freedom and responsibility . . . life and death. But this time the ending would be different.

There were dogs howling, or maybe it was just Gesualdo, and Pietro had to raise his voice to tell me what I already knew: that he didn't have a passport or the money to pay for his airfare, and that his parents would never give it to him. "But maybe I could rob a bank," he said with a laugh. "Or pinch some old lady's purse in front of the post office, or steal some chickens. Whatever it takes to join you over there, love of my life."

I switched off the lamp and lay down on the couch with the phone to my ear. Outside I heard the tires of a motorbike screeching and someone calling Gennaro home: it was the Old World, lit by a perpetual yellow sunset, that was turning in for the night.

I had a dream. Under my rowboat the sea was gulping softly, glassy and so blue it looked fake. What a gorgeous day. Rays of sunlight were being drawn toward the bottom like golden feathers. For a while I just watched them mesmerized.

But where was I? I lifted my gaze. Judging from the hillside to my left, a froth of olive trees that seemed to emerge straight from the seawater, I had to be somewhere near Sorrento. To my right were islands—Ischia and Procida, I was sure, although they looked oddly more like barren boulders than resort spots. That meant that just to the right of Procida I would see Naples. It was my compass.

But Naples wasn't there. With mounting fear, I took a better look at my surroundings. That steep land wasn't covered in olive trees, after all, but shrubs, Mediterranean scrub that not much farther ahead gave way to cliffs, rocky faces like fresh wounds made by a sea that perhaps wasn't always this innocuous. And those islands weren't actually Ischia and Procida but Capri's sea stacks, the Faraglioni, monoliths rising from the waves to block out the sun and make a labyrinth of the sea.

Now I understood. I'd gone much farther out in my boat than I'd thought: I was at Punta Campanella, the tip of the Amalfi Coast, the furthermost edge of the Gulf of Naples, the point of no return. And beyond, the open sea.

Only meters from there, in fact, the water went dark like squid ink all the way to the horizon, that line without a beginning or an end where sky and sea could finally unite. It was the very seam of the world and it terrified me. I couldn't fathom how I could have drifted this far from shore. Had I gone fishing and fallen asleep to the soothing rhythm of the water going *plop, plop* beneath my boat?

Maybe I did know the reason I'd gone this far out. Vesuvius, barely visible behind the ever-present haze over the bay, was erupting but without making a sound. The sky above the volcano was blooming in shades of gray like a black-and-white image revealing itself in the developing tray. I watched that silent film without emotion. I didn't dare look behind me at the void my boat was carrying me toward even though it gave the illusion of being suspended in the same spot. Yes, there was no doubt, the current was taking me out to sea, but ever so slowly so as to make the separation painless.

Dear Heddi,

I love reading your emails. It's like you're in the room with me; I can smell your scent of yogurt, the salt on your skin. I miss you so much. No matter what I'm doing, my thoughts always drift to you. I can't help it.

My health has improved. I thought that once I felt physically better the confusion in my head would clear up too. But now it seems that I can only see with greater clarity just how very complex my problem is.

It's the same old multilayered issue. The outer layer is my parents. Obviously, leaving for a completely different world without a return ticket wouldn't make them happy or leave them indifferent. The heart of the problem, though, is the land. Maybe it's the way I was brought up, or rather the way I was conditioned, but I just can't imagine being the owner of my books and CDs alone. They gave me a house, the one I live in, and they gave me some land, which provides me with a small annual income: with constant care and management it gives me the security of knowing I could survive even in a nuclear war. The land is where my roots are. It belonged to my ancestors as far back as anyone can remember. And I can't leave it for good or, even worse, sell it. I would have to live a stone's throw away or at least not as far away as New Zealand. So I've come to the conclusion that to crack the outer layer of my worries (my family) all I have to do is resolve the core of the matter (the land). But how?

It's no easy feat. To this you'll say that I'm trading you for material possessions, for some things . . . but it's not that simple. I would love to be with you and live the life I imagined not so many years ago: travel the world, see new places until we find one we'd never want to leave again. But I don't know if I'm able to grab my destiny by the horns, or if I want *it badly enough. I can only hope to come out of this mess quickly, and hopefully without turning it into a big ordeal to all concerned (but that's the hardest part).*

Probably at the end of the novel I'll write, the readers will come to see (or perhaps I will too) that I'm just a coward, that I didn't defend my love for you and therefore my self-love, due to cowardice disguised as fear and laziness (a fine combination, don't you think?).

Many times I've tried really hard to ignore or somehow drive away the part of my life I shared with you. It's a futile and even harmful thing to do. It's like you're in my blood. I don't have one thought, one feeling or action that is not related to what I learned from you. Actually, it's more than that: I was like a parasite with you. I sucked everything I could out of your life.

We were young and naïve. I was naïve and so were you. In my own way I loved you madly, just like in my own way I have never stopped loving you. But my curse, my hereditary defect, my environment make me make all the wrong moves. I let myself get dragged down by inertia, I let myself get carried away by the current. That which one moment I desired more than the air I breathe all of a sudden becomes intolerable. It's probably because I'm only human, but I have yet to meet other people with my same stupid logic.

Now I'm a bit tired, of working hard all day and tapping on this stupid computer keyboard (maybe I prefer to write by hand but I've never realized it) . . . I'm tired of everything, it seems.

I hope that these few lines will shed some light on the situation but I'm sure they won't, without underestimating your intelligence, which never ceases to amaze me. My hope is to see you soon and to read more of your thoughts.

Ti voglio bene,

Pietro

33

RITA FIBBED at work in order to take me to the airport. It seemed fitting that she would be the one seeing me off now since she'd been the first person to greet me at the train station all those years ago. I crammed my suitcase till nothing more could fit in, figuring that those last two books and that pair of jeans could be brought over later by Pietro.

I'd left out the Roman effigy and set it beside the alarm clock so I could sleep near it. I hoped that tomorrow morning I wouldn't be stopped at the airport for theft of cultural artifacts. But that statue, I realized, wasn't the only gift Pietro had given me that was imbued with history: all of them had been, starting with those old songs he'd put together for me. I'd only ever given him new things. I myself was new, an amalgamation of random bits all thrown together, just like my potato dish, of dubious yet ordinary origins, which I reinvented each time I made it depending on the ingredients I had on hand. And I wasn't so sure this was such a bad thing after all.

Without our things, the room reverted back to its implausible size: the low ceiling, the tiny opening that was a window in name only. The port was doused in sunlight. It was still afternoon, but it already felt like the day was over.

As I was dragging my suitcase to the door, something caught my eye: a small scrap of paper sticking out from under the mattress. On it was

Luca's number in Varese written in Tonino's sloppy handwriting. It must have fallen long ago from my book bag. I picked it up, smoothing its creases and then carrying it downstairs along with my luggage.

There was only one last thing to do: go visit Angelo in the Sanità, the only way to say goodbye before I left. I missed that boy. Maybe I just felt like walking too.

The trash collectors must have gone on strike again because Via De Deo was bursting with refuse. Garbage was spilling from the dumpsters, and the air was a full-bodied mix of pork rinds and coffee grounds. I saw a few *zoccole*, rats of the man-eating kind. The storekeepers and shoppers on my street appeared unfazed by that visual and olfactory frenzy, but I opted for a shortcut.

The sun was abandoning the Quartieri, becoming a privilege of the highest floors. Down in the streets, like the anonymous one I found myself in now, darkness lingered like hard luck. My shoes smacked the big, square *basoli*, moving from one to the next as if across a giant chessboard. There was a bad vibe there. In a ground-floor home a woman painting her toenails threw me a suspicious look. I suddenly became fearful. There wasn't a specific reason why; there was nothing unusual about the street or the woman. It was a generic fear, a caution planted by the guidebooks on Naples when they write about its narrow streets: hold on tight to your bag, be on your guard, or better yet, don't go down them at all.

I took another side street. Had I been down this one before? It was hard to say: even after all this time, all the streets looked the same. I walked surefootedly so as not to betray my uncertainty, not to myself and definitely not to that young boy wearing filthy, oversize slippers and stalking me with his eyes. I had two choices: either trace one of the straight lines down to Via Roma or follow one of the perpendicular streets that would eject me out into Piazza Carità. After all, the Spanish Quarter possessed a mathematical symmetry.

My feet chose to turn right. As soon as I rounded the bend, I was flooded in light as though someone had flashed a spotlight on me, and I had to squint. An entire block of buildings had been demolished or had collapsed, leaving a crater in the neighborhood. The sun thus had free rein, but it wasn't a pretty sight. As if to discourage street kids and their dingy soccer balls from getting any ideas, a wall, heavily graffitied, had been shoddily built around the ghost of the building. I was disoriented by that dazzling and at the same time dead space that broke the geometrical laws of the Quartieri. Starting to panic, I dove into the first left-hand alleyway.

I'd strayed far from Via De Deo, that much I knew: I couldn't even hear its comforting bustle. All I could hear was a toilet flushing and water coursing through pipes and my blood throbbing through my veins. I was lost but I kept on walking. The real danger was in stopping.

I ran my eyes up the façades of the buildings. High above, the last sunlight was an orange juice being sucked away by a straw. It was getting late and I had to get to Via Roma as quickly as possible. My footsteps gathered speed, aiming for the next side street, searching for a straight line—any line—that would take me downhill. And there was one right there.

No sooner had I turned the corner than I came to a halt. I knew that place. The low walls barricading the street, the scaffolding bracing the brittle stone, the harem of pigeons and the bed of cardboard, and on top of it, sprawled out like an undefeated general, the big black dog.

Checkmate.

The birds, frightened in turn by my intrusion, burst into flight. I had to duck to avoid them in their clumsy escape, but all the same I felt the breath of those many wings and their papery feathers lifting my hair and brushing against my forehead. Only then was it just me and the beast with his glazed-over eyes as soulless as black pearls.

I stood there paralyzed, fearing that if I made a move in any direction, the dog would pounce on me and bite me with those hard, yellow teeth. I knew he had it in him to do just that, judging from his battered body, a map of battles scribbled in black scars that glistened in the dying light.

And he was undoubtedly faster than me. My eyes darted left and right in search of the quietest, most submissive exit. Yet I was unwilling to retrace to my steps: turning back just wasn't an option.

All of a sudden, I noticed that the first wall, the one being used as a clotheshorse directly behind the dog, had an opening that wasn't obstructed like it had been last time. It was just wide enough for a moped to fit through . . . so surely a person would be able to. I realized in fact that all the walls had a small opening. Should I go for it? I thought to myself.

Again I looked at the dog, his scars expanding with each breath. Feeling bold, I took a step in his direction but I wasn't looking at the ground and kicked an earsplitting plastic bottle across the cobblestones. The dog bared his teeth and I retreated.

But something inside, maybe that gambler in me, again pushed me forward toward the beast, who despite the heat wasn't panting but breathing through his nose like a bull. His black-leather nostrils widened as he sniffed the air, picking up my human smell invading his territory, and his blank eyes too were rolling this way and that as if looking for a thief in the night.

Suddenly I got it. The dog smelled me and sensed my movements but he couldn't see me. He was *blind*.

Placing all my foolish hope in that intuition, I held my breath and edged toward him. I came close enough to feel the heat rising off his body, the foul steam coming from his nostrils. His muscular head tattooed in wounds turned right and left trying to locate me, but I didn't give him the chance. With a surge of adrenaline in my legs, I darted behind the dog toward the opening in the wall. I heard him stir on the cardboard but I kept going, not daring to look behind me as I slid through one passageway after the other, until I'd gotten past the entire block forever in need of reinforcement. Once I was out the other side, for some reason I burst out laughing.

I took a street that looked promising, and indeed it took me to safety on Via Roma, where the anarchy of the Spanish Quarter might seem like nothing more than a strange dream. However, instead of continuing on toward the Sanità, I headed back in the direction of Via De Deo. I couldn't be sure I'd find Angelo at home or even recognize his decrepit building, still standing only by some miracle. Besides, to be honest, I was a little tired.

After talking on the phone with Pietro for over an hour, I got into bed with an issue of *National Geographic*. Despite worrying I wouldn't hear the alarm clock in the morning, I felt at peace knowing that soon (two or three months at most was Pietro's guess) we would begin living the life we'd dreamed of for so long. Leaning back against the wall, I was flipping through the glossy, saturated pages of an article on the Islamic peoples of China when I felt it.

It was a push from the wall behind me, like a stranger jostling me at a crowded concert, so rudely it even moved the mattress. My first thought was that it had come from Gabriele's room; I almost called out his name, though I knew I was alone in the house. When the wall gave another push, I grasped that it wasn't the wall that had pushed me but rather the mattress, with me on it, that had thrown itself against the wall. Like in a boat on the sea, the mattress slid shoreward once more, and this time the wall and the mattress began knocking together repeatedly, like teeth chattering in the cold. I even considered the possibility that someone was shaking the bed. The *munaciello*! That cheeky little spirit was getting back at me for not having offered him any coins when I'd moved in. It was a split second of the most sober madness. Only when I saw the glass vibrating in the window frame and the makeshift bedside table clicking against the wall did I finally understand.

An earthquake. I threw off the sheet and the magazine and hurled myself barefoot down the stairs, making a dash through the living room and straight for the front door. I didn't open it. I stood there on the threshold, wrapped in the shadows, my heart thundering and my head wondering if this was the end or just the beginning.

I waited. Sinking to the floor in my underwear, I ran my fingers through my hair. My hand was trembling, but I felt proud of myself for remembering Pietro's advice to run for shelter under a doorway and for having chosen, without stopping to think, the doorway which in our illegally built house was probably the strongest. However, it hadn't been a conscious memory at all but rather an instinct, like a nomadic memory I'd always carried in my bones.

The house was still now. How could the neighbors not be yelling themselves hoarse over this in the courtyard? Maybe they were asleep or too wrapped up in their ridiculous squabbles to notice that the earth had moved beneath their feet. Admittedly, though, it had been a minor tremor and a short-lived one at that. I couldn't have said I was disappointed, but I became aware of the fact that I'd actually wanted to experience an earthquake or an eruption. Or rather, I wanted to take part in something truly big and powerful—a release of latent energy, an explosion of truth.

I felt like calling Pietro to tell him what had happened and be enfolded once more in the velvet of his good night. But at this hour I ran the risk of waking his parents. And as my eyes scanned the living room resting in the semidarkness, I saw the crinkled slip of paper with Luca Falcone's number.

On impulse (or maybe not) I grabbed it and dialed, quickly so that I couldn't change my mind. As the phone rang, I looked out the window and spotted—so low in the sky it looked like it was emerging from the Spanish Quarter itself—the finest sliver of light, as fragile as a splinter of glass but practically blinding in its intensity. The moon, mother of the tides and the only witness to the fact that even geological time isn't truly linear but comes full circle, and that for every goodbye there's always a return.

My old friend picked up; I recognized him straightaway from his peaceful voice. But since he wasn't expecting my call, I said, "It's me. Heddi."

From: heddi@yahoo.com

To: tectonic@tin.it

Sent: February 8

Dearest Pietro,

You write so well. Thanks to all the emails you've written me, I've finally
understood once and for all that you do love me, in the Neapolitan sense of
the word. But I know something else, too: you won't come to see me or take
me away. I'll spare you the unpleasant task of having to tell me yourself.
The truth was right in front of me all along . . . how could I not have seen
it earlier? You tried to tell me in every way, now and years ago, but love is
hardheaded . . .

They tell me that when the first Englishmen came to these remote shores
they tried to buy land off the various Maori tribes—dense, muddy forest
that was practically impassable. In exchange they offered money and
goods, and the Maori took these gifts and laughed in their faces. They
laughed. *How absurd, they thought, to think you can buy the land!*
Because in their worldview the land can never belong to man: it's man
that belongs to the land. In fact, Maori call themselves Tangata whenua,
literally, "people of the land." You and I will always love each other,
Pietro, more than anything, but you belong to your land and I'm destined
to be here.

Oh, destiny . . . I've decided: if I did want to get a tattoo one day I know
what it would be. Not an image at all but a word. And it wouldn't be destiny
or even knowledge, but the Maori word aroha. *Aroha is a sublime concept
of love:* it encompasses generosity and the creative force of the spirit, and
involves not only the heart but the head and all the five senses . . . and
probably that sixth sense, too, that led you to me.

You won't ever come here, and that's the way it should be. I won't hold it against you, I couldn't possibly, because thanks to you I experienced a kind of love that few people in the world have the privilege of knowing, and for that I will always be indebted to you.

Yours,

Heddi

Dear Pietro,

How are you? I'm writing to you with pen and paper, like you always preferred, like maybe I always preferred too. I haven't heard from you in ages. It's been almost a year since I told you about my engagement (and buying the house); thanks again for your sincere congratulations. I don't know if you got my short email from Vietnam or the one I sent you from Cambodia (we were traveling with Barbara, my dad, my brother and his wife) . . . you didn't reply. If I don't hear from you now and then, I feel something is missing from my life.

We got married on the beach in the month of February. As you can see from the pictures, it was a beautiful summer's day—actually, four beautiful days because the festivities lasted that long. Beach, music, lots of food. My dad took charge of the barbecue, Mamma Rita made spaghetti with shellfish. Guests came from all corners of the world, including Ivan and Snežana and—you won't believe it—Luca Falcone! He just appeared from the crowd with the same ease as always, as if he were simply walking toward me in Piazza San Domenico and not at the ends of the Earth. In perfect Falcone style, he stayed for only two days . . .

But my wedding isn't the only news I wanted to give you. Do you remember that novel you always wanted to write as an old man? Well, I wrote it . . . I hope that you don't mind too much, and that you'll want to read it. It turns out I remembered everything; evidently, my amnesia was merely transient.

Please let me know how you're doing, otherwise I'll start to get worried. I hope that you've found or will soon find everything you desire and deserve, and that you won't feel regret when you look back on our story, which (in the novel as in real life) begins and ends with you.

h.

From: tectonic@tin.it
To: heddi@yahoo.com
Sent: April 16

Dear Heddi,

Where should I begin? I'll begin with the obvious. Today I got your letter. I can't describe the little leap my heart gave when I came home from work to find it sitting on the mantelpiece. I should have expected it, though, because today I witnessed a very strange phenomenon. I was putting some tools back in the truck in a spot where I spend most of my time. It's just outside Monte San Rocco, in the hills surrounding it, where there aren't any houses whatsoever and all you can see are the "giants" (the windmills). I was alone, absorbed in completely trivial thoughts. Then I clearly heard, very close to me, the sound of an animal. The voice of an animal. It took me a few moments to figure out what it was: a small white owl perched on a metal pole. It was looking at me and belting out its song. I thought about how odd it was to see an owl during the day, in such damp and cloudy weather, and I thought of the Greeks and their belief that owls are Minerva's messengers. But I decided on the simpler explanation that that little bird had a broken clock and had confused day with night. But in the end it was a messenger!

I must admit, however, that I felt I would hear from you sometime soon . . . I hoped so. I didn't write to you earlier because, even though I live a zillion kilometers away, I wanted to leave you in peace . . . I'm glad the wedding went well. I'm happy for you, believe me. I couldn't not be, looking at the photos you sent me. I truly am happy.

As for the novel, I'm not hurt at all. I'm actually excited and even a bit moved that I'll be able to read, along with thousands of other people that don't know us, the experiences we shared, where, when, and maybe even why . . .

I'm surviving in this wolf lair. I somehow managed to overcome all the small-town corruption of this place and about six months ago I found a job. Like with my last job, I'm not exactly working as a geologist. Maybe I don't even like the profession as much as I used to.

I work as an electrotechnician for a company that runs windmills. They've built a plant for creating aeolian (wind!) energy in the countryside around Monte San Rocco, and I'm responsible for making sure the windmills run well. When they break down, it's my job to fix them . . . often that means going all the way to the top (they're 80 meters tall) and spending a lot of time up there . . . I call them my fifteen Moulin Rouge girls. It's strange but the first thing I see when I wake up in the morning is actually them, from the window at the top of the stairs. I make sure that they're all spinning, that everything's good. Only then can I go downstairs to the kitchen and have my coffee in peace. It's a job that some days I find satisfying and other days I don't, maybe just because the work itself is unusual, dangerous, difficult, even modern . . . I don't think it's my be-all and end-all. It's just a phase, a challenge, maybe a game.

Over the last year I've spent some time abroad, a month in the north of Germany, practically Holland, for professional training. I learned a lot about the people there. Then I spent a month in Spain, in Don Quixote's Mancha, to really learn about the job. I even learned Spanish. I speak it pretty well. Again I have you to thank for taking me by the hand to see the world. I would have never left Monte San Rocco if I hadn't met you, if I hadn't fallen in love with you . . . and my English. You won't believe it but even after all these years I'm still decent at speaking, reading, and writing it. I use it at least three or four times a day to speak with people on the phone in Germany . . .

Gabriele lives in Barcelona. He's teaching in an Italian school but finding it hard to fit in with the people there (I'd told him it was like that). Our parents are getting older. Despite their ripe old age, they get by pretty well . . . they grumble all the time and have all their same old habits . . .

I've found a girlfriend. Or rather it's more accurate to say that she found me. It didn't take much searching: she lives 50 meters from my house. She has a degree in languages (from the Istituto Orientale, a coincidence?). I think she loves me. She puts up with me. She's very patient with me and my mood swings. She tolerates my absences . . . I care for her a lot. But I'm not able to love her like I should. Like she deserves.

I should tell her. But as always, I expect her to be absolutely understanding, impossibly so. I don't know. Maybe I'm just afraid of being alone.

What a joy it is to look at the picture of you two on your deck. But the bougainvillea behind you is in dire need of a good pruning! Don't think ill of me: I only said that because your letter sitting before me has the scent of a life I desire and I know I will never be able to have. I feel a bit like a prisoner, not a prisoner of a place or people but of my own character, which by now has taken on its irrevocable form. I love to know that you exist, even at an enormous geographical distance.

You did the right thing running so far away from me. Had you gone to any other place, I probably would have already come to visit you. I really did book a ticket to New Zealand. I had every intention of joining you there. But it was probably a good thing that I didn't go. I would have only ruined the balance and the life you've made for yourself down there. For a while I would have acted like a man in love, perhaps till the time came to sow the field, and then I would have run away like a coward. In the end, I think our love story really was a novel.

Heddi, what can I say? You were always wonderful to me, you gave me every chance possible, more than once . . . but I felt tired, overwhelmed by events, afraid and with a life ahead of me that was too different from the one I was cut out for. But I have a whole lifetime to think it over and regret my mistakes. I accept it, that's all I can do, knowing what I sacrificed.

It's hard to move on from those years, that period, those people, you . . . How will I ever be able to show you how much of my soul, my skin, my life belongs and will always belong to you, even though our lives are spinning around the globe in opposite directions? Have I already told you that I've decided to tattoo your name? I think I'll get it done this summer.

I'm happy for you. And I'm a little bit happy for me too. I don't know why . . . I guess it's like being given the go-ahead to do new things and set new goals (even though unfortunately I don't have any yet) . . .

I love you. Please don't ever forget me,

p.

P.S. I have a gray cat and she's just had three kittens: two of them are black with white paws and one's a tabby.

ACKNOWLEDGMENTS

I would like to thank Naples first and foremost for all the experiences I had in its narrow streets, and I hope I can be forgiven for any errors made by my memory, the only map of the city I had.

I wouldn't have been able to write this novel without the support of my family and *whānau* (Maori for "relatives and lifelong friends"), especially my husband, Kevin, and our two young boys, Elio and Mattias, who made sacrifices.

Thanks to my friends, in particular my three Kiwi girls, for their endless enthusiasm even when I seemed like a lost cause. A special thanks to Costantino Pes, Sonia Cerasaro, Ester Monti Reid, Mary MacKinven, and Rina Ziccardi; to Elena Bollino for urging me to take a leap and instinctively knowing what the right form for the title was; to my elementary-school teacher Donald Bufano, whom we recently lost and who long after fourth grade encouraged me to keep writing about southern Italy, which he loved so and which ran not only in his blood but in his soul.

I wouldn't have had the guts to write in Italian in the first place if it hadn't been for the premonition and conviction of my friend and travel companion Shelley Sweeney, otherwise known as "the witch doctor." My deepest gratitude goes to my friends at Giunti publishers, who more than new friends feel like old ones I've found again, and in particular to Antonio Franchini, who was somehow able to hear my voice from so far away.

A NOTE FROM THE TRANSLATOR
AND AUTHOR

I was as stunned as anyone to discover one day that, despite a lifetime of writing in my mother tongue, I could only truly express myself in the Italian I learned growing up and smartening up in Naples. This novel is that eureka moment. But when the time came for me to translate it to English, my newfound literary voice still felt so fragile I was afraid I'd lose it. Yet as an English teacher, translator, and copyeditor, how could I possibly shy away from the challenge? And who, other than me, could divine the true intentions of the author? Translating myself turned out to be stimulating and fun. I paid a great deal of attention to sound, trying to retain some of the alliterations, for example, and to recreate what Italian readers have described as the "freshness" of the language in the original. However, whereas my somewhat naïve lack of linguistic prejudice in Italian allowed me to, for instance, stick certain adjectives onto certain nouns in unexpected ways in my native language, where I know fully well what's "acceptable" and what isn't, I was constantly aware of the risk I might bend the words or force the syntax too intentionally, thereby losing the sincerity—*the heart*—of the novel. The most challenging passages to translate were those that involved physical intimacy or Neapolitan dialect. That said, my sense that some of these nuances may have been unavoidably lost in the English edition is compensated by the tiny but delicious opportunities to go even deeper behind the scenes and thus reexperience the same beloved places and faces and voices, but this time through your eyes.

Here ends Heddi Goodrich's
Lost in the Spanish Quarter.

The first edition of this book was printed and
bound at LSC Communications in
Harrisonburg, Virginia, August 2019.

A NOTE ON THE TYPE

The text of this novel was set in Fournier, a typeface first developed by French engraver and typefounder Pierre-Simon Fournier (1712–1768), who was noted for his decorative typographic ornaments and his standardization of type sizes. Stanley Morison of Monotype released the version of Fournier seen on this page in 1924. Fournier has a greater contrast between thick and thin strokes with little bracketing on the serifs that produces an open, clean look on the pages that is both distinguished and friendly.

HarperVia

An imprint dedicated to publishing international voices,
offering readers a chance to encounter other lives and other
points of view via the language of the imagination.